The Blood Knows

Vincent N. Perales

Copyright © 2011 Vincent N. Perales
All rights reserved.

ISBN: 1467908762
ISBN-13: 9781467908764
Library of Congress Control Number: 2011960306
CreateSpace, North Charleston, SC

For Leah. It is possible. Just try.

"Deep into that darkness peering, long I stood there,
wondering, fearing, doubting, dreaming dreams
no mortal ever dared to dream before."
— Edgar Allan Poe

Chapter One

Mechanical mastodons roam across highways to nowhere. The honk of car horns and the signs of stilted life outside my window are not as annoying as the sounds from a wannabe hip-hop artist in the 1st nearby apartment. His beat-box machine is loud; his vocals are an awful, tone-deaf belch of noises and lyricism. Monotone beats vibrate through the walls, chipping pieces of wood and paint off wih each sonic boom.

"Come on, bro!" I yell, slamming my mighty palm against the wall. "I am a man who works from home! Your distraction makes it hard to concentrate! Could you lower it a few clicks back? Pretty-please?"

My neighbor's response is to turn the volume up, not down.

I slam my hand again, then give up. I've complained to the manager before, once or twice. I get the impression from his lack of responsible cooperation that he doesn't care. My middle finger to him, and the corrupt system in general—an insult that fell on incompetent, uncaring minds.

Ashen Apartments isn't the kind of place where my opinion matters much anyway. They can abuse me because it's cheap; I wouldn't be here if cheap wasn't my sole option. Splinters, nails, and open live wires poke out through the cracks; the kind of fun stuff kids love to accidentally fall on. I always eat out because an army of roaches crawls over my clean dishes and holds them hostage.

It's the middle of a heat wave in September, and my AC is stuck on tropical humidity. My clothes are drenched in putrid alcoholic sweat, and the water here is so damn rusted that I have to go to the YMCA to get a decent bath.

My biggest gripe revolves around the apartment staff not bothering to clean the blood off the carpet from the police raid a few months back, before I moved in at such a low discount rate. Come on, that's just rude. They had the courtesy to seal the bullet holes, but is it that hard to at least bleach the stains? The blackish yellow stains are an eyesore and probably a health hazard; I know that much from hanging around crime scenes to do my stories.

Still, the TV works. Ashen Apartments doesn't get a normal set of stations. Sure, we get the satellite programming that's included in our monthly bill, but it comes with a unique set of rules. Depending on the day, I have a roulette of fixed stations to choose from. It's now 4:00 p.m. That leaves me with the option of watching soft-core, the Weather Channel, or dubbed cartoons. Fake sex never got me off, and the weather girl lost that loving feeling when she popped out a kid and got real ugly real fast.

That leaves just one choice: Russian-dubbed *Looney Tunes* with Spanish subtitles.

"Baby, do you have a dollar?" Heather asks, lollypop hanging from her cracked lips. I look toward the long-legged, pink-haired, teddy-wearing seductress sitting on my couch. Before her are several pills inside a disposable Tupperware bowl. She crushes them with her nails. What powder remains on her fingers she puts in mouth, scrubbing between her teeth and gums.

"You don't have one?" I ask. She says no. I take a sip out of my pickle jar turned wine glass and tell her to wait. I struggle to reach for my wallet and find a dollar. I open the wallet, but nope, no money there. "Do you take a check?"

She says that's fine but pays me no eye contact. She's mesmerized; the eccentric foreign dubbing is too great to ignore.

Heather looks better than she did an hour ago, when an ill green colored her skin. She fell onto me as I opened the door. I don't know what kind of bender she was on last night, but it meant she would put out if I took care of her.

There was a problem, though: she wouldn't put out if she overdosed or passed out. I had the medicine to postpone both, if for just a second.

"You feel up to it, Cynthia?" I ask.

Heather awoke from her sleepy haze, annoyed that I called her by her first name. "Just give me the check, Claire," the fiend using her voice hissed. Her fiend needs to be fed. I open my checkbook and hand her the check I had planned on using to pay my credit card bill. She rips it in half, twists it into a tube, and up goes the powder with a quick sniff.

I give her the biggest look of disappointment. "Great." I go to my checkbook and void the torn check. "Now I have to write a new one."

Her smile points at me. "Shouldn't have called me 'Cynthia.'" Heather only goes by her first name when she's cashing checks from Sparks Ultra Lounge, where she works as a waitress.

But I have no time think of how to respond to her abuse of my checkbook. I look at the clock on the wall and am reminded I have a deadline. I need to ghostwrite the stupid review Ralph West hired me to type.

So I look busy and pretend to write. The only person I need to fool is me.

Heaven comes when the weasel on the pill dances with the cells in her brain. She melts into the couch and falls out of her teddy. Her beautiful brown skin glows under the orange hue of the burning bulb above. She bites her lip, squeals a little to distract me, and closes her eyes.

My phone rings. Brought back to reality, I take a swig of wine and answer with a hello.

"Hi, my name is Oliver Greene, assistant district attorney. Am I speaking with Mr. Claire Walker?"

"This is he. Are you calling in regards to my inquiry about Kenny Daniels?"

"Who?"

How can he not know who Kenny Daniels is? Kenny Daniels: the man who sunk the battleship that used to be my journalism career. He's the reason I'm stuck doing graveyard work for the *Eye Tribunal* and ghostwriting crap for other journalists.

I tell Greene all this, but he says, "No, I'm just an ADA. I don't personally represent anyone."

"Well, Mr. Greene I have a deadline, and I'm a busy man. What is this about?"

"Stop killing my glow," Heather says as she throws a pillow two feet to the left of me. There is something to be admired in how quickly she goes from zero to Major League pitcher. But I won't stand for a naked junkie on my couch being rude.

I point my finger at her and say, "Shut up, hotness! I'm on the phone!"

In defiance, she picks up a coaster and takes aim. I retreat to the bathroom before she can fire at me. A prisoner in my own domain, I make sure to bring my wine.

"Mr. Walker, you don't know me, but I handled the Paxton H. Chambers case."

I knew Chambers by a better name, a name I gave him and a name I repeat now, "The Slowburn Arsonist." My voice takes on a gruff edge from the last gargle of wine; the itching in my throat will take time to go away on its own, but I scratch anyway. "What about him?"

"Actually, I'm not calling about him. Well, sort of, not completely. Let me explain. I'm handling his case, and I had intentions of calling you to see if you'd possibly testify against him."

"That's strange. Wasn't your case open and shut? You guys should have everything you need on him." Greene agrees with my statement, so I ask, "Why you need my testimony?"

"As I said, Mr. Walker, I had intentions for a possibility. If I have to call on you, could you testify against him? I need to make sure the DA can reach you in the future."

Despite this being a detriment to my schedule, I agree to it. To make sure Slowburn never takes one step as a free man ever again, yeah, I'll testify. But Slowburn is second priority. Greene has another reason for looking me up, so I ask again why he's calling me.

"I want to solicit your services," Greene says, invoking the image of a smooth-operating snake tempting me with dirty fruit. "A case I'm working on involves a man accused of murdering his fiancée. The victim's name is Dorothy Finley."

"I don't know who she is."

"She and several of her friends vanished while on a camping trip a year and a half ago. Her body was recovered inside an abandoned water processing plant, located near Jaune's Vin Lake and Forest. Dotty was her nickname, if that helps you remember. Everything happened around the same time you encountered Chambers. You were even in the police station answering questions at the time we were interviewing her suspected killer."

"Nope, still doesn't ring a bell. Who's the suspect?"

"Darius Renton, son of toy tycoon Gordon Renton."

I feel my teeth crash against one another. I've done my best to block out Gordy Renton, the jackass from my less-than-fond memories of high school. I'd done a good job until now; I hadn't thought about him in eight years. He was a rich, spoiled brat destined to inherit Carcosa, the multimillion-dollar toy company. It was only fitting that Gordy had offspring equally spoiled and corrupt.

How lovely.

"So the kid is rotting in prison while waiting for the needle?" I ask.

"The case is still ongoing. We fought tooth and nail to build a case against him. But his trial date keeps getting pushed back for various reasons. Been a few setbacks. Darius is a free man on eight hundred thousand dollars' bail."

How I yearn to ever taste that kind of money. Must be nice to be a trust-fund baby. Tough break he's out on bail; gross injustice is what I say. Not my problem. I want to hang up on Greene just because he said Gordy's name. Everything about that guy puts me in a prickly mood. As I say good day and good night, Greene stops me.

"Well, we can't find Darius," Greene says. "He's been roaming around unaccounted for the past three months."

I tell Greene I don't work in any branch of the law. "I'm just a journalist…well, a ghostwriter at the moment. But I plan on being a journalist sometime in the future. I'm a complete stranger to your case."

"I understand that, Mr. Walker. But I need to know the extent of your relationship with Gordon Renton. This is why I called."

Without thinking about who I'm talking to, I yell, "I went to high school with that no-good son of a bitch! That asshole used to bully me and get away with it because he had daddy's money and influence. I hate him more than I hate Kenny Daniels! Twenty years of festering hate. To hell with his family!"

The burst of built anger feels good.

Before I can say more, I pause: Joe Renton is all right. I can't hate Joe.

"Here is the situation, Mr. Walker. Legally, Darius is supposed to be back for his trial date, which is two months from now. The DA's office has several cases with too much going on and can't spare too many resources in tracking his whereabouts. They don't see Darius as much of a priority at the moment."

I scratch my chin and let out a whistle. "A suspected killer isn't a priority at the moment? What would the state consider a priority?"

"Look, I can't get into the details, but several very important cases are on the verge of collapsing. We're spread very thin, and the state is willing to gamble on making Darius Renton's whereabouts a minor priority. But if Darius has fled, I need to know to start looking. If he's hiding, I need to know what rock to turn."

"Did I mention I am a writer? That I have no skills in actual detective work?" I brush my teeth with my finger to get the bitter wine taste out of my mouth and snicker. "You must be desperate if you're asking a guy like me."

"Technically speaking, yes, I am. I wouldn't be asking a potential witness for one of my cases to help with another unless I was desperate. I know you're a journalist, not a cop or anything, but if you know Gordon, you should know he's not in good shape. He has had bad financial and health problems recently. From what I hear, everyone turned their backs on him. He's very eccentric, these days...not that he or his family were normal to begin with. Believe me, I've tried getting people to open him up, but that didn't work. What he needs is a friend from the past, someone he has history with."

So this is Greene's pitch. He wants me to rekindle the old high school flame with Gordy, regaining his trust and find out where Darius is. When I do, Greene takes over, making sure Darius is tagged properly by the police and the DA. Greene will pay me a nice little bonus if it got that far.

Greene's proposition is simple enough. I can't say no to the money he's offering. I spy on Gordy, lie to him, find Darius, and return to my business. The prize is better than what I'm making ghostwriting for Ralph West and the rest of the losers at the *Eye* anyway.

Then I get the itch.

This same itch got me into the whole fiasco with Slowburn and Kenny Daniels. That little voice whispers over my shoulder, haunting me, tempting me to take a shot that would lead to better opportunities. A voice for suckers; a voice that comes in an itch.

Screw it. Couldn't hurt to do it this time. What's he going to do? Accuse me of plagiarism and tank my already-shot career? Besides, I'm already buried underneath a rock in terms of lows.

No matter how far you dig, dirt remains dirt.

"I'm kind of having a lull in my career; I need a little something-something on the side," I say. Greene asks what I mean. "My intuition tells me there is something shadier going on at the Renton home. If I find anything, well, I want to make a story out of it."

Greene doesn't like the idea. I pitch a little harder.

"I can make you seem like the shining hero if you want. The lawyer who went above and beyond in the pursuit of justice. Oliver Greene, action attorney. Written by the multi-Pulitzer winner Claire Walker."

"Fine. Just report to me whenever you find something."

I tell him we have a deal. After he gets my bank information to wire me some cash, he hangs up. I give myself a high-five and do a shuffle. Time to celebrate and not bother with Ralph West's article.

Ever since the whole Kenny Daniels incident, I have suffered endless setbacks. I'm buried, doing graveyard stories and secondhand mulch for other writers. My life is full of seventy-hour-plus weeks, going in at ten in the morning and coming home after two in the morning the next day. When my luck is bad, I have to go right out at four in the morning on my days off just to get a chance at leftover work.

Always being tired gets boring. I'm tired of doing other people's work. I'm tired of having to either work myself to the bone or starve.

I want to run after the hard scoops, fight away all the vultures scrambling for evening news. I want thirty deadlines a day, making fifteen before lunch and fifteen after lunch. I want to get through my day piss-drunk and angry at the world.

Sure, this is what I'm currently doing, but goddamn it, I want work of my own choosing, published under my own name. I'd choose my battles and get paid an actual salary instead of nickel and diming myself for crumbs and pennies.

This new story will be my revenge and my redemption, and Gordy Renton is the key to both. Will he remember me after twenty-plus years? Will he still be an ass? What if he's changed? Can I even stand to be in the same room as him? Can I forgive? Can I even gain his trust? Why did Greene really pick me, of all people? How could he go from the Slowburn Arsonist to finding Darius Renton?

I'll worry about all that later.

Since Greene doesn't bother leaving me any information to find Gordy, I need to consult the white pages. After that, I'll work on my lie. Staying in Gordy's good graces will get complicated when the very touchy matter of sons and murdering is brought up.

I creep out of my bathroom. The first thing I notice is that my neighbor has turned his shitty music off; the void is absolute, pronounced. But there is no silence. Relaxing, jazzy music plays on the radio, the kind that invokes lonely nightscapes, the bitterest, blackest cups of coffee, and smoky rooms filled with quiet, lovelorn strangers.

Heather has a lit cigarette hanging on her lip. She drowns in her own sweat, her feet resting on the multiple phonebooks on the stand. One hand bounces along to the tunes, while the fingers on her other hand rub from her breasts down to her naval.

Her sweet, strawberry smell puts a smile on my face.

I reach underneath her feet to pull out the white pages. When I do, her foot presses against my chest. She taps her toes above my heart. "What are you doing, baby?" she asks.

"Need this phone book. I'm working."

She shakes her head. "No, you're not."

"Then what am I doing?" I see her reach over to the bowl and dip two fingers into the bluish powder. She uses her free hand to signal me to come forward, so I do. Her fingers go to my nostrils, and I breathe in the blue. What little is left on her fingers goes between my tongue and gums; she lets out the little sexy squeal she likes when I lick her fingers.

"Come here, baby, I'm cold."

Chapter Two

Gordy Renton lives in the prestigious Hollywood Sunset district. How old the mansion is, the exact number of rooms it contains, or even what style it is are lost to me. The fancy design could woo the rich, the all-knowing house shoppers, but it helps me as much as a picture of water would help a man dehydrating under the Texas sun. I do know that the fancy Renton mansion was paid for by the original patriarch a long time ago: paid not with toys, but with money donated by ignorant church sheep he preached to. If I had a better voice I could have been have been a pastor and acquired a flock.

This is a talent I do not possess.

No, instead I undress the truth, paint it with glitter and gossip, and then kick it back to the masses. It's a cheap living, yeah, but I get by. It's not my problem if anyone has to deal with storms of criticism and scandal to get a decent hot plate.

At least that's what I did before Kenny Daniels handed me a journalistic death sentence.

What an asshole.

But Gordy was warm to me when I called; much to my vexation, he even went out of his way to call me brother. This was a far cry from back in the day.

For four straight years he hounded me, beat my ass, and gave me shit for being poor and for being named Claire. I was too much of a pussy to fight back. I was content with being a statistic for the school and legal system, a prime example of where they had failed. They promised to curb the bullying and teach tolerance. Instead, they took federal money and bitched about parasites on opposite sides of the aisle keeping their politically correct utopian dream from happening. My parents made it a point to not ease my growing pains, otherwise they would have avoided naming me Claire.

That was the worst part: having a name that lost its masculinity sometime after the 1920s. The least they could've done was name me Clair, but no. They had to make my life suck in every way. I would tell my parents something now that I'm pushing forty, and am the age they were when they had me, but they're dead. Many things left unsaid had made me bitter over the years. Talking to Gordy brought out a ton of harbored resentment. What a crock.

Yet Gordy invited me over after just a few minutes of talking to him, even after I mentioned I was a journalist—and I made sure to mention I am one. I might be in disgrace at the moment, ghostwriting to get by, but he didn't need to know that; I'm still a journalist. And later on, I don't want him accusing the shark of biting the careless swimmer when I write my piece on his family.

So I drive over to his side of town and get buzzed through the mansion gates. Gordy opens the front door and waves me in. I'm taken aback by how much Gordy has changed.

Gordy was a brown-haired wooly bully back then. His skin was kissed by an overdose of carrot bronzer, and his porcelain-capped teeth reflected his reflection of a reflection when he looked into a mirror. He was a plump boy then, with malice fluffing up his leftover baby fat.

Greene said Gordy had become eccentric, and people couldn't deal with him, but this old man can't be Gordy. He looks like a grandpa in his seventies, not a man just a hair over forty, who should be in his prime. He has hollow, junkie eyes with purplish bags underneath, and his sunken jaw is unshaven in places. His skin is filled with white, wrinkly spots. All the weight is gone, leaving just saggy meat on bones.

"Gordon?" I ask.

"Just Gordy. Not Gordon," he says. "How you doing, Cabbage?"

My old nickname throws me off guard. I myself wasn't the skinniest of boys, so I used to prepare and eat small sandwiches instead of cafeteria food. I liked cabbage more than I liked lettuce, so I used that in my sandwiches instead. Everyone in school found out. I was dubbed Cabbage. It's not the best story, so I don't tell a soul. I'd forgotten all about it until now.

I smile for a fleeting second before shoving the smirk back in the bag. This is business. I won't let myself get emotionally involved, as it might make my dark, scathing piece on him harder to write.

Gordy leads me into his home. I had hoped to get out of the heat, but Gordy's home is just a lighter shade of hot than outside; I should have told him to chill in the car—at least my AC works. Even worse, the weatherman says it's going to get hotter over the next few days. I wipe my brow; my arm comes away covered in an ocean of sweat. I look for a place on my body to wipe it off, and realize I'm drenched. Gordy doesn't have this problem, though; in fact, he is shivering.

What I wouldn't give for a little cold comfort myself.

I am surrounded by empty cardboard boxes filled with what I assume is Schrödinger's cat litter. The way things are arranged puts me on a path that Gordy claims leads to the mansion's den. Any furniture and trophies to ooh and ahh over have been covered in unmatched bed sheets.

"Moving?" I ask.

"Maybe. Haven't decided. Getting rid of stuff, not sure what," Gordy says. His voice is a raspy mess. He keeps chattering, but hesitates repeatedly. Between each hesitation, he holds his mouth and looks around for cigarettes that he doesn't have. He does this despite telling both of us over and over that he doesn't have any.

We reach the den after an extended wander. Gordy finds a corner to huddle in while I take the edge of a desk as my chair.

Gordy asks how life has been treating me. I lie. I tell him wild stories about my golden days as a journalist for the paper, anecdotes I pass off as of my own. He seems satisfied with the answers, but he looks bothered. He stares blankly at the door, then at the windows. He makes no attempt to look at me. He rocks in place while chewing his fingernails down to the cuticle.

Gordy is a burnt-out carcass. He has to be on drugs. What kind? The bad stuff, no doubt. But his jitters and tics unnerve me, and I need to break his silence.

"How's the family?" I ask

"Wife died. Stress gave her a heart attack." I give my condolences, which masks my contempt for his wife. She was the high school sweetheart Gordy knocked up. She was as spoiled as Gordy. What was her name? Lisa? Tonya? "Denise couldn't take the stress."

I would have gotten it eventually.

"Darius is my only son…"

"How old is Darius?" Gordy says he just turned twenty-three. "Where is he?"

"You don't know, do you?"

"Know what?"

"My son was accused of murdering his fiancée."

I force surprise into my voice and say, "Oh, that is terrible." Unable to keep a straight face, I turn my head. I stare at empty beer cans and vodka bottles overflowing from a tiny trashcan. Empty to-go containers are filled with old food stuck to the Styrofoam. Bugs have made a nice little village inside old pieces of cheese pizza and Mongolian beef. The smell is rancid. I turn my attention back to Gordy. "Tell me what happened."

"Hurts too much. Can't do it, Cabbage."

Stress comes over me as I search for a discussion topic. My fingers snap; the answer is so simple. We can talk about Joseph Renton, Gordy's older brother.

Everyone liked Joe, including me. Joe looked and acted nothing like Gordy. Very nice guy, very humble, and real smart too; runner-up for valedictorian the year he graduated from our high school. He could have been anything he wanted. He had a mean kick; he could have been a pro soccer player. From what I vaguely remember, he went into anthropology instead. So I smile, hold out my hands, and ask, "How is Joe?"

"Joe died a few years back, Cabbage. Everything went bad after that. Darius went to jail. Denise died too. Everything went bad."

Joe's death comes as an unexpected shock. The good die while the wicked live.

Gordy's rocking and verbal go faster. "All your fault, Joe! All his fault…"

"What did Joe do? Was it something illegal?" Gordy says no. "Was it something morally questionable?" Gordy again says no and becomes more agitated by my persistence. I realize that a game of twenty-one questions is not a smart choice. "I'm not trying to pry. If you don't want to talk about it, Gordy, I understand."

Gordy nods with a twitch and says, "I'm sorry, Cabbage. Not used to talking so much anymore." Gordy stands up and motions for me to follow him.

We walk back to the hallway, then take a turn into a dark corner. Two rooms are located in this hidden part of the mansion: one to the left and one straight in front of me. The one to the left does not interest me. The one before me, however, has my full attention.

White, see-through plastic covers the door. The cover stretches from ceiling to floor and is held with red tape. Behind the plastic there is another layer of thicker, solid white plastic, molded to the door like a body cast. It's sealed in red tape in multiple horizontal and vertical directions. In the corner is a hole where a hose of some kind can be attached. I make out a few biohazard symbols stuck to the plastic and a warning about harmful fumes being inhaled without proper gear.

Gordy stands in front of the door, rocks back and forth, shakes his head, and says we aren't going there. He mentions that it was Joe's room, but I can't see it.

"Why not?"

"The smell won't leave. Scratches, can't stop the scratches," Gordy mumbles as he points to the other door. "Darius's room is there. Joe's stuff is there. Important stuff."

We enter the room and immediately nothing sits right with me. No bed, no dresser, no belongings to gauge what kind of person Darius is. There is a desk with a yellow notebook in the middle, two giant stacks of paper on each side of the desk, and one very large stack located behind the notebook. A trashcan is filled with what looks like hundreds of spent black ink pens.

A beautiful wooden music box is the only thing that stands out on the desk.

The other side of the room is filled with rows and rows of stacked papers. They are as high as my chest and go all the way into the closet near the entrance of the room. I examine several random pages and find they are blank. I pick out more random papers…all blank.

So Darius is a tree killer. That much I knew.

My attention goes back to the papers on the desk. Sticky notes identify each stack, yet they still leave me confused. I read a green sticky first, off to the left of the desk, "Castle. Puppet. Ghosts." I look at a blue one, off to the right side of the desk. "Ape. Sand God." Then I look at the red sticky taped to a pile on the desk, behind the notebook. "Scarecrow. Black Fairy."

I pick up the notebook and examine it. Wordless. I examine it further and notice that a pen had been pressed against the pages. There are traces of ink on several pages.

Either the lines were erased or someone, Darius I assume, traced over something written elsewhere. It seems like an asinine thing to do. Why not just take a picture or scan what you want to copy?

On the last page, one legible sentence is written.

"Let me sleep, salaam," I say. Then I repeat it a few times. "What does salaam mean?"

"Peace," Gordy answers. "It's Arabic for peace. It's also a salutation out of respect. Done with a bow. Done with a right palm to the forehead."

"Strange sentence structure. So what was Darius doing?"

"Following Joe's research."

I ask if Darius was an anthropologist.

"No, he studied oceanography. Picked up Joe's research after he died. Became obsessed. Obsessed." Gordy's shivering affects his whole body, and he begins tapping his head against the wall. "Can't understand any of it. I get angry when I try. The scratches scare me. Don't know, don't want to. Need help. Help me, Cabbage."

I rub the back of my neck and look away. The last thing I want to do is help Gordy.

But his face becomes desperate. He senses my hesitation, holds his hands tight, and shakes them at me. I move behind the desk in case he decides to strike me. Now I see why none of the people Greene sent wanted to deal with Gordy.

Gordy lunges from his spot and says, "I'll pay you, Cabbage!"

When you don't have any, all monetary offers look good.

So I push down the creeps he gives me. I move away from the desk, put on my best sympathetic look, and ask, "What do you need, Gordy?"

"Please, find Darius."

I almost say yes. Then I realize why I am here. Greene hired me to find Darius, and if Gordy is asking for the same thing, I have a bit of a problem.

"Darius is all I have left. I don't care if he did it. I just want to know my son is alright."

The way I see it, Darius doesn't have much to look forward if he comes back: a deranged father and a trial date as welcome home presents. If I murdered my chick, I would have sold everything and moved to a place with poor extradition laws.

Still, it is comforting to know in a situation like that, despite being accused of a monstrous thing, there is someone who cares about you when no one else will.

"Please, Cabbage," Gordy says, almost on the verge of tears. "I need to find my son."

"You don't know where he might be?"

Gordy shakes his head. "The last time I talked to him was two months ago. He brought these papers in." Gordy points to the papers stacked along the wall, "then he told me he was going away. Going to help Dotty. Something about eating. Going to stop the Strangers."

"That...doesn't help me much, Gordy."

Gordy reaches over to the desk and grabs the notebook. "He follows Joe's footsteps. In the pages. He'll die. Like Joe died." Gordy's sudden twitch makes me back away.

It's hard to imagine that simple pages are capable of killing someone, but I find myself concerned. If Joe really was killed, then I understand Gordy's worry. So I ask how Joe died.

Gordy rubs his stomach and looks away. "No, Cabbage. Too painful. Scratches."

"Okay, Gordy, so you're going to pay me to find Darius?"

"Yes. But not just that."

I ask him what else.

"Find out what Joe was doing. Find out what Darius did after picking up from Joe. Please. I need to know."

Gordy points at the papers. I look real long and hard at the papers, all ten tons of them around the desk. This is the last thing I expected to go down. It's the same shit I'm doing for the bastards at the *Eye Tribunal*. Find a story hidden in the papers. Make it happen on a deadline, and get paid dirt because you are an accused plagiarizing fuck doomed to do this kind of work forever.

I stop myself from letting out a bitter moan. Instead, I give a soft smile, nod, and curse Kenny Daniels for putting me in this goddamn situation. Then I tell myself, hey, this could be bigger than Slowburn. And it could, if the cards fall in my favor. This is my ticket out of the cesspool that is the *Eye*.

In the back of my mind mostly I want to know what happened to Joe...and maybe figure out just what the hell happened to Gordy. I'd have plenty of time to figure out both, now that I was getting paid by two people to do the exact same job. Neither one would be the wiser.

Chapter Three

"Ralphie, baby," I say into the phone while doodling Ralph West hanging himself. "Gordy Renton. Come on. You know this is money."

"Goddamn you, Walker," Ralph yells. "I wanted that review done yesterday, but instead you're working to find Gordon Renton's wayward girl-killing son."

Ralph is but one of many parasites who use my services, but he uses them the most out of pure laziness. My other main antagonist of late is Stephanie Quinn, but that's more out of annoyance. She calls me constantly, asking me to go over her blog. She wants to turn it into a novel that she can sell and I can find later at the supermarket stand of overpriced, underperforming bestsellers. I pretend I have too much work on my plate to read, but incognito I do read it—whenever I can get my laptop working. It is a massive train wreck of fan fiction, dedicated to a guy she met over the Internet and got engaged to after knowing him for just six days. Smutty, self-fulfilling garbage laced with rough sex, plot holes, Mary Sues, and adverbs.

An absolute train wreck. I love it.

But Ralph has no redeeming qualities, no way I can amuse myself with his shortcomings. He's a slime ball filled with incompetence and nonfunctioning higher functions, dropping terrible projects with last-minute deadlines on me. He hopes I can get him out of his hellhole, not knowing that I secretly work to shove him further down it. Despite my best efforts, he gives me even worse assignments to work with. I can't say no, since I need the money.

I make my annoyance known to him by chewing my bubblegum at max capacity.

"And chew with your mouth closed," Ralph yells.

My left hand, the one not doodling, puppet-talks; a stand-in for Ralph's physical presence. I draw some eyes, a mustache, and a mouth on my fist. It quacks and mimics every word Ralph says. If it wasn't my own left hand, I'd stab it with my writing pen out of spite.

"I'm not paying you unless I get that review."

Holding out for that review is like me closing my eyes and praying that my neighbor's rapping suddenly gets good. Or getting the managers to call a proper exterminator to deal with the sudden scratching behind the walls from the rats.

It won't happen.

"Look, you pay me shit, and you treat me like shit. I'm trying to sell you a better story."

"At least I'm not a plagiarist," he says.

"Then what do you call me ghostwriting your shit? Honest work?"

"This isn't about me, Walker."

"As a matter of fact, this conversation is all about me."

"Look, Walker, you plead like a whiny little bitch for work and do the low-cut, under-the-table work because no one will let you publish a story on your own." Ralph stops to laugh and chew on what I assume is food but just might be a dirty dick. "How could you steal from Kenny Daniels? He did nothing to you. Who do you think you are, Stephen Glass?"

"Well, Glass wasn't a plagiarist; he fabricated his stories. You're probably mistaking him for someone like Jayson Blair. Now he was a plagiarist. But you wouldn't know this because you're an incompetent fuck who hasn't been promoted past reviews and wedding announcements in over seven years. If you want this so bad, do it yourself. I'm getting paid more money to do this thing with Gordy Renton than you ever offered me to do your travesty reviews and shite wedding paragraphs. I can sell this to someone like Stephanie Quinn or Ross Turner. I'm sure hot-tits and the drunken sportscaster could use the career boost."

Before he can retort, I hang up on Ralph West. A few seconds later, he sends me several text messages, calling me very dirty words. If only he had talked this dirty to me before, our relationship would have been better. But love is over, Ralphie, and I've just got to let you go.

Four big boxes filled with files from around Darius's desk now sit on my own writing desk. I don't know where to begin; I realize I overestimated just how much work this would take as I flip through random papers. Many are written in German, French, and what I assume is a type of Middle Eastern text. I know none of these languages. In the past, if it wasn't American, I didn't bother. Now I have to deal with thousands of pages written in languages I don't understand. I slap myself for not reading what I took before I took it.

My cell phone rings. Greene's name flashes so I pick up.

"What happened, Mr. Walker?" Greene asks.

"Better than expected. Gordy Renton was very open to me. He doesn't know where Darius is. When he got wind that I was a journalist, he asked if I could use my resources to help him find his son."

"He doesn't suspect anything?"

"As far as he's concerned, I'm helping out with his son's whereabouts. Gordy told me he isn't interested if his son is guilty or not. He just wants to know Darius is safe. Plus he's lonely, desperate, might be susceptible to influence, and doesn't know I hate his guts. Just as planned."

"Well, it looks like you have a handle of things. I guess you can take your time."

"Wait, aren't you in a rush to capture Darius?"

Greene yawns. "Not really. There are other important cases to worry about."

I scratch my chin and let out a laugh. "How about *America's Most Wanted*?"

"Law enforcement doesn't want to get involved. Waste of time and money, honestly."

"So what about the courts? Can't you file a motion to subpoena or something?"

"That's not how the courts work, Mr. Walker. He's out on bail. I just need to know where he is, where his hiding spots are, in the event he doesn't show up to court."

"He is accused of killing a girl, no? You'd think he was kind of a risk to the general populace and should be found immediately."

"He's also responsible for the deaths of her missing friends. But that's not important."

"Wait, what?"

Greene repeats his statement.

"Whoa, hold your horses, buddy. You said Darius was accused of killing his chick. You didn't say anything about him being responsible for the death of Dotty's friends. You just said they were missing."

"It doesn't matter—"

"Hell yes, it matters! Bro, you're asking me to go after a suspected killer. This isn't what we would call 'professional.' I mean, this is something you should leave to actual people who handle this stuff. Like the cops, or even a private investigator…" I bite my hand to stop speaking. I tell my inner Claire to shut up with a punch to the thigh. I'm not a person in a position to be lecturing my source of income.

"It's not the details that are important," Greene says with a sigh. "Find Darius. No need for details."

"Come on, I'm a journalist. Details matter to me. You left out big important details, bro. I mean, shit, if this guy is a serial killer, I need help. Come on, bro, you work for the city. You're trying to nail the bastard." Greene lets out moan that irks me. I don't like things that irk me. "Can you give me anything to help out?"

"I'm afraid I can't do that. I just can't."

"Then what about giving me some names of the others he supposedly killed? I can interview the associates and relatives myself."

"I don't remember any off the top of my head."

"What the hell, man? You worked the fucking case, how do you not know?"

"Those details really aren't that important."

"Then what about the Finley girl?"

Greene lets out another groggy moan. "She's dead. Isn't that all that matters?"

"What?"

"Look, it's complicated. Okay, the police, the courts, and myself included, poured hours and hours of work into trying to clinch a conviction. We had problems with the jury, witnesses, evidence; things happened with other cases that just snowballed from there."

"Get that nonsense out of here! Not my problem you couldn't do your job. I need information, I need people to talk."

"Not gonna happen, Mr. Walker. The case is still pending. I can't reveal certain things."

"A guy kills a bunch of people, and no one, including you, gives a shit that he is still out there and not behind bars? You're just gonna leave it at that? That's a crock, man."

Greene growls and something bangs on his other line. "I can find someone else, Mr. Walker! I don't specifically need you!"

"Yeah, you could, asshole, but you knew what you were getting into when you came to me. I'm a journalist. I'll remind you again, just in case you didn't hear me several times before: I'm a journalist. I uncover stuff, I write about it. I do what I do, otherwise I don't eat. Now, I already told you what I had planned on doing. This should have brought up a red flag somewhere in your mental facilities. If you're having issues with it now, knowing who I am, why ask me to find Darius Renton? I had zero involvement until yesterday."

Greene laughs, and I ask what's so funny.

"Well, Mr. Walker, truth be told, you were recommended."

"Huh? Recommended?"

"Someone who was originally there for Darius's arraignments—but Chambers was brought in at the same time. So he caught Chambers's arraignments by chance. Heard what you did, read your article about the ordeal. You left an impression on him. Said you had a 'good smell' about you, probably meant a good nose for sniffing out things."

"Great, I have a secret admirer. When do I meet him? I hope he's cute."

"You won't. He prefers to be anonymous. All you need to know is he found out about my problems with Renton's case and told me you had a personal connection. So I did a little research and found out Gordon bullied you. I figured that would be good enough motivation for you... especially since you got tanked for accusations of plagiarism."

"Man, what the fuck do you know?"

"I know you're a pathetic loser who needs the cash. I would hope you'd keep your mouth shut and do this as quietly as possible. Honestly, I don't care if you write a thousand-page thesis on the Rentons that wins you millions of accolades and awards. All I want you to do is find Darius. So do you want to keep rocking the boat? Or do you want to make cash?"

I say yes, and Greene hangs up before I can respond. What a jackass, putting my life in potential danger because he has no interest in helping me out. I understand if he's burned out, but come on! I could friggin' die here if I'm not careful! Glad I didn't tell him about my side job.

I want to get high; my best stuff comes about that way.

Heather, queen of the drugstore rodeo, has my medicine in more than one way.

While I fiddle around with my cell phone to call her up, I dig into one of boxes on my writing desk. I pull out Darius's old yellow notebook. A few sharp pencils are needed. I have to scribble on the pages and hopefully read what has been imprinted onto them. With at least five hundred pages to go through, carpel tunnel will become my enemy.

I put the notebook to the side and resume searching the stack of papers. I find a fax from Charles Benson, PhD, of the Southern Miskatonic University's Archeology Department. Science jargon litters the page, and I don't understand any of it. Still, legible English catches my attention, as do digital photos paper-clipped to the pages.

The pictures show a forest with fallen trees and rotten stumps. What looks like burned stone, from the ruins of a mansion or a castle, stains the bare dirt. A note in the margin reads: "German Castle Ruins. Est. 1500 CE."

Information on the fax sends me back into the box to look for its sister fax. Attached is a picture of two very long swords lying on a table side by side. They both look ancient, but the blade marked "Sword A" looks much older than "Sword B." The message attached is very simple. I read Benson's words to Joe Renton:

"Joe, I have some wonderful news from the German dig site. One of the Zweihänders we sent in was given a carbon data analysis and compared to another from the era. Do keep in mind the original machine broke down several times upon use. The second, newer machine we used also broke down from unknown technical difficulties. But we fixed the second machine, and the results are astonishing. At first we thought it was just more glitches or faulty software; multiple runs, however, came back with the same results every time. Simply put, despite being made in the same era and in the same region as Sword B, Sword A has decay putting it back to around 1800 BCE; not its later 1500 CE creation date. Let that thought settle in for a while. A two-handed greatsword, made of iron, made in the Bronze Age over two thousand years before its type, the Zweihänder, and all other Iron Age swords, would be created. Isn't it amazing? Isn't it scary? It makes no sense! And I can bet you everything, from the castle rubble to the trees at this dig site, will give off these insane readings! What is causing it? Your suggestions worked! This trip was a success! Is Afghanistan next? What do we do next?"

Joe had written a response to Benson.

"I'll send you more funding for Germany. Yes, I believe Afghanistan is next. We are going to change human history, Charlie. We will set human destiny."

Those are some heavy words.

But it is beyond me, and it does not matter in my search for Darius.

I put the papers to the side and focus on a thing that interests me above all else. The beautiful, wooden music box that was originally on Darius's desk now sits in my hands. I am mesmerized by the color of it, a color I didn't notice until just now. I can't quite say what kind of red, but it is very rich, very vivid.

How could I not notice this? Why did I not remember putting it in the box of papers?

I play around with it for a bit. I turn the knob underneath and wind up the device inside. When I open the box's lid, a wonderful chirp comes out. Metal teeth comb against the tiny metal music sheet located inside. A beautiful tune soothes my ears and the deepest parts of my ego and emotion. I smile and rotate the music box. Inside is a dedication.

To my lover, Joseph.

Aw, isn't that sweet?

The music puts me in a very good mood. With it playing right next to me, I decide to go through the boxes and see what other wonderful gems I might find.

Chapter Four

Even behind these iron bars and cracked mason walls, the first impact is still the loudest. I imagine the bones breaking, the flesh tearing, and the liquid splattering from each hit. The battle is waged miles away, yet I can see the trenches filled with barbwire and men in gas masks. They charge at one another, rifles in hand and the presence of God and country behind them, pressing them to take the fight to the enemy. The machines roar behind them, carving pieces out of the world with oily treads and burning lances. Metal sky crawlers hurl bombs and leave hellfire over the green.

Mortars fly into the trees, sparks shine brighter than the stars. The crushing sound of stone and dirt explodes, signaling where the rounds have fallen. The smell of gas burns the air miles away from where I sleep. My eyes burn with a sensation that is not natural; a chemical burn. Bullets take flight before and after the rounds crash, hurtling across air from chamber to target. The delayed sound of these deathly trumpets is carried only after they hit their note.

A fine bloody play deserves no less.

Even with the skirmish going on outside these prison walls, my ears hurt the most from that first gunshot, that first explosion, that first dying wail that broke my ignorant view. I knew none of this several months ago, until the first impact shattered what I knew of the world and of human nature. Only these prison walls can keep me protected from the violence outside.

I wanted no part in this; I refused to fight. I would let other sons kill one another, but not mine. I would keep my own son sheltered from being asked to pick up arms in the name of God and country. I did not want my child to stain his soul with another's blood.

I want to start over, away from this violence.

But there is something in the blood. Something in it that makes running and fighting impossible. The horror can smell you. It will follow you if you smell right.

And I smell like a banquet.

So it followed. It thirsted. It yearned. It spoke to me, and I felt its teeth press into me.

The world knows I am of a forsaken lot. The roaches, the flies, the rats: they avoid me. I am kept in isolation in hopes that Pestilence itself, festering in my wounds, takes my life away, if only out of pity. My fellow prisoners scream in agony as they are preyed on by something invisible, feral.

It is but a matter of time before it is my turn. Until then, I will answer their persistent questions, since it will be their turn too. There is nothing I can do. The decayed cell walls won't protect me. Neither will the feeble firearms of the guards. I'm not even sure they will still be around anyway; they probably will flee from the hopelessness of their situation long before they become a target.

For a fleeting moment, I allow myself to wonder how my family is doing. Thinking about them makes me depressed. It's my fault if anything happens to them. I should have escaped with them when I had a chance. A terrible thought arises: "I should be more concerned with myself."

Whether I like it or not, soon all my worries will be about just me.

The rain starts to pour down, as if God is trying to start a second flood and wipe away the bloodshed. Cracks in the floor allow water to flood part of my cell, all the way up to the ankles. I don't panic anymore when it happens. If it ever got high enough, I would try to drown myself. I begged for hypothermia to take me away, but instead the tainted water agitates my wounds and makes me weaker.

None of this bothers me. I fixate on the battlefield. Not on the soldiers. Not on the shells. Not on the carnage. I stare into the middle of it, looking for the horror behind it all. I find myself looking for the Pale Stranger from afar. I know it's there. Because I fear, I know it is out there, searching for me among the fallen.

The blood knows it will get to me before the other preying on my fellow damned does, before the sickness eats away my health.

And I pray God will kill me before it does arrive.

Chapter Five

"Baby," Heather whispers into my ear. I am slow to respond. I look at her stoned eyes when she blows cigarette smoke past my face. "Why are you being so quiet?"

"Oh, sorry. I lost track of what's going on. Been at this for a while." I picked up the stuff I was working on. I explain I was piecing together what Charles Benson had written to Joe Renton about the German castle ruins. She looks at a paper with some German on it; cigarette ash falls all over it. She stares at the paper funny then stares at me funny.

"What are you doing reading German?"

"Oh, I'm not. I don't understand a damn thing without a translation."

"Then why are you reading German without a translator?"

"I'm trying to find somebody. Trying to see if there's anything I can use in these papers to help me do so."

"Yeah, you told me that a hundred times over the phone."

"Did I tell you I'm getting good money coming in from two people?"

Heather nods. "You also need a tan bad. You're going full vampire on me. Not the sparkly kind, though, that would suck balls."

I agree. Then I notice four people loitering around in my living room. I don't recognize any of them, don't even remember inviting them in. "Um, what is going on?"

Heather grins and whispers into my ear, "We are celebrating, remember? For you getting some good gigs?"

"No, not really. Sorry, I'm zoning out here."

She nibbles my ear and laughs a little laugh. I ask who they are. "The people we are going to be partying with for the next forty-eight hours. Remember now?"

I shake my head.

"Sorry, I've been trying to work here. What do we have to play with?"

"Shabu." A wild party man wearing a black silk shirt with gold and white omega symbols all over it appears. His long, greasy hair, unkempt beard, and sunglasses despite it being nighttime put me on guard. I ask him what Shabu is. "Ice, baby," the party man hisses.

"I'm not a big meth person. Like the rush. Don't like the rotting of the teeth."

The party man accepts my challenge, pulls his gums apart, and shows me pearly whites.

"Fuck that hillbilly shit," he shouts before reaching into his pocket. He pulls out a small, foggy glass toy shaped like an angel statue. "This is Shabu. Ninety-six point three percent crystal methamphetamine right here. This doesn't come from a meth house. No sir, this comes from a Japanese or Filipino science lab, made with lasers and chemicals and designed on a microscopic level. Only the best; Walter White perfection right here. Gonna chop this little girl into pieces, mix it with some caffeine, and smoke it. Probably get four hundred hits out of her. But one hit from this, and you're always gonna want it on the menu."

"Well, I like where this party is going now." I purse my lips and nod. The wild party man lets out a wild cry and goes over to the couch, where the other candy kids hover. Heather slithers onto my lap, wraps her arms around my neck, and gives me a peck on the lips. I grin. "I like where this is going too."

"Hey, bro, can I ask you something?" the party man says.

"You just did. But sure, ask away."

The party man pops his collar to fan himself off. "Can you turn on the AC?"

"Nope. Trying to lose some weight. Need my sauna to be hotter."

So party man leaves, leaving me and Heather to make out. After sucking on my lips she spins around and uses me as a chair. Curiosity has stricken her. She goes over the things that have been translated into English. She targets the file titled "German Count," only because some of it is in English. A citation from Benson says that although the count was nameless, Benson nicknamed him the Yellow Count. Underneath the citation, Joe has written his own note. Around the time he got the notes about the count, Joe had been watching the movie *Nosferatu*, so he gave the Yellow Count his own nickname: Graf Orlok.

Ah, so this story is about a real-life Dracula? Interesting.

The summary of this mystery man begins with the castle the count resided in—or rather it begins with the lack of information surrounding it. The ruins tell a tale of a marvelously built work of art that stretched for half a mile and had multiple levels above and below the surface. None of this interests me or Heather. If I want to learn about old cribs for decrepit, rotting corpses, we can watch classic reruns of *Lifestyles of the Rich and Famous*.

Not much was said about the count. Most of the information about him revolved around what type of count he was. The two men argued over the different types of titles the ancient count could have held. Benson honestly thought the Yellow Count was a Rheingraf, because the count had commanded a presence near a river, where the ruins were found. However, Joe Renton wrote that he thought Orlok was a Landgraf; a theory he couldn't prove, as he didn't know if the count was part of the Holy Roman Empire, and he couldn't confirm what the count did in life.

I think they argued over this trivial stuff like this just to prove who was smarter.

As with the castle schematics, I'm not interested in titles or a history lesson. Hell, I failed my history courses in both high school and college; I'm not even sure Heather finished high school. He was a count. That's all that matters.

At the end of this file is the myth that surrounded his death.

"Looks like we have a winner," Heather says.

Jackpot indeed.

The Yellow Count's legacy was tainted with infamy. According to the tale, a young stable boy serving at the castle had fled to one of the nearby towns under the count's rule. The boy was half dead and covered in blood when the townsfolk took him in. The boy explained that the count had everyone serving and living on the castle grounds locked in. With no way out, the count and several of his guards had begun to hunt everyone down, one at a time.

It wasn't just an ordinary slaughter. The myth compared it to fox hunting. The count was the hunter, and would pick sections of the castle he would hunt in. It was ritualistic, methodical, prejudicial. This had been going on for days, and the boy barely escaped with his life.

The villagers became enraged. They took arms and stormed the castle. They killed the count's guards before capturing and beheading him. What became of the castle was unknown. The charred ruins suggest it was burnt to the ground sometime after the count was executed.

Benson said there was more to the myth than he thought. Pieces of historical truth verified the myth, but they were spread over countless unrelated documents in German history. The story is there, Benson promised, it just needs to be brought together. He promised he would let Joe Renton know when he uncovered it.

The date of this file precedes the picture of the two swords with freaky carbon dating timestamps by two months.

"So ghoulish," she says in between lighting another cigarette.

"You know, I can imagine someone running around, you know…" I make a chopping motion, imagining an ax in my hand. "I think all the count really wanted was just to ax them a question." I change my voice into something demonic and chop at her. "I'm going to chop up the pretty girl in front of me!" Heather pushes me and gives me a sour look as I laugh.

"That's not funny. You shouldn't say things like that. A bunch of people got killed by a deranged royal. That stuff happens all the time in countries with corrupt leaders. You ever think about that?"

"Ah, come on. Don't lecture me. It was a joke."

"What do you think happened to that poor innocent boy?"

I shrug, which makes her push me again. "Seriously, Claire, I don't like scary stories. I need to know he had a happy ending."

"Scary stories don't have happy endings. Not real ones, anyway."

"Well, that whole thing gave me the shivers. Something about it is creepy and wrong. Just what the hell are you doing with this anyway?"

"It's just a myth, baby. These are just stories. And besides, I'll hold you if you get nightmares." I put my hands on her thigh, rubbing up and down to warm her up. She lets out a little squeal, takes out her cigarette, and kisses me. The kiss turns into licking.

"Hey, lovers, you ready to party?" the wild party man asks. Heather takes a drag of her smoke, then puts it in my mouth before launching off my lap. It is wonderful that, when it comes to drugs, I know where her loyalties are. Not that I blame her.

So I release my passion on the cigarette, kill it, and put the butt in an empty soda can.

Everyone but me sits Indian style around the coffee table. The tinfoil is placed down, the sharpened butter knives come out, and the glass pipes are placed side by side. Poor little angel is cut into hundreds of little pieces then ground into powder, but it's a necessary sacrifice to take us to a chemical heaven. Joining in the fray right now would have been a party indeed; it looks so yummy. The allure of getting blazed on some quality, high-grade crystal is a tempting devil.

But my interests lie with the boxes of papers. I still can't make out why Darius Renton would be interested in his uncle's work. Joe was an anthropologist. Darius was an oceanographer. What does the study of the ocean have anything to do with homicidal Germans? Making matters worse, I have yet to find an opinion or comment from Darius himself. Without his thoughts, knowing what made him tick or plotted, I have nothing to go on.

Maybe he was just reading his uncle's work. Something fascinated him.

And if this was the case…then maybe he ran off to Germany to study ruins.

The very thought made me sweat, more than I was already.

If Darius really killed a bunch of people, maybe he is now overseas killing beautiful European babes and causing an international incident. I don't have a passport to go chase him across international waters; I don't even have the authority to bring him over in case I found him. Plus I hate flying. I really hope this isn't the case. I want to get paid doing the least amount of work. Playing crime-stopper is not a good career path.

As I begin to wallow in self-pity, an idea comes to mind; it's terrible really, as I don't want to do legwork today. I should find Charles Benson. Maybe he will know what to do.

I just need a number.

So I start scanning through the various boxes for Benson's personal information. Flipping through the pages, I find more articles, notes, faxes, memos, and personal emails from Benson to Joe. The jargon makes my head spin. The very thought of having to hire a geeky nerd to translate both the languages and the science lingo makes my stomach hurt worse than the chili bean sauce I had earlier. I find no phone numbers, but I do find an address for the Southern Miskatonic University.

Before I can call, something catches my eye. A newspaper column, dated five years before, with a postcard stapled to it. Small, quick, and lacking certain details, the article tells of Charles Benson's demise. He and sixteen off his staff were killed by insurgents in Afghanistan while investigating a ruined royal palace. U.S. Marines exchanged fire with the insurgents for two days. The skirmish ended when an airstrike was called in to eliminate the insurgents' hiding places deep inside a mountain. Unconfirmed reports said over forty insurgents were killed during the battle and airstrike. Two marines were also killed in action.

I'm glad I never joined the military. I don't think I'd have the stomach to be killed.

So I couldn't ask Benson for help. Dead men thousands of miles away don't tell me any good tales, not the important ones involving me anyway. The thought of Afghanistan is not my idea of an autumn vacation. I see no reason why Darius should, or would, go there. It's still a hotly contested place.

Hoping to find something more, I flip to the postcard stapled to the paper. The timestamp for the postcard is a day before Benson was reported to have been killed. A big red "Return to Sender" covers the postmark. It was written by Joe to Benson.

"I'm sorry, Charlie," I read in Joe's voice. "I never wanted this to happen. Despite what has happened between us in the last few weeks, you are my friend. I am sorry you feel this way about my decisions. I hope we can put this past us and move on."

Benson never got the postcard of apology. Words were left unspoken. Bitterness of unknown sorts was left unresolved. Should have e-mailed him or texted instead.

Still, I wonder what Joe was apologizing about? Why is Darius interested in what happened between two colleagues five years ago?

But as Heather now points out, it's time for me to stop working and break bad instead. There will be plenty of time to waste chasing ghosts and locating a suspected killer. With the stress yet to come, I must indulge now. So I put the thoughts of working on the backburner and get ready to head into outer space.

Chapter Six

Hour fifty-one, I think. Exact date: forgotten. Location: bathroom.
 Heather is passed out in the bathtub, talking in her sleep about something indecipherable. I pay no attention to it. My mind was on something important.

I had 102 used Popsicle sticks, held together by the melted remnants of sticky mango ice cream. By my feet are about two hundred more used Popsicle sticks, a dozen empty water bottles, an unlimited supply of used Jolly Rancher wrappers, glue, and multicolored duct tape. I didn't need the scissors after all, but you never know.

What was I doing with all of these items?

I am building a house. A house for a family, yes, and I built the family too, out of little sticks and Jolly Rancher wrappers and tape. I gave them each a smiley face and heads with cigarette ash. They would be my make-believe family for the rest of my lunacy, which had no known end in sight.

Heather comes half to life. She places her hands over her face, and coughs. She mumbles, asking if I have any spare water bottles around my feet.

I shush her with a ferocious shush. A master needs his silence.

And when I do finish, I will find a way to move in. For that to work, I have to build an add-on. Not enough sticks. Need more. They have some at Home Depot. Lumber sticks.

I can just charge it on my credit card.

"Baby, get me a glass of water," Heather says as she twists and turns in the tub.

"No time for water. Can't leave. City Ordinance will cite me if I leave the house unfinished. Need to finish before the permit expires."

"Please? I'm thirsty." Her lips are as cracked as mine. When she taps at her lips, thick, dark blood oozes out. She keeps licking at the fresh wound, thinking it's water, which it technically is made of.

"How about orange juice?"

She says no.

"Mangos? Strawberries? Bananas? Milk? Smoothie? Gatorade? Pedialyte?"

Still no.

"How about water?"

"Water sounds lovely." I hustle over to the bathtub. I turn the cold water on, then hobble back over to my house. The pipes rumble before erupting. Bitterly cold water blasts her in the face. "Thank you." She moves around in the tub to accommodate the sudden intrusion of water. She cups her hand at the edge of the tub to catch the spill and laps it up like a cat. She smiles, rubs her stomach, and gurgles before swallowing. "How did we end up in here?"

Good question. I lost track after the thirtieth hour.

Everything between hour fifteen and twenty-five was all clean, clean, tweak, clean some more, and clean once more before tweaking again.

Hours ten through fifteen, we ate very light and took a few pills to help with the sleep deprivation so I wouldn't be lost in the mad psychosis that was no-sleep tweaking. I know there were some beer and shots in there; I do remember going to the liquor store.

Hours five through nine were strip-club hopping. One of the girls dancing, I had been waiting like a year and a half to see her tits. Totally worth the price of entry. After that, we went rave surfing. We rolled and did some blow.

I do remember having a threesome with Heather and another girl who came back with us from one of the clubs sometime during hour twenty-two between cleaning and smoking ice. After that, I remember going to the store for more Popsicles and lightbulbs after the tweakers used my good bulbs to smoke out of; I had to go back shortly after that for more candy and fruit.

Just another endless party that leads to lost days and fun nights.

It always ends up like this, whether I want it to or not. Most times I ask for seconds.

My brain gets pretty fried from my little endeavors. Even now, I know that soon the upcoming body crash will hurt all over. It helps in tiny amounts that I take a power nap sometime during these wacky shenanigans. Normally, I don't dream when on a binge. Dreaming just isn't possible for me under such intoxicating circumstances. But dream I did… this time.

The dream was of a little boy running in the woods with a pretty girl holding his hands. She was much older. Could have been his mother, could have been his sister—hell, she could have been his lover, the lucky little player. But both of them ran, scared at what would happen if they stopped. Boy and woman were more animals fleeing than they were rational humans.

Something evil was giving chase. There was a tall, lanky man galloping toward them. He was made of impossible white, made of a dreamy haze. His hands were colored with the blood of many. Behind the lanky pale stranger were several wolves that he may or may not have commanded. Wolves like people. Wolves like reptiles. Wolves like things not considered wolves. Every possible combination that could be spliced with canines was there. They melded and twisted together like a big melting pot of unnecessary. My imagination, even in dreams, was tested past its threshold.

"A pale stranger, yes, that's what he is." I find myself repeating the phrase, until it loses all meaning and leaves my mind.

Without admitting it, I knew I shouldn't have read creepy stories before taking drugs.

Heather nods. "Yeah, I saw one not too long ago."

"Really?"

She nods again. "Probably a hallucination caused by the drugs, though."

"Or he was really a creature from in between dimensions, looking down on us disapprovingly."

We both nod at the possibilities and resume what we are doing for a moment.

"Tell me something, Claire," Heather says between helpings of rusty water. "Who is the guy Slowburn?"

"Eh…" I don't want to talk about him. "How do you know about him?"

"Before I broke your bathroom door handle—"

I stop her from speaking and examine the door handle. She didn't just break the handle: the door had been kicked off its hinges, and there are several knife stabs, flame burns, and scribbled faces in the cheap wood. I tilt my head, not surprised that I didn't see the door torn down, then I ask, "Are all Mexican women that violent?"

"Only when provoked."

"And what provoked your wrath?"

"You were shouting something about how City Ordinance was going to get you."

"Oh, sorry, that was the drugs talking. Although," I stop to stroke my chin, "the possibility of them citing me for not having proper permits to construct this house is about a seventy-one percent possibility." I shake my head. "Need to finish just in case they bring the pit bulls down."

"Don't change the subject, Claire. Paxton Chambers. Slowburn. Who is he?"

"Well, missy, how do you know about him?"

Heather explains that she was going through my closet to find Easter eggs of speedball hidden in my lair. When she found no eggs in sight, she moved to the closet. She found dozens of empty cardboard boxes I used in my journalism days, to hide inside and infiltrate enemy territory. Hidden among them she found a cardboard box unlike others: it was filled with papers and sealed with duct tape. Thinking goodies were hidden in it, she cut the tape off and dug in.

She found several awards, two plaques, a framed article, and a picture of me at the hospital with the burn victims of Slowburn. I am more proud of the picture then I am of awards and plaques; neither paid me, and all I got out of them was the bottom of a night crawler heap. But that photo, yeah, I was real proud of it.

"You had a wrapping around your right arm."

I laugh. "Second degree burns. My hair has grown back."

"So tell me the story," Heather says, using her toes to turn the shower down and give her a better ear.

My involvement with Slowburn started two years ago. It had nothing to do with him, but rather it was about the string of arson attacks in old buildings in and around the historic district. No one cared too much about it, except for the people who ran the historic district. The buildings were of cultural significance, which was just bullshit in my opinion. They wanted to renovate the homes and sell them for millions of dollars to stupid people willing to buy into the lies about making the city significant. There was nothing significant about kicking out the homeless people who squatted in these abandoned places.

He used slow-burning lamp oil to set the places ablaze. A typo in my first printed article about him, combining the words "slow" and "burn," gave him his name, although not at first. It was only when Paxton Chambers, a twenty-nine-year-old real estate agent for the historic district's renovation project, decided to burn homeless people instead of rotten homes that the typo become his moniker.

For almost a year he played his game. He would find sleeping homeless people when they were alone. He'd dump lamp oil on them, and then throw a match. None of his victims died, but they might as well have. The first two or three had minor burns. Then Slowburn used more oil on them. When he didn't get the desired effect, he switched to gasoline. Many of the homeless left, so he followed them to other parts of town. Some started to hang out in groups, so he stalked them, picking them off when they were vulnerable.

"Mr. Walker," I say, as I remember for Heather the many letters and phone calls I received over my time on the beat. "How close are the police to catching the Slowburn Arsonist? How soon can he stop terrorizing our streets?"

"Did you answer them?" Heather asks, as she puts her forehead on the rim of the tub.

"There was nothing I could tell them. The police had nothing to go on. By the time my infamous encounter with him happened, he had moved onto taping up his victims and watching them squirm before setting them on fire. He never stuck around after igniting them until that point, and it was partially the reason why none of his victims died. He was going to change that; make sure someone died. On the day of our showdown, Slowburn decided to use his methods on a seven-year-old girl he found while she was walking home from school. Police found homemade napalm in his car and at his home."

Heather holds her mouth against the tub. "Oh no. That's horrible. What was he like?"

"Quiet young man, very polite, very calm; his boyish looks belied the monster inside him. I met him once or twice at one of the city's many meetings in regards to Slowburn and the burning of its historical buildings. Just polite hellos, byes; he didn't seem interested in me or what I was writing about. Did everything in his power to keep himself hidden from the police."

On that fateful day, I was doing a follow-up on the rebuilding process for a few of the old homes. The presence of Chambers outside the burned wreckage of Slowburn's previous arsons did not send any red flags my way. He was on the Restoration Committee, so he was at every burn site. It was part of his job. Perfect cover, really.

He was near the basement of one of the burned homes, going down with gasoline. The little girl he had kidnapped was down there, bound and gagged. I approached him to do an interview with him, if only because he was there at the time and because I wanted to get home early to catch some much-needed sleep. Get Chambers out the way, pretend he was someone important, and then be on my way.

So I climbed down the basement stairs, approached him, called out his name.

Before I noticed the little girl tied up in the corner, he chucked the gasoline can at me. He had a small blowtorch. He flipped it on and tried to singe my face off. He damn near burned my eyebrow off. Came at me and gave me a burn on my right forearm. Screamed for help, a few of the neighbors heard me and called the police.

While I'm not much of a fighter, neither was Chambers. He was so determined to burn my face that he forgot how to duck and dodge. He tripped over himself when he missed me on the third pass, so I punched him in the back of the head. He fell forward and busted his head open on one of the basement support beams. I tackled him and held him until the police arrived.

That was my big rumble with Slowburn. Rather unimpressive, thinking about it.

"I was sent to the burn section of the hospital to treat my burn. I met several of Slowburn's victims who were still in ICU. Despite their pain, they wanted to meet with me. Shook their hands, was humbled by their gratefulness. There's nothing more inspiring than a disabled spirit. It felt good that I eased their minds; their tormenter was now locked up."

I didn't enjoy bouncing around the police stations and the courthouse, but I wanted to make sure that Slowburn was getting the shackles and not the free pass. I'd seen it too many times before with people like him. I was surprised that mysterious someone who sent Greene my way remembered me from that day. Might buy him a beer if I meet him.

"That's sweet, baby. You should've made it big after that."

I scratch the back of my neck and shake my head. "Yeah, well, I was introduced to a guy named Kenny Daniels. 'Show him the ropes,' my editor told me. Surefire way to get a promotion with all going in my favor." I spit to the side. "Worst mistake I've made so far."

I'm sure if those burn victims could see me now, they would have nothing but disappointment for how my life has turned out. There was once a time I was proud to talk about the heroic thing I did. Now I'm lucky if I ever tell that tale, and why the box is locked away.

My apartment phone rings. Heather and I cringe in pain from the sudden telephone ring. This marks just the third time I have heard that phone ring in the few months I've lived here. The first time was from a debt collector looking for the previous tenant who, I reminded them, was killed in a police raid. The second time was a guy calling for directions to a bar downtown. I wobble over to the telephone near the front door.

"Ahoy hoy?" I say.

"Mr. Claire Walker? Is that you?" Greene's obnoxious voice oozes through the phone and into my ear. Goddamn greasy lawyers only call when they want something, and that usually is money. I let out a gag. I feel a rant coming on now that memories of my former glory have been shaken up and let loose on my conscience.

"Wasn't expecting you so early in the day. How can I help you, Olly?"

"Please don't call me that, Mr. Walker. And it's not early, it's two p.m. I've been trying to reach you the past two days on your cell phone, but I have gotten no response. I had to call your apartment manager for your number."

"Well, excuse me, princess, but that's early for a hardworking journalist like me."

"Excuse me?"

"Now, Mr. Greene, I know you hired me to find Darius Renton, but frankly, these past few days I have had zero input to go on from any of the sources I've asked. Including you. And I've paid good out-of-pocket money to get some leads. Leads you aren't helping me with."

"What leads? What sources?"

"Can't tell you that. That's the first rule of journalism, Mr. Greene. If I betray my sources, I can't call myself a journalist. No. I can't call myself an honest man. Now, for attorneys, being honest might not fly, but for a guy like me, it's about one thing: the truth. Not what I think is true. That don't matter. No, it's about what the truth is. How it happens, that's how I report it. I have to get out the truth to the people. They are what matters."

"Mr. Walker, I hired you to find Darius Renton. Not preach."

"Frankly, I don't give a damn what you hired me for. You're interrupting me while I'm doing some important investigative journalism. You're interrupting the truth. And worst of all, you won't help me bring the truth about Darius's transgressions to the public! This sick person has to be brought to justice. Or more people will die, like Dotty Finley, like the people whose names you held out on me. And you won't..." I hold my finger up high in the air, "you won't help me. You have given me nothing to work with. And if you fire me for not doing my job, then it is my American right to write about this travesty! That I report your lack of transparency! Your lack of compassion for the victims! Your lack of respect for truth and justice!"

"Okay, you win, Mr. Walker. Just stop rambling. Give me a second." Greene says something to someone in the room before clearing his throat. "You free after seven?"

"Anything for you, sweet cheeks."

"Okay, I'm going to bring you some files on Darius Renton. I will also take you to the crime scene where the police found Dotty Finley. Will that satisfy you, or are you going to preach more bullshit?"

Greene hangs up after agreeing to meet up with me, making me promise to never call him sweet cheeks again. Ah, the joys of being on a binge. My confidence is rocket high. My tongue and mind are sharp and lethal. I feel invincible.

Heather walks out of the bathroom. Water soaks into the rug where she stands. She goes to the center of the room, takes off her clothes, an item at a time, until she is left naked. She walks to the kitchen, grabs her cigarettes, and goes to the bedroom.

"You coming to bed, my personal hero?" she says in a sultry voice.

I would in a hot minute.

But I need to finish the home first, before City Ordinance shows up.

Chapter Seven

Oliver Greene is a muscular forty-five-year-old, standing about six feet tall. Gray haired, he has a very round face, a strong chin. and a thick neck. Those teeth of his are too damn blunt and damp with chewing tobacco—just like a hyena that dips. He would seem scary to anyone facing him in court, but his hands betray him. They are soft to the touch, like touching a girl's skin. It doesn't match his macho imagery. He must be a hit with the ladies. Or boys. It's not a problem if he does, but I can't quite tell if he likes either. He has his nose above everyone else. Narcissistic bastard. Probably enjoys money more than sex. I wouldn't be surprised if he has sex with his money. I wouldn't trust a child with him and expect him to not eat the kid if it meant he could get ahead in life. But people trust him to get the job done, to win, and to devour their firstborn child if necessary just so they can win.

Greene is everything I expect of him.

Yet it is Darius, the man I've been hired to find, who surprises me. He is nothing like I anticipated. At least not from what I read on paper.

The doctor who did the psychiatric evaluation on Darius did not paint him in a positive light. Neither did his cellmate, his classmates, his teachers, or his friends. No one is going to vouch for him, let alone deal with him; though to be fair, the resentment extends to the entire Renton clan. Whatever impolite or derogatory term could be used against him is thrown at him with great force.

The consensus is unanimous: either throw him in a solitary cell forever or execute him, but under no circumstance should he ever be let out again.

He is a wicked man. So wicked that he is the incarnate of all that could be considered evil. He is so evil, in fact, that no one can stand to be around him for more than a few minutes before becoming "ill" and "unnerved." His mere presence makes people frightened that he is going to attack them.

One massive report repeated this over and over. I get bored.

The next report is more interesting. It omits all the hearings, all the statements, and focuses on the history of the madman behind such heinous acts.

Darius is a lanky twenty-three-year-old boy, standing at five ten. Blue eyes and light brown hair. Chipped front tooth from a skateboarding accident as a kid kept him looking like a kid when he aged. Straight-shooting, with As and Bs for grades, didn't drink, didn't smoke, didn't curse, didn't even talk unless spoken to. Never went to jail prior to Dotty's murder, never went over the speed limit, drove a fuel efficient car. Went to a nondenominational church every Sunday, stayed after to help out with charity work. Became a vegan when he went to college for oceanography, chose marine biology as his specialization. He picked that degree because he wanted to save marine life and spread understanding about the wonderful creatures that live under the water.

This was a menace to society? This was the incarnate of evil?

I remember that Paxton Chambers was like Darius in a goody two-shoes kind of way.

No need to question myself anymore.

"We had enough evidence and witness testimony to get him the needle," Greene says.

"Then why did he get bail?" I ask. Greene's sneers at me for a second before putting his eyes back on the road. "Do you have a legitimate answer?"

"I don't know. Things happened."

It was a common theme I had noticed in the past hour, from reading or hearing Greene speak ill of him. Everyone hated Darius. No one wanted to give him a chance. Yet they couldn't give one solid reason why, if that much. It was of their opinion that a proper beheading was the answer, no other alternative.

"Can you think of anything?"

"Goddamn it, Mr. Walker!" Greene hits the steering wheel with his palm. Such reactionary outbursts are common during the drive as I ask about Darius. Every outburst is followed by silence, an ugly look, or both. What follows is a change of subject, an attack on my character, or both. "You look strung out. Are you tired or just on drugs?"

"A bit of both: they balance each other out."

"Drugs are illegal, Mr. Walker."

I shrug. "What recreational activities I do are none of your concern, Olly."

"Please stop calling me that."

"Fine. Just drive me where we are supposed to go, and I'll leave you alone."

We don't talk at all for the next ten minutes or so. I rub my eyes before returning to Darius's saintly record before his life was ruined by a little thing called murder. It's sad to acknowledge that this kid, prior to his fall, reminded me too much of Joe Renton. He resembles nothing in his manners or upbringing like Gordy, even though he looks exactly like his father.

Both men have a passion for soccer. Both men love classical music and theater. Both men enjoy helping out at the Southern Miskatonic University's ballet program. Joe was a big funder for the project. Through the program, Darius became acquainted with Dotty Finley. She was a star ballerina; she gave its program some legitimacy. Joe was a big fan of hers, and it was through him that they ended up becoming a couple. Dotty had a bright future ahead of her. Many offers were extended to her. There was even talk about her joining actual theater productions or dance troops.

None of this happened. Whatever dreams she had were left unfulfilled.

I really don't want to write a scathing piece about Darius or Joe. I didn't even want to do one about Dotty Finley. I signed up to make Gordy look bad, but even now I am having doubts.

What made you flip, Darius? What made you kill your fiancée?

And when did I start giving a damn?

We arrived at our destination, Jaune's Vin Forest, without me knowing. Greene parks at one of the rest stops then tells me it's a mile hike to the abandoned Vin Lake Processing Plant. Vin Forest is foggy, one of its defining features. Among of its other defining features are the thick oak trees that block the sun and the poppies that litter its grassy areas.

"This place was very popular for suicides," Greene says, breaking my sense of serenity. "The constant foggy environment made for a perfect cover. There was a myth that said anyone who wandered around in the fog got lost."

"Bro, I really did not want to know that," I say with the disgust. "I've been reading fucked-up stories lately and don't need any more weird nightmares. So please, don't."

"Oh, don't worry, there hasn't been a suicide in years. Jaune did a fantastic job of cleaning up the forest's image. It was a popular tourist spot until a year ago."

I roll my eyes. "Let me guess. Bigfoot started batting people away with tree stumps?"

"Actually, people have been vanishing from the forest. Runners, tourists, and explorers have disappeared. Abandoned cars have been found, and missing backpacks and purses turn up in the most remote parts of the forest."

It was uncomfortable enough that Darius was a suspect in a girl's murder and unofficially suspected in the disappearance of several of her friends. This forest was at the center of it. So I snicker and shake my head. "You going to blame that on Darius too?"

"No, smartass. I just thought you might want to know since you're a journalist."

"Believe me, I didn't. And if you need to hold my hand because you're scared, don't."

"You know, Jaune is such a small town they couldn't properly prosecute Darius. So they sent him up to the city so we could deal with him. I bet you're interested in knowing the details of that, aren't you? Since, you know, you want," Greene holds out his fingers and makes air quotations, "'all of the details to the case.'"

"I'm not giving you the satisfaction of boring me to death with the inner workings of your legal system, jackass."

"Fine. Let's do this so I can be done with you and go back to more important things."

I grab my backpack from the backseat before descending the long, gravel walkway with Greene. Fog makes it hard to see what is past the trees, or when the road sharply curves. But it doesn't take long to see the outline of the abandoned Vin Lake Plant. Greene attempts to give me a tiny history lesson on it while we walk, but I pay no attention to him. Dark, rusted, and derelict, hoodlums hang out there and people died.

That is all the important stuff I need to know.

A gate with the chains broken greets us when we arrive, the padlock scattered in pieces everywhere. Greene stands by the fence and proceeds to text on his phone.

"You coming?" I ask.

Greene rolls his eyes. "I'm busy. I'll wait here."

"Come on, bro. I don't know where to go." That isn't a lie, but it isn't the truth. I had seen the building's layout on paper. But I have no sense of direction. A toddler could have handed me a map of scribbled lines in crayon and I wouldn't be able to tell the difference between that map and the one Greene had.

"Heads up," Greene says before tossing me a high-powered flashlight. "You wanted to come here, so go on your own and look stupid when you don't find anything."

I smile. "But I like to look stupid when I can help it, Olly."

"Goddamn it, stop calling me that!"

I laugh as I get on one knee and search my backpack. The first thing I find are the one hundred dollars' worth of scratch-off tickets I purchased at the gas station on the way here. I won a total of three dollars and a medium slush. Not the worst investment I've made. I push them to the side and pull out some of Joe's research notes. I brought them along to see if I could understand more about what he was doing. It's been a failure. My major issue is still trying to separate all the foreign language papers from the ones I could understand.

"If you don't mind, can you separate the English-speaking papers from the non-English-speaking papers? Please?" I give Greene cracked-out puppy dog eyes.

Greene gives me a sullen look. "Absolutely not."

"Stop acting like a girl who got felt up in a Burger King bathroom. Here," I reach in and pull out the music box that used to belong to Joe. I wind the music box up, and then place it by Greene's side. "Ain't it pretty? Cheer up, sourpuss." Greene didn't cheer up, but I did. I stretch out my limbs before turning on the flashlight. Then I give my uncooperative boss a scary face when I place the beaming light under my chin. He doesn't respond. What a jerk.

So I move through the broken gate, across a catwalk, and then down some dark stairs. Past the stairs is a narrow path that breaks into different pathways, before looping back to the entrance I arrived at. Rust, more rust, and just a sprinkle of damp rust for an added measure are painted on everything.

A couple of offices have been ransacked, with graffiti and filth left behind to say hello to whoever came by. Broken panels, control switches covered in dried mud. My feet squeak with leftover trash, ranging from used coffee cups to empty food cartons to burnt needles and used balloons.

Some gravy parties had rocked here once upon a junkie's dream.

A series of metal bridges stretch from one side to the other. Underneath the bridges are a series of tunnels. Water used to run here, but has since dried up. I assume the lake drank all the plant's milkshake up with a large straw.

I could wander around this place aimlessly for a good twenty minutes before having seen everything it has to offer. But I don't want to chance Greene suddenly getting the urge to take off without me. I stick with the plan of doing investigating. I pick one path, the one marked on the map, and cross that metal bridge.

I come upon a hallway with a series of doors. To no surprise, each door is protected by strands of yellow police tape in various states of decay, with holographic police stickers covering double padlocks and sealing the doors shut for what could be forever. The stickers tell of different dates for different crimes: rape, vandalism, drugs, murder—all that wonderful stuff currently being electrified and simplified on television for a viewing audience.

But this is the real deal, no Holyfield—all its grim grit, none of the glossed glamour. If I am unlucky, I will witness some of the leftover trauma embedded in the walls and floors. That stuff is near impossible to clean up, no matter how hard you scrub; and in a place like this, they don't even bother bringing a mop.

Dotty's murder scene will be no different. I know what Greene told me on the way here. Dotty was found ripped open, her bones cleanly cut. Darius was found holding her mutilated body with one hand and a sharpened screwdriver in his other hand, covered in her blood and skin. His prints were all over her, all over the entire scene. Scratch marks on his chest and neck matched the skin underneath Dotty's fingernails. Items belonging to her missing friends were scattered all over the room, despite there being no traces of them.

It took many police officers to pry Darius off Dotty's body.

Not a single person is said to have to come back since that day.

Why they just didn't tear this fucker down is beyond me. All they need to cleanse this forsaken place are a few sledgehammers and a bulldozer. They should erase this horror so no one has a reminder of what transpired.

I match Dotty's murder date against the other dates on the door. I expected to see the remnants of an unspeakable crime, but I am stunned at what I find. Each door was made out of steel. Each door has taken its share of repeated licks, but each of the sealed doors is still sealed.

No one is getting in without some serious power tools or being a master of unlocking.

But the door to the room where Dotty's body was found has been shredded open with what looks like a double-bladed chainsaw with lava teeth. I examine the doors. Claws did this, like a bear's or a lion's.

The thought of a wild animal tearing through a steel door terrified the badass out of me. I'm no animal expert, but I have questions just looking at the door. Is it even possible for a large animal to do that without harming itself in the process? Are there even any wild, deranged bears, possibly with claws made out of chainsaw blades and lava, running around Vin Forest?

The only witnesses are a dozen roaches, but they aren't talking. Not the biggest fan of snoopers, I imagine; they probably think I'm going to snitch them out to the exterminators. I tell them I don't roll like that before entering the room.

The walls are covered in newspapers. The papers aren't old. Most go back from a few days to a few weeks ago. A strange language I vaguely recognized is written on the paper in different colors and different textures: some pen, some markers, some paint, some mud.

The words warp into a mosaic eye.

Most words go over my head, but I do catch one word in particular: "Salaam." I read the wall further. By its side is written "As-Salaam." I count both words at least twenty times. I don't recognize the other words, but I assume they are Arabic. I think I see a few Spanish and German words in there too.

I take out my phone and make a quick call to Gordy.

"Hello?"

"Gordy, it's me, Cabbage. I'm where they found Dotty's body."

"Why are you there?"

"Trying to find out as much as I can. I have question. You told me the word salaam meant peace in Arabic. Do you know what As-Salaam means?"

"One of the ninety-nine names of Allah."

"Are you familiar with Arabic?"

"No. Did research. Darius repeated certain words. Over and over. I caught him repeating similar phrases. German, French, Spanish, Mandarin, many other languages. All variations of peace and God. Not any particular god. Just any variation of god. Why are you asking? Did you find something?"

"I found the phrases written on the walls of the room where Dotty Finley was found. These words make up a giant eye. Does this mean anything to you? Like did Joe or Darius mention anything like this?"

"No, not at all."

I shine the flashlight over the room for more clues. As I pass over the random words, which I assume were written by Darius, I come across a blank portion of wall. Instead of one large eye made of words, a dozen or so smaller eyes have been drawn in different shapes. I see something shiny underneath a long pipe, hidden from view.

So I kneel down and look underneath the pipe.

I find something that looks like a shrine. Old candle wax has built up a small mountain on the floor. Inside the wax are necklaces and rings that would be impossible to dig out with my fingernails. Pictures of a young woman I haven't seen before are pasted in the tiny area. She has long red hair and freckles in her white face.

Most of them are solo shots, but a few have Darius in them as well.

I take a photo of the shrine with my phone and sent Gordy the photo.

"Is that Dotty?" I ask.

A few seconds later, Gordy confirms her identity but mumbles, "What is that, meat?"

"Huh? What meat?"

"Hole in the wall. Behind the pictures."

I crouch lower to see what he means. Behind the pictures, hidden underneath the abundance of candle wax, is a hole I missed. It's not small, but not glaring either. I probably missed the hole because I was too busy looking at Dotty's pictures.

In the hole, I see two things. One is a bone of rotten, half-eaten meat. The other is a note attached to the meat. The words are written in big block letters, very easy to read and written in English.

"This will have to do for now, my love," I read off the paper. "It's not what you like. I promise I will get you another real soon. Forgive me." Gordy mumbles something. "Gordy? You okay?" His mumbling gets louder. The few words he speaks are gibberish. "Listen, I'll call you back and tell you what it is." The line disconnects.

I stare hard at the meat. It is rotten, half-eaten, but does not smell. No different from any ground meat I can find at the supermarket. Could have passed for sirloin or steak had it not been so decayed. I even see the Y-Mart logo on the paper; might have gotten the food from the store butcher.

I have no emotions about this slab of dead flesh wrapped in a paper.

But maybe it tastes good, had it not been toxic.

The lack of a smell bothers me. Something like this should be rancid and horrible, but I get nothing. My sense of smell isn't dead; I was able to smell the oak trees and the grass of early autumn before I came down here. It bothers me more when I realize there is no smell in the building.

A flapping of newspaper wallpaper near the shrine reveals a hole behind it. I tear back a piece of the paper and look in. The hole goes back very far and, like the one under the shrine, there is dried blood from where meat was stored. Torn bloodied papers litter inside. Must be a hole behind every last newspaper, where meat would rest and rot inside.

Something catches my eye. Hundreds of torn, bloodied papers extend past where I can see with the flashlight. I see long strands of hair coating the endless cavern like spider webs. I see chewed-up human fingers embedded in the concrete walls. I see pieces of scalp and skullcap stabbed into the concrete.

My high has long since passed. But none of this troubles me. It should have. I just stare, mesmerized by this sudden perversion.

What else is in the hole? How deep does it go?

Can I somehow enter?

My eyes tremble. I see myself not in this room, but in one of the locked rooms nearby in the hallway outside. I see a naked man sits at a table, facing away from me, praying to someone. Every inch of his skin is tattooed with blue eyes.

The eyes on the back of his head open up and stare at me.

A sudden jolt hits my ears, bringing me back to this room. It feels like liquid fire has poured into the cavities housing my eardrums. The ripple of pain fires throughout my body and takes a jackhammer to my skeletal frame. I stumble away from the hole, spinning around in circles before the pain subsides. I rest on a pillar with my fingers in my ears.

Goddamn it!

I scream as loud as I can. I rub my hand over my face, feeling a torrential fall of sweat spray my clothes and skin. I take some of the loose newspaper off the wall. I dry myself off before tossing it to the side.

Out of the corner of my eye, I see someone lying flat on her stomach in the hallway. The figure is of a small girl, covered in dark liquid. I think it's a small girl, but it could be a small boy. Hard to see her in the dark; I can't make out what she looks like or what she is wearing.

The liquid bubbles off her. She remains perfectly still.

I aim the flashlight at her. Yet it's still too dark. I notice the flashlight isn't on; that it has been turned off.

My finger hovers over the on button.

And it won't press down.

"Hello?" I say with a stutter. She doesn't respond. The girl picks herself up with her arms and sways from side to side, slowly at first, then speeding up.

She howls silently before crawling away down the hallway.

The tall shape of a man flashes by the hallway in the direction the girl crawled.

He looks just like the pale stranger in my dreams.

Another sudden zap hits my ears. My muscles instantly contract, and I fall to my knees. I cover my ears to protect them from a physical assault, despite not hearing or feeling anything enter them. Something has invaded my body through my ears. I panic and huddle in the corner, trying to look at every inch of the room at once to make sure nothing else is going to attack me. Something begins to rush over me. My body shivers.

But it isn't an outside invader; it is all from within.

It is my sense of smell coming back. The pain I'm feeling is the sudden putrid odor in the air that threatens to poison me. I'm choking. This personal terror has assumed control of my every sense.

Incomprehensible fear has a shape, if such a thing exists.

I cry out for help and pray to God someone out there hears me.

Chapter Eight

Rocking back and forth in my chair and staring at my cell phone was not how I wanted to spend my evening. It would have been a horribly wonderful waste of time if what had happened a few hours ago did not occur. It's one thing to not do anything, to be happy being lazy at my absolute maximum. I hate waiting. I am very impatient.

Being forced to wait by my cell phone for an answer from Greene and the police is agony in its simplest form, a silent insanity that creates invisible noises to make up for the lack of actual sounds. I want to be talking. I have to be receiving information.

I need my journalism fix.

Greene and the police are not making the process easy.

This heat is getting to me; everything I touch sticks to my skin. My fingernails are chewed raw. I'm acting like a fucking junkie, and I can't keep still. I'm ready to bounce through the neighbor's walls and give their families the surprise of the week, though I doubt it would last for longer than a second before I catch a bullet for breaking and entering.

Is it so wrong to wish my crappy rapping neighbor would put out a bad beat now and break this torture and give me something else to think about?

My sole light, the one thing keeping my sanity from spilling through my eyeballs, is the red music box. I forsake my jams on my radio for this newfound lover. It becomes my glory box, a temporary salvation that usually comes in a powdered or liquid form.

The soothing tunes aren't enough, and neither is the injected magic. Something needs to happen.

My cell phone's sudden ringtone shakes me off my chair like an abusive husband.

"Hello?" I yell into the phone.

"Baby, don't yell, I'll go deaf," Heather's lustful voice sways into my head.

"Oh shit, I'm sorry, Heather." I let out a sigh before falling back into my chair.

"You sound stressed," Heather purrs. I imagine her swaying from side to side, rotating her head with closed eyes; it's a recurring habit when she purrs. I calm down just a tad. "Wanna give me a reason to be proud?"

"On an ordinary day, I would say yes, but, um…this isn't really a good time."

"Please? Don't make me beg. I want to see you."

"I have to deal with the police and a shifty lawyer. You shouldn't come over."

Heather laughs. "And? I can wait in the bedroom. Hey. Do you have any more of those scary stories? I wanna read some more."

"You said you didn't like scary stories."

"Really? Oh, well, I changed my mind. I'm a modern chick, you know."

I get off my chair and walk over to the table with the boxes of Joe's papers. I would love to scare the shit out of Heather and worm my way into an easy lay, just to take my mind off what happened earlier. But she gave me an idea: teamwork.

I tell myself this is going to take more than just Claire Walker, a few uppers, and an Asperger's focus to figure out what the surfing fuck is going on. It's not like I can just call up someone at the *Eye Tribunal* and ask for help. No one will help me. I'm the leper they go to for cheap labor, not the leper they heal.

But Heather doesn't know any better. Put her to work. She's not Kenny Daniels. She won't take credit for helping out and screw me over.

Two is better than one.

She agrees to come over, and I hang up. I take incentive and call Greene. I'm tired of working on his schedule. Greene picks up. "Olly, Walker here."

"I told you not to call me that, Mr. Walker. I don't call you Clarissa, asshole."

I am taken aback by my name said in anger. Lounge music plays in the background. Two females laugh near the phone, calling Greene by name. "What do you want? I'm in the middle of something."

"Bro, what is going on with what I found in the plant at Vin Forest?" I don't want to mention the human remains. Just saying it Jackie Chans my acid reflux into my ass. Even if it didn't, I still have a hard time uttering things like "body parts," "half-eaten flesh," "shrines to a dead girl," and a hundred different ways of spelling out God in the unhealthiest ways possible. I'll never look at drawings of eyes on newspapers, or any kind of hole, the same again. Hell, I'll never look at sirloin the same way again, period.

"You know, it is a long process." Greene's voice is drawn out, uninterested. He blurts out some naughty things to the girls nearby. They say something even dirtier to him. Makes even me blush.

"It's good to know that to get in the good graces of a crooked lawyer all a woman needs is to be capable of harlotry. No need for decency or morals. Straight to the whoring." I say it loud enough so the women can hear it over the phone. Greene apologizes to them, but why bother? I'll keep going. I can keep embarrassing them all day with my misogyny.

Letting out a little anger on perfect strangers is good for my soul.

"That was uncalled for, Walker."

"What can I say, princess? I'm a jealous beta. My complex is caused from being a guy named Claire. You might think I'm an asshole but I'm just flowing with traffic here. What's your excuse for being a date rapist?"

"Please stop with the names, Walker."

"Oh, I will when you give me something to work with."

"Listen, I have nothing right now. The police are trying their best. They put in a ton of overtime checking for fingerprints and variables. The coroner's office needs to examine what they found. I need to file court reports. Results take times. A few weeks if we're lucky. A few months if we're unlucky."

"Results? What kind of results are you talking about? The cops just stood there like morons. They looked into the different holes and shrugged. I handed them the shrine! I showed them the pictures! I told them about what I found at Gordy Renton's home. And not a single one of the bastards jotted anything down."

"You know, I worked very hard today on this."

"You stood by and did nothing but text while I stumbled upon pieces of dead people! If the police found more remains, maybe they belong to Dotty's missing friends."

"Walker, I don't appreciate you implying I wasn't trying." Greene lets out an arrogant, probably forced, laugh. "Who am I kidding? Who cares about some missing people from a few years ago? They are probably long dead anyway. It's no use crying about it if they can't find the bodies. That's less work for me. I'm not going to act unless I get the word. Do the same."

"You son of a bitch! That's someone's missing loved one. You got me into this mess because you wanted to bring Darius to justice. And now you're telling me not to care?"

"I have other important things on my plate. The DA's problems were in the news all day before you had me go on your little road trip. I'm surprised you didn't inquire about it. Look it up right now. You'll understand what I'm going through."

"Believe me, I want your justification just as much as you do. And I would try to verify it right this second if the TV wasn't playing Ukrainian pop videos and my laptop had a working Internet card and a battery lasting more than five minutes." Greene laughs. "What's so funny?"

"I really think you should find out before bitching to me about what I should be doing."

"Oh really? Is it more important than finding a suspected serial killer?"

"You're a journalist. What would you say about several convicted criminals going free because the iron-clad cases against them fell apart?"

"I'd say sucks to be you."

Greene laughs. "Sucks to be you too. Are you willing to be a five-second hero again? Tell me what you think when you find out."

Before I can retort, Greene hangs up. Just what the hell are you talking about, Greene?

This game is rigged in everyone's favor but mine. What a crock.

The power of prayer is the only way I'm getting a miracle out of this.

My phone rings. I expect Heather or someone like Ralph West asking me to do a last-minute project for them. When I check the caller ID, all I see are zeros broken in different places. I almost don't answer it, expecting it to be a telemarketer. But if it is, I'll take my anger out on them so they would either never call again or put my hilariously angry rant on the Internet. A misplaced fetish of mine is to have a dance remix of my rant make its rounds across the world and possibly put me on a reality show. So I answer.

"Are you Claire Walker?" a male voice asks.

"This is he. Who is calling?"

"My name is Levitt Brower. I'm a photographer."

"Are you from the *Eye Tribunal*? You need me to do a story for your photos?"

"No. I heard you are looking for Darius Renton." His voice is very quiet, very peculiar. I can't get an accent or a hint of emotion, like I'm talking to a robot. "I would like to help you."

"How did you know I was looking for him?"

"I understand your plight. The disinterest of the people around you. The open hostility. The lack of help in finding the truth."

I ask him how he knows what's going on.

"I know your situation all too well."

"Well, if you do, then what is your stake in this?"

"I simply want to help you find Darius. Do you know a Professor Charles Benson? He taught archeology at Southern Miskatonic University?"

"I don't know him personally, but I know of him." I search my desk for a pen and a paper. For the first time, I have what might be a lead in whatever it is I'm doing. "What of Benson? How you know him?"

"I was in Afghanistan five years ago with him and his research team. I was the photographer assigned to his dig outside the ruins of a palace he had discovered. My job was to record all findings they unearthed. As you might have guessed in your search for Darius Renton, his uncle Joseph Renton was a friend and colleague of Benson. Joseph paid for everything. I became acquainted with Joseph via letters, e-mails, and phone conversations during the expedition. After Benson died, I kept in touch with Joseph until his death two years back. Darius picked up where his uncle's work stopped."

"Tell me then, Levitt, just what was Joe doing?"

"Unlocking the forbidden secrets of the world."

I become curious. The journalist in me asks, "What kind of secrets? Was there really anything left to discover with all our advances in technology, knowledge, all that good stuff?"

"They wanted to find out the stuff we weren't looking at. They wanted the primordial." Then Levitt goes quiet, as if he wants me to respond.

I don't understand what this "primordial" thing is, but I decide to roll with it. "Did he succeed in finding the primordial?"

"Yes and no." Loud static muzzles our conversation. The reception is fine, but I have a hard time talking or hearing over the sudden hissing buzz. "I'm afraid I have to cut our conversation short. You must stop Darius from continuing," he says.

"Continuing what?"

"Read Joseph's research notes. The answers are all there."

"Great idea, but there is a problem. Most of these papers are written in languages I can't understand. I don't even know where to look."

"You will in time."

Darius went mad after all, but so did Joe and Benson, according to this photographer. This is my best lead so far, but I'm left with more questions and no solid angles. The static starts to hurt my ears, but I can't end it here. Before I get cut off by either static or pain, I need to ask one more thing.

"Do you think Darius Renton killed Dotty Finley?"

"He killed all those he is to be suspected of and many more to come. But he isn't responsible for her missing friends. And he didn't kill her. She's not dead."

I was floored by Levitt's statement. I ask him to repeat his claim, and he did.

"Stay away from where Dotty's body was found. It's not safe there yet."

"Too late for that. I don't think I'll ever sleep normally again after this."

"Sleep is all you'll get until you don't."

The phone disconnects. I search through my call log only to find that the number didn't save. All it saved are broken numbers. This isn't the first time my phone has done this. I need a better phone, but I don't want to buy into another two-year contract and pay out my ass when I live day to day. So I toss my phone to the side and read what I jotted down.

Levitt said that Darius was responsible for murders he is suspected of. Did that mean he killed those people whose parts I found at the Vin Plant? Are there others? And what did he mean that Dotty is alive? Darius was found near her shredded body. Or was it her body?

Joseph's notes are an even bigger mystery. Levitt thinks I will be able to suddenly translate half of this stuff on my own. I'm just a two-bit ghostwriter and sometimes journalist when they let me out of my writing cage. I can't do this on my own.

The apartment phone rings before I can find a rhythm of self-pity.

"Claire Walker," Levitt says over tremendous static when I answer. "Go to Gordon Renton's home. Darius has a secret hiding place in the dining room. There is more stuff there. Take all the papers you find belonging to Darius in his room."

The phone goes to a dial tone before I can ask him anymore questions.

None of this makes sense. With nothing else to go on, I grab my stuff and head out to pay Gordy as visit. What else am I going to do besides bake in my apartment?

Chapter Nine

For the past half hour, I've waited outside Gordy's home. I try calling him, but my cell phone continues to spaz out. Heavy rain fogs the windows in my car. A potential heatstroke is alleviated for now, if only to give way to neck-choking humidity in a few hours. All it does is make looking for Gordy harder. The weatherman on the oldies station made me moan when he announced more heat and humidity are on the way.

My car seat is not the nicest or comfiest place to be reading a manuscript the size of *Atlas Shrugged*. Painful memories of painful English assignments during my college years rush over me. At least I can read this bastard as opposed to Ayn Rand's piece of elephant shit—or any garbage assigned back in the day by my elitist college professors. So what if I was a C- student? None of that means nothing now. I got my degree. I paid my dues. Yet I can't help but feel like I am back in school, searching through thousands of pages and finding the right combinations of words to write my paper.

The whole manuscript, minus a few parts, has been translated from French to English; it was written sometime in the early 1960s. The manuscript consists of a back-and-forth conversation between two men: a psychiatrist whose name is only referred to as Friend and a retired doctor by the name of Lien Foch, who had been living in an old folk's home since the end of World War II.

The first part of the manuscript is dedicated to Foch's early life, or rather what little was known of his life in general. While his nationality was French, he had moved to the Netherlands as an adult to study medicine and psychiatry.

He became a doctor sometime before the turn of the twentieth century. Prior to the First World War, he had moved to Germany, where he offered his services as a personal physician to German officers in the military. He became acquainted with a man named Sigmund Thieriot, who had the rank of captain in the German military.

World War I happened. Thieriot was assigned as a warden for a prisoner-of-war camp in an unnamed part of Europe, which also doubled as a temporary medical outpost for the Central Powers. He had pulled some strings to get Foch named as the physician at the prison.

Exactly why Thieriot had a civilian doctor stationed at his prison was not discussed. Friend had made a linear note suggesting that Foch might have played a role in extracting information from captured prisoners. He had no evidence of this, except for handful of cryptic phrases uttered by Foch in passing that he quickly dropped after bringing them up.

The next part described Foch's physical condition. Foch was a ripe old eighty-two-year-old when the sessions were conducted. He had suffered a stroke when he was in his late sixties. He suffered a speech impediment and had been confined to a wheelchair since. He was half blind in both eyes; one was caused by trauma to the retina, the other by old age. He said it was caused by an accident during World War I, but he would not discuss how he received the wound. He was partially paralyzed in his right arm; most of the muscle from his wrist to his bicep had been removed by trauma also caused during that war. Again, Foch would not say how he received the wounds. Every time Foch was asked, he would ramble off into something cryptic before changing the subject.

Most of the conversations Friend and Foch had started off with Foch discussing what he wanted to talk about that day, from the changes in art culture to the advances in cinema to the beautiful music that he heard emerging from the United States. He was a cultured man.

But conversations always shifted back to his time with Thieriot at the prison.

The next part of the paper discussed the prison itself. It wasn't a real prison. It was converted from a large old abandoned orphanage.

The conversion process had stripped it to the bone. Concrete and steel reinforced the bare parts; hundreds of cells were made from the small assortment of rooms that once housed children. No more than a month or two of work was put into turning the orphanage into a functional prison before it was commissioned for use. While it was also meant to be a temporary barracks for wounded soldiers, it almost never fulfilled that secondary purpose.

Foch had spent the entire year of 1915 and a portion of 1916 at this prison. At its peak, the prison housed over two hundred prisoners of war, ten wounded soldiers, and twenty-five guards. Foch mentioned countless times how the prison corroded from the quick, but improper conversion. When pressed further, he would talk about how there were never enough medical or food supplies to go around between the prisoners, the few wounded, the guards, and Thieriot and Foch themselves. Weeks, then months, would go by before any shipments were received. Then the shipments just stopped coming. By then, they had stopped receiving orders.

During the last month of his stay, there was a skirmish between Allied forces and the Central forces outside the prison walls. It was a brutal, bloody battle. Because of trench warfare, neither side could gain the upper hand. It was a slow, tortuous campaign that bled out both sides. It lasted almost a week. Eventually, the fight was brought to the prison itself. Everyone who had remained at the prison when the fighting started had perished.

All but Lien Foch.

According to records, Foch had wandered off for several days. He almost died from his wounds when he found refuge in a village almost a hundred miles away. He recovered and exiled himself from Germany, returning home to France. He was never prosecuted for any type of crimes after World War I, as he was just a civilian hired by the enemy. The manuscript went into just why this happened, but I wasn't interested in the laws of foreign governments.

For years, the French government had tried to piece together the full extent of his involvement. Friend made his intentions known early. He wanted to know just how and why Foch worked for the Germans and what happened at the prison. But like a record set to repeat, Foch wouldn't budge about what went on at the prison. Many had come before Friend, trying to declassify as much of the hidden aspects involving the war as possible. All had failed.

The sessions with Foch and Friend had gone on this way for about a year. Friend recorded everything they talked about, no matter how repetitive. It was a hopeless task getting a stubborn, crippled old man to spill the beans. But Friend stuck with it. Like a stonecutter pounding the rock, he hoped the next slam of the hammer would crack it.

Then one day, Foch responded in a way Friend wanted but didn't expect.

"I'm going to burn," I read in what I imagine was Foch's voice: old, shaky, and tired.

"What do you mean by burn?" Friend asked in what I imagine was his voice: French.

"If hell exists, I'm going there when I die. I'm going to burn for what I did. And that is not enough punishment for what we have done. May God damn me, may any God damn me. What we did to humanity is beyond unforgivable."

What kind of war crimes could Foch have committed to need damnation?

Foch's words were underlined many times, black ink bleeding through the page and almost tearing through it. There was a citation from Joe next to it.

"God has damned all of us," Joe wrote, "but if there is no God, then we have damned everyone. No one to blame now but us, Charlie. We should have seen their warnings. I should have never sent you out to the mountains with those people."

I flip through the pages and see no other comments or citations from Joe.

Why are you speaking in absolutes here, Joe? What happened? How does an event that happened almost a hundred years ago have anything to do with you or Darius?

My phone vibrates. I'm having problems with the numbers breaking, but I can answer.

"Hello?" I say.

"My flame, why don't you answer your door?" Heather says.

"Aw shit." I drop my head to the car horn, which lets out a toot that is smothered by the sound of rain. I darted off without telling Heather I was going to Gordy Renton's home. Then again, if I did remember, it's not like I could call out with a messed-up phone. "I'm sorry, baby, I had something important to do. My phone is on the fritz, and I couldn't tell you because I can't call out." Heather let out a loud wheeze following a laugh.

"It's all good, baby."

I ask if she's mad.

"Nope. I forgive you."

"So what are you going to do if I'm not there?"

"Wait for you outside, what else? Maybe I'll take a nap outside your door. Better hurry or someone might invite me in to their place and have some fun with me."

I laugh. "You wouldn't let that happen."

"I'm always on the prowl for something better, so I just might. So you won't ever forgive me, so you won't ever forget me. You're not mad at me for being the way I am, baby?"

"It's all pillow talk to me."

Heather purrs, "Hurry up, would you kindly?"

"I'll try." She hangs up on me.

Heather is a strange woman. She is half my age, yet that doesn't bother her. I still can't understand what she sees in me. We met at a party and I took her home for a quick lay.

That is all I saw her as. That was a year ago.

She always makes quips about wanting to leave this ghetto city behind. She's always looking for something better, in a man and in her life. That girlish dream of a knight sweeping her off her feet and making things all right is all she talks about.

Yet she keeps coming back like a lost puppy. Like she has nowhere else to go.

Her clinginess is almost suffocating at times. Her persistence at tempting me with her body and with worldly vices is unwanted at times.

And yet I keep letting her in.

She always whispers how much she loves my brown hair and my brown eyes, how she loves it when I don't shave for a few days so my stubble pricks her skin when she rubs my face. Most of the time, I think the drugs speak for her. But once or twice, I knew there might have been sincerity behind her words. At least I wish there was.

Maybe I'm just lonely. Or maybe I want to settle down soon. I'm not young anymore.

But Heather isn't the marrying kind. And neither am I. She deserves a guy who will treat her right. She has her whole life ahead of her; she shouldn't be wasting it on me or her lifestyle.

I don't know what to think right now. Too much stuff on my mind. I still can't figure out just what Joe and Benson were doing. There isn't a single shred of transparency with anyone involved. And Levitt's words sent a shiver down my spine; it makes me wiggle around in my car seat with an uncomfortable twist. Just how did he know what I was looking for? Is his interest really in Darius, outside of his connection with Joe and Benson? Why did he claim Dotty wasn't killed, and how does he know Darius is responsible for those chopped parts despite not being there to see himself?

Or is he trying to make a profit?

That makes perfect sense. He's trying to scare me off the case. There has to be something valuable in these notes. Levitt worked with Benson in Afghanistan and had an arrangement with Joe. He knows the ins and outs of these pages. He could be throwing me off to make a play and some cold cash. It's not like I know where to look for the buried treasure anyway. And both Joe and Benson admitted they found something that would change the world. It's just a matter of snooping around and uncovering it.

Still, it's a fact I can't deny: Levitt's the only person to be up front so far. He told me where key information might be hidden. It might help me move along. I have to give him a reasonable benefit of the doubt.

I just had to find a guy, but I can't even get that done within a reasonable amount of time. I'm not a private eye. I did get some cash out of it, so it's not a complete loss. Despite pissing off Ralphie West, I'm sure I didn't completely burn my bridges with him. I could kiss his ass and do his toilet work to get back in his good graces.

The future is rainy with a chance of tornados ripping me a new face.

And now I ask myself: Is the money really worth it? Do I want to keep moving? Are my bills really worth trading safety and health for?

I'm not a hero, despite my act of serendipitous heroism involving Slowburn. I have no personal stake in any of this. I did that gig, and it got me where I am. If there was a time machine, I would definitely have punched myself to stop me from going to that burnt house that day. But since there isn't, I can do the next best thing.

All I have to do is put the car in drive, chuck the notes onto the flooded sidewalk, and head off to go have me some fun. That seems like a good idea.

But so do many things. It all boils down to needing the money and needing to eat.

If I'm going to leave, it will be to get a cup of coffee to keep me from falling asleep.

My yawning is getting to me. The car lamp's ugly orange glow is hurting my eyes to the point the lids are about to staple themselves shut. The clock says 11:12 p.m. Man, this day sucked balls. I should have gone and scared the paleness off my ass tomorrow, but I had to tweak-preach Greene into taking me to Vin Forest today. If I had waited till tomorrow, at least I would have been rested for it and not exhausted from staying up almost three days in a row. If I had waited, I could have been on Valium prior to my stupid attempt at crawling into a tiny hole.

I pull down the visor mirror and stare at myself. I lecture myself in the mirror, "Of all the dumb things in my life, I have never wanted to crawl into a hole with fingers. You tweaking dumbass. Wait, I can't even use drugs as an excuse. I was sober; tired, but sobered. What gave you this suicidal idea of climbing into a tiny hole?"

A half-decent job of blocking out what happened at Vin Forest's Processing Plant goes to waste. I just had to remind myself and let the heebie-jeebies get all up in my grill again.

Passing cars catch my attention. I have high hopes one is Gordy, but it's not. I fall back into my seat and let out a yawn that almost dislocates my jaw. In my rearview mirror, I see a pale man made of haze standing in the rain about a block away. He walks toward my car. Behind him, what looks like a floating torso made of leeches follows.

I really need to lay off this scary business. Man, I am tired.

I think I'm going to close my eyes for just a second. Just a sec...

Chapter Ten

We were all small at one time or another.

I grew up about two hundred miles from here, near two mountains that surrounded my village to the east and the south. We were farmers, though my village was becoming well known for wood-carving and clock making. I remember when my father took me to see a cuckoo clock being made in its entirety; it left an impression on me.

I wanted to make clocks. I wanted to live in the village and make beautiful wooden clocks. But I was the eldest of nine children. Making clocks wasn't my destiny.

No, I was to inherit the farm from my father, who had inherited it from his father.

Not that I was disappointed. We never had any real worries on the farm.

I do admit there were times during the winters that things were harsh. Food was very tight during that time. Crops were hard to harvest, and it was hard to earn any profit. Sacrifices had to be made at times. But it was tight for everyone else, and that made it more bearable when things seemed hopeless.

I wouldn't have to worry about finding work. I worked from home. I never had to leave home, except to travel for items necessary to keep the farm functioning.

Life was more or less stable. It was a good as life was for anyone born in my shoes.

As a boy, my job was just to help my papa. He was not a strict man.

I remember him fondly for being more lenient with me than my siblings. He let me play when I should have been working. When my siblings caused trouble, they got punished. I, on the other hand, committed no sins in the eyes of my papa. I always guessed it was because I was going to be running the farm one day. Maybe he did not want to burden me with an animosity that I might take out on the farm itself. Or maybe he wanted to instill a kindness that I would pass on when I had children of my own.

But he did have one rule. It was a family rule, one his father learned from his own father. It was a rule trained into each of his children from the moment we could understand words.

It was the one rule none of us dared to break.

As I got older, I found this rule funny—so funny that I would tell people visiting the village about it. It seemed silly and odd to them, a reminder of an archaic time that was slowly being replaced with changes in technology and culture.

They found it funny until they came to my farm. The joke, the humor, never lasted.

The villagers knew better. They knew what it was; they knew it all too well. Despite it being a family rule, the villagers who knew of it had passed down the rule themselves from earlier generations, from families who never left the village and never would leave.

Everyone who lived in the village made it a point not to come to our farm for that very reason unless they had to do business with my father, and then later myself. Their business didn't last very long most times. We never had parties; we never had guests.

All because of this one rule.

We lived on a hill, and my home was built facing toward the village half a mile away. The fields were in front of the house. It was a strange layout compared to others.

When we did have livestock, the animals were kept in a small barn located in front of our garden. We rarely kept livestock, as they either were very hostile or very melancholic when placed in the barn. Most of them escaped, died trying to escape, or died from malnutrition. Those that escaped tore their way out of the barn, destroying whatever effort we put into keeping them.

Harvesting was easier and more profitable for our family anyway. It was inconvenient to keep rebuilding the barn after every animal escape. We had the village to buy whatever meats or produce we needed. Because of this, the issue of owning a consistent supply of livestock was never brought up.

The actual home we lived in wasn't our family's original home. My grandfather built his home behind where our current home stood. But he decided to build another in front of it, and that was the home I grew up in. The old home still stood, but it was filled with dust and cobwebs. He never gave his reasons for building two homes and not using one. When I inherited the farm, I had planned on adding an expansion connecting to two. That never happened. I was always sidetracked by either work or chores. So instead I used it as an extra shed.

Behind that house were several large brushes, planted in three rows. The first two rows were kept by the women in the household. The first two rows looked very pretty, but the third row was unkempt. Most of the bushes were withered and dead. The women never bothered doing anything with them. The idea of tending to them was never brought up. It was just a fact of living on the farm that no one touched the third row.

A little way off, behind the third row of shrubs, was an open field that led toward the Black Forest. Standing in the middle of the field facing the Black Forest was the Scarecrow.

The rule concerned that Scarecrow.

No one was to approach the Scarecrow under any circumstances.

The Scarecrow was of a leaning man. He was tall, surrounded by branches, with a large wooden stump for feet. His head stared up at the sky. Either the tree held the Scarecrow in place, or the Scarecrow had been carved out of the tree. The tree was a type alien to the Black Forest. Its branches were darkish green and the bark got darker until it reached the bottom of the trunk, which was a rotten yellow. The Scarecrow was faceless, the blank front of its head colored an unusual off-white.

The details are murky, I confess, as my father never went into the details of its origins completely. The Scarecrow had been there since before my grandfather moved onto the land and built his farm. The man he purchased the land from claimed the Scarecrow was there before he himself purchased it, and always had been there.

The elder villagers told tales of this Scarecrow, and young children used it to scare one another. There was a legend of a man with a cursed bloodline. Centuries ago, the man's ancestor was part of a cult that roamed these forests. The cult worshiped a devil. They sacrificed an entire village in its name for greater power. The cult was killed, but the man's ancestor remained. The devil chased him and then his descendants all over the country. The man, wanting to free his bloodline, was to kill the devil.

He did this by building the devil a body.

Using the flesh and blood of the devil, he fashioned it to a tree and carved it into a man: a Scarecrow. The devil came to life, and unable to move, the man struck the devil down. He freed his family and his bloodline. But it came with a cost. The flesh and blood of the devil was toxic. The man became ill from handling it. He succumbed to his wounds years later, dying in agony.

The Scarecrow, they said, is all that remains of the vanquished devil.

I never knew for sure what the actual truth was. What I did know, what I accepted long ago, was that it's a superstitious tale told by superstitious people, clinging to ancient traditions they refused to change. They refused to see beyond the village.

They refused to see it was just a man-shaped Scarecrow carved out of a tree. A man, either as a joke or on superstition, carved it. That was all I needed to know.

My grandfather was one of those who believed. He designed the strange layout of the farm based on his rule of avoiding the Scarecrow. As a child, I didn't know any better; I was scared like everyone else, but also mischievous, daring enough.

My siblings and I stared at the Scarecrow for hours on end, to see who would last the longest. I couldn't last for more than a few minutes. It was like staring at the sun, and after a while I swore I'd go blind. To be honest, it was an ugly thing to look at anyway, like staring at a dead animal and watching it get eaten away by the insects and boil under a hot sun. It was also sickening to the stomach; repulsion would make one of us sick and quit before we puked.

Then there were the sounds. We always argued about what we heard, or where we heard it. Sometimes I heard a grunt. My siblings argued with me, saying they heard a squeal or a bird. We could never pinpoint where the sounds came from. I heard them from behind us. One sibling said they came from the left, while another argued they came from the right. We even heard the sounds come from high above and underneath the dirt. They never lasted more than a few seconds.

Of course, none of this happened as an adult.

But I never went by the Scarecrow, even when I inherited the farm. I honored the rule.

"Every day it's the same," Thieriot said. "Stop telling ghost stories, Johan. Tell us what we need to know. Tell us where your allies are."

I stared at Thieriot and said, "My siblings moved away one by one and started their own families. I inherited the farm, just like my father had intended. I met a young girl who worked at the village pub. Her name was Hilda, and in time she would become my wife. We had two daughters and one son. My children have her blonde hair, her fair skin, and her blue eyes."

Thieriot thrashed his arms. "Give me names, Johan!"

"I'm glad they didn't take after me. My daughters Claudia and Franziska are too young to decide what they wanted to do with themselves, but Xaver my son decided early on he wanted beyond the farm, beyond our small village. I respect that, and now thinking about it, I think he made the best decision."

"That's enough for now, Johan," Foch said as he grabbed Thieriot by the shoulder to keep him from tackling me. "He'll talk in time. Let him tell his life story." I laughed. The two men stared at me. Foch then asked, "What is so funny, Johan?"

"We are all going to die before the week is over. Can't you hear the Black Fairy singing? Can't you hear her wings flapping? Can't you hear her preying on the wounded? She's coming for us. She'll kill us all."

Thieriot came over to me and placed his hands around my neck. He growled as he squeezed tight, "Playing insane won't protect you, traitor! If you don't talk, I'll kill you!"

This was how my encounters always ended. And like every time before, Foch stopped him before it went too far. The guards took me back to my cell to rot. As the lights around me faded, I prayed, "Don't stop next time, Warden Thieriot. I want to be spared my fate. Death is relief. Death is salvation. Come sweet death."

Chapter Eleven

"Hey, Cabbage, wake up," a voice says to me. The voice repeats, this time accompanied by a shake and the wretched smell of pizza and tequila. My eyes refuse to open. When they do, I find Gordy standing slouched, a bag filled with liquor bottles and frozen pizzas in his hand.

My body is stiff; the left part of my neck down to my waist is numb. I feel dry slobber on my face from where my face was mashed into the seatbelt. How long have I been asleep? The clock on my car says 3:07 a.m.

"Damn, I was tired," I say with a yawn that almost dislocates my jaw.

"How long you been here?"

"Came around eleven." The rain had stopped sometime before I awoke. I get out of my car and stretch the parts that refuse to work. "What took you so long to get back?"

"Playing bingo. Didn't win. I like bingo and drinking. Only time I'm happy. Sleep well?"

I shake my head. "Had the strangest dream." I skim over the manuscript involving Foch while waving it to Gordy. "I was dreaming about this. That's strange."

Gordy asks what I mean.

"There is no mention of a Johan in here. Was just getting into the details before passing out." I stare around my car, then around the block, down the street, and under my car.

Why am I jittery? What was I doing before I fell asleep?

"Maybe osmosis," Gordy says, patting me on the shoulder. "You don't remember."

I nod. "Yeah...yeah, you're probably right." Oh shit, I was supposed to be meeting with Heather. I check my cell phone and see the battery is dead. I can't call her and apologize. Damn it. "I need to talk to you, Gordy. It's about Darius."

Before I can say anything, I remind myself about what happened at Vin Forest. Gordy's face lights up when I mention Darius. He stands closer to me. Eager, desperate, worried. He tries in pathetic attempts to control his twitching. He waits for me to say something.

"Did you find him? Is he okay?" he asks. "Please say something, Cabbage."

Seeing Gordy like this...I don't have the heart to tell him about what I saw. Or what Levitt Brower told me.

"No, Gordy. I didn't." Disappointment washes over Gordy. "But there might be a hidden spot in your dining room that Darius used to hide key parts of Joe's research. I'm asking for permission to look around your mansion."

"Sure. Come on in, Cabbage. Want pizza?"

My stomach rumbles when he asks, so I nod. Binges have a habit of keeping me from eating because, really, all I want to do is keep getting more trashed.

Now free of the fiend, I need to feed.

We enter Gordy's home and go to the kitchen to prepare the oven-cooked Supreme pizza. Just thinking about it makes me drool all over my chapped lips. But this ruptures the dry skin on my lips. After wiping the blood off, I fight the urge to gnaw on the cut, but it's hard. I compare the feeling to a dog combing through its hair to pick off a flea. I'd rather be eating, and I want to chew on something. Wish I had gum, or candy.

Gordy lets me plug in my phone to charge while we wait. When my phone gets enough juice, it vibrates with several text messages from various people. Heather is among them, asking where I am. There is Stephanie Quinn, begging to read my blog. Someone I don't know asking me to proofread his son's essay. Another from someone asking me to write apology letters to both his mistress and his wife for getting caught with a transvestite hooker; it wasn't him, he swears.

All for shit pay of course. No other kinds of offers come my way.

The rest are from Ralph West, demanding I get in touch with him. He sounds like an insecure teenage girl waiting for a response to her "Will you be my BFF?" query.

Sure enough, he calls. I answer, "Ahoy hoy, I'm covered in bees!"

"Walker! Hi, it's Ralph West. We need to talk. I'm kind of in a bind and really need that article done. I'll pay you extra. Do you have time?"

"I have to return some videotapes. Talk to me next week."

"Wait! Walker—"

I hit the disconnect button. It doesn't work. To hang up, I unplug the phone and hurl it at the floor. That works.

"Angry much?" Gordy asks while poking at the shattered pieces of my phone with his foot. I jump on the electronic parts. Have to make sure there is no fucking way it will ring.

"Blood sucking parasites! The whole lot of them, I swear. Won't leave me alone." I wipe my head and crack my neck. "I'm sorry, Gordy, let me pick this up."

"No, let me help." Gordy grabs a broom from the pantry and sweeps up the broken phone. "You seem stressed. Why? Covering headline stories? Important deadline?"

I lean on the counter and scratch the back of my neck. "Gordy, I haven't had a single article published in over a year. Not in my name, anyway."

Gordy asks what I mean.

"I'm not allowed to get published in the *Eye Tribunal*. I'm a ghostwriter for other writers there. That's the only kind of work I can get."

I explain the circumstances of just how I got involved with Slowburn. Gordy is unfamiliar with the case, since it happened on the same day Darius was accused of murder. After I tell him that story, I tell him how I got involved with Kenny Daniels.

For a few weeks afterward, I was given celebratory pats on the backs, lip service, all that neat stuff. Kenneth Daniels was brought in to the *Eye Tribunal* and needed some guidance. I was warned in advance that Kenny was the nephew, cousin, or illegitimate son of the man who owned the company, Frederic Johnson. A soldier's order was given to me: show Kenny how to write and I would get a big promotion. This was my big opportunity.

What they didn't tell me was that Kenny was an opportunist and a con artist. When he couldn't finish deadlines he cut corners. When he couldn't cut corners, or even do the bare minimum, he started to hijack pieces of my unfinished stories from my work computer. Not like I noticed when he turned in dozens of reports and articles in his name, but written by me. I was high all the time. I binge wrote many articles as backup in case I didn't have anything to write about, or needed to pull something out of my ass when I just plain forgot to write. I must have had at least a hundred stories saved for rainy days; never bothered to lockup my computer either.

The son of a bitch didn't even bother to change anything in his submissions. The editors never caught it, or paid attention really, because of who he was. His stories always got the golden stamp of approval; his work was saved from the chopping block, and printed as is. Then again most of it was regulated to the back, stuck somewhere in the paragraphs dedicated to car reviews and stock suggestions. Nobody read that shit.

Everything came to a head when I wrote a small piece on a drug lord who used to hang the bodies of his victims on a bridge as a warning to his victims. Many of the lines were lifted verbatim and reappeared in Kenny's article about, unsurprisingly, the unexpected link between cats and psychic connections. A lovely anonymous reader, goddamn them for reading that day, noticed the similarities of our works and brought it up to the big wigs. A "scandal" was on our hands but none of my editors or fellow journalists would do anything against Kenny Daniels. So it was then turned over to big man Frederic Johnson himself to make the judgment call.

And despite hundreds of small articles I did, despite my yearlong literary dance around the Slowburn Arsonist, all before Kenny Daniels even stepped foot at the *Eye Tribunal*, Johnson chose Kenny Daniels over me. Most of my back catalogue was gotten rid of, and the online stuff I did was hastily passed off as Kenny's.

"Worked my way the hard way little by little over an eight-year period. All ruined because of one thief everyone sided with. That's nepotism at work. Now I know how Nikola Tesla felt when Thomas Edison did him raw. Maybe I'll get vindicated by history a hundred years later. But I'll be dead by that point, so I won't be in the caring mood then."

"They did you wrong," Gordy says. "Why didn't you sue them?"

"Believe me, I tried. Kenny Daniels's sugar daddy paid whoever I talked to and had them ignore me. Easier to have me crucified, rather than admit that a family member of the big boss stole work from an employee and passed it off as their own. And if I went beyond them, like gone to another paper with proof of what happened, my rampant drug use would have been made public. No one likes a drug user. Hard to believe, easy to silence, and I'm allergic to handcuffs."

"Then why didn't you quit?"

"I never had the best grades, Gordy. I was a terrible student in high school and college. The only reason I got the job at the *Eye Tribunal* was because one of their journalists got fired for driving drunk in a school zone when the kids were getting to school. They needed to fill the void, and by luck I got the job. If I quit, I could never work in the city again. No one will touch a plagiarist in the writing community. They let me keep my job, but I couldn't write. I had to go back to copyediting, which turned into ghostwriting."

I don't have any higher connections, no next of kin. If I'm dead in a watery ditch somewhere, they'll just let me bloat before burying me in some unmarked grave, next to all the unidentified, unclaimed, and unloved.

No one is looking out for me. I'm just a nobody in the long run.

Gordy places his hand on my shoulder and smiles, "I'm really sorry, Cabbage."

I shake my head and say, "Don't be. This is what I get for being a nice guy, for being a hero." I snicker and point at Gordy. "For doing lots of drugs when I wasn't supposed to be."

The sound of the stove buzzing makes us focus on eating. We head to the dining room and split the delicious pizza. I multitask eating with examining the dining room for a hidden compartment. There is nothing in the pantry and there is nothing in the cupboards. Nothing under the tables or chairs, just in case Darius had been sneaky-sneaky about the proper definition of hidden compartment.

Underneath the rug, I find the compartment Levitt had told me about. The boards are marked with scratches. Gordy's twitching had been controlled, but now it becomes very erratic. I ask him if he is okay. Gordy doesn't respond, other than to slap the twitching off his face.

When he calms down, I pull the boards back. Inside is a huge hole filled with video cassettes. There have to be at least a hundred tapes inside. A portable black light is hidden among them. I turned on the black light.

The tapes illuminate with florescent letters. Each tape is marked with a date. It takes us a good five minutes to take out all the tapes from the hole.

"When did this get here?" Gordy asks. "This hole wasn't here before."

"Darius must have put it here sometime before he got arrested, or after he was released."

"But why?"

"I think Darius was paranoid about something. Might have to do with Joe's work."

"What have you found out?"

"To be honest, I can't quite make it out. I got a call from this photographer who worked with a colleague of Joe's, a Professor Charles Benson, at a dig in Afghanistan. Joe and his associate were trying to uncover something big, game changing, according to Joe and Benson."

"Game changing?"

"Yeah. It wasn't an issue at first when I read about it, and it had no relation to me searching for Darius, but the photographer said it was important. Been rocking around my brain for the past few hours. What could Joe have been doing?"

"Any guesses?"

"Well, Joe was an anthropologist and this guy Benson was an archeologist. There is one way they would be working together and that might have something to do with the origin of the human species. Or something our ancestors accomplished."

"What makes you say that?"

"Aside from the wild guess I just pulled out my ass, quite a few things are leading me to this conclusion. Benson had been bouncing around using Joe's funding. He went from Germany to Afghanistan, and possibly France, sending Joe back tidbits. At a ruined castle in Germany there were two swords from the same era, but one of them is two thousand years older than it is supposed to be."

"Is that possible?"

I shrug.

"I'm not a history or science person. The nerds might be onto something. Maybe time travel is possible. Oh, that's a good angle. Or maybe aliens are involved. No, I'm just reaching with that." I cough, close my eyes and shake my head.

Gordy laughs. "Aliens would be game changing, don't you agree?"

I laugh right along. "No shit. Aliens are kind of scary. But wouldn't Joe be on top of that? As an anthropologist, I mean. If humanity is his thing, why did he not go with Benson?"

Gordy stares at the tapes and sighs. "A girl kept him here."

"Oh? Wouldn't have thought a studious person like Joe would be bogged down by something as precarious as a relationship."

"My brother, my brother." Gordy smiles. "All he cared about was studying. The pursuit of knowledge. You know he never dated in school?" I shake my head. "Academics was his life. Human history was his passion. I'm surprised he didn't join the seminary, given his monkish lifestyle. His sole joy outside of knowledge was theater. You know he donated tons of money to the school's theater and dance programs? Then a girl came along…for so long, he never was interested, then he gave in. And she just devoured his time. I'm surprised he had any time for what he loved. That's why he stayed behind. Why that guy Benson went alone, with Joe's funding as his backing."

Gordy's eyes start to well up. He says he was glad Darius took after Joe.

"I miss them so much, Cabbage."

"I'm sorry, Gordy."

"It's okay, Cabbage. Thank you for trying. At least I know a bit of what Joe was doing. You'll find out where Darius is. I know it. I have faith in you."

"Well, I haven't had much to go on, to be honest. The papers I took from Darius's room are written in foreign languages that I can't read. But the photographer was the one who told me about this hidden hole. So I might have to start using him for help. Unfortunately, he told me Darius is going to do something and he needs to be stopped. He didn't say what, but it has everything to do with Joe's research."

"Might there be someone after him?"

"Possibly. I'm looking at the possibility that there is a good buck to be made in the notes. Outside of the human history element, there could be treasure involved, or some rare find that someone would kill for." Then I remember the ominous words Levitt said about Dotty and about the possibility that Darius was behind other murders. I look at Gordy, who looks at me with a crooked smile. "Gordon, do you think Darius killed Dotty?" Gordy scratches his neck as he rocks back and forth. "I need an answer."

"No! Darius worshiped Dotty. All he had was devotion. Like Joe."

What I want to say is that there might be proof Darius is a monster. Instead, I say, "Everyone is convinced Darius is a monster."

"No!" Gordy yells. "He's a kind boy! Never hurt anyone! He was sick. That's his only sin. Just like his uncle."

I ask what kind of sickness.

"Wanted to find the truth."

"What truth, Gordy?"

"About the world. That there was more. An afterlife. A god. A soul. Deeply religious. They went to church Sunday. Every Sunday."

"So Joe's project might be about trying to prove the existence of a higher being?"

"Maybe. I think so."

"Okay, good, Gordy. We are getting somewhere. I need to ask you something. It's going to sound stupid, but I need to ask it anyway." I take a deep breath, then exhale. "Did Dotty really die?"

Gordy tilts his head at me. He laughs. "That is stupid. Kind of. Dotty's dead. Got to see her body. Many times. In court. At the morgue. Dead as dead."

"The photographer who contacted me said that Darius didn't kill Dotty because she wasn't dead. What do you think he could have meant by that?"

Gordy shakes his head.

He isn't going to answer, and I'm not going to press him any further. If I tell him about Vin Forest, he might go off the deep end. All he wants is Darius back, probably as much as he wants to find out just how deep Joe's project went.

There are certain mysteries I need to answer…out of curiosity and commitment.

Gordy grabs my hand and shakes it. "Thank you, Cabbage."

"For what?"

"For visiting me. I'm lonely. You're my friend."

Nothing but sincerity in Gordy's words. I don't know what to say to him after that. It's hard to imagine how to react when someone who treated you like shit for a good portion of your life calls you their friend. It happened, and I have no response. I just nod and tell him I had to be on my way. Before I take off, I invade Darius's room and do what Levitt said.

I grab all the papers and stuff them into my car.

Now why do I need these papers? And why did Levitt tell me Dotty wasn't dead?

Chapter Twelve

Curiosity punted the cat down the ravine, but only after I get my beauty sleep. I wake up midday and spend until sundown searching for a device that can play back the tapes I found. With all the advances in digital technology, I thought there would be a surplus of tape-based devices. Darius was not kind enough to leave a playback device. Hell, even the place I purchased the playback device from wasn't kind enough to have the playback device in stock. If I wanted it, I needed to place one on backorder and wait a month to pick it up from the store.

I had to con the device off a technophobic wedding photographer who refused to change with the times. He bought the last one on backorder and just so happened to pick it up the day I showed up. The cause of finding out what was going on with Joe and Darius sets me back three hundred bucks, even though its sale price is just twenty.

But a month was a long time to find out what was on the tapes. By then Darius could have been caught and my investigation, and payment, would have ended with an apprehension I had no part in. The rip-off would pay for itself, I hope, but it still stings.

After sulking about being taken for a fool, I plug the thing to my TV and hit play on the first tape I randomly choose.

Joe Renton appears on my seventeen-inch screen. I had high hopes something interesting would happen. Instead, Joe is reading a book, and for the next thirty minutes he keeps reading his book. I leave to go get some McDonalds, come back, and he is still reading the book.

Damn, Joe, you were a slow reader.

I stop the tape and pop in another. This one is a little more interesting. Joe is stuck in the corner of his room. He looks around, focusing on the door. He looks frightened of the door, despite it being nonthreatening. Maybe Joe, despite being a prudish scholar, had a bad drunken experience with it. I've had plenty of those in my day.

Instead of watching him repeat the same thing for a few hours, I fast-forward the tape. It takes about five minutes to go through a four-hour tape. Sure enough, the only thing he does is pace around the room a few times before going right back to his corner to stare at everything, but mostly at the evil door of doom.

I pop in another tape. This one is of a cooking session in the kitchen. The next is of him watching television. Another is of him organizing his research notes in his room.

Every action he does is minimalistic, more so than the indie movies in theaters but without the quirky, ironic music. Every action is without life, and with the exception of the one where he stares at the door of doom, is without emotion. Annoyed, I take the black light to every tape. They span three years.

There is no way in hell I'm going through hundreds of hours of tape just to watch someone pick their ass.

Something catches my eye. One of the tapes is different. It has Charles Benson's name written on it, along with the words "Session One." So I place the tape in and hit play.

It was a clear, sunny day when the video was taken five years before. Mountains of sand and rock are everywhere, with an actual mountain towering over everything else. The camera stops moving. Several people are excavating a building. They look young, and all of them are speaking the American English I have been dying to hear during the multilingual reports of Joe and Benson. I identify U.S. Marines by their fatigues and large guns, talking among themselves.

"Levitt, get over here and record this," an old man with a proper Midwestern accent says off camera. "Hurry! You're paid to record, not to slack off!"

"Yes, Professor Benson, coming, sir," Levitt Brower says as the camera shakes from his jogging. I find it shocking that there is actual emotion in Levitt's voice. He sounds like he is from Southern California.

Charles Benson, on the other hand, was a doppelganger for Edgar Allen Poe, had Poe lived into his sixties, sported a goatee, and had a penchant for cargo shorts and a linen coat jacket over a black Mastodon shirt.

"Did you notice what we are trying to accomplish here, Levitt?"

Levitt shakes his head. "No, sir, I have no idea what you are doing. Care to explain to the home audience what you are trying to do?"

"First, take a look around us."

Levitt does as Benson asks, then shrugs. He asks what he should be looking for. Benson taps his knees and strains himself when crouches down. I can hear his old creaky legs pop and crack. I'm not looking forward to my twilight years, or bending over on shot kneecaps.

Benson puts his hand underneath the sand and pulls it up. He holds it to his face, sniffs and gives the horizon a once over glance. "Afghanistan is a majestic place, filled with complex cultures and histories, spanning generations, and changing constantly throughout history." Benson lets the sand fall from his hand. "But one thing that usually stays the same is the land. Afghanistan has a wide variety of vegetation, rivers, wildlife and climates. It very rarely changes except for outside influences. You know what makes this place different from everywhere else?"

"No, sir. What is it?"

"This place is a desert."

"And? There are many places in Afghanistan that are subjected to desertification."

Benson nods. "But this place is only a desert within a strict area. There is plenty of water and vegetation in these parts to grow out and overtake this barren wasteland, but they all disappear immediately before the ruins. The sand starts and ends here, except for the path leading to the mountain behind us and to a small local village nearby. And this sand is not like normal sand. Go on, feel the texture of it."

Levitt grumbles and the camera shakes to the side, like he is saying no with the camera. "Don't want to get my hands dirty. I'll take your word for it."

"The texture feels more like flour than sand." Benson presses hard on the sand and it turns into dust. "But it's brittle and turns into nothing when force is applied to it."

"So it's more like dirt then?"

Benson waves his hand around and shrugs. "I was thinking moondust, but not toxic or sharp. You know, moondust is a big hurdle if we ever want to conquer the moon. Messes up the machinery and makes us sick if it comes in contact with our skin."

"So this place is like the moon? I thought this was archeology, not astronomy."

"Don't be silly. This sand isn't suitable to build on. You just don't build a palace of particular length, or anything, without a solid foundation. This sand wouldn't hold up something that heavy when erosion, and other weather elements, came into effect. This place wouldn't be perfect for a palace, let alone the Amir. But they did it, and here we are."

"Just perfect for what you are doing, correct?"

Benson gives off a huge grin. "I guarantee you that when we send fragments of these ruins and the sand back home, it's going to give off the same readings as in Germany." Benson is excited as he gets back up and shows Levitt around. "Most of the buildings we are excavating look older than what would have been built for the Amir of Afghanistan during this time. It's exactly like at the Yellow Count's castle. Or as Joe affectionately calls him, Count Orlok. The architecture should be eighteenth to nineteenth century design when we unearth it in its entirety. But on a microscopic level, after we do proper dating on it, we will find that it is several hundred to a thousand years older than it is supposed to be. Everything here will be older than it looks and should be. Even the sand has an expiration date here."

"What are the implications?"

"The implications are a game changer for the scientific community and humanity as a whole." Benson crouches, picks up a handful of sand, and lets it drop. "Imagine for a minute that everything we think we know about time and reality is wrong. What if there were certain places on Earth where, under the right circumstances, time accelerated? Do you have any idea what this means for things like agriculture? We could possibly solve world hunger by using these places to rapidly grow crops. Months of harvesting would instead take hours or days. The possibilities are fantastic!"

"But you're an archeologist, professor. With all due respect, I'd think you should leave world hunger to those scientists. Aren't there other things you can do with such a place?"

Benson is deep in thought, stroking his goatee. Levitt had made a good point. Just what was the point of an archeologist and anthropologist worrying about hunger problems anyway?

"Well, I am thinking about the short-term effects this could have on humanity. I know Joe Renton is trying to think of what effect it might have on bodies. I speak on his behalf when you think of what it means for things like evolution. He wouldn't want to recommend people sitting here to age at an accelerated rate, but in the case of animals, we can have irrefutable proof of evolution working before our eyes. What would have taken generations, we could see firsthand in days or months. And we can catch the different changes from previous generations on film and see what causes them. But I know he is a God-fearing man. I am not. We haven't found his God yet anywhere in this desert, or anywhere else. This doesn't sit well with him. Not one bit."

"So if time accelerates in these pocket areas, doesn't that mean we are aging faster?" Levitt's voice is shaky.

Benson laughs before his face contorts. "Well, I didn't take that into account. But look at us. We are all fine."

"If we aren't aging fast, then doesn't that mess with you theory of accelerated time?"

"Quite possibly, but the facts are embedded into the stone of the building, and possibly the sand itself. Time has accelerated the aging of the Yellow Count's castle ruins and this palace for the Amir. I'm sure if it happens to us, the evidence will be irrefutably within the blood." Benson holds his forearm out and taps it to make the veins pop out. "Then we will have organic proof of accelerated time. We will go down in history. You, me, and everyone here working hard to help prove this theory…" Benson pauses midsentence to look up at the sky. "Maybe there is a catalyst. It's going to take some time to look at all the possibilities."

"How has the scientific community taken your findings?"

"Not so well. They want more proof. They are in denial. What we have discovered messes with many science laws. This is taboo." Benson approaches the camera and says, "And I wouldn't doubt that they'll use all their powers to bury it. Just like they buried the cures for cancer and certain diseases."

"And how does the nearby tribe feel about you desecrating this area?"

"Oh, don't be so negative, Levitt. As a matter of fact, they haven't said anything. We tried approaching them, but they ignored us. Quiet people. So no harm, no foul."

A loud gunshot ruptures my TV speakers. There is shouting, followed by more gunshots. Everyone ducks behind the marines, who give chase in the direction the shots came from. Levitt follows them, despite protests from Benson and the other archeologists. Half of what they say was inaudible. At first I think it's the TV being shitty until I realize it's the camera.

I huddle closer to the TV to a clearer sense of what was being said. The camera stumbles around before it falls behind several rocks.

"I saw it, goddamn it! Don't you tell me I didn't see a fucking thing! It vanished into the sand just now!" a soldier named Jefferies yells.

"This is the third time this week you did this, Jefferies. Heat and dehydration are getting to you," another solider named Cruz says. The soldiers surround the man, disappointed and angry. A soldier comes up to him and grabs him by the shoulder. His name is Torres. Jefferies pushes his hand away.

"Don't you push my hand away, Private!" the soldier who had his hand pushed shouts.

"Sir, I know what I saw! It's been following us since last week!"

"Commander, let's just send him back. He's losing it. And he's scaring the shit out of everyone with random discharges of his firearm," Cruz says.

"Maybe we should look?" a balaclava-wearing soldier named Rankin says.

"You honestly don't believe him, do you?" Cruz asks.

Rankin shrugs, and then points to the place where Jefferies was shooting. "Without us here, these archeologists would be easy pickings. It doesn't hurt to confirm what Jefferies thought he saw. Maybe we can ask the Hajji village nearby if they seen anything strange. They know this area better than us."

"Come on, Rankin. Seriously. He's gone bat shit. It's one thing if they are insurgents, but he says he saw a fucking monster. A monster that has been chasing us all week, mind you. A monster. Let that sink in." Rankin and Cruz stare at Torres, waiting for him to give an order.

"Tell me what you saw in detail," Torres says. "Convince me, private."

The tape stalls and ends there.

"Oh, come on!" I slap the playback device's shit around. I take out the tape to see that it has really run out. "That's bullshit!" I flick the tape to the side. I scan the rest of the tapes for more of the Afghanistan sessions.

A tape marked "Session Two" comes up. I put it in, press play, and watch the same four-man group of marines talk. They are walking down a narrow dirt road, descending the sides of a mountain. They talked military jargon. I pretend I can understand them.

"Keep your mouth shut, video boy," Torres says.

"But what if I need to interview the villagers?" Levitt asks. Cruz laughs and pushes the camera away, almost making Levitt drop the camera.

"Rankin, don't translate for him if he needs to ask them something," Torres says, and Rankin nods. Jefferies spends the entire time looking around. Torres grabs Jefferies and says, "Try not to shoot any kids."

The village they come upon is decrepit. The homes are broken down; the water pails are filled with a terrible black goop. Livestock has been left to rot underneath a blazing sun, with vultures casting shadows from high above. There is a single man with a turban-covered face hammering away at one of the homes far away.

The group is about to approach him when they see another man carrying a dead goat into a hut. Rankin and Torres go inside the hut, with Levitt tailing them; Jefferies and Cruz stay outside. Inside the hut is a table with dead animal parts accumulating flies. The man throws the dead goat down, takes a large knife, and begins chopping.

"Ask him if he has seen any missing Americans, or foreigners, who worked around the Benson's dig site," Torres tells Rankin after handing him several photos of people.

Rankin approaches the man and asks him what Torres said. The man turns around, his face is covered in red tribal tattoos or something along those lines. His eyes are emotionless, unresponsive, like there is no one in the driver's seat. Rankin continues to speak as he shows the photos.

The man says something to Rankin in anger.

"What he say?" Torres asks.

Rankin turns to Torres and says, "He asked us what the fuck we are doing here. Asked why we are interrupting their god's banquet."

Levitt turns the camera to the angry man, who vanishes into the back. The angry man returns a few seconds later with large hatchet and a look of murderous rage.

He reaches back and strikes the camera.

The lens is cracked into a million tiny kaleidoscopes. Levitt screams, which is muted by the firing of the marines' guns. There is the barking of orders, the firing of bullets, and horrific howls I never thought could come from a human mouth.

A soft knock on my front door makes me jump. I pause the tape and hold my chest. My heart valves refuse to work. I'm not terrified of the actual door knock. I'm terrified at what was going on in the video. Why does this video scare me this much?

After wiping my brow, I go to the peep-hole to see who goes there. There is a man in a sleeveless, unzipped white hoodie and black jeans. The hood covers his entire head, and he keeps his head tilted down toward the peephole. He is shirtless under the hoodie.

What I pay attention to most is not how he's dressed but everything else.

His arms and his chest are tattooed with blue eyes on almost every patch of skin I can see. Underneath some of the tattooed eyes are worn scars, fresh scars, and open cuts. Some heal, others fester with infectious rot. It looks like he has just lost weight, as parts of his skin have stretch marks.

He knocks again. After a few times, I become unnerved.

"You wouldn't by any chance be here to fix my air-conditioning unit?" I ask in some stupid attempt to break his repetitive knocking.

"You disturbed her," he says. "I can't forgive you."

"What, you want to file a complaint? I'm out of forms." I laugh. He slams both his arms against the door over and over, busting open the wounds on his arm, spilling blood. I see him reach for a screwdriver in his pocket and jam it into the peephole. The tiny glass shatters. I bounce back, almost tripping over my couch.

"I'll kill you!" The door handle rocks around. What he hasn't taken into account is that my door has four locks and two deadbolts, reinforced by the building manager when the police broke it down last time. He isn't getting in that easily. "Open this door right now! Make it easy on yourself! Beg for her forgiveness!"

"Nah, I'll call the cops now and beg later." I shake my head as I pick up the apartment telephone and dial out. As I wait for a dial tone, I hear a laugh in my room.

I turn my head to see where the laughter came from. The dial tone turns into static.

"Get out of the room!" a voice shouts over the phone line before it disconnects.

I drop the phone out of fright. The slamming of the door gets harder. The screwdriver grinds into the wood around the handle.

This guy isn't going to stop.

His tattoos seem familiar. I mean, I know where I saw them, I have the name on the tip of my tongue. But the words never come out.

My mouth loses sensation with each attempt at saying the words. I drift in and out of consciousness as I force my mind to speak in absence of my voice. The more I want to say, the more my body is refusing me. I need to listen to the voice on the phone. I need to escape.

But where do I go? The madman is at my door trying to get in. The only way out is through the window. Four stories up I'll break every bone on the way down.

Yet…that feels like the best choice right now. My body is telling me it is the right choice.

More laughing near my head shakes me. "Who's there?" I ask.

The only thing in the room, besides the notes and research, are the large stacks of papers I jacked from Darius's room. Another laugh comes from the corner where the papers sit.

I stare at the papers. I pray that I am just imagining things.

A pair of glowing eyes, belonging to a pale face made of liquid, shines from behind the papers. They stare deep into me…

Chapter Thirteen

Sharp pain runs up my face and into my ears, waking me up. I lay flat on my stomach against a carpeted floor. I don't know where I am, don't know how I got here. It is very dark and cold. I can't stop myself from shivering, and I can't adjust to the darkness engulfing the room.

A burning sensation touches my abdomen like a hot pike trying to poke at my organs. Moisture saturates my shirt. There's wetness all around where I lie. My hand presses deep into the wettest part of the carpet. I bring my hand close to my face and struggle against the darkness to see what liquid I am surrounded by.

A light bulb pops on. I'm blinded by the unexpected light for just a second before it turns off. Then it turns on again. Off again. Between the pulses of the light, I get a good look at what is around me. I'm in a room filled with empty bookcases. A smashed TV rests by a smashed mirror. Papers lay scattered everywhere.

Underneath me, blood stains the carpet. Blood stains my hand.

A gaping wound has left a hole in my stomach. The bottom part of my ribcage is showing, my intestines threaten to fall out. I breathe in gasps, but I don't panic. I struggle to cry, but I feel no pain from the wound.

The only pain comes from between my ears.

"Still alive?" someone asks from behind me. I fall onto my back as I turn around. A man sits in the corner of the room with a record player by his side and earphones on. By his feet is a bloodied knife that I imagine had been used to carve a hole in my stomach.

He's aged quite a bit since the last time we meet. Yet I recognize the man, much to my horror.

How is Joe Renton still alive?

"Why Joe?" I ask in reference to the trauma he inflicted on me.

He has a frozen on look on his face. I don't know if it's in response to what I said or if he had it to begin with. He isn't looking at me, however, but behind me. I'm too weak to turn around and see what he's looking at.

"It's all your fault, little bitch," Joe says. "You ruined everything. You said I would find God if I did what you said. You said I would understand what it means to be human. I trusted you. Benson is dead. They all died because of you. You were my angel. You ruined my life." Joe unplugs the earphones from the record player. Loud opera music echoes across the small room. "I am going to miss this. All of it. Such sweetness. I wish I had more time." Joe sighs and let the earphones slide out of his hands.

He reaches to his side and pulls out two long, silver needles. Despite having no strength, I pull away from him the moment I see him point the needles at me.

"This is the only way," he says. "It will only hurt for a second. Don't cry, little brother."

"No, Joe! Please don't!" My pleas fall flat as Joe turns up the opera music to the highest level possible. I close my eyes and pray this is not to be my end.

Instead, a scream followed by a moan then a sigh overpowers the opera music.

My eyes open. Joe has stuck the needles deep into his ears.

Fluid pours out in small amounts. Joe's eyes twitch open as he digs the needles deeper; his face distorts into a half smile of pleasure.

He pulls the needles out, then stabs them back into his ears.

"It hurts…it hurts so much. But I feel good. I feel so good," Joe says in a loud, high-pitched voice. "I can't hear it anymore. I'm happy now." Joe pulls the bloodied needles out, lets them fall out of his hands, and stands up. He wobbles over to where I am, steps over me, and leans down. Thinking he is going to strike me, I cover my face.

Joe instead picks up the music box dedicated to him from an unknown lover. My fears subside. I feel comfort staring at it. It is a wonderful little thing made of wood and metal. Joe has the same affection for it. He turns it around in all directions, smiling at the inscription inside, and then he turns the dial underneath the music box.

The familiar music I have grown to like does not come out.

An explosion of pain ruptures inside my ears. The cause for my agony is a distorted, horrible sound. Alien and unnatural is the best I can describe it; it's inhuman, no doubt, but everything comes in phases.

The first phase is a schizophrenic mix of a dog, cat, pig, and a goat getting murdered all at once. There are more animals, but those are the ones I recognize, the ones I focus on. The wails stretch out over a period of what seem like years. Flashes of animals getting butchered flash before my eyes. Each cry forcefully invokes the painful images.

The second phase is even worse than the first. It is a series of human voices that aren't human at all. Each voice is scratchy, rigid, and mechanical. They talk over one another and under one another. The voices are all speaking the exact same thing, but in different ways. Some laugh, some cry, some yell, some sneer, some climax. Words between them go forward and backward. The voices and words speed up and slow down, all at once.

There's no way of blocking any of it out. My brain tries to decode the incoherent babble against my will. Every second it continues, the more the pain in my ears pulses through my body. But I need to know what is being said. It is almost recognizable if I just pay attention a little more. If I can just concentrate just a little harder, I will understand.

I have to know. I need to know. I need to focus harder. I am willing to become undone by the pain, to even inflict pain on myself. Just so long as I know what is going on.

Deep down, my body knows what's going on; it knows what's being said.

Underneath all the babble is a solitary voice, a quiet voice, a whisper. It speaks at all times, never stopping. Yet in doing so, the voice takes all the time it wants. And it takes forever to utter just one syllable in the faintest of voices.

Then comes the next syllable. And then the next syllable.

All deliberate, all orchestrated. There is no rush. I am going to have to wait for it to finish speaking. There is no escaping it, no blocking it out, no denying it. The finality of its words will be heard.

You can still hear me.

I tremble at the sudden weight of the voice. Despite it being barely audible, it shakes the very foundation of my body. Every inch of me shivers, every inch of me burns. I feel a million pounds of pressure squeeze me from all sides. I feel like I'm being pulled apart. The pain freezes me in place. There is no escaping now that this voice has spoken.

"Leave me alone!" Joe's voice trembles. "Let me sleep! Please let me sleep!" Joe turns around in horror and looks at the room. He falls to his knees and sobs uncontrollably.

This is what you wanted. I have so many things to show you.

The voice keeps repeating its promise over and over. He looks at me and screams. He screams loud, but his scream is crushed under the repeating words of the voice.

Joe puts his hands deep inside his mouth and begins pulling his jaws apart. His jaw goes in opposite directions at a ninety-degree angle. Out of his mouth a gush of blood streams like smoke into the air. Everything it touches is warped into a void; the whole room bends to its will.

Before the room becomes encapsulated, I stare in the direction Joe is staring.

Inside a cabinet I see a pair of tearful eyes staring at me.

A young girl whimpers. A young girl laughs.

Then my world turns red. I am eaten by a crimson haze. Left swimming in sky of red by morning, I take my sailor's warning. Only when a hundred years pass, do I escape. But it isn't delight that meets me.

In my hand is a piece of sharp metal with tiny bits of my palm's flesh hanging off. My fingernails are torn to the bone; behind me is torn window grate and broken window covered in my blood. My wrists are marked with a hundred cuts, small and large; tiny shards of glass are inside the wounds. My chest is covered with stab marks from the metal.

This ledge I stand on, this edge of life, is too sharp for me to bear. I can feel it in my blood. Through the walls I hear wailing. I hear, feel the scratches on the walls. They are trying to get in; they will get in. And a hundred feet down, others stand waiting for me. If I do nothing, they will climb up the steep walls of the building to catch me. Or the orderlies will bring me back in and lock me in a solitary room with no exits. All that will do is lay me out for them to find.

I think of nothing as I step off the ledge. Tumbling down for the few seconds I have left, I have no time for reflection. No greater understanding, no regrets. All the pain, all the hatred, all the fear, will be over.

God has abandoned me. Death is my sole saving grace. Come, sweet death.

The Pale Strangers will come for me no more. Now I can finally sleep.

Please let me sleep. Please never let me wake up.

Chapter Fourteen

The sound of the telephone wakes me up. I am sleeping on my bed, back in my apartment, and I have no hole in my stomach. Thank god for that—I love to eat, and I need my stomach to do that. I am not contemplating suicide or jumping off the ledge of a building.

My apartment hasn't changed, but things are different enough that I notice something isn't right. The subtleties cannot be ignored. But the insistent ringing of the telephone demands my attention first. I stumble out of bed and go to the front room.

"Yeah?" I answer.

"Walker, Ralph West here! I thought long and hard about your pitch, and I want in!"

"What pitch?"

Ralph laughs. "The one involving Darius Renton. We talked about it yesterday."

I don't even remember talking to Ralph West yesterday. The last time we talked about this, he outright rejected me and was pissed that I didn't do his review.

"You probably got fucked up last night, didn't you, Walker?"

"Yeah…yeah I did." I reach for my wallet on the coffee table. My money and my cards have not been touched. I know my cards weren't used, otherwise there would be receipts wrapped around them. "Ralph, do you mind bringing me up to speed? I'm at a loss for what we talked about." I force a laugh and blame it on my imaginary partying.

"You called it 'The Renton Conspiracy.' You stated how Darius Renton, son of toy tycoon Gordon Renton, was being set up by a corrupt judicial system to take the fall for something he may or may not have committed. How despite there being exculpatory evidence, and enough reasonable doubt, the court is trying to convict the man anyway. And you were going to write about how ADA Oliver Greene is conspiring to get Darius convicted."

What? When did I do that? I don't remember any of this.

The last thing I remember was seeing what happened with Charles Benson's expedition in Afghanistan. Some madman attacked the camera, and there was gunfire. Then there was a man at my door attacking it and those eyes behind the papers in the corner. A phone call warning me.

Then I saw Joe Renton stick needles in his ears and tear his head apart.

Wait…those eyes in the corner.

I turn my head to look at the corner. The paper stacks are all knocked over.

Was I dreaming? Was I just hallucinating?

"You still there, Walker?" Ralph asks.

"Yeah…one second. I'm checking something." I put the phone down and race to my kitchen to see if I had cooked up some drugs. The trash is empty. My fridge is empty. There are no bottles of liquor around. The sink is bug free for once, but the dinnerware has been smashed to pieces; it's like the roaches rioted against the corporate dish machine for being too sanitary.

That's when I notice how annihilated the apartment is. Large growths of mold have replaced impossible-to-clean carpet stains. Chipped paint and cracks mar every inch of wall. In the living room, cassettes have been broken in half, the tape spread all over the floor like silly string. The few tapes that remain are hidden in different parts of the room.

I look at my writing desk. While Joe's research is untouched, I notice that the many of the thousands of blank pages have been scrawled over. Some were left blank, why I don't know. The yellow notebook is in the center of my desk. Sharpened pencils rest on top of handwritten pages. I know, somehow, that I authored these handwritten pages.

My handwriting is precise, clean, without errors. I take a brief glance at the title of the pages I had written.

"Darius's notes," I say.

"Walker, you still there?" Ralph asks.

"I am. Listen, Ralph, I need to call you back. Something's come up."

"Well, take your time. This will resurrect your career, buddy. This is the redemption you have been looking for. Fred Johnson will see to that. Anyway, take care, friend."

I hang up and dwell on the exact words Ralph said to me.

Ralph West is a prick. Ralph West is a lazy piece of shit. Ralph West has never once been nice to me. Ralph West is not my friend. And sure as I could be, Ralph West is only interested in his career. Just what has caused the sudden change in his character?

Just what the hell is going on?

My apartment telephone rings again, spooking the hell out of me. I answer to a minimal amount of static.

"Claire Walker? Can you hear me?" Levitt says.

"B-barely," I stutter. "I'm freaking out, man." I sit on my hands to keep them from shaking. "I don't remember anything. Do you know what's going on?"

"What do you last remember?" I tell him about Afghanistan tapes, about the creepy dream involving Joe Renton, about Ralph West's odd behavior in accepting a story pitch that I had no recollection writing. Then I mention how my entire apartment was rearranged almost beyond recognition.

"You're being indoctrinated."

"Indoctrinated?"

"You'll end up in places you don't know. You'll experience things you've never experienced. You'll go from point A to point X without knowing anything about experiences B through Y. It'll get worse. Your body hasn't started falling apart on itself, and your immune system hasn't turned against you. But it will."

"Dude, stop messing with me. It's creeping me out."

"You can choose to believe me, or not. What happened to us in Afghanistan happened to Darius, Joseph, and now you."

"I need some answers, damn it, not scary stories to tell in the dark!"

Levitt's hum follows a sigh. "Alright, then, how can I be of assistance?"

"What the hell happened in that Afghanistan village?"

"First, what did you see in the tapes?" I tell him that the last thing I saw was his camera lens getting a money shot with a deranged villager's hatchet.

"So what went down?"

"Oh, the whole thing was interesting. We were going to search for Benson's missing group of archeologists. The villagers attacked us. The marines opened fire on them. Men, women, children—they were killing anything that moved. Bullets didn't stop them, though. Neither did the falling bodies of their friends and families. Wave after wave, they kept coming, forcing us to retreat. A few days later came the aircraft that dropped the bombs. That ended our little journey and a whole lot of lives." Levitt laughs. "I almost forgot about those tapes. Forgot I sent them to Joseph Renton. So much carnage, so much nostalgia. They must have enjoyed them back home, just like I did making them."

"Carnage and nostalgia shouldn't go hand in hand."

"They don't, normally. But as a photographer, you're always looking for the perfect shot, the perfect story. Just like a journalist. Don't you agree?"

Rubbing my neck, I grudgingly agree. Then I ask, "So was Benson able to get in touch with Southern Miskatonic University or the scientific community and show his findings?"

"That's something you'll have to find out on your own. But it's safe to say that he died a charlatan in their eyes, as quickly forgotten as the archeologists who died along with him."

"I'm guessing you didn't like Benson."

"There was an incident where he shot at me, but that was forgivable. His sanity slipped down a slippery slope, but I think he was broken before Afghanistan, never to recover. He walked smack right into his doom; he took all but the cowards with him. I have nothing against him, other than his inability to see what was going on around him. Too busy focusing on the beautiful flower, ignoring the giant python right behind it, ready to grab him and crush him and swallow him whole."

"Okay, this might sound stupid, but was there any treasure found? Any relics, artifacts?"

Levitt snickers. "Whatever could be found was destroyed by the United States' million-dollar death machines. What? Plan on treasure hunting, Mr. Walker?"

While playing cool like Nathan Drake seems like a good idea, I instead say, "No…" before writing the word "treasure" just to strike it off. "So what else happened in Afghanistan?"

"Sadly, my time is very limited. You'll just have to read Benson's notes and find out the rest of the tale for yourself."

"But I don't know where to look. Let's meet up, discuss. I'll buy you something to eat. Maybe we can do something together."

"Physically, I cannot join you because of circumstances that have me tied up at the moment. I'll hold you to your offer when we do meet. I love to eat." The ungodly static hit Levitt's side. "Now, I have to let you go, but I will keep in touch with you. Find Darius. Please, you need to stop him."

The phone goes to a dial tone. Levitt didn't give me a chance to ask just what Darius needed to be stopped from doing. What did he mean by indoctrination?

Not having a clue, I jump into my couch, dislocating the furniture from its resting spot and making it slide several inches across the floor.

I should have never taken this job.

My phone rings again. Man, I'm starting to hate that phone and its insistent ringing. I kick the phone off its cradle. The receiver bounces off the floor then dangles from the cord. I bark into the phone with the driest voice I can muster. Static almost burns my ear off.

"Walker! You set me up three days ago! You tricked me! You've been working for them this entire time!" I recognize the voice as the guy who tried to break into my apartment.

"Easy, tiger. Back the fun bus up before you wreck," I say. "You came at me, man. You tried breaking into my apartment. I don't even know you."

"You won't take Dotty away from me."

"Dotty? Wait…Darius Renton? Is that you?"

"She told me about you. She told me you ruined her meal. You had the police destroy her shrine. It led you there. It wanted you to kill Dotty and me. You're its servant, aren't you?"

"Darius, listen to me. I'm a journalist. I write for the *Eye Tribunal*. Your father asked me to find you. Everyone's looking for. They are worried about you, man."

"Stop lying to me! Greene sent you! You want to fry me and keep me from worshiping my angel. Or maybe you're just working for it, aren't you?"

"Who are you talking about, Darius?"

"Stop trying to trick me!" Just like with Levitt, the static gets worse. I grip the arm of the couch and squeeze tight. "My angel wants me to kill you. She needs to be fed."

"Who needs to be fed?"

"My angel, Dotty."

"Darius, listen to me, man. I don't care what you're trying to do. I knew Joe. He was a good guy. He was nice to me in high school. I'm trying to find out what happened to him, and I'm trying to find out what happened to you. Please, I don't have a single clue about what is going on. Talk to me. I need your help. Help me solve this puzzle." Darius screams words as the static reaches its apex. My ears can't take it anymore. I drop the phone, collapse to the floor, and cover my ears.

"Help me!" Darius's voice echoes across the room through the small earpiece. The dial tone takes over, but Darius's plea for help festers into an explosion of emotions. His cry doesn't resonate from within my mind. No, it comes from somewhere more ancient, something passed down through my bloodline, everyone's bloodline.

Something inside me boils with fear and empathy for Darius. I stare at my forearms, then at the rest of my body. My blood knows these feelings.

I hurry to the table and examine my copy of Darius's notes.

"Like a vast ocean they swim around," I say. "They are no different from a wild animal, but I compare them more to sharks. Our reality is like a vast, watery desert to them. They have senses superior to those of any creature on the planet. They track us from hundreds of miles away, pinpointing where we last were. It's not human or animal echolocation, but more primordial. It's not that great, since it takes them so long to travel and they can only see the remnants of a trail from where we stood to where we went. I don't know if it's friction or a part of their world that I can't explain with science, but they are very slow to enter our reality. They are incredibly patient, incredibly persistent, though. They just don't stop chasing you. Ever. While I still have my sanity I will write out more."

Just what are you talking about Darius? If not animal or human, then what?

"The sigils are the key. With one, they can see out; with more, they can influence; and with many, they can come into our world with ease. It can be any word or any picture. No magical combination, no taboo assortment. Something that is drawn. Has to be drawn."

Sigils? Drawings? I see none of that.

"I can hear the whispers too. That's a warning that they are near. But it's the scratches. Some of them like to scratch. If they can leave deep scratches, that means they are almost done traversing through the realities. Or they can influence it from what they are. Either way, that means they are here. Can you hear them? They won't leave me alone. I can't sleep anymore."

I move further down the page.

"I've asked in every language I possibly know for peace and sleep. I've asked God in every speaking tongue. I'll stick with English, but I like the way As-salaam sounds. I'm tired of saying Yahweh anyway. Even better, salaam by itself means peace. Maybe if I say it enough he'll hear me. Let me sleep, As-salaam. Let me sleep, As-salaam." After a few repeats Darius stops. "My hand hurts. I'll just stick with salaam. "

None of this makes sense.

"Let me sleep, salaam. Let me sleep, salaam," I repeat for page after page. An endless repetition of his mantra continues with each turn.

The madness stops in the middle of a blank page before continuing. Just one phrase.

"God has damned me. Whoever reads this, please kill me. Kill me before I kill more."

A knock sounds on the door. My heart stops for several beats, and my lungs shove out all their air. I remember this feeling from when I was in high school. I kept staring at a pretty girl, so she sent her friends over to tell me I was creeping her out. If I kept at it, I was going to get my ass beat. This feeling is a million times worse, but somehow I am a teenage boy again, terrified at the consequences of my actions.

I zombie-shuffle toward the door and notice the peephole is crushed. Now I am left with no doubt that Darius tried to break into my apartment. If what Darius said was true, he confronted me three days ago. That meant I have no recollection of a period of three days.

I am beyond terrified.

The knock continues. I put my ear to the door and listen.

"Who is it?" I say. A woman cries outside the door.

"Please, baby, open the door," Heather says. I let out a loud sigh of relief and rush to unlock it. Heather pushes the door open and gives me a tackle hug.

"Why are you crying, baby girl?"

"I thought you had gone crazy."

I ask her what she means.

"I saw this crazy man hacking away at your door with a screwdriver. Then he stopped, covered his ears, and screamed. Then he looked in my direction. He was feral, baby. And I saw this ghost of a woman covered in black bubbling water floating behind him, like La Llorona but not crying. Oh God, I have never been so scared in my life." Her tears and mascara soak through my shirt. Her fingers dig deep into my back. Her shivers run across my skin. Her voice breaks into pieces.

She is a scared child in my arms. So I hold her tight and shush her.

"What happened next?"

"She blinked away. Then he ran at me and knocked me over. I didn't see him again, but I heard his screams for a long time after he ran." I hold her at a distance so I can look at her face. I rub the tears off her olive skin. "I knocked on the door and pleaded with you to open it. You didn't. I looked under the door. You just paced around, making grunts as you walked. I left after an hour. I came back the next day and the next one after that. You kept doing that, baby."

"But you came back to check up on me."

"Every day." She nods and kisses me on the neck.

I nod, kiss her forehead, and let out a sigh while saying, "Thank you."

I have to figure out what's going on. But for the moment I can just be happy and not worry about that.

Chapter Fifteen

Heather has been quiet since I started talking. She's paying attention, I think. I am on a roll about what I discovered. I tell her that something very bad is going on. Though the totality has yet to be seen, I'm convinced that the worst is to come. Unnamed forces caused the demise of Joe, if my "dream" is anything to go on. Darius has been eroded in both mind and body; a shell of a deranged person is all that remains.

She just nods, takes an occasional cigarette puff, and nods a little more.

"You're not going to say anything, are you?" I ask.

Heather shrugs. "I don't know what is going on, baby. When we last talked about any of this, you were trying to separate unreadable walls of text from disturbing fairy tales."

"These aren't fairy tales. This happened. All of it."

"Not to be a bitch, Claire, but how can you be so sure?"

I understand she has to feed the fiend and cushion herself from my verbal onslaught. Her haze is a temporary fix; it won't last. If I was sitting where she is and cooked up after a traumatizing ordeal involving a man stabbing at a door with a screwdriver and a disembodied ghost floating behind him, I would be unsure of everything too.

Still, she's the one person who is willing to listen. Greene is a dickhead whose moral compass is so fucked up I'd be surprised if he could find his way to the bathroom. Ralph West is playing a card on me I can't call. I don't know his angle, but I'm sure he is up to something. Levitt knows what is going on, but I can't keep him on the phone or get a complete answer out of him. Gordy? Shit...I don't know what I'm going to tell him. I think I understand why he is messed up and in poor health.

And if what is happening to me happened to him, then I have him as an example of what my future is going to be like unless I do something.

"A guy named Levitt told me that everything in these files is true." I tap my writing desk, and then pick up some papers. "Things that went down in Afghanistan headed out our way. Then there is the issue of three days I don't remember. Somehow I managed to write someone else's thoughts in this yellow journal, tear up the apartment, and pitch a story to Ralph West."

"You sure you don't remember anything?"

I shake my head before taking a place by Heather's side. She puts my arm over her neck, hangs closer to me, and rubs my chest. "Maybe you should see a doctor."

"I don't have insurance. Besides, a doctor wouldn't see me unless I was bleeding out of my eye sockets. Damn health care system is all screwed up, ya know."

She tells me she knows all too well about healthcare, then tells me she has a brilliant idea.

"You can stay at my place."

"Huh?"

"Live with me. I can keep an eye on you." I'm sure she feels my heart bounce off a trampoline a couple times. I feel my face turning red, and my neck gets a little tighter.

"Nah, that's not a good idea."

She asks me why.

"If Darius comes by, I don't want you to get hurt. There is that lingering possibility he is killing people right now, after all."

Heather lets out a long, dull laugh. "But you'll protect me, won't you?" She rubs her fingers across the stubble I've grown. She bites her bottom lip and gives me a soft kiss. "My own personal hero who puts away arsonists and saves young girls like me."

She has a point. If another blackout is possible, it'll be safer if I have someone keeping an eye on me. I quickly bury that idea when I remember her saying she saw me pace around my room, grunting, for three straight days.

I mean, what if I harm her? What if I get out and harm some kids?

If I ever came to my senses after doing something terrible...no...I dare not imagine. I wouldn't be able to live with myself. I'm not taking any chances.

"Sorry, doll. No can do." She tilts her head, her expression becoming stone. She moves my arm away from her and puts distance between us. "You understand, don't you?" She gives me a small nod without looking at me. Knowing full well I disappointed her, I just rub my face and try to change the subject. "How about you helping me clean up this place, then going through these papers? Two people will make this go faster."

"Okay, I can do that."

We get up and start picking up the pieces of my broken apartment. She takes the kitchen while I take the area around my writing desk. Little by little, I unwrap the tape from the corners. Then I dig through the room, playing "Marco Polo" with the tapes that are hidden among the trash. I find about fifteen tapes that aren't ruined. The black light is somewhere, but I'll worry about it later.

The blank papers I took from Darius's rooms are no longer blank, except for the hundred or so that are still untouched. Using pencils, I had scraped over them, then scraped through them; they are more lead than trees now. They are useless outside of looking dark, troubled, and mysterious to a younger crowd, but I'm hesitant to throw them away. Heather stays away from the papers; she doesn't want to toss out anything that might be important later.

Why did I do that? Was I trying to draw something but didn't like the end result?

I wish I left myself some notes about everything I did during my blackout.

After stacking the useless papers in a corner and stacking the useful papers in little rows on my desk comes the sweeping and filling of trash bags. Broken glass, torn paint, dust bunnies...cleaning while stone-cold sober sucks. I wish I had the help of a few junkies. They'd make quick work of this place. But then again, they might freak out over the talk of ghosts, killers with screwdrivers, and shady lawyers. Especially the part about the lawyers.

An hour or so later, we finish. I spearhead the cleaning of the writing desk; it's about ten minutes worth of backbreaking work. Three separate stacks are now arranged on my desk.

The left stack reads "German Count," the middle stack reads "Prisoner," and the right stack reads "Afghanistan Ruins." The yellow journal of Darius is useless to me, other than proving he is crazy or proving Levitt right with his ominous predictions.

Right now, finding out what happened to Levitt is the key. Not only is he directly connected to Benson and Joe Renton, but the tale he is involved in is the most recent. If I can get up to speed on what happened in Afghanistan, maybe I'll find some common ground with Levitt. Despite his mysterious motivations, he's the only sane person who knows anything or is willing to help me. I grab the Afghanistan stack, while Heather grabs a chair and sits by me.

I split half the stack with her. We get to work.

"What are we looking for?" she asks.

"Look for anything involving a man named Levitt Brower or Charles Benson." I give a glance over at my TV. "I don't know for sure what tapes are left for us to watch. They are marked with florescent ink; I can't find the black light anywhere. We can go through them one at a time after we at least go through these files together. Are you up to this?"

She says yes.

We spend a few minutes looking over our halves. Heather doesn't find anything useful, but I find excerpts from the journal of Private Aaron Jefferies. I grab her and read along with her.

Jefferies made notes of the strange things happening around the archeological caravan that he and his squad accompanied. The reason his squad accompanied Benson's staff was because they might be attacked by hostiles, as the dig site was located just a few miles away from a battle zone between U.S. forces and insurgents. Not wanting to have an incident on their hands, the U.S. Marines agreed to lend out Torres's team.

It all started just moments after they left the base.

"I saw someone hiding behind the rocks," I read out loud. "No friendlies were outside. Thinking it might be an insurgent preparing an attack on HQ, I tell Torres. He phones back, we get out the cars, and sweep around to check who was there. Nothing at all. We resume our drive to the dig site. When we get there, the guy I saw outside the base was standing on a hill. Now it took us 'bout two hours to get there and we were hauling ass; no other cars around, no birds in the sky on our drive to the dig site. No way this guy could have just outrun us on foot and got there before us. I get out the car first and make an approach with my firearm pointed at him. I order him to stay where he is with his hands up. The man waves his hand at me and sinks into the sand. Rankin follows me. We do a sweep of the area, and I dig into the sand. No one there. Rankin saw nothing so Cruz busts my balls for being jittery."

The entry skips around several days and between sentences. It is clear to me that Joe most likely omitted all unimportant information related to the entry. Just the bare essentials remain.

"I keep seeing that guy. Casper-looking motherfucker looks like he has ice fog coming off him. He stays about half a mile outside our perimeter, and before anyone else can see him he vanishes. Over the course of a week he circles around us, waves at me, and disappears into the sand. Next time he shows up I'm gonna shoot at him."

I saw the aftermath of Jefferies' plan on the tape with Benson and Levitt. Jefferies shoots at this person he keeps seeing. His squad accuses him of being dehydrated and losing his mind. I tell Heather about it and promise to show her—if the tape isn't destroyed. From here, I see the entry that connects Session One and Session Two in the village.

"A couple of the archeologists went missing over the course of the night. Nobody wants an incident that'll piss off the people back home, so we have to go look for them and bring them back. Don't really want to bring the paparazzi with us, but it ain't my call." The entry ends there, before beginning again with chaotic handwriting. "We killed them. Twenty-three dead. The villagers were insane...feral. Shot a kid in the head, didn't kill him. He just got back up and kept coming at us. Put him down with a second bullet and a third to make sure."

"That is horrible, Claire," Heather says as she rubs my arm. "Who would kill a child?"

I try not to think about it as I read the next entry, which is a scribbled mess.

"The caravan is gone. The dig site is empty. Blood everywhere. From over a thousand yards out, some guys, with the red tattoos like the people we eliminated, are gathering. There are at least fifty of them, armed with assault rifles. Rankin pops a few of them off with a Barrett. They don't move. Even when their buddies splatter besides them, they don't fucking move. They just stare at us." The entry skips to another page. "At least four hundred around us now in a circle formation, two hundred yards out. We are hunkered down in dig site. Our radios and electronics aren't working. Still the bastards won't move! What are they planning?"

A few pages are filled with blank space and ink spots before a small sentence appears: "I saw an ape!"

Heather grabs my arm and lets out cracked laugh. "Are there apes in Afghanistan?" she asks with a raised brow.

"There are no apes in the Middle East, at least not any wild ones," I say to calm our suspicions. I read the next entry. Then I cover the paper with my hands.

I stare at my hands before cupping them together. I make sure to read without showing Heather what the next part says.

No, I'm reading this wrong. This can't be happening.

"What's the matter? Something spooky?" Heather attempts to tickle me behind my ear, but it doesn't work; my head twitches instead. I can feel an expression of dread paint my face. She pushes me away. "What's wrong, Claire? You're scaring me."

"Baby, I need you to do me a favor," I say as I reach into my wallet. I open her hands, stuff some cash in, and close them tight. "Can you go buy us some beer? Whatever you want. The store is just around the corner. Please?"

She stutters as I help her up from the chair and crumple the page with a closed fist.

"What's going on, Claire? You're white with fright, baby." She puts the money in one hand and rubs my forehead. "Baby, you're sweating. Tell me what's wrong."

"Just get us some beer." She shakes her head and stumbles to the door. She tries to speak but doesn't. I help her out before slamming the door shut. My shoulder drags alongside the door, and I slide down. I make sure her footsteps vanish down the hall before I open my hand and read off the page.

My hands tremble, and I stutter to utter any words. I stop trying. Instead, I read in silence.

The pale ape was hairless and malnourished. Its face was skeletal and made up of pieces of rotten skin and muscles. Its bottom jaw split open like a bug's. Dozens of faces littered its body, and hundreds of tendrils stuck out of its body like worms and wiggled around. The ape stomped and ran up and down the top of the mountain for hours upon end. It carried one of the bodies of the missing archeologists and smashed the corpse on the rocks of the mountain until it was just ground meat. Then it ate part of the corpse and let out a roar that sounded like glass grinding against a chalkboard.

The beast charged the men with the red tattoos. Four hundred against one. They didn't stand a chance. Bullets didn't faze it, nor slow its charge. It barreled through them like a cannon busting balloons made of meat and blood. It pounced and stomped on them; they were suffocated under the sand and rock until they became one with the sand and rock. The surviving men with the red tattoos retreated into the mountains. The creature didn't give chase.

Rankin fired several explosive cartridges from the Barrett at it. The creature split in half, but reconnected itself using the bones from the dead. The bones became one with its body, like an exoskeleton.

Now aware of the troops' presence, the ape stared at them from afar while devouring the dead. For hours, it did this.

Soon, Jeffries wrote, it was going to run out of food.

I put my hands in my hair and pull. I shake my head. I deny everything I just read. My head bounces off the door. My hands shake and my eyes water. I have no reason to be scared, let alone emotional.

None of this shit happened. This dude is crazy. I mean, Benson was killed by insurgents. That's who was behind it. And they got rid them with large bombs, just like the paper said.

I yell, "This is the worst story I've ever heard. Worst description of a monster ever! What is it supposed to be? Bigfoot? The Yeti? There are no monsters!"

I toss the paper aside as I force a laugh. I thump my chest with my fist and tell myself that a man doesn't cry. But I don't believe in my bravado.

I fight with myself, and I lose. I curl into a ball and pray not to read anymore.

My mind is stable, but my body rebels. Why is my body defying my mind?

My eye strays to my writing table. I stare, but not at the papers. I focus on the music box. My expression is the same as Joe's. I am terrified of this box, and I can't say why. But I need to know why he was so scared. I need to understand why I am so scared of reading further.

I must know why this music box has frozen my body in fear.

I approach the table with small steps. My brows and lips twitch. My heart refuses to work when I pick up the box. Superficially, the box is okay; there is no indication of blemishes or scratches. The beautiful red captivates the eyes. It's perfect in every sense, yet my shivers continue.

"For my friend, Joe." I read off the engraving as my fingers reach underneath and twist. I prepare for that unholy sound. But air rushes from my lungs. I hear that sweet music hit my ears and wash away all my negative feelings. I'm able to wipe the tears without debilitating tremors. A laugh passes my mouth and lets in a few more.

There is nothing wrong with the box. I have no reason to be afraid of the box.

But I refuse to look at the pages from Afghanistan. I refuse to finish Jefferies' entry.

I'm going to look at the other stuff. Yeah, that's a good idea. But before I continue with anything, however, I'm in need of a beer. I hope Heather brings back something strong.

Chapter Sixteen

The heated breeze brings both relief and a sting. Empty beer cans from the twenty-four pack lay by the side of the bed, and I struggle to find at least one full can. Heather is cuddled under the pillows, asleep. Her snoring drowns out the wannabe hip-hopper's crunk mess next door and the passing car sounds coming through the open window.

We had a strange, emotional reunion when she came back from the store. It led to sex, but I hadn't been planning on it. It was more of a distraction than anything, really. Until now, I had forgotten what transpired two hours before.

With her asleep, I can suffer for my pursuit of the truth, alone.

Afghanistan has nothing more going for it outside of the tapes. Jefferies' journal ended abruptly. I don't know how his tale ended. Levitt has to answer some of my questions next time.

For now, the story behind the Yellow Count from Germany is my mission.

Benson's research notes split into two paths. The first involve the actual ruins of the castle themselves. Benson spent over a year, going on two, devoting his life to the ruins. There are sketches and opinions regarding how big the castle was, how many people lived in it, when it was built, all that stuff. None of that helps me. The second part, which becomes more prominent, absorbing a massive amount of the later pages, is dedicated into reconstructing the history behind the Yellow Count.

With the exceptions of the Yellow Count's name—as his and everyone's names have been stricken from history for reasons known only to the region—there is more fact and truth glossed over or omitted from the original tale that I read a few days before. The count had been blacklisted from written history, so little remained for oral tradition. It took Benson almost two years of constant work to piece together the fractured story.

The Yellow Count was not the tyrant I first imagined. He didn't subjugate or oppress the people who lived under his command or in the region. He was born from royal bloodlines and given his title at a young age.

He was ambitious, but kind and wise, very devoted to country and faith. When he was not tending to civil matters, he tended to the needs of the nearby towns and villages. He had no problems helping them in times of famine and sickness, even helping till the soil. His castle remained open to everyone, and he offered his listening ear to whoever came to him with troubles.

The primary position the count held was that of jailor. Benson theorized from studying the castle's layout that the prison was underneath the castle itself. The count jailed all kinds of prisoners, but he specialized in housing political prisoners who opposed the Holy Roman Emperor. Benson had pictures of the torture devices that were used at the time. Vises and spikes, prongs and heat—disturbing methods from an uncivilized time we pretend never existed. Using these barbaric tools, the count was ruthless to those who opposed the Holy Roman Emperor. He was lenient to other prisoners, but most of his prisoners weren't the kind he showed clemency.

Joe got the idea of naming him after Count Dracula, or Graf Orlok, because of his ruthlessness and cruelty to the prisoners he tortured and executed. Joe thought he had a bloodlust that needed to be fulfilled, but, really, he was just devoted to his cause.

"Orlok's devotion proved to be his downfall, just like Joe." I whisper.

It's the cryptic things that make me wish I could talk to Joe.

Glossing over the page, I find a small article on a new player to the tale. The Yellow Count married a young peasant girl Benson called the countess; Joe had no witty name for her. She was known around the region for her beautiful singing voice.

Benson stressed how jealous and paranoid the count was. The count refused to let her leave the castle and only then under the watchful eye of armed guards.

In the end, he was justified. She refused to practice his faith. She was known to dabble in witchcraft and was a member of a popular cult that practiced hedonism. Benson thought the cult practiced a form of ancient Satanism, or perhaps they melded old pagan deities with pseudo-Christian demons.

Her beauty and influence made her a target for the cult. The high-ranking cult members tried to use her to gain favors from her husband. This was no secret to the people who lived under his rule, including him. He knew she slept around and engaged in questionable practices. She had carnal, greedy, mortal desires, bound and urged by her flesh. She needed them fulfilled, and the only way was through self-indulgence in taboo behavior.

Yet the count desired his wife. He just wanted his love reciprocated. So he let her do as she wanted just to keep her happy. He even imported large amounts of orpiment to bathe the castle in her favorite color to appease her. Orpiment is also referred to as King's Yellow.

But one thing she could never have, something the count could never give her, was her own kingdom. She wanted to be queen, and if that were to happen, her husband had to be a king.

This is why Benson called him the Yellow Count: he wasn't a king—that was a position he could never attain. He was resigned to being a devoted servant, and being a count was the highest he could climb.

In time certain members of the cult the countess belonged to were accused of taking part in a campaign to overthrow the Holy Roman Emperor. The bold plot was halted before it could come to fruition. The cultists were driven out of Germany or put to death upon capture. The countess, however, was spared.

The Yellow Count used his power to save her from certain death. Yet she still had to pay for her part in treason. The Yellow Count agreed to keep her as his prisoner under his castle. He built a special cell to keep her comfortable. His servants kept her in the lifestyle she had grown accustomed to.

Life went on, and it seemed like nothing had changed. Except it did.

Heather opens her eyes and asks, "You find anything yet?"

I turn the pages over to keep her from reading. "Just another scary story."

She dances her fingers across my chest. "Is it any good?"

"Sort of. Not my kind of thing."

"Can I ask you a question?" I tell her yes. "Do you love me?"

"You know it." I move her hair to the side and kiss her on the forehead.

"I am happy I have you, Claire. You treat me good," she says, with a yawn and a grin. Her arms sneak under my stomach and squeeze. Her head rests on my shoulder. The cuddles get more sexual, but it's all just foreplay for a wonderful waste of time.

Pillow talk happens for an almost an hour. Hopes, fears, dreams, and plans get mixed in with sensuality, dirty talk, and laughs. For almost an hour, I pretend there is some future between us so that she can pretend we are a real couple. I make believe that the past few days never happened, that instead I had been here in her arms.

If I try hard enough I can just forget…

But in between each breath, each kiss, each whisper, each blink I am reminded: all of it happened. There is something horrible out there. There are things I never wanted to know.

I don't pry her arms away when she falls back to sleep; her comfort and warmth helps me pick up at the paragraph where I left off and continue reading.

Several things disturbed the nearby villagers. New prisoners were brought in from all over the country, many of whom were to be executed just days after arrival. Heavy construction materials were brought in from all over to build something beyond the castle walls: a bigger, labyrinthine prison. Exotic devices were purchased from different corners of the world, strengthening rumors that the count was performing horrible experiments on his prisoners. But this was never proven.

Most unnerving of all were the whispers revolving around the count himself. The few appearances he made outside of his castle showed a disintegration of physicality and mentality, despite his being a man in his youthful prime. His hair had become white, and his skin lost all its color. He was slouched, with a hump protruding from his back. He mumbled to himself, and roamed around in circles without talking to anyone or responding to outside stimuli. He saw fewer of the villagers, heard fewer of their problems, and had fewer guests over the years.

I stopped, and reread the part about the count's description.

The connection to Gordy and Joe makes my hands jitter around so much that Heather moves. Is there a connection between the Renton brothers and the count in terms of their health and minds failing before their time?

My fingers turn the next page and almost tear the corner.

Orlok's servants were ordered to stay within the castle grounds at all times. At first the isolation was not very welcome, but then it became a willing choice of self-exile. Those who had left the castle to attend to outside business were known for being very melancholic and aloof from the rest of the world. Most were never seen again after a certain point.

A strange mist formed around the castle. It was small at first but refused to go away. Months passed by, and the mist grew. Odd, pale-colored people hung around outside the castle and traveled in the mist, but never outside out of it. Wildlife abandoned the area, plants stopped growing. The villagers heard growls, squeals, and an assortment of animal noises from creatures not of the region inside the mist. People reported fleeting glimpses of unimaginable beasts that pounced, and of eyes that shined a hypnotic and sickening flash of colors before fading away.

They were called the ghosts in the mist.

Those who wandered into the mist for too long vanished, only to be found later as a pile of bones for the crows and the worms to clean.

Crippling fear tiptoes its way out of my stomach and into my bloodstream. I tense my body and force the fear away with an invisible broom.

Not this time. I must know what is going on, and what I got myself into.

I turn the page and read again.

A stable boy escaped the castle. The original tale said that the boy rallied the villagers, who, upon hearing of the crimes the Yellow Count had committed, stormed his castle and executed him. That was the original myth I read. Benson had uncovered the lesser known, "alternative" story that went in a different direction and had a different outcome.

The stable boy never said what happened, and he was not alone. There was another survivor. She was a handmaiden and also the sister of the stable boy. The siblings escaped together and attempted to go to one of the villages. When they arrived, however, they found nothing but mist—the very same mist they had so desperately tried to escape from at the Yellow Count's castle. So they ran for days, chased by the mist and the ghosts inside.

Leading the ghosts was a pale creature, more devil than man, made of haze.

Why does this sound so familiar?

I swear I've heard this before, despite reading it for the first time.

Not wanting to be derailed by my sudden case of déjà vu, I turn to the next page.

The siblings came upon an army resting before a battle. The army, Benson said, belonged to a group of knights called the Order of the Yellow Moon. Their battle standard was black, with a maroon crescent hanging over a dark yellow full moon. Benson made a personal memo to Joe that he couldn't find more information on the Order, or who they were fighting. Joe sent him a message back, suggesting that they might have been imperial knights or a band of mercenaries.

One key figure Benson did identify among the knights was a man named Götz. The knight wore fluted armor made of dark gray iron that bordered on black; Joe nicknamed him The Black Knight after the infamous knight in *Monty Python and the Holy Grail*. Benson replied that this knight kept his limbs. Joe replied that he wasn't defending a bridge against the king of the Britons and his patsy.

The exchange makes me laugh when it shouldn't. Nerds to the end; how embarrassing.

"What's so funny?" Heather asks without opening her eyes.

"Nothing. Go back to sleep. Sorry I woke you."

A few minutes later, her snoring resumes, and I continue with the story.

The boy and his sister told Götz what happened at the castle. Everything came to a head a week before they fled. The mist had invaded the very cracks of the castle walls, and the servants began to hear and see strange people out of the corner of their eyes or down the hallways. If the horses and animals hadn't been locked up and kept from moving, they would have raced through the castle in an attempt to escape.

The Yellow Count went to visit the countess in the castle's dungeon, as he normally did. On this particular day, however, things changed. The count rushed out of the dungeon, covered in blood and crying hysterically. When everyone inquired about what happened, he mumbled on and on about her being a puppet controlled by the castle.

The countess was no longer his wife.

She had become one of them, just like the ghosts in the mist.

Orlok assigned several of his men to the job of walling off the prison dungeon entrance, leaving the remaining prisoners sealed down there, still alive. After they finished the seal, his men barricaded every exit and entrance inside the castle. No one was allowed to leave.

The castle itself was an enemy, but they couldn't leave.

The ghosts in the mist were trying to break in.

For days, maddening, agonized screams echoed through the cracks of the stone floor. The prisoners begged to be released. They prayed for death. Then the cries stopped.

The servants tried to leave en masse. They bullied their way past the guards, but when they stepped outside the castle gates, they saw dozens of ghosts with shimmering eyes in the mist. Some of the servants were taken immediately by the mist. Others fled back inside.

Brother and sister were outside the walls when it happened. They saw the horror in its entirety. The count barricaded the gates and shut the massive doors, leaving the two siblings outside alone. That's when they ran for their lives.

And that's how they made their way to the Yellow Moon's camp.

Götz, having heard the tale, decided to take several of his men back to the castle to confront the Yellow Count. The brother was forced to stay back with the resting soldiers while the sister led the way back to the castle.

My palms are sweaty and my heart is racing. My emotions are strapped onto a rocket. This rush is unlike any other…and I can't explain why it's happening. It shouldn't be. Not from just reading.

But I want to know more.

Benson claimed there was political turmoil and subtext in the Yellow Count's tale. Germanic culture and history were so deeply hidden in this tale that he didn't have enough time to search for it properly. He theorized that the ghosts in the mist were enemies of the Holy Roman Emperor. The countess was a traitor and had been influencing her husband. The ghosts in the mist were trying to stage an attack on the Yellow Count. Götz, knight of the Order of the Yellow Moon, and the rest of his men were loyalists dedicated to wiping out enemies of the Holy Roman Emperor. Either that or they were a band of mercenaries hired to do assassinations by proxy.

That was Benson's theory.

"I don't believe in goblins or ghosts," I whisper Benson's words, reading out loud. "God is as much a fairy tale as these ghosts in the mist. These monsters are flesh and blood people. They are long dead. Come on, Joe, why bother with this one? We aren't going to find anything about your imaginary deity, or humanity. I'm tired of being stuck in this part of Germany already. You should be with me out here, not with that little ballerina tart. Hope you don't turn into the Yellow Count on me. Now, don't think I'm not grateful. I am. Funding for this expedition wouldn't have been possible without your aid. Southern Miskatonic University has a shitty budget, but we both know that."

I might be inclined to agree with Benson had I not seen or read about Afghanistan first…if Heather hadn't seen a ghost…if I hadn't seen a creature with shining eyes appear in my apartment. If these things hadn't happened, then I could get high and laugh at the terrible idea that there might be something otherworldly that exists alongside me.

Ignorance does have its perks.

I reach a paragraph that refers to the original fax of the pictures of the two old swords that Benson found at the ruins of the Yellow Count.

"I should have never doubted you, Joe! You hit the jackpot several times over!"

The tale of the Yellow Count ends there. No continuation, no denouement. It just ends. Unless there is something mixed up with the other papers, I am left yearning for more answers. The last page is what I read days before: Joe and Benson claiming to have the thing that would change the world. They had proof in the swords. Afghanistan was yet to come.

High hopes, big dreams. I'm sorry, guys. Deep sorrow and regret float to the surface. A cruel causality found both of you. Now I fear it has infected me, just like it infected Darius.

I kiss Heather on the cheek.

I pray she does not let me go. For a moment, I hope she loves me more than I love her.

Chapter Seventeen

An odd series of nightmares wake me up. When I open my eyes, Heather is sneaking around the room in search of the rest of her clothes. She stops when she sees me panting and drenching my blanket with sweat. She comes over and brushes my wet hair aside.

"You all right, baby?" she asks. My hands rub against my skin in search for invisible wounds. I move toward her hands and feel them, and then I move my fingers across her face. My breathing is heavy, and I can feel my lungs seizing, like I'm drowning. My hands wrap around her; I hold her tight.

"I'm alive," I say.

"You had a bad dream?"

I nod.

"What was it about?"

"I was in a chapel. A really gorgeous chapel made of beautiful white stone, polished to a blinding mirror shine; had hundreds of pillars and a thousand pews. And there was this…man in regal cloth. He was at the altar, kneeling, praying. He was in tears." As I say it, I can feel my eyes starting to water. Heather wipes away my tears before they can fall. "The walls started to crumble down. I could hear the scratches, the voices, trying to break in. Feral monsters, changing shape. Trying to get in. And I was praying for forgiveness."

"Why were you praying, Claire?"

"Because I had my men kill my people. Men, women, children. I killed them to spare them. I did it out of love and pity. They didn't need to suffer. I did it to protect them from the ghosts in the mist. I did it to protect them from what was underneath the castle. I did it to protect them from her."

In reality, I had done it to protect them from the primordial ghost who abandoned his kind for a feast, all for himself. In my dream, he was my true enemy.

There is no hope for me but in death.

"I'm sorry you got scared, Claire," Heather whispers. "Remember, it's just a nightmare."

"I just..." My voice stutters and my hands shake. "That was worse than death. Whatever was trying to get in was worse. No one deserves that."

Heather picks up the files from my nightstand, waves them around, and then tosses them on the bed. "That's your problem, darling. You read this screwed up stuff before you sleep, and your good night becomes utter shit. I tell my nephews and nieces that, whenever they want to watch a horror movie. That's the only advice I can give you."

I force a laugh. "You have nephews and nieces?"

Heather pushes me away. "Are you serious, Claire? I only talk about them all the time." She hops off the bed, mad that I forgot, and resumes putting her clothes back on piece by piece. Despite my attempted apologies, she doesn't listen to me.

Typical woman. There is no point in telling her about the other half of my dream.

There were smoking craters and broken trees, mud and trenches littered with barbed wire and landmines. Spent ammunition crumpled under my feet as I walked with my son across the killing zone. We were trying to get back home; when we did, we found our home ablaze.

Hundreds of dead soldiers were impaled on stakes. Blood and flesh of the dead soldiers drained through the stakes. A thin, tall, pale stranger I recognized stood on the roof of the burning house, staring up at the sky. The stakes came out of his stomach by the hundreds, stabbing deep into the earth then piercing upwards through the ground again, and into the flesh of the dead.

He noticed us and gave us a wave.

He called me by my name, then asked me to wait for him.

This is what woke me up.

Overwrought, I stumble over to the bathroom and lock myself in. I fill up the faucet and dunk my head in the water. My reaction is a confused feeling; part of me can't deal with the rust-tainted water flooding my nostrils, and another part can't deal with the sudden liquid chill punching me in the face. Yet the rest of me keeps my head submerged, only to come up when I almost suffocate.

My sudden masochistic move serves a purpose other than getting me wet and half dead: it proves that I am both awake and functioning, unfortunately.

When I leave the bathroom, Heather is sitting on my couch. She tells me she has to go earn some money at Sparks Ultra Lounge. Despite my desire to tell her something, words pass unspoken. My wordless speech leads to a kiss on her cheek.

I show her the door and say good-bye.

I lie in bed for an hour, but all I do is toss and turn. I move to the couch and realize I am unable to find a comfortable position. I go to my writing desk and pick the last stack I have to complete: Foch's World War I story. My eyes feel like they're being poked with jagged glass every time I blink. Too damn tired. No way am I getting any more work done on the legibility side.

Frustrated at being unable to read and unable to sleep, I search the room for the black light. Twenty minutes of searching and I don't find it. Figures. So I sit on the floor in front of the TV. Blindly, I am going to have to figure out which tapes remain. Finding a Session Three and beyond is the best-case scenario for me, though any clue at all would help.

Yet each tape I eject and replace with another shows endless hours of Joe doing mundane things. My impatience grows alongside my fatigue.

Is there a point to any of this? Why the fuck did Joe bother making these tapes?

My answer comes with an erotic twist.

Dotty Finley is in the camera's crosshairs this time. She is dressed in bluish pajamas, with her hair done in pigtails. She has light makeup on her face, and her lips crackle with the gum she pops. Her pink toenails curl against the carpet; her fingernails tap against the desk she sat on. She isn't looking at the camera; instead, she's staring at the darkest part of the room.

I don't snap to it, not at first, but there is familiarity to the room.

"Take off your clothes slowly," a male voice booms from behind the camera. Dotty hesitates to unbutton the top of her pajamas. "Do it now!" The voice's heavy breathing almost ruptures my TV speakers. The camera shakes wildly, fingers popping up in front of the lens and adjusting the focus. "I'm waiting," the impatient man huffs.

So Dotty does as she's told. She strips piece by piece. Her skin is naked for the camera to see. The man who barks orders at her tells her not to hide anything with her hands, so she places her hands behind her back.

I'm embarrassed to see her like this. Maybe it has to do with her being dead. Or maybe it's because I'm watching something private, intimate. I know my checks are blushed, and I squirm with childish effort to look away.

"What now?" she asks.

"Tell me what to do." Joe Renton says as he grips Dotty by her hair, sniffs her all over before licking and biting near her neck. "I need to know what to do. Tell me, please, I beg of you."

I'm stunned by what I'm watching. My head turns to keep from watching, to tell myself this isn't real. My hands reach up and cover my ears to block out the moaning and groaning from my TV. The physical act of their sex becomes more depraved, more violent with each barking of Joe's orders, with each cry of Dotty's voice, with each passing frame of tape. This sadism inflicted on her, possibly going as far as rape, leaves me with utter repulsion. Disbelief jars me, and I feel dirty all over.

Dotty was Joe's lover. But I thought she was with Darius. No one told me.

I feel like such a fool for being the last to find out.

Disgusted by seeing a man I respect having his way sexually with his nephew's girl, I take out the tape. I put in another tape, hoping to find something mundane to clear my mind. This next scenario plays out the same with Dotty and Joe, except for two things.

First, Dotty looks very unhinged. She doesn't have that innocent, girlish quality to her anymore. She looks feral and possessed, with risqué clothes and a cracked shell of a face. She has aged badly, like a long-time drug user who didn't know when to stop.

The second important thing is that Darius is in the shot, not Joe.

"Hit me," Dotty commands Darius.

"No, I can't," Darius says, staring at his trembling hand. Dotty grabs his hand and starts licking his fingers. Then she clenches his fist and places it next to her cheek.

"Your angel commands you to punch me. Hard. You'll do it if you love me. You do love me, don't you?"

Darius nods. He lightly slaps her across the face. She demands to be hit harder. So he slaps her harder. She wants to be punched. Then he punches her. Dotty laughs, moaning with delight as she bleeds. Darius doesn't enjoy himself, and he cries as he hits her hard enough to knock her out.

She falls to the floor, laughing all the way down. She gets onto her knees, lifts her bottom high in the air, and spanks it. Darius stands confused. She has to spell it out for him, saying, "Come on." He nods again, throws off his clothes and gets on her. While they are having sex, she keeps looking into the corner of the room, at the closed door. Just like Joe in the other videos. But unlike Joe, she is in ecstasy.

Not wanting to sit through the rest of the tape, I stop it and pop in another one.

This tape gives me a black screen. The screen goes to static before going to black again. Loud banging comes from my speakers, but the screen doesn't show. Indecipherable yells, clanking metal, the sound of ripping wood all merge with one another. Loud breathing, grunting, and the sound of shuffling feet eventually overtake all other sounds.

"Let me in!" a man screams in agony. I recognize his voice. "Give me back the papers!"

After a few minutes, an image pops up. Blinking eyes stare at a carpeted floor.

Am I watching through the eyes of someone? Is that even possible?

The door on the video is getting hit by a man outside. I see a hand reach for the phone and press the disconnect button. The hand then dials out and puts the phone in front of the blinking eyes. I recognize the number being dialed.

Wait...it can't be. This was from four days ago, just after I blacked out. This is my apartment. Darius was outside my door trying to get in.

This is...me?

"*Eye Tribunal*," a man answers. "This is Ralph West speaking."

"Ralphie, baby. It's me, Claire Walker," a disembodied voice says into the phone.

No. That isn't me talking. That voice is not mine. It's metallic, sharp, deep, and dry. It reverbs across the TV speakers.

Am I seeing out of my eyes or someone else's?

"Goddamn it, Walker, check your fucking phone. I'm getting a shit ton of static. Feels like I'm getting raped inside my brain."

The voice pretending to be me laughs. "Sorry…I'm having phone problems. Listen, I have a story pitch for you. It's about Darius Renton."

"No, Walker. Not a chance. We went over this."

"You need to hear me out again. I need a partner on this." A loud shrieking laugh shakes the vision…my vision. The banging outside gets louder.

Ralph says, "Jesus, what the shit was that?"

The blinking eyes turn to the corner of the room. Behind the large stacks of blank papers, the shimmering eyes of something terrible glow. A pale face made of dark oil melts through the papers, showing me just what was hiding behind it when I blacked out.

A woman with hundreds of sharp teeth, a split jaw, and a tongue lolling from the rift in her face stares at me. She is crawling on the ground like a dog. Talons two feet long emerge from each of her fingers. Bones covered in muscles like spider webs stretch far from her back, turning into what look like angel wings. Her skin boils with bubbling black. She sways from side to side so fast she blinks in and out of existence. Her eyes shine so bright that they blind me.

This is the same "girl" from the abandoned Vin Forest Water Processing Plant. And here she is again, in my apartment.

The fake me laughs deeper, deader. "I'll take care of it. Call you back in a few."

Immediately, the blinking eyes stop blinking and everything comes crashing down. My body, no, that fake pretending to be me, slumps to the ground like a toy whose batteries suddenly ran out. I can see hands and feet convulse as the screen starts to darken. But before it goes black again, a large, lanky, pale man covered in haze comes forward and lunges at the girl. After the screen darkens, I can hear breaking things. Unearthly wails and the dying howls of butchered animals fight among one another. This goes on for a few minutes.

There are no more sounds after that except for the sound of grunting, heavy breathing, and feet shuffling. Then comes a small knock.

"Claire, please, baby, open the door," Heather's muffled cry comes through.

The tape ends there. The TV goes to static.

I can't move. The revelations and fear stun me into paralysis. For a few minutes, I cannot move, and when I do, it is by inches. My hand reaches for the eject button, and the tape slides out.

Utter fright comes over me when I examine the tape. There is no film in it: just a blank cassette shell. I drop the tape and crawl away from it. I huddle underneath the writing desk, knocking everything off. The papers fall everywhere, and to my surprise something heavy falls behind me.

It is the missing black light. I grip it, turn it on, and hold it close to me like a flashlight. Little by little, I slip toward the cassette. The closer I get, the more sweat I bleed and the more breath I inhale. From a distance, I can see words on the tape, glowing in florescent ink.

Hello, Claire.

I immediately jump away after kicking the tape under the couch. I return to hide underneath the writing table. The black light flies out of my hand, but I am too scared to grab it. For at least ten minutes, I stay crouched in a fetal position and stare at the cassette. The words shine from afar, as does everything else in the room.

My eyes pick up something to the side, among the stuff that got knocked off my desk. The blank pages that weren't destroyed in during my blackout glow bright. I reach for one of the pages, pull it to my face, and examine it.

One large eye made up of words is painted in a spiraling circle.

It's just like in Dotty's shrine in Vin Forest. Just like the tattoos on Darius.

Every single blank page I took from his room has the same eye drawing. But why make them invisible to the naked eye? What is so special about these eyes?

My senses dull.

An idea pops in my head as I stare at the drawings. I get out from under the desk and go to the phone. I search through the caller ID for the past few days, ignoring everything until I get to yesterday's call log. The number Darius called me from has an area code matching the town of Jaune's. I scroll back three days to find out that Darius made repeated attempts to call my apartment phone. All from the same number, located somewhere in Jaune.

I hit redial. A chirpy musical tone is interrupted by a female voice, "Hi, you've reached the Vin Lake and Forest Touring Center. Our business hours are from—"

I hang up. Now I know where Darius is.

He doesn't have any other hiding spots. He's in Vin Forest. While the police didn't find him at the abandoned water processing plant, he never was too far away from it. After they left, he returned to his haunt. The answer was in my face the entire time…so simple, so easy. He's been hiding in plain sight the entire time. Yet I ignored it. Was it out of stupidity, or did I know the entire time? Did I pretend I was oblivious?

Regardless, I know now. I did it. My job is done. For both Gordy and Greene.

I can stop now…I'm done.

No, I'm not done. It's not that simple, none of this is.

I know this won't end with me telling them where Darius is. There is no walking away into the sunset. Knowing what I saw on that tape, some of my actions are not my own. That means Levitt was telling the truth. This means that, quite possibly, some of Joe and Darius's actions are also not of their doing.

Everyone involved in one way or another with this research project is messed up. These files, those tapes, are proof there is something very wrong with the world.

One thing is for sure: I am not alone when it comes to these monsters—and I have to get the bottom of this before something terrible happens to me.

Chapter Eighteen

Southern Miskatonic University is a fifteen-minute drive from my apartment. I find out before arriving that it is a sister school to the Miskatonic University back in Massachusetts. From what I hear, bad stuff went down at the bigger sister school, so they expanded south to get away from all the bad press—something about morally unethical lab experiments, missing students, deranged professors, and strange hauntings plaguing the campus.

But the younger sister campus is smaller than the pamphlet suggests. The size of the campus was touted, but unless there is something below the surface to give me a chocolate sundae surprise, well, I have to disagree with you, Mr. Recruiting Brochure. Even worse, you underclassmen and faculty aren't impressing me much with your team spirit. Everyone here looks so dreary. I didn't expect this from a college mill town with hard-lined country roots and blue-collared working class people. As I roam around the campus grounds and poke my snooping nose everywhere, I manage to find one girl. Just one! Nothing but dudes here; it wasn't advertised as an "all-boys school."

I make it a point not to trust a school that has a squid with wings in a cowboy hat as its mascot.

My anger at this school began three hours earlier. I was walking around campus, trying to interview lost souls who could give me info about Joe Renton, Dotty Finley, and Charles Benson. The plan worked in theory, at least when I played pretend with the mirror. Yet my experiment failed. This is why I stick to journalism.

It's not that words weren't spoken. People did in fact speak to me about the dearly departed. Some buttered up the dead, while others would shit on their graves if they got a chance. Very specific things were said about very specific people.

Then it all went bad.

First was Dotty Finley. Those who commented on her claimed she was an excellent drama student. But she excelled as a ballerina. She had performed the lead in college productions of the *Nutcracker* and *Swan Lake*.

Some guy with a weird textbook called *Ebion* said, "She was so brilliant. She was art on legs." He looked like a hipster, so I don't take his word for it.

Her grades weren't the most impressive, but that wasn't a major mark against her. Her star was destined for the theater. The other courses were just a pretense to say she had things going for her outside a wardrobe.

Did she have any other hobbies outside of theater?

None. They all said she was a homebody. Kept to herself; didn't have many friends. Nice girl all around, but nothing impressive about her. She became even more reclusive prior to her death, appearing with fresh cuts and bruises all over her face and body. Everyone assumed it was directly related to Darius Renton's odd behavior.

Except, in reality, it was Dotty who asked to be hit.

I know several unsavory men who would have loved to know her when she was alive.

Their response became indifferent when I showed them Joe's research. Then it became hostile when I showed them the blank page with the eye. I took the liberty of making the image solid with various colors. It made it easy on the eyes; I think I made it a little too fabulous.

"Get lost, you pedo jackoff," the hipster tells me. I guess he didn't like my colored picture. "How about I curb stomp your mother's face with my dick?" What dirty mouths on them. No respect for their elders, either. Shouldn't allow them to breed.

The discussion of Joe yields the best and most vocal negativity.

Let me see, what wasn't said about him?

According to the masses, Joe was the following: a creep, a deviant, a freak, and a child molester—the endless train of assorted names continued long after it became unfashionable.

Joe would be found wandering around campus, talking aloud, and staring madly at everything. Rumors ran rampant that he preyed on his female students, offering grades for sex. Yet there was never any proof. No smoking knife, no blunt force trauma with a banana peel. Nothing solid except for gossip that didn't tie back to the butler and the bloody gloves. Reports and lawsuits were never filed against him, despite the constant suggestions that there "must" have been something. He was too weird and too unstable to be left roaming around unchained.

This leads me to an assumption that the only thing keeping Joe from getting called out on his wacky antics had to be his work. Joe was runner up for valedictorian, after all. Obviously, he had to have done something right during his fifteen-plus tenure at the university to merit not getting canned.

So I ask the campus honchos if any of his work is left for me to read.

"Everything was lost after his accident," a school official tells me. Either it was stolen or misplaced, but it is unanimously agreed on that whatever happened, it did the school a favor. The administration likes to pretend he didn't exist.

Some loyalty the school instills.

My fried brain with cheese thought it would be a great idea to show off some of Joe's research, including the page with the fabulous creepy eye on it, to see if anyone knows about either.

"Are you on drugs, son?" a janitor asks me. Not wanting to get called out for being a tad high at the time, I just walk away.

Now Charles Benson. No one remembers him well. No one remembers him ill either. His character was a mystery to the students. All they know is that he was killed in a terrorist attack in Afghanistan while researching ruins. He spent most of his time overseas, doing big research programs for the archeology department. When I questioned if such international ventures cost the school big bucks, I got a unanimous, big fat no. He was at first criticized for taking trips to both Afghanistan and Germany to conduct archeological projects, but he did it using little of the school's money.

Benson had a financial backer. I already know it was Joe.

Charles Benson had big aspirations for something that would set Southern Miskatonic head and shoulders above all the big, expensive Ivy League colleges. But the details of just what are fuzzy, a result of being dead and forgotten for over five years.

Again, I know the answer. Joe and Benson had uncovered something that theoretically had the power to change human history. They found areas where the laws of time and physics broke.

Unfortunately, they also uncovered the nightmarish creatures I call the Pale Strangers. It's an appropriate name, I think, yet it's also a phrase I find myself repeating when I drift off into deep thought.

As with Joe's work, not a single record of written data or research is left at the university.

I humor myself about why he was forgotten. He was killed while doing research for the school in Afghanistan. Didn't they hold a memorial for him? Did they create a scholarship after him? Did they even dedicate a cobblestone with his name etched on it?

Nope.

Once again, I show people the eye picture. It comes as no surprise that I receive a harpy's helping of sharp caws.

This is becoming a disturbing trend among the people I talk to. No one wants to bring up the past, but mostly they don't want to deal with me. They are just fine pushing everything deep in the dirt and keeping it buried.

By a certain point in my day, I am baking underneath the sun. By a certain point, the word gets out to everyone on campus that a certain unhip dude is going around and overall being an unsavory beast. That's when the call is made to bring in campus security.

I am kicked off Southern Miskatonic grounds, by rent-a-cops no less.

Oh well. I am too old for school anyway.

Still, the feeling of being ostracized for something I didn't do stings. I was defeated long before I started this race.

My shiny new phone that set me back six hundred bucks buzzes in my pocket. I answer, "My bitch better have my money."

"Mr. Walker?" Greene says.

"Oh, hey there, Olive Oyl. You don't write, you don't call, I was worried you had a new lover in your life." I force my laugh to annoy Greene.

"I called you earlier! Where have you been the past week? I've been looking for you."

I don't mention my blackout or the horrible things I've seen. Instead, I lie and say I've been doing undercover work behind enemy lines. Greene finds my humor lacking, then demands to know where I am at that moment.

"Well, I just got kicked out of Southern Miskatonic University. The school discriminates against the poor. Help me bring a suit down on them."

Greene's gasp gives way to stuttering. "Why are you there? Is Darius there?"

"No. I needed to find some things out for myself about his uncle and his fiancée."

"Why are you doing this? I told you that is none of your concern. Your job is to find Darius, Mr. Walker, not bring up the past."

"Bro, you don't really know what kind of mess you got me into. And I know where Darius is." I wait for him to say something. He doesn't. "Something wrong, baby boy?"

Greene whispers, "You found him?"

"In a manner of speaking. You don't seem too happy. I can throw the information back into the sea for another catch if you desire."

Greene clears his throat. I hear him get his slither back. "Then tell me. Go on. It's what I pay you for."

"First I want to meet. Can you drive to Southern Miskatonic?"

"Can't you come into the city?"

"Hell no. I'm on fumes, rolling around in a '72 Plymouth. You come here and bring me some money. I don't like the idea of being caught under the thumb of a sunstroke, in a '72 Plymouth no less, if my car sputters out."

Greene says he'll be there in twenty minutes.

So I wait in my car with the AC kicked up to eleven. I turn on the radio, kick my feet on the dashboard, and massage the throbbing bunions on my feet. My socks are so drenched I don't bother putting them back on, lest I get raw feet.

Greene arrives a few minutes later than he promised. Not that I mind much. I'm never on time. Heather likes to complain about my lack of punctuality, but I remind her I never come early. She likes that about me.

With Greene there is no handshake, no proper greeting. All I get from the grumpy bear is an evil eye and a slick tongue. "Stop doing drugs. You look like shit."

There aren't enough drugs in the world that can make my problems go away, that's for damn sure. Not like he'd care.

"Mind your business," I say. Greene looks around, looks in my car. "Yeah, jackass, Darius isn't in there. Thank you for asking."

He folds his arms and leans to the side. "So where is Darius?"

I flap my collar and let out a yelp. "Sure is hot out here. How about a nice place with air conditioning?"

Greene rubs his nose and laughs before saying, "Okay." He points across the street to a tiny, pink Mexican restaurant. He holds out his arm. "Lead the way."

"Oh, don't worry, someone has to wear the pants in this relationship." I brush past him, making it a point to just miss thumping into him. We cross the street and go into the unpronounceable Mexican cantina. The cool air flows down my back, giving me instant relief. Why I didn't do this sooner is beyond me. In front of me is an ice chest filled with domestic and imports; the temptation is too great, so I grab a domestic.

We find an empty table; I crack open the beer. Bitter liquid quenches my thirst, but even better is when I rub the icy bottle against my forehead, bringing my temperature down a couple Fahrenheit's. Damn, that really hits the spot.

Greene ruins my mood by reminding me that I had made him come meet me.

First, I have to bring him up to speed with my encounter involving Darius, an encounter that Greene is sure to not have seen coming.

"Darius showed up at my door a few days ago. Tried breaking it down with a screwdriver. Scared the ever living fuck out of my girlfriend." I hold out my finger to make Greene wait; my beer is more important.

As expected, Greene has a hard time reacting to my claim. He fidgets around in his seat, and his words have trouble taking form. He tells me to continue, and I oblige, but only after I satisfy my throat with fine beer.

"Darius was mumbling something about how we would never have Dotty."

Greene's brows raise, his fingers tap his knee. He crosses his legs and lets out a few unnecessary coughs.

"I'm surprised he would go through the trouble," Greene mutters. "I expected Darius to be in some different part of the country or maybe across the border."

I give him a smile and raise my bottle at him. "Same thing, bro!" I point at him then at myself. "Great minds think alike." I throw out my fist so he can bump it. He doesn't bump it. That makes me a little sad.

"How did he know you were involved?"

I scratch my chin, thinking of what most likely happened and using Darius's own words. "Darius was near the Vin Forest in Jaune when you and I paid Dotty's murder site a visit. I'd go as far to think he was hidden somewhere in the abandoned plant when we arrived. Didn't find him since your people didn't do a full search. He watched us go in, watched me freak out, watched you be lazy, and watched us tear up Dotty's shrine with the police. I say we did a good job of pissing him off."

"Then why didn't he come after me? Why didn't he go after you then if you were right there in the building, just a few walls away?"

"Good question. I didn't take that into account. But after that incident, he proceeded to call me several times over the past few days. Called me from the Vin Lake and Forest Touring Center to be exact. He went back home."

"That makes no sense. Would he go back there after the police tore it apart?"

"Maybe that's the only place he got left. Gordy ain't harboring him." Greene stumbles all over himself. I can't believe it myself. I pause and stare at my beer before continuing, "He sounded like he was in pain. He's hurting. Don't know why, though."

Greene laughs. I ask what's funny. "Yeah, he's hurting in some sick, twisted part of his head. He's insane! It's obvious he killed Dorothy Finley."

I give him a hard stare and chose my words carefully, "Darius sure believes she isn't dead. You did find several pieces of missing people; not rocking the boat, but that kind of strengthens his claim. Might have tagged the wrong girl. Mistakes do happen."

Greene scratches the back of his head, and his laugh this time flutters. "Dotty was dead and buried. I personally held the autopsy report confirming it. Her body was properly identified."

Then why are you shaking, Oliver? Why don't you believe your own version of events?

Greene holds his chest and stares past me. "So you are certain that Darius Renton is at the abandoned Jaune Plant?"

I nod. He asks me what else I know. I don't say anything. I finish my beer and spin the bottle on the table. Greene pesters me. I keep silent.

Whatever information I haven't told him doesn't account for much in the long run, but to Greene, it is lifesaving gold. He needs to earn the rights to the hostage information by answering some of my own questions.

"Did you know Dotty Finley was having a relationship with Joe Renton before she met Darius?" I ask.

"What...what kind of relationship?" Greene asks while messing with his tie.

"Come on, Olly, we ain't in kindergarten, don't play dumb. It was a one-sided sexual tryst. Joe was the master, and Dotty was the servant." Greene is very surprised. He really had no idea there was a connection between the two. I laugh. "Wow, man. Like for real. It was the worst-kept secret. Everyone knew Joe had a weird fetish for young female students, and Dotty was just the flavor of the week."

"Then...then it's motive!" Greene slams his hand on the table. "Another reason Darius killed Dorothy."

"Ha! Darius knew about it. He even had tapes of them banging. Kept them real hidden in his house for however long it was, probably a couple years." I peel off the labels off the bottle. "Now, why would he wait so long to kill his fiancée? Why would he let his anger bottle up for that long before exploding on her with a screwdriver? Why was it that the fresh bruises and cuts on her body and face were caused at her urging, to feed her sexual devil? Did you know Darius wanted no part of it?"

Greene spurts, "I demand you give me that tape. Give me everything you have on Darius. This is new evidence that can be used against him."

"That wasn't the deal, hombre. I was supposed to find Darius, and I did."

"Fine, I'll simply get a subpoena and bring you up on obstruction charges."

"What the fuck ever, bro. It's not my fault you're a shitty lawyer to begin with. None of what I have will help you. Period. You got your shit to convict him."

"Well, I need what you got. Otherwise Darius might go free, like Chambers." I stop my motor mouth from firing anything else at Greene. I ask him to repeat his claim. "Chambers and a bunch of other suspects might make bail because of stuff that has been going on at the DA's office and at the courthouse."

Goddamn it. I find myself growling, "What do you mean, he'll make bail? I thought you had everything you needed to get a conviction?"

"You don't watch the news, do you?"

I stand and so does Greene. "Unfortunately, I haven't had the privilege."

"There was a major accident today at the courthouse. Several witnesses waiting to testify were killed when a car lost control and collided into the courthouse. Including the little girl you saved last year. She was testifying against him today; she and her parents were killed."

"Isn't that convenient!" I shake my head in disbelief. "I'm not even going to begin questioning why witnesses from different cases were all huddled in one spot. That's just asking for a fucking contract hit, let alone a tragic circumstance like several tons of metal crashing through the wall!"

Greene looks at the ground. "There's more bad news."

"Oh, Jesus Christ, what now?"

"A couple weeks back, we had a bit of a flood downtown. Some of the evidence…got washed away. We recovered some. Still trying to recover the stuff involving Chambers."

I smack my hand against my forehead and let out a laugh. I can't believe what I'm hearing. "I've heard of corrupt systems pulling this shit. How incompetent can you all be? How hard is it for you all to convict a couple of society's fuckups?"

"Now wait just a minute!" Greene holds his hands up.

"You know what I'm really looking forward to? Being in a situation where you fight with someone at the club and meet them again later in the night for round two. In my case, I'm super looking forward to going to Walmart at three in the morning, doing my shopping, and finding Paxton Chambers waiting for me in the hardware section. It's going to be fucking marvelous!"

If it isn't disembodied monsters, blackouts, and serial killers with screwdrivers, it has to be this: a vindictive person I put in prison. I chuck my empty bottle away before walking back to the cars. Greene tries to get in front of me, but I dodge him.

"Please listen to me, Walker," Greene says. "I want to call you to testify against both men if it ever comes to it."

"Can you guarantee Darwin won't be putting me down for an award?" Before I bust Greene's chops even more, I hold up my hand and look away. My conscience starts to seep through. I saw what one did firsthand, and I knew very well what the other was doing while still on the loose. The last thing I want is two maniacs running lose and harming more innocent people. So I sigh and nod. "I'll do it."

I agree to give him the tapes. We get to my car, and I pop open the trunk. I reach in and pull out random pages of the paper from the box marked Afghanistan; the tapes are hidden under this stack. Greene asks me what the papers are. I say, "Joe Renton and a colleague of his, Charles Benson, were onto something big. Something world-changing. Not my words, theirs. In Germany, they found several swords and a broken-down castle as evidence that time can be altered; all science mumbo jumbo that I'm sure the nerds in academics would splurge over. That's not my concern. None of it, I don't give a damn. What I do care about is this." I reach into box and pull out homeboy's journal that involved that ape.

"What is this?"

"It's from a deranged marine, and it's one of the few documents in written English. I have an eyewitness who was in Afghanistan at the time who can confirm the existence of such creatures." I stop to shake my head and laugh. "Yeah, it sounds stupid. I don't believe it myself. Hopefully, I can meet this guy and confirm my suspicions. Go on, take a look. I'll get you the tapes in a second."

Greene sits on the hood of my car and scans over the pages while I search.

Everything is fine. Then he gets to the page that I marked with the red ink: the page with the description of the ape on it.

I expected hostility or indifference, but not this.

His hands tremble, and his mouth and eyes get smaller. His skin burns a bright reddish-white. I see tiny hairs spike all around, and he stands and straightens his body. Little whimpers break through the short breaths he exhales. About now, the stomach-tearing sensation grips him.

I had the same expression yesterday. Not anger. Fear. Absolute.

And I didn't even show him the picture with the eye hidden on it.

"Why…why are you showing me this?" Greene asks as he turns around, expecting some massive sucker punch to wallop him off the planet.

"Thought you might find it interesting."

"I…I have to go."

"Wait, what about the tapes?"

"Something has come up; they aren't important anymore." Greene lets the papers slide from his hand, and his elbow catches the box I placed next to him, knocking all of its contents over. I crouch to the ground and pick up as much as I can as he attempts to slip by me. I stand up and block whatever direction he aims at.

"Oliver, I need to ask you something very serious. Have you had any lapses in time or memory, like blackouts?"

Greene's empty expression with dilated eyes give me my answer.

"You get the hell away from me!" Greene places his hands on my shoulder and pushes me away. "You're fired! Off the case."

"For what?" Greene starts to walk down the rows of cars to get to his. I press him more as I keep up the pace. "You have, haven't you? You experienced the exact same thing that I am, didn't you? So did everyone else you sent." I reach forward and grab his shoulder. "You got me into this, you three-piece-suit-wearing shark! You tell me what you know!"

Instead Greene reaches into his pocket and shoves some cash into my hand. I had told him what he needed to know, I think, and I realize now my job is technically over.

"Forget your help. I don't need you to help me convict them. Don't ever talk to me again. I knew listening to him was a bad idea. I should have never hired you." Greene cocks his arm back and motions forward with his weight. I take a few steps back, catching my leg on the curb and trip over myself. I cover my face with my arm. Through my fingers, I see Greene fumble with his keys and open his car door. Tears flow down his face.

"Please, I need answers. Please don't leave me like this," I whisper. "What have you seen?"

"I'm sorry, Claire. I'm sorry for everything that has happened and will happen. Please don't hate me." Greene takes a look around before jumping into his car. He starts the engine, takes off and almost nails a couple students walking across the parking lot.

That's when I notice that the paved blacktop is burning hot, and I jump off the ground. Pieces of rock and dust are pressed into my palm. I dust myself before heading back to my car. A man is picking up the papers beside my car.

"No, sir," I say with an embarrassing chuckle. "You don't have to do that." The man moves away from me, and I kneel to pick up everything that Greene dropped. I stare up at him and extend my hand. "Thank you for helping me."

I can't see him completely. I see the blurry outline of an impossibly tall man hidden by the sun. I squint and look down. His feet look like a man's, but I can't describe them. Why do I think they are hooves? He extends his thin, long, boney and pale hand to me. As he is about to touch me, he leans toward me, his face obscured by some nightmarish fog.

Hello, Claire.

I...feel...sleepy...

Chapter Nineteen

The air is dense, dry, and super cold. I'm lying on my stomach and feel a pressing sensation all around. Absolute darkness surrounds me. I try to move my arms, but they only move a few inches in any direction. My fingers rub against the surface I'm lying on. I feel jagged, blunt, icy rock underneath sandy dirt.

I feel like a caged animal and begin to panic. The cold presses down on my pores and into my nostrils.

Where am I? How did I get here?

An eerie bluish light burns about twenty-five feet away. As I wiggle around, I realize there is enough room for me to wiggle onto my hands and feet. Unaware of where I am, I fall back on a childish need to crawl toward the light. This is the one certain thing I could do.

The light grows and grows, so I crawl faster.

When I do get to the light, I realize it isn't just one eerie glimmer, but many glimmers attached to a series of electrical cables. The cables have thousands of tiny lights in them, illuminating the long tunnel they run across. Dozens of these light lines extend on the walls and on the ceiling, stretching in two different directions for an eternity.

I poke my head into the long tunnel. It's slightly bigger than the crawlspace I'm in. I'll have more room to operate in but not by much. I take a moment to look at my surroundings. I'm in a cave, I think. My hand reaches out and breaks off a piece of the cold rock above me. The rock shatters into soft sand, no, more like flour. I wipe my hand of the dust and look around.

I have to pick one direction and move forward. There is light both ways, so I'm sure one is the exit. Has to be. If not, I'll just go the other way.

The exit just has to be somewhere.

I climb into the crawl space and march forward at a snail's pace. Then I notice there is a physical weight on my back pushing me down. I'm wearing something heavy. When I look down at my chest, I see what looks like a hiking pack strapped around me.

So I was…hiking? I don't remember buying any hiking gear. Hell, I've never been camping. The outdoors never appealed to me.

The further I go, the more crawl spaces and chambers I discover. They exit off to my sides. A few were finished, while a few were just started off. Some of them only go a few feet in, while others are dark, endless campaigns I refuse to challenge.

Despite an urge to try one of the holes, I don't.

These holes are not meant for me.

I stick to the plan and follow the ever-extending light forward. A few minutes of crawling feels like an hour of hard labor. The weight of my pack is starting to wear on my knees and my palms. The sand feels soft but the jagged rocks mixed in make it feel like I'm crawling on sharp ice cubes. I feel that after a certain number of shuffles my hands will become raw and bleed. The foul air is wearing down my lungs.

I'm fatigued as a marathon runner, despite just starting. The cold is giving me uncontrollable shivers.

Being lost forever seems very possible.

The crack of metal smashes my eardrums. The echo vibrates across the crawl spaces and ricochets from the walls. I stop moving and turn my head to hear better. Another crack echoes. Then comes a series of loud grunts and belligerent yelling. The sound comes from the direction I am crawling in.

My curiosity and growing desperation to get out of here make me crawl faster. I feel tiny blisters form on my wrists, yet I keep up my pace.

Then something catches my backpack and yanks me back; I smack chin-first into the ground. I bite the inside of my cheek and hold my mouth tight. Blood flows from the bite and mixes with my saliva.

Stupid pack. Out of anger, I kick the wall with whatever tiny force the space allows. The kicked up dust fills the crawlspace and I cough.

I pull my shirt over my mouth, turn my head and see that my backpack is hooked on a piece of rock. Curious to know what I'm lugging around, I first unhook my pack from the rock. Then I lay flat on my stomach and reach around to mess with the zippers. After opening a slot, I reach in and feel something metallic and plastic. I pull it out of the pack and examine it.

A camera. Looks expensive. I don't remember owning this. I reach into the pack again and feel around. There are more cameras in the bag.

Why did I buy a bunch of cameras?

Can't dwell too much on it now. I'll worry later.

I resume my slow march to the noises. After crawling for what seems like an hour, I hear something different. It sounds like a running generator. I poke my head into each dark chamber to see if I can hear or find anything. Nothing, after nothing, is what I find. Before I can ostrich my way into another hole, I see a light illuminate one of the chambers off in front of me. My attention becomes fixed. I crawl to that hole instead.

When I poke my head into this chamber, I see a wide opening that leads to a drop of about fifteen feet. This large antechamber is a solid, four wall piece, illuminated in its entirety by the yellow flood lamp. A generator rumbles on the ground and spreads dust all over the desk sitting next to it. Papers lay scattered and a thermos container has tipped over and spilled water everywhere.

The antechamber is unlike anything I've seen. All four corners seem to be made of rusted metal, covered in massive amounts of sand. A large, cloudy mirror door is stuck in the middle of this metal cave. The mirrored door has glyphs and symbols carved in that I imagine could only be done with laser precision. Standing on each side of the door are silent guardians, shaped as what look like ancient Chinese statues; these metal demons have assorted colored gems socketed into various holes around their bodies.

A room of this kind should have been real old—maybe a few thousand years or more, I think. Yet this kind of metalwork couldn't exist back then; too advanced for its size and design. Only something modern would have made a room like this work.

But this antechamber was just found a few days ago, sealed off from human contact for centuries. How could something like this get inside a mountain?

And how do I know anything about this place if I've never been here before?

A large man with a beard and long hair is hammering away at the ancient mirror door with a massive pickax. Dozens of tools, more properly used to cut through rock, lay broken near the man's feet. No matter how hard he tried, or continues, the mirror won't crack, the mirror won't stain.

He is mumbling mad. Slobber covers his beard, and his face looks skeletal. It takes me a second to recognize who he is. When I do, I do my best not to stutter.

Charles Benson. How is he still alive? He was reported to have been killed by insurgents in Afghanistan over five years ago. Wait…does this mean he has been alive this entire time? Does this mean I'm in Afghanistan?

I don't remember traveling here. I wouldn't even know how I'd begin to fund my expedition, let alone get a passport in a short amount of time.

What the hell is going on?

I try to call out and demand an explanation for what is going on. My lips don't move. Not a single peep comes out. Instead, I find myself reaching around to pull out one of the video cameras in my bag. If this really is happening, then I want to make sure I record this as proof. The camera turns on and captures Charles Benson's madness.

"I'm underappreciated by my fellow archeologists and by the scientific community!" Benson's scream echoes across the antechamber. "Joe said he could make sure I got the help of the anthropologists. No! I found the greatest thing in human history! They spit on me. They boo me. They hurl insults at me and call me crazy! I'm not crazy, I'm mad as hell! And I'm not going to take it anymore!"

Benson stops aiming at the mirrored door and hurls the pickax at the metal Chinese statues. The head of one of the statues breaks. The rusted metal had become brittle over the years and the sudden force of Benson's rage causes it shatters into a hundred pieces. Some pieces hit Benson's face and cut him. A dusty cloud fills the antechamber and drifts my way.

"Joe pays me and gives me shit workers! He sends me out to Afghanistan and Germany! Moving me from place to place for the past year! He tells me we have to keep going, but is he going to help me? No! He's too busy enjoying his fresh honey pot! The little slut has him wrapped around her fingers!" Benson wipes the blood from his face and leaves a muddy, bloody smear. "We sat on the most important find in human history, and he wants his little harlot to get him off! Joe, you traitor!"

Benson resumes attacking the mirrored door.

"You make me your little work monkey, but you won't let any of the information I send you go public! I'll show you, Joe! I'll show this whole damn world. Charles Benson will become a household name! I won't need your goddamn money after this!"

Dotty caused a level of friction that I never imagined possible between Benson and Joe. I didn't know Joe past high school, and I never met Benson, but from all the notes I thought they were good friends. Did she really cause such a wedge between the two?

And why does she seem to be at the heart of everything?

These questions are overshadowed by a familiar sensation: a sharp rise of pressure and noise rings in my ears. It's the exact same thing that happened when I saw Joe in that room, the same sensation that came over me at the abandoned plant.

Oh no. Not again.

The generator beside Benson begins to sputter. The lights in the tunnel and in the chamber start to flicker.

No, no, no. No dark. Please don't let this be happening to me. Please, God.

I look back and panic. A tiny wall of darkness grows as each light is shut off. I see an afterimage of where the light used to be before becoming enveloped in black. The void shoots forward. Pitch black eats at everything, and my eyes cannot adjust—or they refuse to adjust. My mind tries to find light, pretend that it is somewhere around, that I should crawl further down to find it.

The afterimage of light haunts me, reminds me that it's gone forever.

I hear Benson fuddle around in the dark, mumbling something to himself. I hear the crack of plastic. Several glow sticks illuminate the darkness near Benson. He tosses them all round, then hooks one onto his cargo shorts. He kneels down and works on the generator.

Fear grips my stomach, rotting there and chewing away, bit by bit. The claustrophobic darkness is making my body jittery, ready to rip away from my own skin. I try to move around, try to free myself from the enclosure.

I feel a toothy rock bite down into my shoulder. I scream and press down on the wound to keep the blood from gushing out.

Benson notices my cry, reaches into his pocket, and pulls out a small handgun.

"Who's there?" Benson fires the gun in my vicinity. "I'll kill you!"

I cover my head with my free hand in a futile attempt to protect myself. The ringing echo of the gunshot is deafening in such a confined space. "You lost bastards won't take me. You took my digging crew, but they were expendable. They all are. Including those useless marines. Couldn't do their job right. Some elite fighting squad they are!" Benson laughs and shoots wildly. "I can save this place and kill you all at the same time. Nothing but a bunch of goddamn terrorists, all of you! I know they are calling down an airstrike sometime soon, any day now! Damn marines couldn't do the job, so they call down the heavy firepower! So just come out, and I'll kill you quick!"

The gun clicks empty. He throws the pistol aside, pushes the desk against the wall and stands on it. He looks deep into the tunnel I'm in. He sniffs, and stares deep into the darkness. He stops when his eyes meet with mine, despite not being able to see me.

"I should have known it was you. You're a little rat that escaped the mousetrap. Always butting in to my digs. Always harassing me for information. Fine then." Benson laughs and jumps off the desk. "You don't have to be so quiet. But whatever. You don't need to speak. Just watch." Benson waves his hand around as he picked up the pickax again. "You can record my moment of glory." He points toward the mirrored door. "This door hasn't been opened in millennia's. It holds a secret the world tried to bury, tried to keep us from learning! You can tell the whole world, boy, and you can show them it was Charles Benson who did it on his own."

Benson ignores me to resume his attack on the door while mumbling. With nowhere to go, I focus on Benson's chanting. Some of the words are Arabic, I think, and some of them sound like something Darius might have written in his notebook.

A loud wail comes from behind me. I can't turn my head to see what it is; my pack obscures my view. My terror expands past the absolute; tiny increases of sound rattle around my ears and override my senses. My eyes are seeing smell, my ears are hearing taste, my tongue is hearing noises, and my skin is seeing something move toward me in the dark.

Cold is gone, dryness is nonexistent, and the air becomes stale. Disorientation takes hold. I am unsure of which way is up, which way is down. Absolute fear of the darkness comes over me. I huddle into a ball. But

Benson is oblivious to this. He hammers away at the mirror, obsessed with breaking it down. That's when I see it.

In the darkness, there is a bright shadow that stands out on the ceiling. It stands above Benson, floating, unassuming, unimpressive. It floats all the way down like a veil, taking its sweet time to touch the ground.

My desire is to yell out to Benson, to warn him of what is going on. But my voice refuses to speak. If I speak, I will alert it to my presence.

Instead, I watch the veil touch down. The metal walls around Benson have somehow drawn closer to him. I think I'm imagining things until I see the glow sticks on the ground, which had been spread out, are pushing closer to the generator.

It came without me knowing it. Too busy focusing on Benson, I never saw it coming.

My body feels a giant hand press down. It's not a normal hand. No, a hundred long, slithery legs make up its fingers; they are slimy at times, fluid at others. Hairy and prickly in between the crevices, it crawls smoothly and roughly across me. It's a giant centipede or a snake, or even a squid crawling across me.

But I can't see. I don't know what is on me. Yet I know it's there. I can feel what must be a thousand pounds crushing me. My organs are compressed against the rock; a little more pressure, and the soft grains of sand will stab through my skin and into my body. Pain screams all over, my skin starts to tear, and blood rushes out from even the tiniest of wounds. I cry tears first; then blood comes from my eyes.

All over, I feel the hand eating away at my skin with millions of tiny wet mouths filled with suckers, teeth, and beaks.

Breathing is impossible, and when I gasp, I take in less and less.

The glow sticks have gotten closer to Benson, eventually touching his feet.

Benson turns his head. He is greeted by a wall bleeding fluid. A maw forms out of the mirrored door, filled with teeth and hooks and faces everywhere.

The faces freeze my pain. They are beyond horrifying. They are creatures that exist as only genetic memories of my primordial ancestors. They are of creatures that never existed, at least none that any human has ever seen before.

But my blood knows this fear very well.

The wall collapses over Benson. Thick, syrupy fluid fills the cave. Benson is unaware of this, despite looking straight into the door's maw.

His body floats into the middle of the pool. His body is crushed the same as mine. I can hear Benson's gasp for breath muffled by the pool. I see Benson's body pop and compress. Then it vanishes along with the last light from the glow sticks.

Benson wasn't killed by insurgents. He was devoured.

I am being devoured.

The pressure builds on me. I know most of my skin is gone; my muscles are dissolving. I feel my vital organs rupture. I know my heart is tearing apart. My bones are almost ground into dust.

It's just a matter of seconds until it all ends.

Then my body feels the thing wail. The mountain I am in starts to rumble. The cave I am in almost shatters. The weight instantly vanishes and splashes against the ceiling. I look up and see a tentacle of sorts, constantly changing shape. At least, that's what my mind thinks. It is shaking violently, drilling into the cave walls.

This thing is in more pain than I was.

Look at me.

Who said that? My eardrums are gone. I hear no sound, but it wasn't spoken.

No, my mind said it?

I move my working eye around. A few feet down the chamber, I see a lanky creature made of freezing mist hanging upside down. It waves at me.

I've been watching you. There was another, but I like you better. You smell better. Your blood is better for helping me. So you don't have to die. I can save you.

My fingernails snap as I try to crawl to him.

There are so many wonderful things to show you. Let me help you. Just take my hand.

Chapter Twenty

The guard opens the cell door. Cold, rusty steel shackles clamp down hard on my wrists. I used to be terrified every time they clamped down. I used to be scared they would never be taken off, and my hands would rot away. Now these shackles are like a friend, more consistent then meals and communication. I get little or neither of each. The shackles mean I get to talk with someone face to face.

Maybe for just a moment, I'd be treated like a human being.

The guard ignores me during our walk. Ever since I arrived, they've had a very hard time looking at me or even talking to me. They make all attempts to avoid contact with me. Two days after I arrived, they locked me away from everyone. I have done nothing to provoke this treatment. I got the same reaction from everyone but the warden, who did it out of duty, and Dr. Foch, who did so out of curiosity.

The eyes on me make everyone fear me.

As they take me down the prisoner corridor, I see into the cells. When I arrived two months ago, there were at least three hundred prisoners of war piled into these cells. Most were from countries I knew little to nothing about. They spoke funny languages. Not a single one could relate to me, nor I to them. Now the two hundred had been reduced to ten. Just five guards out of three dozen remain; the rest have been called to fight in the battle being waged outside the prison.

To die on the battlefield means they are the lucky ones.

Wrapped bodies of prisoners are stationed in opposite cells from the remaining tenants. The makeshift graveyard outside has run out of places for the dead. Warden Thieriot has no choice but to keep them in the cells until he figures out what to do with them. For now, crucifixes made of wood and held with yarn are wedged between the shrouds, temporary markers for a temporary tomb.

I can't say Thieriot is a bad man in how he treats his prisoners. We aren't beaten, and we aren't tortured for information. Given that the war effort has consumed whatever supplies the prison could obtain, we are maintained as best as he could manage. I think he understands this is a war and each man will one day put his rifle up, take his uniform off, and return home to his ordinary lives—provided he survives.

At least this is what I want to believe.

The remaining ten prisoners' eyes tell a different tale. Their worn, slender frames whisper of a struggle against the bars and walls. Two months ago, they had a fighting spirit. Even in the poor conditions, they had the urge to keep going. Hope is a powerful thing. But something changed. Hope is gone; life is gone. Now they are just husks, ghostly shells that don't respond to movement or calls. They are as lifeless as the bodies of their former cell mates, except the dead have shrouds hiding their decay.

I suspect it has nothing to do with the actual incarceration.

All of this has to do with me.

Even in solitary confinement, I can feel the corrosion creep underneath the floors and bite my skin, severing my sense of pain. Whenever I ate my portions, the bitter bile would destroy my sense of taste with each bite. Even the hallway I am being escorted down has lost its color. Objects are distorted. Lights dim to the point of darkness. The floor and ceiling are extended and depressed, the distance expanded and coiled.

This damage was at first temporary, but with each breath, each passing thought, I could feel it becoming permanent. The physical rot is just the last step, and that happened faster than I could have imagined. I had prayed to have a year at best, a half a year at worst. By then, I would have been dead or freed from here.

Then again, I am being hopeful. Hope left sometime when I was asleep. What is happening to me is happening to these prisoners. And I feel nothing but guilt. None of my horrors should be happening to these men, who have neither a chance to run nor fight.

Their unimaginable suffering and eventual deaths are tied to me; to me and the Black Fairy. It is time to confess while I can, and end this cruel game.

"How are you feeling, Johan?" Dr. Foch asks me as I enter his small office next to Warden Thieriot's. The guards attach my shackles to a hook in the floor. The guards exit while Thieriot stands in the corner with his arms folded, one eye focusing on the clock, the other focusing on me. The smell from Foch's pipe makes my eyes water as he takes my arms and lifts up my bandages. "Are the scars healing well?"

"I wouldn't know. I don't mess with them," I say

"Surely you are curious to see how your health is?"

I shake my head. "I'm a prisoner of war, doctor. There is a battle going on outside these walls, and it crawls closer to us every second. At any moment mortars could rain down on us. My condition, my wellbeing, is the last thing I'm worried about." Foch nods as he dumps out the ash and replaces old tobacco with new. Thieriot unfolds his arms and approaches me with his finger out.

"So you finally admit to being a spy."

Thieriot accuses me of this in every session I have with Dr. Foch. I am mistaken for a spy because of the circumstances of my capture. The soldiers were looking for a spy in their midst, and by coincidence I had been scavenging for food in one of their camps while wearing the uniform of a dead enemy soldier to keep warm. My cause was not helped because I was bearing arms and had battle plans for both sides in my unchecked pockets.

The way things look, I am their spy. So they sent me here.

And every day, the warden hounds me. He demands to know what I know.

"I'm a farmer," I say.

"Admit your crimes, traitor. Men on both sides are dying because of your betrayal. Absolve yourself of your sins and admit your guilt."

"But I am just a farmer. I am not a soldier. I serve in no army."

"Then why were you wearing a uniform and carrying not only a rifle but also transmissions and battle plans for both sides?"

"I can only be honest and say that I had no idea what sides were allied with one another. No matter where I went, I was fired upon and I was lost. I took what I could when I could. I found a man dead from combat and took his belongings. He had a map on him; I used it to find my way to a ruined camp. I took my chance to scavenge for some food, and I was caught."

"You lie!"

It was the same scenario every day. I repeat my claim over and over; he repeats his accusation over and over. He wants me to confess to being a spy. So instead I tell them my life story, in hopes that the warden snaps, or the doctor says my time is up.

I really wish more could hear my tale.

"Enough of this, Warden," Foch says. "Look at the scars on his arms. He admitted to self-infliction. We found him half starved, delirious, and lost. This man is sick. We need to send him to a hospital for proper care."

Dr. Foch has been defending me since I got here. He became interested in my welfare after peeling off my dirty clothes and finding the holes for eyes on my skin. He talked to me, tried to get me to open up about my past, about my intentions. He really believes I am not only physically but mentally ill, that there are treatments for men like me.

"Of course he's sick," Thieriot laughs. "What kind of man carves eyes into himself?"

I nod. "You're right Warden Thieriot. I am sick."

"Oh, you're ready to admit being sick but not admit your allegiances? Ha!"

My situation is not going to get better.

I know of just one option to save everyone here.

"I'm tired. You win, Warden Thieriot, sir. I have been spying for the enemy from the very start. I am a traitor." Foch's brow rises. "Just tell the guards to bring me to the gallows and execute me. I'll admit to whatever you want: names, places. Just make it quick."

Foch stands and keeps Thieriot from cheering. He comes over to me, looks at my wounds, and then at my face. He says, "For a man who confessed to something, you don't seem relieved."

"Just shoot me." I look down and see my hands digging into the chains. My knees buckle under the weight of my body.

Before I know it, Foch shines a candle in my face, but the light is dim. He says, "For a man who freely wants to die, you're scared. No visual stimuli still."

I tilt my head and feel my mouth twist. "No one wants to truly die. But death is sometimes better." A prickling sensation comes from my arm. A small pen stabs between my dressings and into my healing scar. Blood soaks the bandage, but I feel numb.

Foch looks at Thieriot. "Johan is still suffering the same symptoms as the deceased."

"Then it confirms he is the enemy. The enemy carries the plague that has been driving the prisoners mad." Thieriot spits to the side. "Maybe he is the carrier. All of this started shortly after he was sent here."

Foch shakes his head. "This isn't a plague we are dealing with. Johan has had these symptoms for at least a month, possibly more. The prisoners don't last more than a few days." His stare seeps into my eyes. "Johan hasn't gone mad, not yet. He hasn't fallen prey to the whispers the prisoners claim they hear."

Johan, where are you? I miss you, my old friend.

My hands rattle the chain as I press my fingers deep into my ears. I know my fingers can't keep it out when it starts. Still, my childish instincts tell me to do it anyway. It takes me a few seconds to force my fingers out of my ears; I wrap the chain around them to keep them from going back in.

She's coming to get you Johan. She has your scent. I can protect you. Where are you?

Foch continues his examination, his curiosity raised by my rising tension.

"That is because we have had him isolated," Thieriot says.

"Neither of us is sick, and we spend the most time with him. How would you explain that? How only the prisoners he had the least contact with have been sickened with plague and we have not? How come the guards are in fine health?"

Thieriot rubs his chin. "He still admitted to being a spy."

I mouth words I mean to speak. Foch notices me trying to talk.

"What is it?" Foch asks.

"I am not a spy," I say.

Thieriot slaps the wall. "Don't deny it now! You admitted you spied for the enemy! You cannot take admission back!" I focus on the candle flickering behind Foch. My mouth moves, but words still aren't spoken. "Speak up, you mute!"

I play with my fingers and let out a sigh. "I only admitted so that you would kill me. I don't want to live. Maybe everything going on with the other prisoners will stop once I'm dead." I rub my eyes as the sensation of tears runs down my skin.

"What kind of man wants to get killed by admitting to something he did not do?"

"Because I have been on the run. I abandoned my family to save them and kept running. I don't even know if they are alive, if what was chasing me abandoned its hunt for me to go after them. I probably will never see another free day. I probably won't be alive much longer anyway. I am too tired. I'm not seeing very well today. What I want to do is confess the truth today. Confess while I still have a voice." I put my hands through my hair. "What is happening to the prisoners has everything to do with me."

Foch asks me to explain.

"They are banging their heads against the wall. Are they not?"

Foch nods.

"They can't eat because the food won't stay down. They are stricken with fevers, yes?"

Foch nods.

"They claim to hear whispering that is more like machine than man. Yes?"

"So what?" Thieriot says. "You could have heard the guards talking about it when they passed by your cell. There is no way this could have anything to do with you."

I painfully smile, laugh. "Just a minute ago you accused me of spreading a plague to the other prisoners. Now I am not responsible for them going mad and beating themselves to death? You're a strange man, Warden, sir."

"No one said they were beating themselves to death. What makes you think that?"

"I've seen it happen before." I rub an older scar on my head. "Had this from when I was a boy. Happened to others I knew personally. Never knew what caused it, or put them together until just recently, when it happened to my family...all of it. And it's not caused by some plague." Thieriot makes it known he isn't convinced. Foch seems on the fence. "Have you discovered the scratches yet?"

"Scratches?" Foch asks.

I nod and point out at the window. "You might not see what is going on around because there is a war being waged outside. It's perfect for them. We are distracted. The threat of being blown up or shot is a real and terrible thing. The thought of being gassed is a terrible way to die.

But that doesn't compare. None compares to what you can't see. And you can't see with your eyes."

I unwrap the bandages from my arm. It feels like I am pulling off new skin to reveal the old, scarred tissue underneath. The half-infected, half-healing eyes I carved into myself all around my forearms are visible. Both men have a hard time looking at them. The eyes follow whoever looks at them. I admit to them that I never thought I was capable of such self-mutilation.

"These eyes are not natural. I acquired them during my travels without knowing how they got there. Days, nights, I don't remember. But they kept appearing all on my arm. And so did he. I became ill, got real weak. These eyes are not of my own. They are like windows into another world. That's how he found me so easily when I ran. There is no scrubbing them off; no water will make the unnatural ink run. So I did what I had to: I cut out the eyes with a sharp knife. He's blind for now, yet he searches for me."

Foch asks, "Who is blind, Johan?"

"The Scarecrow. He can't see now that his eyes on my flesh are gone. But he can smell me. He is out there, looking for me. I can hear him calling my name at night. He's getting close. I've been in one area for too long. He has my scent; he's had it since I was a boy." I sigh as I look away from the window. "He's somewhere hidden among the fighting, waiting for the soldiers to kill or wound one another."

Thieriot paces across the room, angry. "That's a bunch of nonsense! You mean to tell us that a scarecrow is out there hunting soldiers?"

Foch shushes Thieriot. He is intrigued, confused, but most of all scared by what I have said. Foch approaches me. "How do you know he is out there?"

"The body knows. The flesh knows the fear before the mind does. It can see the monsters around. It goes deeper. The blood knows. The blood can see what our eyes cannot." I cover my arms to spare them from having to look at my wounds.

"What does the blood see, Johan? Who does the blood know?"

I stare at the door, trying to look beyond it. "Another. She is here."

Yells and gunshots sound outside the door. Foch gets behind the desk while Thieriot grabs his sidearm and makes sure a bullet is chambered. Someone bangs on the door, screaming. Blood pours underneath the large metal door.

Thieriot points the gun at the door as it opens. Two guards, pale with fright, torn clothes, and covered in blood, run in. A third guard collapses to his knees, holding his intestines as they spill out from a cavernous wound in his stomach. Foch runs to the wounded guard and tries to stabilize him.

"What's going on?" Thieriot says.

"A dead prisoner came back to life when we were putting another body in the cell! The dead man grabbed him and started biting through his stomach!" One of the guards points to the wounded man. "Some of the bodies are gone!"

Everyone turns to look at the hallway. Dozens of glowing eyes appear out of the darkness, slowly coming toward us. The rotten smell of the dead gets to us first. The burial sheets are still wrapped around them, yet something moves underneath them, staining the sheets with red and black.

At least five of them make their slow, crooked march toward us. The men open fire on the shambling corpses. Bullets tear the dead flesh apart, slowing them to a snail's pace until they eventually drop and twitch. But more glowing eyes glimmer in the darkness. More dead prisoners walk toward us.

Yet I pay no attention to them or the belligerent cries of the men in the room.

I stare at the ceiling. On the other side, I can hear the fluttering of wings.

The Black Fairy has made her presence known.

Chapter Twenty-one

My eyelids open groggily. It hurts. Breathing is hard. I look around and see I'm in my apartment.

That would normally make me happy, if not for everything else going wrong.

My jaw feels like it has been ground into meat, like it's held in place by just a few strands of muscle and flesh. The pain is immediate and immense. Not an inch of me is spared from this agony. I'm on my stomach and have no strength to pick myself up. My clothes are saturated with something wet; it's red, but I can't quite make it out with my face jammed into the floor. So I roll on my back and feel my carpet squish under my body. My eyes force down to see what I'm covered in.

My forearms are covered in dried and fresh blood. Cuts and marks in various states of healing spread like spider webs all over my skin.

"What...?" I cry out in a dead voice. I place my hands on the carpet and squeeze; ooze bubbles in my hand and sticks to my skin. I pull my hand up to see I am laying in what could very well be my own blood.

A sudden jolt of adrenaline makes me rise from the ground and stumble onto the couch. My insides throb.

What happened to me?

How did I see Benson and Foch? Why was Foch calling me Johan?

The uncertainty of what I saw, what I experienced, is overshadowed by something else. Panic recedes under disbelief.

My apartment is beyond wrecked. The couch is shredded, with cotton snowing over everything and metal springs uncoiled. The TV is broken in half, with pieces of electronics embedded in the floor. Parts of the wall have been torn off, and holes have been randomly punched in other spots. A small metal trashcan sits in the center of the desk; the stacks of Joe's research have been shredded into little bits.

The blank pages with the hidden eyes are all gone.

I approach the trashcan on my desk and get a mean whiff of lighter fluid and burnt paper. Fresh ash lay over old. The scent of a flame lingers.

I turn my head and see that my wall has been covered with words in different languages. But they are scratched off, burned off, peeled off. The words were drawn in the shape of an eye, like Darius' tattoos. But there is something different. Something more personal.

These are the eyes that littered Johan's arms before he sliced them off.

How the fuck do I know this?

Not all of Joe's research has been destroyed. A box of untouched stuff is hidden in the kitchen, marked with my handwriting. On the top of the box is the red music box, which unfortunately has been scratched by something, exposing the wood underneath the vivid color.

A wave of pain slams into my forearms now that I am awake. Blood is still breaking through the half-infected wounds. I limp to the bathroom, then dive for the towel rack. I make strips of bandage by tearing apart the towels and dumping them under the rusty water. At this point, I don't care that the water is rusted. I let them soak while I struggle to take off my shirt.

My chest is covered with bruises, both old and fresh, and I have a dozen tiny scratches across my abdomen. Stretch marks wrinkle the side of my stomach, and I notice I've shed a few pounds.

"How long have I been out?" I ask myself, knowing full well I have no true answer. I wrap the wet towel around the wound, firing off signals to my brain to stop being a dumbass and not touch them. As I inspect my battered body in the mirror, my attention goes straight to my face. When I last had control, I was clean-shaven. Now I have a small beard. And damn it, I was proud to say I didn't have any white hairs before. Now I have a couple dozen popping out.

I look old. Really old, compared to how I was when I last showered, before I met Greene. The person standing in the mirror is not me, it just can't be.

I look more like Gordy than myself.

The apartment phone rings. I stumble out of the bathroom, hoping to talk to anyone and figure out how much time I lost.

I lift the phone off its receiver. "I'm here! Hello?"

"You don't sound too good, Mr. Walker," Levitt's icy, robotic voice whispers. As usual, the static is unbearable. "Everything okay?"

"Levitt, oh thank God. Listen, man." I almost fall over from the excitement and catch myself against the wall. Light-headedness makes me want to pass out. I grip my chest, gulping in as much air as I can. "Dude, I need help. What's happening to me?"

"I told you what would happen."

"No, don't give me this bullshit, man!" My voice cracks. I want to cry; I want to yell and punch something. "My body is all fucked up, and I saw things I shouldn't have seen!"

"Like? Tell me what you saw exactly. I am so interested."

"I saw Benson die. He wasn't killed by insurgents. He was…eaten. I was eaten, but something saved me. This wasn't a nightmare! I almost died. And I was seeing Foch, this German or Dutch guy! In a prison during World War I! And I was some guy named Johan. Like I could feel, I could hear his thoughts, I felt his pain. And it was as plain as I am talking to you. I was someone else, I was reliving something that happened. Shit, why was I seeing it? Was it some kind of past life I lived? Like I was reincarnated?"

Levitt doesn't say anything. I can't hold back from screaming into the phone. My rage and my pain and my fear give force to my scream.

"This guy cut out eyes on his skin, made the same just like the tattoos Darius has. And these zombies sprang to life and attacked us! I saw…I saw Joe stick two needles into his ears and scream in horror at something in the corner of his room. I saw him jump from a building that was surrounded by these…sick shape-shifting things…then this horrible looking ghost woman appeared in my apartment before I blacked out. And one of the tapes showed everything from my eyes. Was this all just a dream?"

Levitt remains silent.

"Why did I see Benson die? Why am I seeing everything?"

Levitt's silence breaks with an emotionless laugh.

"Was he killed by insurgents?"

"No. I'm sorry you were misled, but that is just the official story. His body was never recovered. What you saw is what happened. Same thing with Joseph Renton and with the men you saw in World War I. Even the ghost girl who appeared in your apartment. It's all real."

My world freezes in one moment and shatters the next. My life was over, and I have taken a hundred steps past that point before realizing it.

"How did this happen? What caused this to happen?"

"The Pale Strangers," Levitt says. "The Pale Strangers are the root. They are the virus. They are the culprit. They are the origin. They are scary stories told in the dark."

"Pale Strangers? I made up that name for them. Is that what they're really called?"

"They don't have a name. Not a real one, anyway."

"They? There's more than one?"

"Yes. Countless. Endless. They are at the heart of every story you read. Every misery, ever fear, they are the source. I believe Joseph named them individually, those he could identify anyway. You've read their names, right?"

The sticky notes. It was so obvious now. But that meant Joe knew exactly what they were. Why didn't he fight back? Or did he fight and lose?

"So why are some of them named, like the Black Fairy and Scarecrow?"

"Just nicknames. Not like they would have names or need names. Names are to humanize, to identify, to relate, to imprint knowledge. Such things are not needed where they are from or where they go. Fear machines are all you need to know them as."

"What are they? Where do they come from? What is their goal?"

"They are creatures, like you, like wolves and snakes, like lions and hyenas. Apex predators. They come from here, but not here."

I was confused. "Clarify that last part. Here but not here?"

"They might be in your room; they might be outside your door. They might be in your hallway; they might be outside your building. They are there, but not here. All at once."

"That makes no sense."

"It's not supposed to. You're thinking with logic, with realism. Your faith, your experiences, and your understanding of the world makes you doubt. Your disbelief keeps you grounded in what you accept as truth. These Pale Strangers are not of this world, despite being on this world. The laws of reality don't restrict them in the ways you are restricted."

I take the phone to the kitchen as Levitt explains this. I find a half-empty bottle of whiskey behind some plates. The temptation to drink is replaced with the need to disinfect my wounds. It stings but it is necessary. The last thing I want is for evil doctors to chop off my arms.

Levitt's static gets worse. I expect this conversation to end soon.

"Everything is in the papers," Levitt says.

I walk over to the trashcan and take a good look at the ash. If they are so important, then why did I burn and shred the papers?

"Not anymore," I say. "Most of it got lit up. I assume I was the eager pyro."

"Only the most important papers will remain."

I laugh despite my lungs feeling like they are being stabbed with quills. "You don't know a thing about what is going on with me. You're not here."

"Then let me explain what will happen to you, since I obviously am not there. The blackouts will get worse, your wounds will get worse. Actually, you won't be worrying about your physical state's decay, not after a few days when your mind starts to go. Piece by piece, your sanity will begin to slip as new information replaces your old knowledge. You're going to begin to forget simple things at first. Things like what day of the week it is, what a lifelong friend's name is. Then you forget things like what color is what, what sound is supposed to come out. You might forget how to eat, how to breathe. You might not even know who you are. That's when your body is ripe for the taking. Indoctrination."

I notice my hands and legs are trembling. The symptoms will get worse in the coming days. I just know it. Ripe for the taking, the taking, taking. My body will be beyond my control.

My legs cave under the stress, the fear. Yes, I'm afraid. Every second fills me with dread. I feel sick. I feel like something is invading every pore. "Please, stop," I say. The room begins to spin. I can hear the walls moan underneath an invisible stress, I anticipate that the walls will suddenly come down. The static rises to an apex I didn't think possible. "Please, no more."

"Okay," Levitt snickers as the static falls to a more controllable level. "I have to go anyway. You should be getting a phone call soon."

"Phone call?"

"Yes. I helped you get in contact with Torres and Cruz. You know them."

I did. They were the marines in the Afghanistan video. "How do they know about me?"

"They understand you need help. They also know you have certain answers. You need to meet them no matter what. Before other Pale Strangers get to them. No matter what, you must meet them."

Once again, I am unable to ask Levitt many questions. Yet I repeat his words after he hangs up. If there is a possibility of me getting out of whatever I am a part of, these men should know. They were in Afghanistan. They encountered that ape or whatever it is.

I need their help, and they might need mine.

The phone rings. Despite my new mission, I am uncertain what to do. But there are no other clues to go on. I answer the phone. "Hello?"

"You Walker?" a man asks.

"Yes, I am. Who am I speaking to?"

"Torres. We spoke on the phone last week."

"Last week?" So I've been out a week. Torres hums over the phone and whispers to another person I can barely hear. "I don't remember."

"So you're experiencing strange things, huh? So you really are just like us. I didn't think we would ever meet someone else in our situation."

"If you don't mind telling me, what did we talk about?"

Torres said I had gotten a hold of him through the papers in Joe's research. I had mentioned Joseph Renton's name; they asked if I knew Benson. Not directly. I said I had known Joe years before. I had explained my situation, my mission of finding Joe's nephew Darius for ADA Greene. Torres needed to discuss things over.

"You sound more alive now. Not possessed. Sound human, unlike the lost."

"I've heard that name before. The lost. Is that a person?"

"Guys we encountered in Afghanistan. Just a name we gave them 'cause of the way they looked. Might have been better to name something after their red tattoos. Too late for that."

"Are they the guys you fought in the Afghan ruins?"

"Those are the ones."

"What were they after? Who did they work for?"

"No one human, but we didn't know that during our encounter. Through intelligence, we thought they belonged to a terror cell, smuggling people, weapons, and drugs to fund operations around Afghanistan. But that wasn't the case. They were hunting for humans, hunting us."

"What the hell was that ape I read about in Jefferies' log?"

"If you're involved deep like you said you were, then you know. Your body feels it, doesn't it? Feels the fear, the pain?" I tell him I do, then ask him what happened with the ape. "For three days, we fought the lost off before that thing showed up. Chewed them up. Came after us when it finished eating; Rankin pissed it off with some explosive .50-caliber rounds. Something chased it off. We tried extracting survivors, but only Brower and Benson survived. Benson refused to leave. Tried rescuing him when we encountered the lost again. Tagged at least eighty of them by the time we finished, but we didn't recover Benson. He was in the mountains when we had heavy payloads baptize the area with fire. He wouldn't have survived the blast."

"Did you do it to kill the lost?"

"Yeah. Wasn't hard. We sent in the request claiming that we were hitting a major terrorist hideout too hot for a ground operation. But really there was another thing, worse than that ape. Something very big under the mountain near the ruins and the village. A sand god."

"Sand god? How big was it?"

"Very. Me and my partner Cruz flew out last night to recruit Ned Rankin, but he wants no part of our shindig. He's content with running away from those things chasing us since Afghanistan until he drops dead, which I don't plan on doing. We want to meet up with you tonight, after we get into town. Found a nice little Italian restaurant, Giallo's, online. You mentioned certain information was in the files you found that might be able to help us."

"I don't remember, but if you say so. I'll bring what papers I have remaining. You can examine all of them if you want. Anything you can help me discover will ultimately help me."

Torres gives me the information about Giallo's before hanging up. It is 2:00 p.m. right now, and I'm to meet them at 9:00 p.m. With seven hours to myself, I need to retrace my steps.

But seven hours is too much time to wait. Loneliness grips me. I need to know right away what kind of black hole I'm trapped in and how deep this void goes.

Certain questions begin devouring my mind.

Why did I burn the papers? Who can I talk to about this? Is there anything I can do?

Only one person comes to mind. I decide to pay Gordy a visit out of desperation and find out what I can.

Chapter Twenty-two

Outside Gordy's mansion is a caravan of U-Haul trucks. Dozens of men enter the house with nothing and leave with boxes. The motion is as rhythmic as it is mechanical. They rock and roll from shade to shade in an attempt to stay out of the blistering sun.

I take my backpack and sling it over my least hurting shoulder before going to the front door. I slide around the moving bodies and ask where Gordon Renton is. They are in a panicked rush, either avoiding me or outright ignoring me. I grab the attention of a man with a dolly.

"He's in the pool," the man says before shooing me off. He almost collides the wheel of the dolly with my foot, which would have been yet another injury to my battered frame.

I avoid the hostile workers. I make my way to the back of the mansion. The yellow and brown grass has grown past my waist. The pool is empty, and cracks run along its bowl. The scent of dead skunks bakes underneath the sun, giving me a whiff that would have killed me if I were able to breathe normally.

That damn sun isn't going to let up. I can see heat waves bouncing off the concrete.

Gordy is in the center of the pool, hiding underneath a few umbrellas that make for a poor man's parasol. By his side is a bucket filled with ice and water, with a bottle of opened champagne cooling in it. Gordy looks a few shades darker, but it might just be the sun.

He notices me, and his face contorts with concern. "Cabbage, what happened?"

"Got hit by a train. Then another when I was getting up."

"How unfortunate. Here, have a drink." Gordy points to a small ice chest. He opens it, revealing a few kinds of beers. The one that catches my attention is the Shiner. It reminds me of home and will go great with the Vicodin running through in my bloodstream. I pick the cold bottle from the ice chest and struggle to pop it open. Gordy takes the bottle from me, pops off the cap, and hands it back.

Bitter beer courses through my mouth and throat. It doesn't taste like it used to, probably has something to do with the sores inside my mouth. But it will do its job, I hope.

"So what's going on, Gordy? You moving?"

Gordy nods. "I'm done here. With this city, with my house, and with my life."

"Why the champagne?"

"Might as well toast myself. Sold the toy company to my rival Bart Jensen. Big payout. Workers are keeping their jobs. Best possible outcome."

"So what is your plan?"

Gordy stares at his champagne glass; he's a different man than the last two times I saw him. He looks a little more like the teenager I once knew. "Moving far away, across the sea in anonymity."

I smile when I hear Gordy speak almost normally. "You look better than me, Gordy. Way better. I'm jealous."

He laughs. "Best I've felt in years. Body's still gone, but my mind and sanity are healing."

I ask what brought about the sudden change in him.

His answer is Darius.

I almost spit out my beer. I ask what he means.

"Darius paid me a visit. I've decided to call it quits." Gordy holds out his hand and finishes off his champagne. "I owe you a great deal of money. For your time and your trouble."

"Wait. You're calling it off?"

Gordy nods. "Darius came back because of you. You did your job. You look very tired and weak. You need to rest."

"Please, Gordy, explain to me what happened with Darius."

"The short version? He's the reason I'm leaving. I no longer have a reason to stay. Hanging it up, whatever cliché you want to use for quitting. But you want the long version, don't you?"

I say yes. There would be no other reason I'd ask.

Gordy pours himself another glass of champagne and takes sips of it between stares. "He came the day after you discovered the hidden compartment in the floor, when you took the papers from his room. I came home from work to find the entire mansion trashed. I could hear chanting come from his room. So I approached, wanting to know what it was."

There Darius was, in his room, rocking back and forth. His room had scribbles and giant words printed on the walls in a strange black ink. Gordy saw what looked like eyes painted on the walls. Darius was in the corner of the room, kneeling in front of a shrine with Dotty's picture in the middle. Candlewax had melted and stuck him by the knees, shins, and feet to the floor. In Darius's hand was the same screwdriver he used on my door; pieces of skin and hair were stuck onto the steel, and it was covered in fresh and dry blood.

"I didn't recognize him as my son. Not at first. He was much too skinny. He looked older, much older than I last saw him a couple months ago, than what he should be." Gordy stops to stare at his wrinkled hands. "Then again, I know that all too well." He shakes his head and looks down at the ground. "Darius had these crazy blue eyes tattooed onto his skin. When he noticed I was there, after I called his name, he gave me an empty, crazy look."

Darius demanded to know what happened to the papers and the tapes. Gordy told his son that he gave them to me. Gordy said he was worried.

"I really didn't care if he killed Dotty or not. He's my son. I just wanted him to be safe." Gordy rubs his watering eyes and his voice cracks. "I wasn't the best father. Joe took care of Darius more than I did. I never knew him that well. But he is still my son. I just wanted him to be okay. What else can I do as a father, Cabbage?"

"I don't know, Gordy. I don't have children. Never will. Don't know the first thing about parenting. I'd be a terrible dad anyway."

Gordy laughs. "It can be a wonderful thing if you know what you're doing."

Knowing he is sincere, I nod.

Gordy goes off on a long speech, talking about all his proud moments and high aspirations for Darius. I do my best to pay attention to his kind words, his nostalgic words, about a much better time in his life. But at the same time, my concentration breaks. I find myself not wanting to relate to Darius anymore. It wasn't hatred or anything, but a desire to just run. To flee from hearing any more about this man who is out to kill me.

My body's instincts almost prove too strong; I grip my chest in pain and fall to one knee. It is like a hand has reached into my heart and squeezed so hard it won't beat, then released just as I am about to pass out.

"Cabbage, what's wrong?" Gordy asks as he gets up from his chair and picks me up. Pain flares in my forearm where Gordy touches me.

"Please, what happened with Darius?"

Gordy sits back down and continues his story. "Darius spaced out and said it was Dotty who told him that I was conspiring with you to put him away. Dotty said we both are trying to keep him from her. She had ascended and become an angel. She sees all things now." He unbuttons his shirt and pulls it back. I see an ugly bruised imprint of a man's hand and several dried scabs. "Darius did that to me. He told me he was going to kill me for interfering with Dotty's plans, then he was going to kill you." Gordy's hands clench to keep from shaking. "After a few days of not hearing back from you, I began to worry. I was so relieved when you came by. I honestly thought Darius killed you."

I didn't want to tell him that Darius paid me a visit. There was no use worrying him. I tell him to continue, and after a few minutes of pulling himself together he does.

"He chased me around the mansion. So fast, I didn't know he could move that quick. He pinned me to the wall. So powerful. No matter how much I resisted, I couldn't break his grip. He had that awful screwdriver right at my face. It was sharpened to a fine point, more like an ice pick than a screwdriver. The smell of dead flesh, of rotten blood, made me imagine terrible things. He had it right in my eye, ready to ram it in and then…" Gordy stops to look at the sky.

Darius couldn't do it. He wasn't able to kill his father.

"He let me go. Darius fell to his knees, and cried and cried." Gordy cries as he says this. "He said that he barely remembers anything at all. Not the times we played together, not the times we talked. None of the fond or bitter memories. They were all just…blanks."

"His past life is gone, his present is a blur, and his future is unknown," I say. "His life is not his own."

"That's right, Cabbage. How did—"

I raise my hand and shake my head, "Not important." Truth is, I'm beginning to feel the exact same way as Darius, but I won't say this. "Please continue."

Darius told Gordy that he barely remembered anything about his life except for one thing: his love for his father. That's why he couldn't kill him. His love for his father was strong enough to rip away the madness, even if it was just for a fading moment.

"Darius went back to his room and ripped the wallpaper off using the screwdriver, tearing it up and throwing it out. He told me he didn't have much time. While he was doing that, his tattoos ruptured and he bled. His eyes started to bleed too. He kept chanting the entire time."

When Darius was finished, he told his father good-bye. He told him if he ever saw Gordy again, he might not be able to contain himself. He said everything would be fine. He was going back to Dotty's warm, loving arms, and he would explain everything to her. She'd understand in time that she didn't need his father dead.

Gordy sighs and finishes off the champagne. "My son is no longer. Darius is dead. He's possessed by the same darkness, the same monster, that took Joe away. It's only a matter of time until he comes back…"

So this is indoctrination?

Darius has been indoctrinated by a Pale Stranger, probably masquerading as Dotty. Poor Joe…the same thing happened to him. I feel sympathy for Benson as well, all things considered. I think Gordy was also being indoctrinated, but for some reason it failed. Darius, however, hit a point that neither of the others had crossed. He had become subhuman.

Now I'm filled with dread. I know I'm well on my way to flying off the edge, just like Darius. Is this the fate of all people who are indoctrinated?

Is this my fate?

I wish I had asked Levitt. No matter.

"Gordy, I need you to tell me about Joe," I say. Gordy shakes his head. "Please. Listen to me. I know you don't want to talk about your brother. But I've come to a realization that what happened to him…is happening to me." He looks away from me and mutters. I crouch down on my aching knees and stare at him. "The research, everything has to do with it. You, me, Joe, Darius, and a bunch of other people in Afghanistan and Germany going back five hundred years. They were all affected. More like infected."

"Infected?"

I nod. "It's not biological, at least I don't think. It's something genetic." I know I'm reaching when I try explaining this to Gordy. I'm no scientist or doctor. I failed my science courses in high school and college. But it is the only way I can properly explain it, in terms Gordy and I can both understand. "Like, there is something in our blood. I know the blood ain't alive per say, but it has some kind primal understanding of what is around us. It is reacting negatively to whatever it was Joe discovered. And this 'virus' attacking us is making us look the way we do. It's eating pieces of us. So we age, our bodies start falling apart rapidly, and our minds go. Everything about us is turned against us. At least, that's what I think."

"Did Joe know what he was getting into?"

"By the time he did it was too late. I need you to tell me what happened to him exactly."

"Okay, Cabbage. I'll tell you."

Gordy knew his brother was conducting research with a colleague at Southern Miskatonic University, but he didn't know how far it extended. Joe was incredibly secretive. He never told anyone what he was doing. Everything was fine until five years ago. Joe never spoke of it, but he was a changed man. He had become melancholic and quiet, so unlike himself.

I realize the change was due to the incident at Afghanistan. That has to be what Gordy is talking about.

"Over a period of two years, he became incredibly reclusive. He only let one person in the room at that time. His girlfriend." Gordy stops to rub his forehead. "I don't remember much of the details about what happened during these years. My memory has failed with everything happening in my life."

"Can you at least tell me the circumstances behind how he died?"

He put his hands over his face and took deep breaths. "I heard Joe screaming one day. So I went into his room. The next thing I knew, he stabbed me."

In an instant, I reach down and hold my stomach. I flash back to that scene, with Joe sitting spaced-out in the chair with the two needles. The burning sensation of cut flesh and flowing blood. The dizziness, the finite movement, the unbelievable vision.

It wasn't me who Joe stabbed; it was Gordy. I was somehow Gordy. Or rather, I somehow saw and felt what Gordy experienced. Without knowing it, I plug my fingers into my ears, preparing myself for the impossible sounds that I heard through Gordy.

"Joe was surprised to see I was alive," Gordy says as he lifts up his shirt. A very nasty scar connects the flesh on his stomach, sealing the seam of an old wound. "He apologized to me, told me it was all going to be over very soon. That's when he took two needles…I would have died. But we weren't alone."

"You weren't?"

He shakes his head. "No, Dotty was hidden in the closet. She saw the entire thing. She was so terrified, she couldn't do anything until Joe… well…" Gordy can't finish. "She saved my life. Saved Joe's too. Called the ambulance. Went with both of us." Gordy closes his eyes and shakes his head. "It was because of this that Darius met her. She was waiting at the hospital. They didn't hook up then, but they became aware of another. It's really fucked up that me almost dying killed everyone else. I feel responsible."

I put my hand on Gordy's shoulder. "It's not your fault, Gordy. Everything that happened was beyond your control."

"Listen, I have a confession to make. It's about Dotty and Joe…why she was in the room. I knew she was there. I had gone to make sure she was okay."

"She was his lover. I've known for a while."

"Really? How?"

"I'm a journalist. I have my ways." We both laugh, and I pull my hand away.

"You know they weren't always like that. There was no relationship, period. It was a platonic attraction on Joe's end for her. Not her exactly, but her craft. She was a ballerina, you know. He loved her dancing, and he loved watching her perform. She was from a poor family; he agreed to help her get a few grants, help pay with some of her schooling. Purely innocent. He just wanted to help her out, since he thought she could bring some life back to Southern Miskatonic's struggling theater."

But he changed the more she hung around him. He became lustful, jealous, creepy. He was deranged and a hollow shell, never leaving his room or dealing with the outside world unless it was Dotty. However, Joe was not the only one affected. Dotty, the shy ballerina, became a temptress. She started to enjoy pain.

"Darius knew Dotty was with Joe. He loved her anyway, despite knowing about the relationship."

"So that wouldn't have been the cause of Dotty's murder if Darius was behind it?"

Gordy says no.

"Wait a minute. You said Joe was saved?"

"Yeah, he didn't die there."

Instead, the trauma caused by the incident left him a vegetable: a frozen look of horror on his face. Joe was kept in isolation for a few months, never uttering a word or showing responses to outside stimuli.

"One day the restraints were ripped off by an unknown person. Joe had clawed his way through the grating that shielded the window. He broke the Plexiglas window with his fist, shattering it." The invisible, shadow pain afflicted me again. I felt the slicing of my wrists, followed by the stabbing of my chest and limbs over and over. I knew what was coming next before Gordy said it. "Right before he jumped off the ledge, he yelled out that they were everywhere. His blood saw them, and all of humanity's blood knew they were there despite not being able to see them. He yelled out that God had forsaken him. Then he jumped."

Every moment of that flashed before my eyes.

I had seen these events through Gordy's, then Joe's, eyes.

So I ask, "Gordy, do you believe in the supernatural? Or things like that?"

"Never been the religious type. But I started to believe something was out there when Joe was in the hospital."

I ask what he means.

"The patients and the hospital staff dreaded dealing with Joe during the last few months of his life. Rumor is that no one has used Joe's hospital room since his death. They sealed it off. Same way I sealed off Joe's room."

When they examined the room later, Gordy found scratches on the ceiling. They were everywhere: outside on the ledge, outside the door, and in an empty nearby hospital room.

As time passed, Gordy got sick, and Darius started going the same route as Joe. The same kind of scratches appeared at the house. From then on, he found them everywhere. No matter where he went, he saw them. It was like a virus had infected him, forcing him to see these unnatural scratches.

Voices and weird smells came from Joe's old room. Gordy had it sealed off because no matter how many times it was cleaned, the room was contaminated. The disgusting odor drove away most people, and the disturbing noises unnerved everyone who stayed over.

"My body had a sensation that there was something very wrong with his house, and with Joe and with Darius. I couldn't explain it, Cabbage," Gordy says. "I found myself filled with wild emotions. Evil emotions."

He hated and feared his own family. He feared his own house as well. Something evil, as he called it, had seeped in and corrupted Joe's room. But his father had built the house; his house was all he had left. He was too powerless and too prideful to do something about it.

"I know this house has something to do with my body's rapid decay. It isn't caused by simple genetics or a wild lifestyle. It is of something beyond my understanding, beyond what advanced science can explain away. I think this goes beyond what religion can explain."

If there is a good, then there has to be evil. If there is a God, then surely there has to be a devil. But what if there is no God? That doesn't mean there isn't a devil. That doesn't mean evil isn't there.

A devil that our blood knows exists even if we don't. Evil is something the blood knows. The blood knows its unseen enemy.

Scratches appeared on the wall in his room the moment Darius left. Gordy made up his mind to pack up and leave town.

"Whatever there was left to salvage in my life, with what little I have anyway, I'm going to retire and live out the rest of my life in anonymity and peace. No reason to stay."

"Nobody will blame you for leaving," I say.

Gordy stands by my side and stares at his shoes. He whispers, "I have a confession to make. I don't think you're going to like what I have to say. But I need to say it."

I lean into him, whisper back. "What is it?"

"Cabbage, you're giving off the same sensation I've been feeling. That alien, evil, inhuman presence. It is radiating off you like a cloud. With each passing breath, it grows stronger. I confess..." Gordy stares dead into my eyes and says, "I don't know how much longer I can be around you."

"How long have you felt this?"

"Since the moment you were asleep in your car, the day you came back and found the hidden compartment in the floor."

"So am I cursed? Is that what you're saying, Gordy?"

"It was tiny at first. I thought I was just imagining things. I was helpless to tell you anything. You seemed unaware and would've called me insane, like everyone else has."

"You're probably right. But now I believe you. I understand...I won't take any more of your time."

I move away from Gordy and try to leave the pool. But Gordy steps in front of me and smiles. "Even if you are cursed, I'm glad you came by. You're the only person who has visited me. Thank you, Cabbage."

Gordy tells me to follow him into the house. He has something for me.

He hands me a suitcase. Inside is thirty thousand dollars.

"If you're gonna run, just go," Gordy says.

I try not to laugh, but it's hard not to. "I don't think what is going on will stop with me running. I need to find Darius. I need to finish the stories. The case isn't finished yet."

Gordy touches my hand and slips something metallic into it. I open my hand and find a key. Before I can say anything, Gordy laughs and says, "If you're going to keep searching for Darius or the truth, well, you can use my house. Do whatever you want with it. There is a working typewriter in the study if you want it; it's not like I have use for it. Chances are, I won't be able to sell it. Can't sell the broken grand piano in Joe's room either, but I won't step foot in that room and neither should you." Gordy holds the back of his head, sighs, and gives me a sullen look, "Darius is no longer my son. I think he killed someone, or some ones. If you see him, please protect yourself if he confronts you. But if you can, free him from whatever grip it has on him. I failed him as a father. Please, save him if you can. Or free him…"

I know what Gordy is implying; that much is easy, even for a guy like me.

Gordy wants me to kill Darius if I can't save him. As much as I want to believe it doesn't have to go that far, what if there is no other way? Can I bring myself to do it?

Gordy holds out his hand. "I never apologized to you."

"For what?"

"For bullying you in high school. I know you must have hated me for a long time. Or did you forget?" I look away. "I see. These past few years have given me a lot of time to dwell on the past. Gave me a chance to take a long hard look at all the sins, all the wrongs I've done."

He does not want to be alone. He wants just one person he can call a friend.

"It's okay, Gordon. That is no longer important to me. I forgive you." I take his hand and give him a firm handshake. "I'll be your friend."

Gordy weeps and gives me a hug. It hurt at first, but I ignore the pain and hug him back. It's good to know that I have someone to relate to. It is good to know that he will no longer be tormented by the thought of being absolutely alone.

    We bid each other farewell for the last time. Gordy promises to drink something good for me whenever he touches down at his unknown destination. That is a comforting thought. It is nice to know that something so simple can be so wonderful. At least one of us will live.

Chapter Twenty-three

At Giallo, lunch is still being served despite the kitchen going to the dinner menu. I have a few hours before I meet with Cruz and Torres. The place seems nice enough. Fine waiting staff, fine air-conditioning, fine water. The water is the best; it's good to drink something that isn't contaminated with industrial waste. Feeling cool is a second priority, but as long as they bring water, I'm happy.

While I want to believe the answers have been in my backpack, unburned, this was not what I had in mind. The papers involving Afghanistan and the Yellow Count are gone. The pages with the eyes are gone as well. Burnt, shredded, doesn't matter how, but they are gone. And I am the culprit.

But the papers involving Foch are still there.

I put the music box to the side and take out the papers. If what I saw was true, then Johan must be in the file somewhere; Foch must have talked about him during his sessions with Friend. Foch had to have mentioned the Pale Strangers. He had to have won against them somehow. I mean, he made it to the penthouse level of eighty-plus.

There has to be something about fighting them in here.

Though I confess the desire to find out more about the Scarecrow, and the Black Fairy is also on my mind.

While reading the papers, I discover that old crippled Foch told Friend he was ready to talk. Foch was ready to tell his complete story. To confess whatever scarred sins that stained his soul; that was the last thing he had to offer this world.

But this was not to be.

Foch had a stroke a couple days before his scheduled meeting with Friend. They took him off life support at the end of the week. Friend closed his investigation, saying there wasn't enough funding for him to do any follow-up.

Whatever Foch was going to say was left unsaid. His soul was not purged; his mind had not been cleared. He died without letting the world know what happened. He died without warning them about the Pale Strangers. His body was ruined, his mind tormented. Haunted by something he saw, something he did.

This is the fate of anyone who lasts that long.

Foreign stuff is all that's left to read. There is no chance of me uncovering its true message. I don't want to put some poor fool's life in danger to translate it.

I stare at the glass of water and lament. Levitt was wrong. There is nothing for me to go on here except for stuff written in French and Dutch.

Only a miracle can help.

Sweat pours from me despite the restaurant's nice cool temperature. My throat itches. My blood boils with a cold fear. My vision blurs as the pinging in my ears eats all sound.

I panic and try to move, but I cannot budge.

The people around me don't seem to notice. They don't even notice what is happening to them, but I notice them.

They sit there eating their meals while their skin breaks apart like glass cracking. They laugh and talk to one another as a bloody mess streams out and floats in the air like red smoke. The smoke and light bends around a black hole that floats underneath my feet. My body is pulled in, stretching out in the slowest of motions.

There is something in this black hole, something hidden behind the red smoke that circles me like a twister. Fear bubbles to the surface as my body begins to merge with the smoke. I feel hands, feet, mouths, claws, and oil swimming with me. This devouring mass pulls at me.

For an eternity, I fall. My mind is turning to nothing, nothing, nothing.

Insides turn out, then turns in. New skin, or rather old skin, replaces mine. My eyes are pushed out and replaced by someone else's vision.

My bones and muscles break and tear. My pain is substituted with another's pain. The pinging noise turns into something manageable. I can hear someone talking in my ears. I can feel my mouth whisper as I leave this red hell and enter a place more familiar, a place in the past.

The red haze fades from view. I am no longer me. I am now another.

So I speak in a voice not mine, "This is the Black Fairy's work."

Thieriot and Foch stand over several of the newly killed corpses. The two surviving guards point their weapons at the rafters, waiting for the flying beast to make her appearance. The ten surviving prisoners are missing; their cell doors have been ripped apart and blood floods their cells. The other guards are unaccounted for.

"What do you know of this Black Fairy? Why is she called it?" Foch asks.

"A young girl ran away into the forest to join the fairies in the mountains. She wandered around the forest, lost and alone, but found no fairies. A terrible snowstorm made her take refuge in a ruined castle. She found the corpse of the former countess, whose body was transformed into a plant in the middle of the ruins. The snowstorm never stopped, and the despair of being alone broke her. Hate and sorrow drove her mad. Hunger consumed her. She devoured the dead flesh of the ancient countess covered in plants to stay alive. The corpse was cursed, and eating the dead flesh changed her body. She transformed herself into a fairy. Filled with rage toward the world she wandered the forest forever alone. She would kill whoever she met in the forest. And if children didn't behave, or ran away from their homes and chores, the Black Fairy would come to get them and eat them." I look at Foch and say, "The Fairy of the Black Forest is the proper name of this folktale."

"That's a stupid children's tale," Thieriot says.

I help myself with a painful laugh. "So was the Scarecrow in my backyard. As you can see, one of them is very much real."

"So what is she doing here? Did she follow you?" Foch asks.

"I'm not sure she followed me so much as she ran into me. The Scarecrow had been chasing me when I saw her wandering around in the forest in a dirty dress, crying."

"Why was she crying?"

"To lure someone in. From afar, I thought she looked like a woman. I felt drawn to her. I wanted to help her despite having a monster chasing after me. But as I got closer, I got the same sensation the Scarecrow gave me. So I stopped. But she looked normal, like you and me..." I stare at the rafters, thinking she is probably listening. "When she saw me back off, these wasp wings, six of them, protruded from her back. She flew in the air and let out an unearthly buzz of insect noises."

It took me a while to accept that a Pale Stranger was chasing me. But two?

"My mind is still trying to grasp that there may be more of them out there, hidden in the world, amongst us," I say.

Foch gets our attention. He examines two of the deceased corpses and points to a marking on their heads. There are small puncture holes in each of them, barely visible and hidden among the hair. We look at the rest of the bodies and find they have the holes too.

This is different than what the Scarecrow does to the deceased. I saw him devour an entire battlefield of the dead with his spikes. But the Black Fairy hasn't devoured these bodies. Yet they came back to life. It is amazing and disturbing.

When I state this, Foch looks around us and asks, "Then why aren't we being attacked?"

Thieriot nods. "Lien is right. This isn't the best place to be. Let's go to the kitchen." He points to one of the guards, who nods and approaches me. With his key, they take off the shackles. Then he hands me his sidearm.

"Can this Black Fairy be hurt?" Foch asks. I don't answer.

We walk toward the kitchen area, yet they pester me for an answer. To do this, I must first tell them about my encounter with the Scarecrow. Otherwise, they won't understand just what kind of creature they are dealing with. And it is a real possibility that we are going to have to deal with him soon.

"The cries of my daughter Franziska sent me out of my house," I say. "Hilda and Xaver came running out as I darted into the field. We looked all over, but could not find them. I screamed their names. Franziska came out from underneath a hole in the old house. She fell into Hilda's arms, crying and screaming. Xaver looked under the house and found Claudia under there as well, hugging one of the support beams the old house stood on. She did not respond to our calls. It took me, Hilda, and Xaver to pry her off. Her tiny hands refused to let go; her fingernails bent and bled as she scratched the lumber. When I pulled her off, she clung to me and did not let go. I told her to tell me what happened."

Franziska spoke in a crying whisper.

It was the Scarecrow. He was in the barn where they played.

Unlike her sister, Claudia wasn't crying. She was mute, a look of frozen terror on her face. Her eyes shut, but even that didn't stop her lids from shuddering. Her twisted face gave me an uncontrollable shiver and sent bumps all across my skin. She was hard to look at. I hated myself for not being able to look at my own daughter.

We took them in. Franziska cried herself to sleep. Claudia lay still on her bed and stared at the ceiling. She refused to respond to us, or to eat when supper was ready. Hilda stayed at their side while I sat on the porch. Xaver had run to the village to find out if there were any outsiders roaming around.

There was no way the Scarecrow could have come alive. I knew my country was involved in the war. I theorized that it must have been an enemy soldier marching through the forest, a scout perhaps. It had to have been an outside man who scared them, since no one in the village would do something as cruel as that.

That's when I felt it for the first time.

My heart skipped, each beat led to an ever-growing pain that spread further and further through my body. Each breath felt like I was taking water into my lungs; the sensation of drowning made me panic. I tossed and turned all over my porch, falling down and landing hard on my side. My vision blurred. The layers under my skin burned while the outside of me felt like it was going to tear apart.

"I'm sure only a minute had passed, but the minute was an agonizing year. I called for my wife, but only a tiny whimper squeezed from my lips. I forced my body to sit upright. I had to shut my eyes because I had a hard time differentiating between what I saw and what I was interpreting. With the color faded in my vision, objects melted together. Tall crops mingled with the sky, the dirt danced with the grass, and the village caved in on itself. It was so hard to concentrate on what was going on that I became ill from just looking at my hands."

My body fell apart.

I grabbed onto the porch and held on tight. I again called out for Hilda, but a wheeze sounded instead of words. I opened my eyes and stared for a moment to see if Xaver was running back. I focused and focused, but my vision drifted elsewhere. My eyes kept going back to the corner of the field, past the crops to my barn. My eyes wouldn't close, despite the facial muscles forcing down on my eyelids. They stared at the barn; no, I wasn't looking at the barn. I was trying to look past it.

Utter fear came over me. My body cried out in pain.

I felt my body rise. A muffled voice whispered into my ear. Xaver, my boy, was trying to pick me up. While I could not hear what he said, I knew he was crying out, crying for me to get up. Hilda came running out. They each took an arm and carried me up. My knees and ankles almost buckled. I was so helpless I started to cry.

And as I went into the house, I saw. Beyond the barn. Beyond the field.

A Pale Stranger standing from afar. The Scarecrow was alive.

"I blacked out. I slept for two days until I finally regained consciousness."

We arrive at the kitchen, and Thieriot tries saying something but can't. We barricade the doors and sit at one of the tables. "But you said that the Scarecrow was a tree in the shape of a man. A tree is an inanimate object; it can't move on its own. How could it be alive and moving around? And how does this relate to us hurting them?"

"I'm getting to that," I say. "While I was asleep for two days, my family came to a consensus. They wanted the Scarecrow cut down. After what happened, I agreed with them. So I sharpened my ax and went out to the field with Xaver to chop it down."

Thinking back on it, deep down, something was telling me not to go near the Scarecrow. I ignored it. Not out of pride, but because I wanted the damn thing cut down. But as I drew closer to it with Xaver and two axes in hand, I could hear a little voice from down in my stomach screaming at me to run away. Just run. Take Hilda and the children and flee. The voice wanted me to run away beyond the mountains, beyond the borders, into a country on another continent far away from here.

I did not heed the warning.

It was only when I raised my ax to strike it down that I saw.

The tree containing the Scarecrow had been dragged across the field. The roots had risen almost as tall as me from under the ground, stabbing upward like spikes and scarring the grass. What looked like blood had mixed in with the dirt, creating a bubbling mud. It smelled wretched. The Scarecrow had changed shape. It looked more like a man now, with the branches becoming more like limbs.

At first I thought the Scarecrow's limbs belonged to a man's, but then I thought they were like a skinless dog or a cat. My eyes fluttered about, and the limbs became something different, something indescribable. I'm sure they were like an animal's that I have yet to lay eyes upon, because somehow my body recognized them. My body was telling me what it was, but my mind could not decipher its words. Something primordial in my blood was speaking in a wordless voice.

Then I heard the grunt, that familiar grunt my siblings and I pretended we heard as kids. Except it came from all directions and attacked my senses. I wobbled. I held myself up by leaning on the handle of my ax. Xaver came to my side and asked what was wrong. Out of anger, I yelled at him. I asked him if what he saw did not bother him.

No father, he stated, I just see that someone moved the tree and reburied it.

I told him to look closer at the spikes, at the bloodied mud. Did he not smell the foul stench? Did he not see the Scarecrow change shapes before his eyes? My head pounded from the grunting, which had taken on an off-key rhythm.

I grabbed him. I screamed at him not to lie to me. I asked him what he saw.

Stop it, he told me. Stop scaring me, he cried out. I asked him what he saw. He said it was a tree. I called him a liar again. He pushed me away, and I fell to the ground.

How could he be so blind? How could he not see what was before him? Why was he lying to his father? Why did he push me down and deny me?

"The pain became unbearable. It was worse than the other day. Instead of passing out, I was kept awake by the constant grunts. I grabbed my chest, felt my fingers dig deep into the skin, almost clawing it away with my fingernails. Xaver ran to go get his mother."

And I was left alone with the Scarecrow.

I kept focusing on it as the pain grew worse. I couldn't think about what to do. I couldn't pray for divine intervention. I just stared. I stared at its pale face.

A thought occurred to me then. It was so terrifying that I can only reflect on it with clarity. Growing up on the farm, there were no wild animals. Birds would go out of their way to fly away from our home. Livestock would go out of their way to avoid us. I never heard the sounds of insects in the evening. Weather would hit the village, yet our house very seldom saw any of it.

Growing up, I thought this was the best place to live.

It was all because of the Scarecrow. That's what my grandparents found out. My parents probably knew as well. And here I found out, too late to see what was wrong with it.

This place was cursed. The world knew it. That's why the third row of shrubs, the ones closest to the Scarecrow, never grew. That's why the trees were an off, sickly color in the Black Forest behind the Scarecrow. That's why the grass never grew above a certain height and never looked healthy, despite having the best sun and the best rain. Now I realized why our livestock never lasted long. They wanted to get away or die trying.

The Scarecrow's pale face turned to me.

What are you doing? We are friends.

In a panic, I struck the Scarecrow in the face with the ax. The blade embedded itself deeply into his side. The ax got stuck in his thick, gooey blood. His hand reached up and pulled the ax out. From the wound, I saw teeth grow out of its blood and connect with one another, sealing the wound and giving it half a mouth.

Foch and Thieriot's faces sunk when I tell them this.

"So we can't kill them?" Thieriot asks.

I shake my head. "I've fired weapons at him whenever I got a chance. Either he takes the hit or vanishes from sight, only to reappear later. Every wound heals, makes him more grotesque. I don't know what he looks like now, but I'm sure I'll recognize him."

"You said he hunts humans and eats them. So why hasn't he killed you?" Foch asks.

"That question haunts me, Dr. Foch. He had a chance to kill me when I was a child. He was there in my backyard for at least fifty years. But he never made a move until recently. Why? What caused him to come alive?"

Foch snaps his fingers and taps on the table. "Maybe he was waiting for something like this. Many men have died during this war. You said he eats the dead. The wounded and dying are easy pickings. He just swoops into the area and eats."

"No, that makes no sense," Thieriot says. "How would he know this war was to happen? And that it would happen here? You're telling us that it had some kind of precognition?"

"I don't know, Sigmund. This is all new to me. And this is just one of them. We still don't know what the Black Fairy is after. She is not eating the dead."

"Then what is she planning?" Thieriot asks.

"Sir, look!" One of the guards signals us. We follow him to the cellar, where the food and other perishables are kept. The smell of rotten meat hits us. We hold our mouths as we descend the stairs. What we find is horrible.

Hanging upside down are skinned corpses with the heads removed. The skulls and spinal columns are on the ground with circular holes in them. The brains have been sucked out, yet every other part of the body remains.

Foch asks, "Why are the corpses skinned? Why didn't she eat them?"

"I don't know," I say. "I've never seen this before. Does she just eat the brains?"

A loud moan comes from the corner of the room, from behind a very large crate. We aim our weapons and slowly approach the crate. The origin of the wretched smell is found.

A prisoner has been cocooned behind the crate. We lower our weapons and stare at webbing made of silk, dirt, paper, and loose items. Behind the webbing is a prisoner, decayed and rotting. With milky colored eye-sockets and a skeletal face, he groans on, oblivious to our presence.

As we examine him, I see something move underneath his skin. His stomach and his chest expand. What looks like hands and feet press hard against the rotting flesh, trying to claw its way out. I see a face underneath.

"What the hell is it?" Thieriot asks.

"You said The Black Fairy's wings were like wasps, correct Johan?" Foch asks. I nod. He taps his chin and hums. "When I was studying at the university many years ago a friend of mine invited me to an exhibit on the different insects of the known world. It was a fascinating exhibit. The insect kingdom is brutal, almost as much as man's. But insects are not held back by morals or conscience. They inflict unimaginable things on one another in the name of survival. Among the cruelest were the parasitic wasps. They don't have hives like, say paper wasps. The exhibit showed a demonstration of a parasitic wasp and its prey, in this case a cockroach."

Foch explained that each species of parasitic wasp specialized in a particular insect. The wasp would hunt not for the sake of food, but for reproduction. With a precision strike, the female wasp would stab into her victims and paralyze them. She would drag them off into a safe burrow and lay a fertilized egg into the back or stomach of the roach. Then the wasp would barricade the roach in the burrow and leave. A few days later the egg would hatch. The larva would bury itself in the body of the roach and eat it from within. The roach would die and the larva would use the carcass as a cocoon. In time the larva would metamorphose into another parasitic wasp.

"And the cycle would continue again," Foch says. "It's a theory, but I'm guessing the Black Fairy could be just like a parasitic wasp. The prisoners are hosts for her larva. They defend the larva as it eats away at them from the inside; that's why they attacked us. I'm guessing after a certain period of time, the Black Fairy cocoons them so nothing can happen as the larva feeds on them, right about when the larva's ready to come out."

"Great," Thieriot says. "We better destroy the bodies before her brood hatches, then."

Everyone nods. As I dwell on the hideousness of the situation I think hard about the myth. I think about the Black Fairy herself, about why she is doing this. Is she doing this for revenge? Is she doing it to reproduce? Is she doing this for food? Or…is she doing this because she is lonely? Maybe she doesn't want to be alone ever again.

How horrible. How sad.

I feel something wet touch the back of my ear and run down my neck.

I reach to wipe it away and see what it is. It is blood, mixed with some other fluid.

We look up.

A pale, sleek child with no facial features is hanging upside down with its feet embedded in the ceiling. In one hand is a skull and spine. Its free hand has a slit in its palm, with a long umbilical cord attached to a stinger coming out of it. The stinger stabs into the skull and begins sucking out the brain matter. The child tilts its head.

A line appears where its mouth should have been. The sleek skin rips apart like paper, revealing rows of teeth. The child howls at us, and we open fire on it.

Chapter Twenty-four

The forest of yellow wine is in bloom with poppies. Branches slash at my skin, leaves crush underneath my running feet. Though thick fog blinds my sight, I run. Trees knock me over, yet I stand and continue my chase.

Nothing is going to keep me from her. My body is ready.

I scream out her name. I demand she stop running. She doesn't have to make me chase her, she was the one who called me to see her. But she makes me chase. Blood mingles with my sweat like the ancient warhorses from Ferghana.

I must get her. I will get her.

But she is too fast for me. She eludes my every step, anticipates my every move. Her smell lingers and crawls into every breath, driving me to run harder, to sweat more of my blood with every heartbeat.

Echoes from her lips encircle me.

She is calling me. She is requesting me. She demands me.

Remnants of her voice, her scent, lead me further into the forest.

An abandoned building connected by pipes to an empty reservoir stand before me. On the concrete are fresh blood and scratches.

"Darius!" her voice whispers.

Why did she call me Darius? My name is Claire. Claire Walker. I'm not Darius. Why am I responding to her call for another man? Why am I following this girl into this dark, creepy place? Why is there blood?

The urgency to catch her infects my insides. I run through the dark hallways, pass through the empty rooms, and stumble into a dim room. The bodies, limbs, and organs of dozens of slain people are lined up in a circle. Most have been devoured, leaving just tiny fragments of their humanity for me to see. I think I know these people. They were our friends.

Underneath them, an oil canvas has been painted with a grotesque eye, in words that go beyond my understanding of language. They aren't human words but words created in some nightmare. This room is but a yawl to an estuary in the great void.

The horror, the horror. What has my angel done?

Standing in the corner I see that tall pale thing who haunts my dreams. His left arm is gone and all over torso chunks are missing. Fractured pieces, cut pieces, eaten pieces. He is more like a broken puzzle than a man, if he is a man. But from the parts that are gone, the vapors flow out. He heals, and he laughs.

She will betray you. You chose wrong.

No, you're wrong. She won't. She's not like that.

Wait, why am I defending her? Who is this I am defending?

It's not in her nature now, but it will become her nature. You will lose yourself and become less than you are. You will become less until there is none. You will cease to be. You can be replaced. Everyone is. Your uncle was. So will you.

"Darius!" she calls out to me again. I try to yell back; it is not my name. But instead, I run to the other room. There is no resisting. No denying. I need her. I need my religion.

For her, I will walk the fires of hell. For her, I will deny God. I need my angel.

We will find another. His blood will know soon.

"Attention, Walker!" A great force slams against my hands.

Everything is different. A bright, hot light shines down on me. I try to cover my face, but my hands yank against something metal. I'm handcuffed to a long chain attached to the ground.

Where am I? Why am in chains?

"Stop stalling, you son of a bitch!" a voice screams into my ear, freaking me out and almost making me fall off the chair I sit on.

I quiver when I ask, "Where am I?"

"Where do you think?" my interrogator responds. Not wanting to sound sarcastic, but not wanting to play along, I look around some more. Three men stand behind the bright lights. Staring hurts my eyes, and the sole thing that gives them any identity are shiny shields that reflect beams of light.

"A police station?"

"We have a winner!" one of them says with the utmost contempt.

"At least he's responding," another says. They all sound the same: monotone, deep, disgusted, forceful. Perfect triplets, or I'm confusing one person for three. Everything is blurry.

"Can you tell me what you remember?"

"I...I was in a forest."

"No, you weren't. You were at Giallo. You were waiting to meet with someone. Remember?"

"I was?"

A shadowy hand appears from the light and touches my head with two fingers. He presses down, forcing me to stare down. My clothes, my hands, are painted with dry, dark crimson; I am as much glued to the chains as I am handcuffed.

A flood of memories breaks the levy. With each blink, the interrogation room changes.

"What do you see, Mr. Walker?" they ask in unison.

I see myself back at Giallo, sitting still, staring at the pages of Joe's research and the music box. The box's tune is so lovely. I spend the entire time whistling to the soothing song. My beat is off, but with the time I spent at the restaurant and with enough repetitions, I am able to match the music box's sonata.

I had to tell all the boys and girls about its hallowed beauty. I would be a missionary for such perfection. My confession to the world, that despite Joe's madness, he made the best decision by having gotten this box. Anyone who would listen, yes, I'd tell them about it. Yet they never respond. Such a loss for them.

But a hand slams the music box shut.

"Hey there, old sport!" the violator says. That annoys me. My annoyance turns to bitter, loathing hatred in a matter of nanoseconds the moment I see him stand in front of me and take the box.

"Kenny Daniels?" I say.

"Never fear, I is here," Kenny say.

"Why are you here?"

A large hand touches on the sore spot on my shoulder. With a grunt, I turn to face him. My disdain grows when I see Ralph West.

Why were they here? I ask them.

"You invited us here."

"I'm meeting a couple marines for an interview here soon," I say.

"Well you double-booked. Probably forgot you invited us. Must be that dirt you're shooting. Or snorting?" Kenny says.

Ralph laughs and shrugs. "He's a junkie, it don't matter."

I clinch my fist so hard my nails almost stab through my skin. I scowl without looking at them. "Then what are we here to talk about?"

"Well, Claire, you sold us on the idea of this exclusive cover story involving Gordy Renton and his family, some big dark secret that was supposed to be a bestseller," Ralph says.

"You weren't interested the first time. So why the interest?"

"Because, chap," Kenny leans in and gives me that fucking crooked smile of his, "you had some key information about certain things going on. A conspiracy theory, the dark truth about the world. Joseph Renton and his partner had uncovered this, but they were assassinated to keep them from telling the general public about its mystery."

"I figured you fine, upstanding gentlemen wouldn't be interested in a little old ghost story I uncovered." I clinch my teeth and press my tongue against the back of my teeth to keep from growling.

Kenny reaches in further, breathing heavily on my skin. The ugly smell of chewing tobacco between his teeth makes my stomach turn. "You got something good, Walker," Kenny says, "something real good. I'm here to make you an offer." Ralph nudges Kenny, who grins at him and nods. "We wanna deal."

They love the angle I worked on all by my lonesome. They wanted the majority piece of the "untold story" I touted. It was in the *Eye Tribunal's* interest to do a story that would attract so much controversy.

In exchange for taking a backseat credit, both men would gain the press, gain the fame, gain whatever glory came out of it. And me? I would get my job back. I would no longer be a ghostwriter. I would be a real journalist again.

"All your idea, Claire." Ralph claps his hands.

"Just give us what you got," Kenny says.

No. I will not give them what I have. They lied. I didn't talk to them. I know I didn't. I never wanted to work for the *Eye Tribunal* again.

There are more important things going on.

And neither Ralph West nor Kenneth Daniels can take that from me.

Feelings of absolute rage fill me. Motivated by greed, these men do not care what is really out there. What is underneath the underbelly of our sight, of our understanding, of our beliefs. They just want money. I'm not going to let them use me.

I can stop them, right here. I can stop them, right now.

In my hand, I grab a sharp steak knife. This is what I will use to achieve my goal.

Do it Claire. They wronged you. Kill them both. It's what you want, right?

Yes, I will kill them both.

Kill everyone around you. Feed me. It's what you want, right?

Yes, I will kill everyone here to feed you.

"Then what did you do, Walker?" the officers ask me in one voice.

"I…I don't know." My eyes move around to look at the interrogators. I can't see them. Instead I see the people in the restaurant.

But they aren't people. No, they are frozen glass. Glass filled with meat, pumping vessels, beating hearts. Red mist moves from the parts they move. The entire room is covered in this floating, liquid smoke. I feel like I could swim in it. I can smell the mist.

Countless thoughts from everyone in the restaurant flow into my mind. I am hearing their words, seeing their past, seeing through their eyes. I know what emotions they are feeling.

All from the smell in the crimson mist.

There is no way of turning it off, no way of filtering the input coming from all directions. Worse, I am getting vague signals from outside the building. Going out for miles and miles, these faint messages fight for my attention.

Ralph and Kenny are working together, but their minds are plotting against one another. They each try to figure out the best way to screw the other out of a big story like this. And Kenny has no intentions of helping me get back my job. In fact, he is trying to figure out how to get me fired, since I am a liability at the *Eye*.

Both men fear me. I see the demented sinner in me reflected off their faces. The desire to kill Ralph and Kenny grows stronger with each breath of mist. All I have to do is dive at them and slice away, spilling geysers into the air with a vengeful laugh.

You see how we see the world now, don't you?

Yes, I know how you see the world.

If feels good, don't it Claire?

Yes, it feels good. Yes, I want more of it.

Of course you do. Better than any sex, than any drug.

Yes, this is the best sex and best high I will ever know.

This can be your heaven, if you want.

No, my body screams, it's not heaven. It's not even hell. Far worse than that: it is all a lie. My insides throb with pain as I fight against the voice. I will the blade in my hand to stay put, to not move from its resting place.

My blood wills me to not give in.

We have all the time to correct that, Claire. All bends to our will.

"Mr. Walker, tell us what happened next! Stop fucking around!" the voices say together. "What did you see? What did you do?"

"Time froze. My world stopped," I whisper. Everyone in the restaurant stops moving. Kenny and Ralph stop moving. I stop moving. An invisible tomb of fear encases me. Zero movement is for the best.

It comes from the corner of the room. It swerves with a drunk, palsied gait. Its movements are sickening, unnerving; where it steps, it leaves a bloody footprint with pieces of flesh. A featureless pale face with bubbling rotting skin is attached to the neck like a mask. Countless foot-long fingers dangle from the torso, like leeches made of needles, eating away at what they are stabbed into. A coughing, high-pitched wheeze of laughter damn near shatters my eardrums.

The bloody creature sticks its deformed head high and sucks in the misty air. Then it lowers its head and sniffs the patrons in the restaurant. Though they cannot move, I can smell their terror. Their eyes tremble, their hearts almost rupture with each beat. The creature gives them a few sniffs before slithering away.

No, the creature isn't interested in them.

Its dead eyes, filled with leeches and pus, focus on my table. It vanishes in the red misty ocean around me, then blinks back into existence. It continues to blink in and out of reality as it moves toward us.

The creature sticks what seem like twenty or more razor-sharp fingers into Ralph's spine. Ralph lets out a loud, long, deathly gasp. The fingers go through the front of his chest. Then the creature moves its hands apart, splitting Ralph in half. Blood pours in all directions, hitting me.

"You killed all of them with that knife, didn't you? Ripped them apart, Mr. Walker," the three voices drill into my skull.

"No!" I yell. "It's not true! It's all just a big misunderstanding! It was a Pale Stranger!"

Pictures of four mutilated corpses are thrown in front of me.

"You killed Marco Cruz and Ferdinand Torres."

"What? I was waiting for them. I've never met them in person. They hadn't arrived when Ralph and Kenny showed up."

"That's because you killed them before killing Ralph West and Kenny Daniels. You used that steak knife you used to eat your steak. Cut them apart with it. What happened to their insides, Walker? You ate them, didn't you?"

I put my hands over my ears and shake my head. I can hear the crunching of bones and squishing of Ralph's ribcage and lungs as the creature eats them. Kenny stared at me the entire time, crying in fear. The creature still had Ralph's intestines in its mouth when it raised its head and smelled Kenny. A warped grin appeared on its fiendish face. Then it gave me the most venomous smile before resuming its meal.

So delicious. Would you like some, Claire?

"It was a Pale Stranger!"

"You were the only man at that table Walker. Everyone saw you do it."

"No! I didn't kill those men." I pick up the photos and show them to the three interrogators. "How could I have possibly made these wounds? How could I have ripped apart these men using just a steak knife?"

"You just did. Walking around with their blood on you, with that knife on you, like a drugged-out zombie, chanting and smelling people. You were trying to kill them when someone tackled you to the ground."

"But it wasn't me! I didn't kill them! I have papers! I had a music box! They explain everything!"

"You were there by yourself. There was nothing on the table except pieces of the people you killed."

My research, the music box and the rest of my stuff was taken by the Pale Stranger or the police threw them out. Regardless, my emotions sink into the deepest hole possible. All my evidence is gone.

There is no hope for me.

"It's getting late. You'll be formally charged in the morning for the murders of four people. Come on guys, we need to go find that missing cop." The men turn off the lights, leaving me blinded by sudden dark. They pick me up by my armpits and take me away. "Your entire story was funny, Mr. Walker, you might as well just plead guilty. But you know what else is funny? A year ago, you sat in this very chair, giving us a statement to put away a monster you chased. Look at you now; you've become a monster too. Ain't life grand?"

I begin to cry. In front of the police, I break down.

I'm not a monster. I am not.

Chapter Twenty-five

"Hi, you've reached Heather. I'm not here at the moment. Please leave me—" Before the machine can finish, I hang up. My ninth try in the past two and a half hours fails. The operator is sure to hate me if I try again in ten minutes, but I'm getting tired of being defeated. Either Heather is out or she really isn't accepting collect calls from a jail cell in the middle of the night.

Gordy's phone is disconnected. Greene wants nothing to do with me, other than to prosecute me and throw me in some prison hundreds of miles away.

I have no one to call for help. The money Gordy gave me is hidden in a rented coin locker near the airport terminal, but it's not like I can use it to buy the services of a good defense attorney. A public defender, burned out from years of serving or fresh off the boat, will be assigned to me. He will recommend I confess to avoid the death penalty. He will then say sorry we couldn't do better, so peace, fuck off and die, you miserable bastard, but he'll say it in the politest of ways.

Given the circumstances, I don't hate anyone for not believing me when I say a monster waltzed into Giallo and took a chunk out of four grown, capable men. A junkie with a steak knife gutting them and ripping them apart—in front of several patrons, no less, who did nothing but watch—was far more believable. Even if it was four grown, capable men, able to fight off an injured man with multiple wounds. Despite the bodies looking like they were ripped apart from the inside out, something no living person could do under normal circumstances.

Yeah, seems like an open and shut case for the state.

My cell is freezing. For once, I welcome the sweltering heat as opposed to my shivering loneliness. The bland, used-up yellow-grey stripes of my jumpsuit take away whatever optimism hides within. The smell of industrial bleach emanates from the metal toilet and sink. My bed is just a concrete slab two inches off the ground. I can't lay down. I sit with my arms pressed against my chest to keep my wounds from developing frostbite.

This is what Slowburn had endured while I laughed with the cops as I gave my statement just a few rooms away. This is what Paxton Chamber has to live with as he sits in a rotting prison cell. Not that it matters if he gets out. His release is not even my problem anymore.

Now I have the same mark of Cain he did.

The police put me far away from everyone else. With no one in the vicinity to talk to, all I have to do is decide if I want a needle, electricity, or rain of bullets for my going-out party.

"Claire," a whispering voice calls out. "Don't cry, Claire."

It sounds like the voice is all around my cell.

Unable to pinpoint the voice's origin, I sit very still, close my eyes, and ask, "Who's there?"

"Levitt Brower."

I open my eyes and smile, "Levitt! You're here!" I move to the grated cell door and jump onto it like a chimp looking for a tourist snack. Levitt isn't in the hallway or in the giant command area in the middle of my prison block. The one place he can be is in a cell. "Why are you here? Did you get arrested too? What cell are you in?"

"I'm in the cell next to you." Levitt's baritone voice is a welcome sound.

"Why you there?"

"I was around and…I fought to make sure you didn't get arrested. Didn't work out in your favor. Now I'm here with you. So don't cry, Claire."

"I'm just overjoyed to be able to talk to someone I know. Glad there ain't static between us." I press my head against the mesh door. "Tell me…was that a Pale Stranger that killed everyone, or was it me on a psychotic rampage?"

"No, that was a Pale Stranger. He killed those four men, not you."

I'm having a hard time wrapping my head around the concept of a Pale Stranger, and I say this to him.

"They are hunters of another sort," he says. "Think of them as a devolution between man and beast, but not man and beast. That's how the mind sees them."

I ask Levitt what he means.

"Most of what you see is but a glimpse of what they actually are. The human brain can't comprehend a Pale Stranger in its entirety. What one may look like to you looks different to someone else. It's the electrical signals of the mind, the rapid fire memories, getting cut and copied into a single image that is put in place of what it is really seeing. A captive gazelle knows what a lion is, despite have never seen the outside world of a zoo. Humans know what Pale Strangers are, just like they know what fire is."

We operate on ancient instinct. Our bodies produce these horrible images so that we can run. We are not supposed to fight. Even reading about them, like I did through Joe's research, produces the exact same dreadful sensation.

"Where do they come from?" I ask.

"A formless 'pocket dimension' here on Earth is one way of putting it. Like an ocean of a void. But that is just one way of rationalizing."

"What's the other?"

Levitt taps on the concrete, letting out a small echo. "Everywhere around you. There are Pale Strangers in this very room, swimming around, crawling around, floating around. They are around you right now."

I look around, unable to see anything but a dull jail cell. "I can't see anything."

"Trust me, they are there. Imagine that all around you is an invisible ocean. You are a tasty fish. A Pale Stranger is a hungry shark. But you live on the surface water. The shark lives in the deepest parts of the sea. What separates you from it are miles and miles of ocean. The ocean is more like a desert than anything else. Thousands of miles away, the shark feels your heartbeat, it smells your blood, it hears your voices and thoughts."

"But it has to swim to get to me?"

"Correct. But instead of water it has to swim through an infinite void to get to you. Then it has to break through the layers of 'reality' to enter. Then they have to create a form made out of carbon, out of the building blocks that make up life on Earth."

"Carbon? Life?"

"Life on Earth is carbon-based. The Pale Strangers are formless in their realm. They have to create a corporeal form when they come into the human realm, otherwise they cannot physically interact with you. They take whatever matter they find around them, take whatever *knowledge* they have, and create a form. Some are more monstrous, some are more humanoid, chosen for certain kinds of hunting. No matter what form they take using the knowledge they have of the planet, the human mind makes it a million times worse."

I ask why Levitt emphasized the word knowledge.

"Pale Strangers are primordial creatures who want just one thing: food. All life on Earth is food for them. Any knowledge they learn is done to get food."

"Then why hunt humans?"

"Humans are common and easy to hunt. Very rarely are other animals ever picked off. They can sense a Pale Stranger and flee before it can form. Modern humans are too boggled with life's problems and too disconnected from the world around them. Plus, humans taste better."

"So we are all targets?"

"Not exactly. It takes considerable effort and time for a Pale Stranger to find prey, let alone chase it. Under normal circumstances, they won't try unless they are sure they'll succeed in feeding on a meal. Look at the apex predators in the animal kingdom. They are killing engines that need massive amounts of fuel to run, and they expend just as much to hunt. Most are ambush hunters for this reason. The same could be said about a Pale Stranger. When they come into the world, they have a finite amount of time to hunt before expelling their corporeal form and returning to the void. Attacking and feeding uses up great amounts of energy."

The thought is as perplexing as it is fascinating. Pale Strangers are like any carnivore. If what Levitt says is true, then that means these creatures have been around before humanity walked the planet. How else could we instinctively know they exist?

They aren't animals with sharp teeth, Levitt warns me. Individual Pale Strangers in general are of equal strength. But when it comes to intelligence, there is a fine thread that splits them from one another. The majority are no smarter than a wolf. But there are some Pale Strangers that have spent so many years hunting and examining humans that they are not content with just feeding on people.

They have other agendas in mind.

Among these particular Pale Strangers are a select few that figured out how to bend the laws of physics and reality to their advantage. With this knowledge, they have done something that is not supposed to be possible. They have managed to stay in the human world beyond their corporeal forms' expiration date. And they have been able enter the world freely.

These caused the problems in Joe's research.

"Unfortunately for you," Levitt says, "they are the ones hunting you."

I sigh and rub my face. The painful realization there is no textbook, no seminar, on dealing with these things falls on me all at once. At a loss, I ask Levitt to tell me about the Pale Strangers he encountered in Afghanistan.

"The ape picked off those who weren't stopped by the sand god. I don't remember if the ape was killed; if he wasn't, he's still roaming the mountains of Afghanistan. He might still even be chasing after Rankin, for all the things the marine did to piss him off. As for the sand god, the United States military is to thank for its destruction. Scorched the entire mountain that contained its lair. There is nothing in this world or the next that would have survived that bombardment of mechanized death."

"They can be killed?"

"Yes. Their corporeal forms make them vulnerable. But there is always a price to be paid for killing one."

"What do you mean?"

"How much are you willing to sacrifice to slay one, when there are others to deal with? What is your humanity worth?"

I clinch my fists and stare at them. Levitt's words floor me. My shoulder slides down and gravity takes me along. I sit on the ground and curl into a ball. I have no answer.

Tears would flow if I weren't so damn tired.

"Hush, Claire. Don't cry. No need for that," Levitt whispers. "Let me tell you a story. Once upon a time, there was a demon that roamed the lands of ancient China. For untold centuries, it roamed around China's vast deserts, terrorizing and devouring whomever it came upon. Generations told tales of this demon. Generations feared the wandering sandstorms, for fear that the demon lurked within to carry them underneath the dunes."

An army of holy men marched throughout the deserts in hopes of finding the demon and killing it. For a hundred years, they tried. For a hundred years, they searched. Then they found it.

Half the army was destroyed fighting the demon. The demon was defeated, but it did not die. The holy men had neither the technology nor the abilities to kill the beast. For the demon would just come back years later and resume its slaughter.

So the holy men did the only thing they could.

First, they performed a special binding ceremony using the flesh and blood of the demon and securing it to a giant prison. It wasn't an ordinary prison, but one that took almost a hundred years to make, and was made of special metals. Everything was kept together with ancient, long forgotten forms of alchemy; the kinds that could change human history if ever rediscovered. And they used holy sigils that would to keep the creature's maddening influence at bay.

When everything was in order, the surviving army marched out of China, into lands unknown and untold, and carried the prison of the demon far away.

It was a one-way trip. They would stop when the last man died. And they accepted their fate, knowing that their sacrifice was necessary.

For years, they traveled, searching for the best place to house the prison. Yet they wandered in aimless directions. The seals protecting the prison broke rather early in the journey. The demon could have killed them if it wanted, could have eaten its fill, but chose to let them destroy one another. Its mad whispering drove the weakest holy men to murder and suicide.

The remaining holy men had no choice but to find the prison a home. They stopped somewhere in Afghanistan, and chose a large mountain with multiple caves. They built shrines and figures based on their Buddhist beliefs. The prison was placed inside a hidden antechamber made of special metals and forgotten arts.

The last remaining holy men sealed themselves in, and stood guard. They all died of starvation. With no one left to watch over the demon, only a cloudy mirrored door stood between it and the world of man.

In time, the demon would later become a sand god.

"For millennia, it remained in that mountain," Levitt says. "Unable to escape, or perhaps unwilling to return home, it extended its reach. The mountain itself became its nest, then its womb. Its body grew; its presence extended across miles of underground caverns. When hungry, it would devour the land itself, aging the surroundings as it sucked out all the matter on a molecular level. That's the reason why the land itself turned into brittle sand."

"But I thought Pale Strangers had to eat living matter?" I ask as I rub the sweat pouring down my face. My nose runs; I become short of breath.

"Only as a last option will they eat the surrounding world, otherwise they start eating themselves; they can die if that happens. The sand god was waiting for an opportune moment. One hundred twenty years ago, the Amir of Afghanistan wanted to build a palace near the mountain where the sand god lived."

My stomach cramps. I become nauseous and sleepy as my neck tenses and itches.

"The tribe assigned to building the palace fell underneath the sand god's sway. I don't remember which tribe they belonged to, but I'm sure they all taste the same way. Lost forever. The lost."

I throw up.

"The sand god was smart enough to let them keep certain higher functions going instead of just frying their brains and turning them mindless. The lost's primary function was to go around and bring people to feed the sand god. It had grown so large it needed a personal army to keep it fed. Otherwise, it would start eating itself. Their most popular way of doing this is through international human trafficking. Illegals are under the impression they will be smuggled around, only to find out too late they are going to be fed to a giant Pale Stranger."

I lay on my back, unable to move from a sudden paralyzing pain.

"The lost lived not too far away from the mountain and from the ruined, unfinished palace. Benson's archeological team uncovered the ruins, bringing the attention of the lost on them. So they attacked us. The marines fought them off a few times. But they weren't a match for the roaming Pale Strangers who were attracted to the mountain the sand god was in. That ape you read about. It was just but one they encountered."

I grip my stomach and feel my insides are liquefying. I feel my immune system attempting to purge whatever invisible virus has invaded me. I fight to speak, but the pain is too much. Yelps come out instead.

"Pale Strangers are attracted to the presence of other Pale Strangers, especially large ones like the sand god. Food is on their mind, and food is what they want. They are opportunists by design. Many go years between a kill. Such a delicious opportunity…just can't pass it up. For the ape, well, it was a bounty for him. All those archeologists, all those lost. I'm sure there were others who attacked the marines. I was too busy to notice."

"Levitt…can you hear me?" I mouth but can't say.

"I can hear you just fine, Claire."

"What is happening to me?"

"Why, you're being indoctrinated. Your body is acting out the information it is receiving. But you're resisting."

But I'm not resisting. I don't know how to resist.

"Your conscious mind is unaware, but your body is fighting with all its might. You've been seeing things because you didn't resist.

Then why am I resisting?

"Because the more you get indoctrinated, the more you lose yourself. Your body is trying to keep control of itself, and to reject the forceful intrusion. Indoctrination is really a Pale Stranger's way of influencing and breaking a person to see what it wants it to see, or do what it wants it to do. This is what happened with the Lost Tribe in Afghanistan. Hundreds of people enslaved with an overload of information. If the Pale Stranger was so inclined, it could make the person's body flail around with an influx overload, turn them into a lost human, make them no different than a puppet. But, really, that all depends on the mood and intentions of the Pale Stranger at work."

The cuts on my arms rupture. Horror shakes me as my blood defies gravity and streams up the wall, through tiny cracks like a waterfall in reverse. Loud slurping, crunching comes from all directions. Pieces of my skin begin to fall off and climb up the waterfall made of my blood. My muscles, my veins begin to pull upward.

The ceiling cracks and falls on me.

A human eye pokes out and stares down.

So delicious. Feed me more. Give me more. Would you kindly?

Gravity fails all around. I begin to levitate off the ground. I am powerless to do anything but let it happen.

Chapter Twenty-six

Water goes into my nose and mouth. Half my face is submerged. It feels like I have either tripped or taken a hard punch to the face, blacking out for a few seconds before waking up. I pull my head from the water. Deep inside my skull, my brain throbs. I sit in the knee-deep water and hold my head in an attempt to relieve the greater pain with lesser.

I'm at the bottom of a damp, dimly lit staircase made of white-yellowish stone. I wobble when I stand and fumble when I walk. A whiff of decayed and dying meat floods at me from all sides, despite there being no signs of death around. My eyes have trouble adjusting, so I grip the wall and hold on.

Where am I?

Moving my hand around, I notice that, behind me, is a large wooden door. I grab the handle and pull. The door won't open. It's locked. My shoulder leans into the wall as I return to holding my throbbing head. Something metal clanks against the wall. I take a moment to first examine myself, using the water under my feet as a mirror.

I am dressed in dirty black and yellow regal attire. My hands are wrinkly and thin. My hunchback keeps me from correcting my posture. I have a long, thinning gray beard with a streak of black running on the side. I am bald, with just a few strands of hair. My face is more skeletal than human.

Who am I this time?

Am I still alive? Is this a dream? Is this a reliving nightmare?

I reach deep into the pockets. A set of keys is in there. When I pull, I feel the keys weigh on my bony fingers. I lack the strength to balance them into the keyhole without shaking.

The door opens with a creak.

Inside is a large room filled with torture devices. Torches illuminate everything. Iron maidens, wheels to break upon, lathes, racks, and spiked chairs. Countless others I recognize from the history books on tyrants and zealots. All rusted from blood and age.

"Please, my lord," a weak whisper echoes in the room. To the side I see a brazen bull with a fire pit underneath it. The bloodied fingers of a man inside the bull poke from a metal grate just above the door. "Spare me. It wasn't my fault. I didn't do anything."

"It was your fault; it was your fault," I repeat as I grab one of the torches. I go over to the bull and light the firepit. He screams and screams, but I shush him. "If it wasn't your fault, you wouldn't be here."

It doesn't take long for the bull to glow orange. The man's screams grow higher and higher, the scent of burning flesh, his last moments in absolute agony, make me smile with delight. I savor his dying wail with a lick of the lips.

Am I really capable of such cruelty? Do I really have this bloodlust?

But I'm reminded that this isn't the smell I came for. This is not who I'm looking for.

Another door is in the corner of the room. I slowly make my way to it to find that it's locked, just like the first. I unlock it.

A spiral staircase descends, with a gaping hole in the center, to a seemingly endless bottom. I am free to fall for an eternity if I take one step too far. Cells are embedded into the walls, each with a sliding iron door. Thousands spiral down the never-ending staircase.

The moaning of prisoners doesn't unnerve me. Their bleeding cries do not move me. They are all here for a reason. I have no sympathies for them.

Where do I end and where does he begin?

A soothing song calls out to me. A lullaby to close my eyes, to make me sleep; I haven't slept in months. A hymn dedicated to me.

I hobble down the staircase, slow step by slow step. My hand uses the wall as a guide, I put weight on my hand as the fear of falling tries to freeze me solid.

But the singing becomes more pronounced. I have to get to its origin. The siren's call beckons me. Like an insect to a flytrap, she wants me.

I come upon a cell partway down the staircase. It is much longer and larger than the others; it can be broken up into four. The cell is decorated with rich, aristocratic furniture. A comfortable mattress is in one corner, a bronze tub in the other. Drawers are stuffed to the brim with fancy clothes. Yellow silk sheets cover the cell walls; a chair stands between the sheets.

On the seat is the countess.

Her skin is a sickly, wrinkly green; her white hair has streaks of brown. Her purple and blue robes are muddied and bloodied around the folds. Her makeup is thick and misplaced, making her look more like a prepared corpse than a woman.

She moves her head around, her eyes closed, and continues her singing.

"My love," I say to her, "what are the creatures outside the castle? Why are they trying to get in?" The countess stops singing, but keeps swaying her head around, her eyes still shut. "Please! I need to know my love!"

She does not speak.

I rattle her cage doors. I demand, I plead, yet she speaks silence.

"My wife? What is going on?"

She stands up from her chair and slowly walks to me.

"Have you given me a kingdom yet?" she asks in a dead voice. "Have you become a king and freed me from my bonds?"

I stutter, "No, my love, I will one day. Your dream is my dream."

"You promised me. You promise every day that you will give me a kingdom, but you haven't become king. Don't you love me anymore?"

"I do, I do love you." I fall to my knees and reach out my hand. She stops her walk and looks around. "I will give you a kingdom, I swear it."

"The kingdom can wait for now. But you need to prove you love me, my count."

I grovel. "Name your price, my love, what is it you desire?"

"Kill them. Kill them all for me. Feed me."

"What? Who?"

A stream of glassy black oil flows through her closed eyes, cutting through her eyelids.

"Our servants. Feed me. Before they break in, feed me."

I do not understand her request. Kill my servants? Feed her?

My wife holds out her hands and resumes her march toward me.

My body aches with immense pain the closer she gets. I retract my hands and move away from her clasping, lunging hands.

That's when I notice. Marionette strings, umbilical cords of flesh are attached to her back, connecting her to the wall slit. The silk sheets covering the walls begin to move. Something large and long slithers behind it. Hands, faces press against the silk. Something red bleeds through, turning the yellow silk orange and then black. I become ill from her rancid smell; she is the origin of the repulsive scent.

The strings of flesh pull her back. She tugs at them as she lunges closer and closer. Her lips move, but she does not speak in a normal voice. The voice comes at me from all directions, but is not carried on the air. My senses feel an assault by a sound not here in the cell, not there outside it, but here around me. Not male, not female, emotionless, passionate, dull, enthralling. It takes hours in seconds for one syllable, one word to pass over the other, with no breaks in between.

Kill them in my name. Feed me your servants. Do it my love.

She is no longer my wife.

I tumble down the staircase. One of the cells is open. The urge to go in is quickly denied when I see a pool of thick juice oozing from the stone walls. Out of the juice a skinless hand and head reach out for me.

"Help me..." the gurgling voice wails. The muscles burn and snap, the blood vessels pop, and the bones break away. Part of the wall cracks. A long tongue made of tissue, teeth, and limbs creeps out of the crack and wraps around the dying person. It pulls the person into the dissolving fluid.

"They won't feed us much longer. Dead and dying prisoners no longer feed us. I need more," the countess whispers into my ear from her cell hundreds of steps away. "Help me, my love. Kill your beloved servants. Kill them before the Ghost and his mist break through."

With a flicker of her hand, the door keeping her in flings off into the dark, crashing somewhere far away. She lurches out of her cell, the umbilical cords dangling from her back and slithering around like headless snakes.

"Stay away from me!" I yell.

"But I love you. Come here, my husband. Let me kiss you."

I run away from her as fast as I can with my beaten legs. She strolls down, making no attempt to run after me. There is only one way away: down the dark, spiraling staircase.

When I do reach the bottom of the staircase, I find my surroundings filled with the thick ooze I encountered in the cell. The stone underneath me gives way, and I fall backward. Tiny hairs pop out of the cracks, and as my legs touch them, fluid bleeds from the cracks. The stone sizzles and dissolve from just touching the liquid. Underneath this dissolving liquid are muscle and skin, veins and bone, melding with one another and moving together like a single animal.

In the corner is a giant malformed heart, with several face-shaped hearts like tumors, all beating at different paces.

A spot on the giant heart begins to bulge. The layers around the bump tear apart, spilling out a hundred teeth like eyes. All of them stare, following every inch of my movements.

The heart screeches like a banshee. My body is crushed by the sound, sending me to my knees and making me cover my ears to keep out the terrible sound.

From behind the heart, the countess walks on the liquid surface. The screeching stops.

"You can join me. You can join us. We can build a new kingdom together. We can be together forever," she says. "But if you don't hurry, he will come to take us away. He comes with his insatiable hunger. He comes to hunt us."

The rush of images, this infection from someone else's past, fills my eyes. I can feel my memories getting overridden, erased, and replaced.

My brain is not my own, my body is not my own. All is against my will.

"My Lord, why are you doing this?" a servant asks as I strike him down with a ceremonial sword. The other servants flee as my guards chase them down the castle. There is no point. They delay the inevitable.

I am doing it to spare you a fate worse than death.

"Please don't kill me! I have a son!" a girl screams as I stab her with a sharp screwdriver over and over. I take no pleasure in this.

I'm sorry. I have to do this. I need to feed her. Then I can sleep.

"Father, come with us! Why must you leave us?" My children and my wife hold me tight as I try to push them away.

I'm sacrificing myself. He is only after me.

"Here is your gift. Happy Birthday, Mr. Renton," she tells me in front of the poppies.

Thank you for this beautiful gift. You have such a beautiful dance, Miss Finley.

None of these thoughts are my own; they belong to others.

But now they are mine.

And so I say good-bye to my old memories.

Cold concrete and warm blood splatter against my skull as I drop to the floor. My body withers with tremors. The lights in my cell start to flicker. Electrical components all around explode. The hazy visions become just a haze of my perception. Everything is frozen in time; everything is stripped of color. My senses are numb. I am dying of shock.

A tall, thin Pale Stranger stands over me. A blurry cloud of foggy smoke, like ice vapors, surrounds him. I have seen him countless times before, across the same fears in different minds, different eras. He haunts my dreams and my waking days. He has made his presence known at least four times that I know of.

And he is here now, ready to feed on me.

You are but a puppet. My puppet.

I'm not a puppet.

Yes you are. That is why I saved you now. He went too far. I am sorry, my puppet. He is still learning.

Why did you save me? I thought Pale Strangers prey on us?

There are things you have to do for me.

What do I have to do?

Kill for me Claire. Kill in my name. Kill before it is too late. Kill before the seed she is trying to plant grows into a tree you cannot kill. There can be no other like us. She is unworthy.

A sea of jailers comes rushing into my cell. They move my body, but I have no sensation. Their lips move, but I can't hear what they say. They shine a light in my eyes, burning away the nonworking receptors.

They don't see the Pale Stranger standing over me, and they don't notice when it leaves.

A few minutes later, the paramedics arrive.

They are trying to keep me alive, awake, conscious. They snap their fingers at me, trying to get my attention, trying to get me to respond. I don't hear it, can't hear anything but my slowing heartbeat. So I help them the best I can.

"I'm me again," I whisper to the paramedics. "Not the count, not Darius, not Johan, Joseph. Just me. I'm Claire Walker. I am Claire Walker, right?"

The paramedic nods and speaks to me despite not knowing I can't hear him.

They load me onto the stretcher and move me. We pass by the cell Levitt was in. Inside is a half-eaten, half-digested corpse. Blood and pieces of body matter have been pulled up the wall, into the broken ceiling with the massive hole. The police examine the body and seal off the area as we pass.

So I wheeze a yelping laugh. I point at the body and ask the paramedics, the police, the prisoners, anyone who will listen, "How you gonna blame me for that?"

Before I blackout I see him, that wicked Pale Stranger who haunts me, one last time. He waves at me. He calls me friend. And then I sleep...

Chapter Twenty-seven

My hospital bed is uncomfortable. Damn, I hate hospitals. I miss my own bed so much. For the better part of almost three weeks, this bed has been my home. It's a terrible home. The only time I sleep is in-between death and revival. Four times I died from shock and exsanguination. Four times they brought me back to life.

Unfashionable scars slither across my forearms. Chicks won't dig these wounds. The hospital staff has a hard looking at my wounds despite them not being overwhelmingly ugly. They just have that mark to them. A mark of something otherworldly.

The blood knows what caused it. That scent passes from me to them.

Unlike them, I can't escape my skin. I'm stuck with this trauma.

The clock reads 11:00 p.m., and there is nothing else to do. Well, besides watch the Pale Stranger try to enter my room and eat me. Always at the same time too, like clockwork.

First the broken TV in the corner of my room shows static. The little bleeping noises used to terrify me into getting the nurses to sedate me. Now it's just annoying. There isn't much I can do to block or avoid this. I'm shackled to the bed. As soon as I recover, they are slapping the handcuffs on. Murder with a five count is the case they gave me.

Either the state is going to fry me, or this Pale Stranger is having me for a snack.

How lovely.

I lay my head on the pillow. This is how Joe must have felt before he butchered himself just to end his misery. I have none of that strength. I'm too weak to do anything but pray the creature won't find me.

Just for one more night.

I can hear voices now. Small but constant requests call out to me.

Help me find you. I can be your friend. You need a friend right now, don't you?

The Pale Stranger gets better about it. Last week it called me "food" and "dinner." Its voice last week was like a record playing backward against needles. Now the voice is so soft, indistinguishable from male or female.

A chill cools my blood; this I cannot fight. I know what's coming.

The TV turns on and flickers. The channels rapidly run through at random. Distorted images of people and events make a disturbing collage of entertainment chaos. I can feel the images flow into me. I am a receiver for everything.

Pictures of war, famine, terror, anxiety, that's what comes into my skull. My head starts to hurt, as always. Finally the TV stops showing random stuff and goes grey. After a minute, the gray lifts. I'm now staring at a video of myself in the room. Somehow the TV is recording me and showing me back to myself. Then it flickers on and off, showing me the entire room. Then it flashes again, and my eyes dilate when it shows me again.

A black spot is coming out of the wall just behind me.

Haven't seen or experienced this before.

I look behind me, but there is nothing there. I look back at the TV. The growth gets bigger. I see a hand shoot out of the black residue. The goop grips the hand, giving it a second skin of sorts. I can hear animals or things cry out for me. I keep looking up but find nothing.

Soon, another hand pops out, using the wall to pull itself out. It has a split-open head and falls to the sides of its shoulders. I can see its eyes rolling around like spinning spheres. The goop sticks to the split head. Like glue, it starts pulling the head together to form a complete head. Disgusting, screeching bat creatures fly out of its mouth. It pulls itself out with only half a torso; the bottom half has been ripped off by something.

I hear a loud thud when it falls, but nothing is there. I can hear it moan; I can hear it crawl. On the TV, I see it crawl on the floor. Its broken nails scratch against the tile, leaving little indentations. That I see.

Pressing the nurse's button won't work. The nurses cut the power to the buzzer during the first week, after I kept ringing it every time a Pale Stranger tried coming into my room. I do not scream. The creature looks like it is blind. Sniffing around, it searches for me. As long as it cannot see me, I'll be fine.

The monster grabs onto the bed. I can feel it move the bed as it struggles to climb.

It makes it onto my bed. I can feel it moving around my legs.

I keep absolutely silent and still, hoping it will ignore me or lose my scent. It looks at me and smiles, but I cannot see the smile; the TV shows me. These bats hover around its mouth, sniffing along with it, fighting with one another, ripping through the Pale Stranger's face. Its head splits open again, like one giant mouth, with the bats making up endless rows of teeth. Each bat has a voice; a million voices must be speaking at once.

Where are you?

The Pale Stranger howls before falling off the bed. The TV turns off.

My heart and my breathing defy my best attempts at self-control. I can hear it panting, sniffing. I look around but see nothing, yet I know it's there. My blood knows.

Then I stare straight ahead.

A man is standing at the edge of my bed. I can't see his face in the dark of the room. His hands clasp around my face.

"It's here with us," he says with a hush. "Trying to lull, trick us. Clever girl."

I bite my tongue. He removes one hand, reaches around his back, and pulls out a box cutter. Then he lets go of my mouth.

"Who are you?" I whisper.

The blade pops out, and he puts it near my neck. "For what I liked to do to homeless people, you gave me a really lovely nickname. Don't you recognize me, old buddy? Go on. Say my nickname. Say my fucking nickname!"

"Slowburn."

Paxton Chambers puts his face right next to mine, just close enough so I can see him smiling. "I never got a chance to tell you how much I fucking hated getting tackled and held down while the cops beat my ass. How much I hated being a bitch in prison. I have you to thank for that. But it's okay."

The sound of the Pale Stranger shuffling around is not lost on my ears. It moves one of the chairs despite being invisible and physically formless.

"Go ahead, get it over with. You deserve your revenge. I won't fight back."

Paxton shakes his head. "No, you can't die. I need you. We are in this together." The box cutter slices my straps off. "We have a common enemy."

"What?" He helps me up to my surprise, horror, and disbelief. I buckle under my own weight, but Paxton catches me before I hit the ground. It's been almost three weeks since I last walked. Muscles have probably atrophied in parts of my legs. Paxton reaches into his pants. He pulls out a hypodermic needle.

The needle jams into my thigh. I let out a yelp as Paxton puts my arm over his shoulder. I'm awakened by the shot and able to move my numb legs just a bit. The cold sensation batters against my feet, and I dance around to warm them up.

"Gave you an adrenaline and cocktail shot. Walk, don't run. Not like you can run anyway." Paxton helps me walk out the room. The invisible Pale Stranger starts thrashing around, knocking things over. Paxton quietly shuts the door. "Most Chasers can't open doors. If we are lucky, that Chaser will warp into its realm. Can't get out of the room otherwise."

Across the hall is an open door. Inside the room is an old man with flat-lining vitals. No one comes to check on him. I try to hobble over to him, but Paxton stops me.

"They look like caterpillars to me. Poisonous caterpillars who will turn into twisted butterflies. What do they look like to you?"

Before I can answer his strange question I see for myself. Underneath his bed, I see six dismembered heads with glowing eyes. Some have spider's legs propping them up, while others had centipede-like undersides. They are whispering to one another but stop when they notice me staring at them.

They shoot me a grin in unison.

One climbs onto the bed, stabs its spider legs into the old man's neck, and yanks off his head with one clean stroke. The head rolls off the bed, spilling blood everywhere. Five of the monster heads swarm the decapitated head and take it underneath the bed, back into the darkest part of the bed. Loud chomping sounds follow squirting blood and falling brain matter. They feast on the head. The head severer joins them, and a fight ensues.

At that moment, the sole one of them not to take part in the festivities crawls up the bed with octopus-like tentacles. It examines the body, opens the neck wound, and stabs deep inside. The head twists and turns, with its tentacles disappearing, or rather connecting, to the wound. The octopus head fuses itself onto the neck of the dead old man.

The old man's body twitches. His hands move. The flat-lining stops, instead giving stable vitals. The old man's body rises from the bed. The creature turns its head to me and smiles.

Hello humans.

"Jesus Christ!" I yell.

Paxton closes the door and says, "This isn't the first time I've seen this, sadly."

"Not the first?"

He grabs me by my arm and we start walking. "Probably his time, otherwise they wouldn't have done it. Easier to fool us. Staff won't know for a couple weeks or so at most. They'll just pretend to be him. Nothing we can do about it."

Paxton tells me in whispers to walk slowly from here on out. We sneak across the hospital, past the receptionists, the cops, and the patients. People let us walk by. They can't see us, he claims. Or rather, they just ignore us.

Their blood knows we are cursed. They pretend we don't exist.

"Why are you helping me?"

"We have the same enemy." I ask who that might be. "The Chasers. Darius Renton. Can't do this alone. Need your help, Walker."

"To do what?"

"Kill as many of them as possible. Then kill Darius. He's doing something very bad. Something that goes against us humans. But before that, we have to take shelter. We have to eat. You haven't had a good meal in a while, no? I'll explain everything. Oh yeah, one more thing. Did you not notice?"

Slung over Paxton's other shoulder is my backpack. He stops so I can look into it. Everything I had with me, like the files and the music box, when I went to Giallo is still in there. The words of my interrogator pull me back to that day at the restaurant.

"You took the bag?"

Paxton nods.

"Then you were there at Giallo? You saw what happened?"

Paxton nods again. "Well, I wasn't following you at first when I got released from prison. Things happened for and against my favor. Darius Renton got me out. At first I was indebted to him. Now I need him dead."

Chapter Twenty-eight

Picking at steamed green beans, fried chicken, and cold mash potatoes in a cafeteria was not how I imagined spending my evening. At least it has AC.

My apartment was sealed off by the police several weeks ago; there is no way I'm getting in. My stuff is sealed off or in police lockup.

But Paxton was kind enough to lend me some of his wardrobe. Most of his clothes are too big, but I find some that fit me just fine: a gray polo shirt, a hooded green jacket, blue jeans, and sneakers.

Irony is a powerful thing not lost on me. Paxton is eating side by side with the homeless people he once preyed upon. Yet the ones he hunted and burned are ignorant of the hunter in the mist. Then again, I hardly recognize him.

He has a large widow's peak now, with dark brown hair instead of his original light brown. His facial features are sharper from weight loss. A long scar runs down his forehead. He packed on a few pounds of muscle during his short time in jail. No wonder the clothes don't fit.

I don't know if he derives some sick, twisted pleasure from eating next to a possible victim or the loved one of a former victim. But seeing him there eating, with a grin on his face, is disgusting. And no one recognizes him but me.

"You want to know why I did it?" Paxton asks.

"Not really," I say. "This isn't the best place to talk about that."

"I grew up with a privileged life. Went to the best schools, hung out with the best people. That is public record. You wrote about that. But you never knew why. No one knows why. So I'll tell you, since we are friends." Paxton leans over the table to me. "I wanted to see the burning flesh of the lower class." A shiver shoots up my spine. He points to the people at our sides. "Watching their flesh melt and boil under the torch's searing blue flame was so exhilarating. They are lesser than me. And I wanted to show them my power and dominion over them by burning them with a reminder."

I lean into him and whisper, "Bro, shut the fuck up. I don't need your lecture."

"I never thanked you for christening me Slowburn. I find it so appropriate. I like to watch things burn slowly. Still do. Thank you."

"Don't. You're sick and insane."

"Me? The one who saved you? The one who made your career? Thank me."

"Listen, Chambers, just because you saved me doesn't change what happened between us. You almost burned a little girl alive. You immolated countless innocent people. Ruined their lives. And for what? To prove you're better than them because they weren't as well off as you? You're not a superman; not of a master race. You're just a punk with a torch and a fetish. All you ever accomplished was leaving some families to grieve, and a community to fear."

Paxton rubs his face, shakes his head. "Can you even name any of them?"

"Of course I can..."

Minutes pass. I remain silent. My mouth moves, but I say nothing. My fingernails dig deep into the table as I try my damndest to say something.

More of my memories are lost in a sea of others' past lives. I can't think of any of their names or even remember what they look like. So I don't speak.

Paxton nods his head. "We have the same problem."

I shove my food to the side. "Don't compare mine with yours. You wouldn't understand. If you saw what I saw, you'd be as fucked up as me."

"I'm sure I will in time. But what I do know is the Chasers did this to us."

"Why do you call them Chasers? They are called Pale Strangers."

He rubs his chin. "Darius called them angels when we shared a cell."

"You still haven't told me how you and he got involved."

Darius had been arrested and brought in for questioning several hours before I captured Paxton. They were in opposite interrogating rooms, and they shared a cell for a time. Had what went down happened on any other day, we wouldn't be in this mess; someone else would.

"As you said, Walker," Paxton says, finishing his plate and eating what leftovers I didn't finish. "I should never have gotten out. They wanted to give me life without parole. Not that I blame them."

Paxton never cut a deal. He never admitted to anything. He kept his mouth shut—a rather smart thing to do. He was let go by a rather hilarious failure of the system.

First, his trial date kept getting pushed back over and over, because of problems involving the jury selection. Then came problems with judges. Strange, quirky events happened. People went missing, got arrested, got deathly ill. Odd things just kept happening.

"You remember the water main that busted and flooded the downtown two months back?"

"Vaguely…wait…" I point at Paxton when I remember my conversation with Greene.

"Main broke underneath the courthouse: specifically underneath the evidence room. The city kept it very quiet. They thought they could recover the evidence. Most of it they did…except for mine. The stuff I was caught with. Well, it got washed away."

"But the little girl was a witness. I am a witness…" I snap my fingers, trying to rattle my brain for bits of my past life. "There was a car accident, wasn't there?"

Paxton nods again. "Yes, sir. Landed right in the courthouse. Killed everyone in the witness waiting area for several cases. Including the little girl who was to testify against me. Rather tragic. A little loophole in state law allowed me to be granted a reprieve from my jail stay while the DA attempted to rebuild its case against me. Just like with Darius Renton."

"Those are some insane coincidences." I pause, nod. "But it wasn't, was it?"

"Nope. It was all because of Darius Renton. I was able to escape from my prison with his help. Left one prison only to enter another prison of a different kind."

"How was he responsible for all of it?"

"Well, he wasn't. A hatchet and a screwdriver were behind it all. They both were blessed with her blood. With them around, she could manipulate things to a certain degree. She could whisper sweet nothings in the ears of people to influence them; put everyone right where she wanted. She was the goblin in the machine, so to speak. Both items he recovered after the evidence against him was swept away. She told him where to find them so he could continue his services to her on the outside."

"A hatchet? I didn't see anything about a hatchet in his file."

"There were many things not in the file. Darius confessed when we were together that he didn't kill Dotty Finley. He would have gotten away with her murder…if Greene hadn't withheld evidence."

"What kind of evidence?"

"The kind that proves he was innocent. The hatchet and the screwdriver were two of the things that proved Darius didn't kill her, so I know Greene was happy when they were lost. But as for the other evidence, well…" Paxton stops me from asking anymore questions about the case. Darius didn't go further into the details.

Darius confessed to Paxton when they shared a cell that his angel was the girl he was accused of murdering. She wasn't dead. She had "ascended."

She went to go dance with angels. And she would return and save him.

This interested Paxton at the time, before he knew what an "angel" was.

"I asked if his angel could really save both of us," Paxton says. "Darius promised me she would. Every night, he prayed; every night, she spoke to him. Darius said that he felt a kind of brotherhood with me. Dotty had confirmed our bond, which was the price of flesh."

Darius said he would help Paxton escape provided Paxton aid him in his "divine work" after he was freed from the shackles of the penal system. Paxton agreed.

"And you believed him?" I ask.

"Of course not. I mean, I'm not stupid. He was clearly insane. Because really, it would take a series of strange, impossible events to get me out of the mess I was in. But I figured it wouldn't hurt my chances to agree with the madman. After our agreement, Darius got out on bail, and left without another peep to me. I didn't think anything of it. Well, prison life made me forget. Had more pressing matters to worry about."

Then the strange coincidences began happening. The impossible events came true. Fate became dictated by invisible, divine hands.

Just like Darius promised they would.

I find Paxton's story funny, so I ask, "Why do you want to kill Darius?"

"I went to Vin Forest in Jaune to meet him. He said I would see the glory of his angel for myself. Took me to the abandoned water processing plant where she was murdered. On the way there, we talked about you. We both hated you, since you wronged us. After I helped him, we both could get our revenge against you. How could I say no to that?"

I don't tell Paxton that right now, with each blink, my reality is being replaced with another. The cafeteria, the people…even I am vanishing. I'm now seeing what both he and Darius saw, with clarity and with horror.

Paxton went into the room where Dotty was murdered. There Darius had drawn a circle on the floor, a circle made up of words forming an eye. In the corner of the room was a young woman, naked and bound. She begged Darius to not harm her, to just let her go and she wouldn't tell anyone.

"I'm sorry," I say invoking Darius's voice, "she needs her sacrifice. I need to sleep. Please let me sleep, salaam." I see the sharpened screwdriver, my hand clenches the imaginary device, and I see Darius's arm graph itself over mine.

Even closing my eyes, I still see Darius stab the girl a hundred times. Her screams became distorted as the blade pierced different parts of her lungs. She didn't die quickly; her body twitched and wheezed from the different holes where Darius stabbed her. It took her almost ten minutes for her life to retreat from her body.

Then Darius used a rusted hatchet to chop the dead girl's body into pieces. Paxton watched, excited and scared all at once. But his excitement disappeared when Darius put the corpse pieces near the pipe underneath the shrine.

A pale, liquid-like hand reached through the pipe. It coiled, bit, and sucked on the pieces. Then it dragged the pieces into the pipe despite being too big. The bones snapped in half and slid easily after.

I'm happy. So happy. So carefree.

The words shook Paxton. His body started to turn on him; he was in flight mode and didn't realize it. He cried out in repulsion.

"My God, what have you done?" I say in Paxton's disgusted voice.

"You deny her?" I say in Darius's demented voice. I hold my face as both voices fight one another. Darius came after Paxton with the screwdriver. But Darius was not as strong as Paxton. Paxton had learned how to defend himself while in prison; he had strengthened himself. Paxton easily overpowered Darius.

Paxton ran for his life. She began to chase after him. For hours, he ran through the forest, hunted by her. She called out to him, pleading for him to come back. All would be forgiven if Paxton would stop running.

But he escaped.

For the first time in Paxton's life, he felt regret. He felt immense sorrow for inflicting harm on his fellow man, regardless of how low they were. His fellow man should have never been his enemy. All along, he should have never been torching humanity.

This angel, now a Chaser, was the real enemy.

His blood knew this. His blood told him so.

Slowburn dedicated himself to at least understanding his enemy. When he knew enough, he would take the fight to them, so he could set them ablaze. That's why he needs me.

Sharp pain in my ears and my head brings me away from the memories, brings me back to reality. I can feel my nose and one of my eyes bleed.

Paxton holds his mouth and examines my face. He says, "So this is indoctrination…"

I let the blood run from my face and splash against the table. Depression runs over me as I see myself bleed. No one is paying attention, except Paxton Chambers. They can't see me, or they are just ignoring me.

Just like Levitt said.

"What were you doing at Giallo?"

"Darius had followed you there. He was after you, since you raided his shrine, but he couldn't get to you. He said something about you being protected or something while you were in your apartment. After our little incident I tried to chase him down, but had no luck. When I did pick up his trail again, he was hanging around Giallo. I assume you weren't protected by your apartment anymore, otherwise he wouldn't have come out in public. He would have killed you when you left. But he ran off. Well, more like he was chased off."

"By what?"

Paxton shakes his head, "I didn't see. A tall, pale man." Paxton rubs his eyes. "I don't remember him that well. He was too blurry, too impossible to get a good glimpse of. I walked in to see if you were alive and I found…well, you know."

Paxton was going to hightail it out of there, content with letting me rot in a cell like he had, until he noticed my backpack. The papers and music box seemed important. Whatever important information I had could help him in his task of killing Darius and his angel.

After discovering a fraction of what I knew, he decided to spring me. Two are better than one, after all.

As I wipe away the blood from my face, I can see the red cloudy smoke coming off everyone. At first the bodies turn into organic clockwork. Seeing the human body at work makes it hard to look at them. The red mist coming off them enters my nose. I try not to breathe, lest I take in their emotions, thoughts and memories.

But then the people start to transform into blank figurines. They look just like porcelain dolls, but they have wax facial features held together by yarn. I can feel my body heat melt the wax off their faces. The muscles begin to melt alongside the wax, as do the veins and blood. Their bodies become messy blots of running ink.

Even without inhaling the red mist, their beings become whispers in my mind. I can feel my flesh sucking in the information embedded in their genetic codes; it threatens to further erase the ego that is me.

Paranoia takes hold. I can't even tell if they are human or Pale Strangers in disguise.

It'll get much worse, I just know it. Next time I'll know to breathe in the red.

I stand up from the table and sling my backpack over my shoulder. "We need to leave," I say. "It's happening again. A Pale Stranger might be nearby."

Paxton smiles. "It's us versus them now. Now that you feel better, you can help me kill one or two of them. Then we can go after Darius."

"I'm not interested in killing someone."

"But he is an enemy to humanity!"

"I'm not worried about humanity. I need answers. Someone set me up to get involved with this case; I need to find out who did. And the person who knows is an acquaintance."

It takes Paxton a few moments to realize who I'm talking about, but when he does, he gives me the evilest grin. And for a moment, I found myself smiling the exact same way.

I should feel ashamed for relating to him in the tiniest of ways, but right now I don't.

Chapter Twenty-nine

Greene went for his gun when Paxton knocked him down with a single punch. We caught him off guard when he was doing casework in his office. No one saw us waltz but him. If things were different, I would use my newfound invisibility to hang out in the girl's shower room. Just maybe I will someday, if I survive.

Paxton has a blowtorch, his chosen trade tool, no need for the gun.

The handgun is given to me.

"Please," Greene says, crawling on the floor. "Don't do this."

"You caused me a lot of problems, Oliver," Paxton says while adjusting the settings to his torch. "You have this coming."

"Isn't it hypocritical?" I ask. Paxton asks what I find hypocritical about what he is doing. "Greene is human. I thought it was us versus them?"

"It is. But I'm allowed to be a little hypocritical every once in a while. Need to feed my fiend, just like you feed yours."

Funny. I haven't needed to do drugs in a while.

Can't taste the high anymore.

Paxton laughs as he turns the blue flame on. He singes away part of Greene's left eyebrow. Greene screams, unaware that he is being ignored by the others in the office building.

"Don't worry, I won't kill you," Paxton says. "Just gonna set your world aflame."

I stop Paxton from burning a hole in Greene's face. "Remember, Slowburn, we are here for questions." Paxton rolls his eyes and moves his hand away from me.

"You both are monsters. You kill and butcher people!" Greene says. "You both deserve to the death penalty!"

I stare at the handgun in my hand. The cold metal warms from my touch.

Is this what it has come to? Holding someone hostage to get answers?

If things were different, I would be inclined to agree with Greene. But there are more important things going on. And I have a boiling anger toward him that I am trying to contain.

So I point the gun at his head, making sure he feels the barrel against his temple. I say, "I will kill you, Greene. No one will hear the gunshot, no one even saw us come in, even though we walked past them." Greene's mouth and eyes widen. "I'm going to burn anyway for those four people at Giallo. That body in the cell next to mine is getting pinned on me, in spite of my not being able to physically mutilate it. So tell me, Olly, what is one more death to me? Even if I didn't do it, what is your death to me in the long run?"

Paxton gives me a twisted smile. "I didn't know you had it in you Walker."

Greene cries, "What do you want, Walker? Please don't kill me, I beg you!"

"No more running, no more lies, no more deception. Give me the truth, Greene. I want to know the truth about Dotty Finley. And I want to know who set me up to take this case for you."

"What does it matter, Walker? Dotty is dead."

"No, she ain't. Darius said she is alive, and I'm inclined to believe the insane ramblings of a serial killer over you." I point the gun away from him and hold out my arms, showing him my wounds. "You see and hear it too, don't you? You might not be infected like us but you know. The strange sounds, the strange visions. Confusing and horrible at the same time, growing stronger with each encounter. This is the fate I am suffering…and you didn't want to deal with it. That's why you picked a sucker like me in the first place."

Everything around me is falling apart. My idea, my whole concept of the world, what I know of it, has come undone. I would give anything to be ignorant. I would give anything to go back to my original life.

I can't blame Greene completely for what has happened. But by whatever fucked up God could have created these things, I will get an answer out of this man.

"You knew what I was getting into, yet you used me, you caused my damnation. Now give me the truth or pay with your life. What is it going to be, Oliver Greene?"

Greene breaks down in tears as he explains to me that justice failed. Two predators of society went free. The police, the media, and the courts…everyone involved just wanted to be done with the cases.

"My cases were going to be ignored and buried," Greene says.

"I'm not looking for your self-righteous preaching, Greene. I know you withheld crucial evidence that proves Darius was innocent of killing Dotty."

Greene smacks his hands against the floor. "He was a killer! I knew he killed her! I did what I had to do."

"You are right, Greene. Darius is a killer. He has killed several people, even more that I don't know about. But he didn't kill Dotty. What did you hold out? What did the police find?"

Greene finally caved in.

At Dotty's crime scene, a rusted hatchet with bloodstains from various people was found in the hallway. When they sent it back for DNA testing, the machine kept breaking down. So they checked fingerprints while they waited for a working machine. When Greene found out whose prints were on the hatchet, he had it withheld.

"Why was that evidence withheld?" I ask.

"Because Dotty's prints were on the hatchet, not Darius'," he says.

Maybe he wore gloves, maybe she touched the hatchet before she died. That wasn't a good enough reason to withhold the hatchet, yet Greene did just that. During her autopsy, Dotty's fingernails were checked for skin and hair. The marks on Darius's body came from Dotty.

However, this wasn't brought into evidence for one very important reason.

Underneath that were skin and hair belonging to her missing friends, in addition to several other missing people unrelated to her case. These people had gone missing months prior to her demise. Their personal belongings had been found scattered all over the forest.

Greene's horror story when we first went to the abandoned plant ricochets in my mind.

This means Dotty was responsible for the disappearances and death of her friends—and other people I don't know about. I was aware of her character change, but I am completely blown away by the thought she is capable of something like this. There were no hints. I just knew she was troubled.

Why would she do that? Was she infected like Joe? Was she indoctrinated like me?

The news scrambles my brain. I wasn't expecting this new mystery. It's going to take some time to digest what Greene just told me.

"That wasn't the biggest part of it," Greene says as he pulls at his hair. "Dotty was ripped open from inside. The coroners proved it with an autopsy. That means something came out of her and killed her. She wasn't killed by outside trauma."

"So Darius couldn't have killed Dotty," I say. "Even without all the strange circumstances happening, you couldn't let the evidence come into play."

"Terrible of you, Councilor Greene," Paxton says. "To bend the rules of the law to your own benefit. That kind of thing should get you disbarred."

I rub my forehead. "So why hold that out, Greene? You have no personal stake if a suspect goes free or not. It's your job to let the case run its course and move onto the next one. Due process and all that bullshit I don't understand. Why be a crooked lawyer and take a chance to let Darius go free if you got caught?"

"Because I was trying to make a name for myself," Greene says and points at me. "Just like you, Claire Walker. No one wants to see a pretty girl get ripped apart and later blamed for the disappearance of her friends. Darius was convenient. Plus, my boss wanted it that way."

I stare at the ground. "I've heard a ramble like that before. Convenience is always best."

Greene laughs. "Doesn't matter anymore now, does it? You said Darius is a killer. It's only a matter of time before the police connect the dots."

Paxton laughs and scares Greene with the blowtorch. I can't help but smile at Greene's fear of getting burned, both literally and metaphorically.

But I came here with a very specific reason in mind.

"I honestly do not care about that anymore," I say. "Now, who told you to hire me?"

One day, a month before I got involved, Greene had received a call from a man with valuable information. He told Greene that Dotty's body was no longer at the cemetery where she had been buried. He thought nothing of it until all the weird coincidences knocked most of his cases out of commission.

Becoming ever more paranoid, Greene got a court order to double check the caller's story.

"After we dug, I knew something was wrong," Greene says. His hands tremble, he can't look at us straight. He mumbles, "Her coffin was ripped to shreds. Talon marks from the inside out…like at Vin Forest."

As they inspected Dotty's grave, they found tunnels emanating from every corner of her coffin. The soil was eroded in a way that made it seem like a massive worm had borrowed out of her grave. The graveyard keepers did further investigating and reported that the tunnels went to other graves. Over twenty total, all of whom were freshly buried within a week of Dotty.

The corpses inside each grave were half devoured, half melted away.

The revelations hit me harder than I want to admit. The answer I get weighs me down. I crouch to the ground, holding my head in disbelief.

Dotty is a Pale Stranger.

How can this be? How could someone *become* a Pale Stranger? There is no way. Impossible. Levitt said they are creatures from a void existing over our reality. They hunt humans. We are their meal. How did Dotty become one?

"There is no way," I say, shaking my head. "A dead person can't be a Pale Stranger."

Paxton stands forward, "Who's a Chaser?"

"Dotty Finley. She was turned."

"Wait, Walker, I thought this angel Darius worshiped was just using Dotty's identity? At least, that's what I came to believe."

Greene laughs, "You both are mad. Speaking gibberish to one another."

"What do you mean, we are speaking gibberish? Have you not seen the Chasers?" Greene tells Paxton to listen to himself. "I'm speaking normally."

I hold my head again. Sharp pain runs over me. "He doesn't understand us. We *are* speaking gibberish to him."

"Well, this is new on me. What happens next?" Paxton says.

Fever rips across my forehead. Sharper, far more immense pain cuts through my body. I fall forward onto my hands and knees. My white blood cells are blindly attacking everything still healthy inside, in attempt to purge this supernatural virus plaguing me.

As I try to stand a sudden spasm sends me down again, and the gun slides from my hand. Greene tries to go for it, but Paxton stops him with the flame to his face. Paxton lets out a high-pitched squeal as he digs the blowtorch further into Greene's cheek.

"Paxton, stop!" I yell as I try to tackle him to the ground. He avoids me this time, unlike last year, and I slam into Greene's table. My shoulder damn near dislocates from the collision. The smell of burned flesh and rubber makes me choke.

"I'm sorry, I just had to do it," Paxton says. "Might have to again. Do I have to, Oliver?"

Greene rolls around on the floor, screaming in fantastic pain. I rush his side and hold him still. Before Paxton loses himself, possibly torturing Greene to the point of being unable to respond, I need to know.

"Oliver! Who told you to hire me? Goddamn it, tell me!"

"A photographer!" Greene screams. "His name is Levitt Brower!"

"Impossible," I mumble. "No, there is no way. It just can't be."

But it was true. Everyone Greene sent to deal with the Renton family quit outright. A stranger wouldn't do. Greene needed to find someone who had a history with the Renton family. It didn't matter who it was. Levitt would help the man Greene hired, one way or another.

All Greene had to do was stay back. Darius would kill Greene if he confronted him.

"Brower said I wouldn't taste good anyway. Not enough fat on me. When I couldn't find anyone, he gave me a call. Told me about you. How you were involved with the Joe and Gordon, how you were in the police station the day Darius was found. He said he remembered you."

So Levitt set me up? That meant he was there at the police station when I came in to write my statement. He knew the Pale Strangers would come after me. But why me? Why did he send me into a hopeless situation? Was he hoping I'd get killed?

"Walker, your nose," Paxton says, pointing at me.

I reach up and feel warm blood pouring from both nostrils. My left eye is filling with blood. While staring at my forearms, I can feel the stitches warp and try to tear apart my healing wounds. The muscles in my legs tense, my lungs take in less air each time I breathe.

"You're going to burn for this, Greene," I say, placing the gun in my pocket. "You'll never work again as a lawyer. Someone more worthy will be upholding the law in your place."

Greene laughs over his pain. "And what about you, Walker? They won't believe anything you say of me. You're a killer on the run. What happens when they catch you?"

"They won't catch me. Or Slowburn." The blood drips from the gauze around my wrist, runs down my fingers, and splatters against the floor. "Besides, the law is the least of our worries. And your career is the least of yours. Because I have news for you brother: the Pale Strangers are going to come after you. I have no sympathy when they do get you."

We leave Greene to wallow in his pain. My threat to him is hollow; there is nothing I really can do. No one will believe me. But I wanted to scare him, and hopefully I did. As much as I want to hate him, I can't. He didn't know any better. If he learns anything from this, he should get out of the city and forget about me, about Chambers, and everyone involved in Darius's case.

Maybe deep down, I just want someone else to make it out of all of this alive.

Gordy did. Maybe Greene can too.

When we get outside of the office building and back onto the streets, I am blinded by a thin mist that becomes like dense smog, and smells of sulfur. Paxton coughs with me, our eyes tear up, and pressure squeezes us.

Who goes there?

The sudden shock jolts us both. A Pale Stranger is around.

"Where did it come from?" Paxton asks as he looks around.

"I don't know," I say, doing my best to stare through the impossible mist.

Where are you?

We walk into the middle of the street to get a better view. Paxton turns his torch to the highest setting possible. I aim the gun outward.

"I never fired a gun before, just letting you know, Chambers."

"Noted, Walker. Please resist the urge to accidentally shoot me in the face during this time of crisis. I kind of like my face."

This wasn't the time, but I snicker. "I'll try either way."

We are expecting to see a monstrosity march our way. A few minutes pass. Nothing happens. But my body aches, my blood boils cold. The

Pale Strangers are around. It isn't safe to move unless we know which way it's coming from.

My ears pick up what sounds like people walking.

I squint to see several shapes take form. A block away from us, I see silhouettes of eleven people in dark, dirty coats. They stroll toward us. I can hear them whispering gibberish. My thoughts become scrambled.

One leads the pack, holding a very large black umbrella and wearing a large hat that covers his face. He is whistling a tune that I recognize but can't remember. His tune becomes another tune, then another. My mind recognizes them, but I can't say what they are. Confusion leads to anger at myself. This whistling is more debilitating than their whispering.

The blood knows they are Pale Strangers.

Yet there is something very different about them.

My body starts to react to them in a way very different from the times at the hospital, Giallo, and at the police station. It is a different kind of fear.

This fear is from another.

They once had a different form. More feral, like wolves in a forest, like wolves in dreams—now they look just like normal humans. They once attacked the Yellow Count's castle. Over five hundred years later, after half a millennium of hunting people, they made their way all across the ocean. Thousands of miles away from their original haunt, they are hungry. And while they no longer retain their original forms, it is clear they use the same methods to prey.

The Ghosts in the Mist point at us. Then they show their changing faces and wail.

There you are!

All eleven break into a sprint. Some collapse and become one with the mist, some run on all fours, while the leader continues his casual stroll while whistling.

We run for our lives as they chase us down the street and into an alley.

Chapter Thirty

We cling to a chain-link fence and climb up. Paxton lands on his feet while I land on my ass. He picks me up and we run down the tight alleyways. We pass dumpsters, knock over trashcans, step into puddles, and almost run into brick walls. We come up a series of stairs that lead to another alley and more stairs. The world around us gets smaller as the buildings shrink, the turns sharpen, the paths grow narrower, and the debris blocking our escape thickens.

"We need to get out of the alleys," Paxton huffs.

"Damn straight," I say. I feel battery acid–like reflux spreading into my lungs and heart from the running and shifting of the contents in my stomach. My legs ache; the last time I ran was twenty years ago in gym class, and I was the fourth slowest. My wounds make it harder to keep up with Paxton.

Yet the chasing mist, defying physics and gravity, is a huge motivation to keep moving. The will to not die a horrible death is stronger than my body's desire to suck at running.

The ones on foot jump from rooftop to rooftop; they take a few seconds to look down on us before resuming their chase. The whispering, wailing, and howling of the Pale Strangers attacks us from different directions. I surmise they are using sound to confuse us, corral us, control which path we take. Or maybe they are toying with us.

But staying in the alleys is a deathtrap. We need an open area to avoid them. It takes us a few minutes to find an exit. When we do see an opening to take our running to the streets, the smog is waiting for us, as is the lead Ghost in the Mist, who is standing in the middle of it, twirling his umbrella. Unlike the others, it looks like he has yellowish-grey vog coming off him; the volcanic sulfur burns our senses and suffocates us.

"Goddamn, how fast is this fucking guy?" Paxton says.

I pant and hold my knees. "They've been doing this for centuries. They know all the little tricks and reality hacks." I look around for a place to run. Two blocks away is a shopping center, with a Walmart-type knockoff chain called Y-Mart. It's open twenty-four hours. Plenty of room to walk around and hide. I point at it. "Let's go there."

We run the two blocks, then climb up a paved hill. A giant empty parking lot stands between us and the store. A security guard is rolling around in his truck, minding his business. He doesn't notice two wanted men being chased by a living mist and several inhuman monsters.

Probably happens to him every day, though. Complacency does that.

Inside, the lights shine bright on an empty store. There are beehives of workers passing us, restocking the aisles, cleaning up the store, and acting very bored. They don't notice us, but I wouldn't notice us if I had their job.

We head to the opposite side of the store and focus on the entrance doors. The mist arrives, but to our surprise, the mist doesn't enter the building. Instead it cuts in half. One half chills outside while the other half transforms into at least twenty humanoid Pale Strangers in dirty black coats. These ghosts scatter as they enter Y-Mart.

"I don't think bullets are going to kill them," I say.

"Any bright ideas, Walker?" Paxton asks.

I nod. "Let's go to the meat and dairy section."

"Hungry much?"

We jog across several aisles to the corner of the store that houses the deli, seafood, dairy, and meat products. I grab some of the packaged meat and tell Paxton to do the same. My fingernails dig into the plastic and tear it open. I toss the contents onto different parts of the floor. Paxton follows my lead. I tell him to remain very still, all the while holding a frozen pig's head in my hand.

Maybe the Pale Strangers are indifferent to some types of meat. Maybe they will accept frozen, processed food. We humans do it all the time. So do some animals.

If my plan doesn't work, we are in serious trouble.

Several Ghosts in the Mist arrive after a few minutes. They approach us casually, like they aren't actively trying to hunt us. I might not even be able to tell them from regular people under normal circumstances. I wonder how many victims they have done this to.

They circle us and sniff us. Staring at them is impossible to do and impossible not to do. Their faces are in motion, vibrating, constantly changing, yet they remain very still. Kind of like a mockingbird in flight.

I begin thinking they are trying to make sure we are the same men running away. They want to make sure they can get us. Yet at the same time, they seem more interested in what we are as opposed to what they want.

Of course, this ploy is to test our resolve, I'm sure. They want to see what we will do in the presence of them. They want to see our horror rise above the skin, to see if we can handle our breath control.

This is their hunting method.

So one tries touching me. I make my move.

I toss the pig's head to the side. Immediately they pounce on the meat. Some chew on it, others turn into partial mist made of knives and slice through the frozen flesh. The feeding frenzy is mesmerizing. Paxton and myself are taken by the way they devour the pig's head till only hairs of bone remain. After they finish the pig's head, they move to the other meat.

We still have their attention, but all they do is stare. They're too interested in feeding on several hundred dollars spread all over the floor. But they don't take their unmoving eyes off us. When they are done, their appetites are going to send them after us.

"They are just animals, after all," I say. "Just looking for a meal."

"More like starved piranhas," Paxton says.

"Amen to that."

For a period of time, we circle around the store. No rush, just walking at a slug's pace, minding our business. We follow their movements, only a few try to follow us; a couple of them moved onto the ice cream section after finishing all the meat.

I guess even Pale Strangers like to cool down after a long hard day.

Now I feel sorry for the employee who has to explain the inventory loss.

We learn a couple things from this encounter. The Ghosts in the Mist have a hard time tracking us. They don't use their eyes, might have terrible vision or their eyes are useless and just for show. I don't know how the other Pale Strangers do it, but I'm guessing all of them feel us. I think they can sense our electrical field, like a shark does. I tell Paxton this after observing them pass by when we move through the electronic section.

The Ghosts nearby look confused, like we had disappeared from their radar. They know we are around, but they have difficulty tracking us because of electronic interference, I think. They start examining the controllers for the consoles, the computers, and the radios.

"Has to do with them being primordial," I say. "They evolved to hunt flesh and blood creatures. They aren't used to our advances in technology. Or rather, they never evolved for human advancement. But they are curious. Our devices are strange to them. Just like most other animals." Paxton nods, accepting my theory.

I'm understanding what Levitt told me. I half understand what Darius blabbered on about. There are plenty of things I don't understand about them, but seeing them like this makes me wonder about their history.

Do they have a culture? Do they have a community? How did they come to be?

As we pass the hardware section, I hearken back to the few early college days I can remember. I worked in a store similar to Y-Mart to make ends meet. The people pissed me off. They brought their whole families, complete with smelly, ugly, annoying kids. And I was expected to be their babysitter. I would walk by the hardware section and on busy days think about bringing a chainsaw to everyone in the building. I just needed some peace and quiet.

I tell Paxton this to pass the time.

"That was childish of me back then," I say. "I didn't know any better. Didn't have patience. Didn't want to be nice to anyone."

Paxton says. "We are just animals, but ones of a higher order. It's in our nature to dislike others who are not us."

"Like them?" I point to the Ghosts in the Mist.

His face twitches as he shakes his head. "Abominations. Creatures like them shouldn't exist."

"But aren't we humans just like them? Don't we deep down have sick, twisted, perverted desires to prey on others?"

"Don't be ridiculous, Walker. The Chasers hunt us."

"We hunt ourselves too. We might not eat one another, except in some cultures, hell sometimes we don't even kill one another, but we do go out of our way to destroy our fellow man." I stand by one of the TVs broadcasting the news. "How can it be news if it's the exact same thing all the time? Global warming, mass famine, Mother Earth betraying us; war on drugs, war on terrorism, war on the poor and middle class; revolutions in other countries and impotence in ours. People are arguing, yet there is no action. The world is dying, and we don't give a shit. Why should they care about otherworldly creatures? They don't care about pollutants killing us second by second. Indifference has always been our fatal flaw."

"Your philosophical statement is amusing, Walker. But humanity isn't on trial, and it is still us versus them. We are the hunted." Paxton points to the Pale Strangers eyeing the monitor with the weather on it. "They are the hunters. Why are you relating to them?"

I spit to the side, stare deep at my hands. "I'm not. My sanity is slipping, and I don't sleep anymore unless I pass out from blood loss or get my body hijacked. My waking moments are spent thinking about them, and I haven't had much else to think about but them. It's fucked up, but these Pale Strangers put things in perspective."

My issues in life had always extended to my fellow man, to the bullshit they gave me on a daily basis. I just worried about how I was gonna get paid, how I was going to eat, and how I was gonna score the next high. It was a simple, boring existence. Being a journalist, then a ghostwriter, made me more jaded and content with wasting away my life. It wasn't going to get any better, no matter how many times I lied to myself.

My problems most of the times were of my own doing, and blown out of proportion to give myself some self-importance that wasn't deserved.

It's an American way of thinking. It's a human way of living.

But there are terrible things at work behind the scenes. The curtains have been lifted, and I've seen a part of the world I never knew existed.

"As fucked up as it sounds," I whisper, "maybe the Third World country kids starving to death have it better. I wish I could switch places with them and enjoy my slow, rotten death…but I wish my existence, my fate, on no one. And that's all I can really think about now: how another's horrible existence is better than mine. I can say that with certainty."

My memories of lost days are disintegrating. All I have left are these wild, twisted thoughts. They shield me from the harsh reality that there is something otherworldly on this planet and it's after us.

I'm on the verge of cracking.

"That is some desolate, despairing shit, Claire Walker."

"That's all we have, Chambers, desolation and despair. Why? What do you feel about our situation?"

Paxton laughs. "Hatred. Rage. Fear. Three easy, primal emotions. Don't need much more. Learned that in jail even before I found out about the Chasers. Had to get stronger. Otherwise, I'd be dead."

"There is no point in fighting. We can't win against them." Paxton asks what I plan on doing if I won't fight. "I got money stashed away. I'll take it and run, for as long as I can run."

"Well, I'm not running until Darius and his angel are dead. I'll erase their heretical existence with beautiful fire."

"You don't even know if you can kill them. Darius maybe, but he is human. Dotty is a Pale Stranger. She's a nightmare incarnate. You can't kill a nightmare."

"Come on, Walker, you have to know a way to harm them."

I sigh. "The only person who knew anything was a guy named Levitt Brower. His body's rotting in a jail morgue right now. That's what he gets for setting me up. Still, he was the only person who knew what the hell was going on, same thing with the two men I was supposed to meet at Giallo. Dead men don't have mouths."

If only there was a way to talk to Levitt…

The lights flicker, TVs fire off different channels, and the phones start ringing despite not being plugged in. The Ghosts in the vicinity leave without giving a second look, vanishing behind the adjacent aisles. My eye, my nose starts to bleed and the wounds start to open.

Another Pale Stranger? What kind of monster am I getting this ime?

Tremors fill my right arm. I feel dozens of sharp, invisible somethings stab through my fingernails, running up my arm and tearing out of the skin. But there are no wounds. Just the sensation that something has invaded my arm and is causing it to spaz out.

Out of the corner of my eye, I see thin, silk-like threads appear. They control my fingers, then my hand, then my entire arm. My possessed arm pulls me toward a silent yellow cell phone in one of the cases. It bumps into the glass, then clenches into a fist and punches. The glass cracks.

Paxton sees this is not of my own doing when I fall to my knees and try to hold my arm back. He takes the initiative, grabs the gun from my pocket, and shatters the glass with the handle. My possessed hand reaches in and grabs the cell. I place it to my ear.

"Hi, Claire," Levitt's mechanical, emotionless voice says. "Sorry about that. Thought you needed help answering the phone."

What? Levitt is alive?

"Yes, Claire, I'm very much alive."

I stutter, "How did you survive the jail cell? I saw your body."

"Not mine. Had to borrow it. Cop was first on the scene. He messed up my host real good so I needed a new one. Didn't last long, but they never do."

"No, this is a trick. You're pretending to be Levitt. He's dead. You're a Pale Stranger using his likeness. Trying to confuse me."

"This is no trick, Claire. And I hope you're not mad at me. All the times I made you bleed these past few weeks. Still working out the kinks of what I can and cannot do. Not as good as my boss yet; need a few more decades of practice in the human world to do a fraction of what he can. Sorry I almost killed you in your cell too. Wasn't part of the plan. Then again…you did say food was on you. Took that a little too literally."

Paxton takes the phone from my hand and smashes it against the ground. "We need to get out of here," he says. He wraps his arm around my stomach and tries to pull me away.

I feel a massive vortex of wind slam into us, stopping us from going further. The lights above go black. All electrical equipment powers down except for the TVs. A distorted face shoots across every TV, with its giant features and a large eye made of snow focused on us. Then comes the boom of a volcanic voice that shatters our hearing and paralyzes us. An impossible ringing replaces all sound.

And in that ringing I can hear that powerful whispering voice of the Pale Stranger.

Don't walk away from me!

Paxton falls to his knees, and then throws up on the ground. His ears are bleeding; he is crying. Up until this point, only I could hear the voices in their twisted glory. All he heard before was a garbled mess. This is his first time hearing their voice.

Only now does he know what I feel. Now he knows part of my fear. This is why fighting is impossible. This is why our fates are corroded, and death is the only choice.

I get off the floor and walk to one of the TVs. I look at my possessed hand and scoff. "So you're a Pale Stranger, huh, Levitt?"

Levitt's digital face smiles at me. "Yes, Claire," he says, using the speakers as a conduit. "Have been for quite a long time."

During my vision with Benson, I had been seeing through Levitt's eyes. I witnessed Benson's last moments alive and Levitt's last as a human.

"So you abandoned your humanity to survive five years ago?"

"What seems like a mere five years for you, Claire, has been over centuries for me. I forget how I was gifted to transcend sometimes, or even why. Lost track of myself. But you know that feeling, don't you?"

Levitt admits to me freely that he's happy to talk to a human for once, as opposed to killing us. The other Pale Strangers don't talk. They don't really like one another. Talking to me, seeing me struggle, was very nostalgic to him. He is glad he hasn't lost his social skills just yet.

"So it's game over then? It's time for us to die? You're going to kill us?"

Levitt shakes his digital head, "After all the help I've given you, why would I do that? It's not game over, just halftime, that's all."

"Then what is it you want?"

"Continue what you're doing."

"I don't have a fucking clue at what you're talking about! What do you want from me?" My hand slams across the TV screen, cracking it. My palm receives a small cut from tiny shards, my bloody handprint smears the cracked screen.

Levitt's face disappears. It's replaced by a picture of Darius Renton and Dotty Finely holding one another. Then the screen pans to the room where Dotty's body was found at the abandoned water processing plant in Jaune's Vin Forest.

"Ah, you don't need my help answering this question," Levitt says. "You know the answer. Just beneath the surface. Scratch that itch. Scratch it and make it bleed." Levitt wants me to kill Darius Renton and the angel Pale Stranger. "That's what I have always wanted you to do. That's why I've been helping you, guiding you along. Our little puppet."

I growl, "Why?"

"If you can't figure it out, then you're a fool. Or too scared to face the truth."

"Why me? Why do I have to do it?"

"This entire ordeal of yours has been to better prepare you. You saw what happened in the other stories. You can learn from their mistakes. And your body has become used to the Pale Stranger presence. You won't easily fail, I hope. You better not. Because I really like seeing you struggle. It amuses us."

"Well, if you want them dead, tell me how I can kill Dotty."

"Killing a Pale Stranger is unique to each Pale Stranger. You just have to keep trying different, unsound methods until you get it right. But Darius is simple. You have the tool right there to do the job just fine."

I turn to find Paxton offering me the gun. I shake my head. "If you aren't going to tell me how to kill her, then how am I supposed to do my job? This is uncharted land for me, Levitt. I need a little more information."

"Like a true journalist to the end. How noble of you. If you want information, you know what needs to be done."

"Indoctrination," Paxton says.

"Exactly, Mr. Chambers."

"What if we fail? You going to intervene?"

The TV screen flickers. I see Heather and me naked. It was the last night I spent with her. We are whispering to one another, talking about going on a trip far away. The screen flickers again, showing Heather at her apartment, asleep in bed.

Standing over her is the tall Pale Stranger with the blurry body. She begins to toss and turn. The walls around her start to bleed, then break apart. The tall Pale Stranger's lanky arms brush her hair aside, showing her sweating face to me.

"We have another just in case," Levitt says. "We always do. And we only choose the most delicious."

The screens fade to static before turning off. We are left alone in the dark. Levitt's presence is gone. He made his point.

My emotions overcome me. Tears break from my eyes and wash away the blood. I fall to my knees and scream, "No! Leave her alone! Don't kill her! I'll do what you want!"

Death is sometimes better.

My body's senses don't overcome me. I didn't feel a Pale Stranger around me, yet it is speaking to me. But this voice is not Levitt's. No. It's another Pale Stranger, but I recognize this voice. I twist my body when I hear the whistling.

In the darkness, I see the outline of the lead Ghost in the Mist, with his umbrella twirling around and obscuring his face. Why don't I feel anything? Then it hits me. This feeling. It's the same as when I became entranced at Dotty's shrine. My senses had been lulled, tricked, while I wasn't paying attention.

We were caught off guard while dealing with Levitt.

The lights come on in Y-Mart. And that is when we see for ourselves.

Surrounding us are one hundred black coated Ghosts in the Mist.

"Oh fuck no," Paxton says.

But why aren't they attacking? Why are they standing there?

The waiting asphyxiates us with terror. Their shifting faces burn a permanent memory into our minds while their whispers tear our thoughts apart. The Ghosts in the Mist stare at their leader. They wait for his command.

So he folds his umbrella and places it on his shoulder. He reveals his face. It's not chaotic, not hideous. Glowing scars, smoldering scars, fault lines of scars twinkle along his face. But otherwise he has the face of a normal man in his prime. And I know him.

Oh my God…it's the Yellow Count.

Chapter Thirty-one

It takes three long hours to board and lock up everything in Gordy's home. When we run out of wood, we take any spare door we can find, chop it into smaller sections, and use it to barricade the windows. The one place we don't have to worry about was Joe's old room. It's still sealed; no one can get in or out.

"This should do it, Walker," Paxton says as he finishes boarding up the windows in Darius's room.

"Good." I finish fitting the shackles, then use a drill to tighten the screws. Paxton comes by and uses his torch to melt plastic over the screws and bolts. These shackles ain't coming off without a bolt cutter.

"You sure you want to do this?"

I nod. There is no other way.

"How are you supposed to eat?"

"I'm not. Pretty sure once I'm under the influence hunger won't be my biggest issue." I point to the door. "Don't open that door. Even if you hear my voice, don't trust it. The slit we added is there so you can peek in." Knowing what I did to my room, I don't want to take a chance of roaming around, let alone hurting a random stranger.

This safety precaution comes with a price. At any moment a Pale Stranger can attack us. And we have no way of harming them, let alone knowing how to kill one. Just one of the reasons I'm doing this. I need to know how everything ends. And I need to know the best way to kill one of these unholy creatures.

"How long are you supposed to be in there?"

"Don't know. Maybe a few hours, a week, longer, won't know until it's over."

I sit on the ground and hold my wrists out. Paxton wraps them with tape and padding to make sure I don't get sores or cuts. He attaches the shackles to my wrists, then to my ankles.

If Paxton needs anything, he can use some of the money from the thirty grand. Food, clothes, whatever he can think of to get. If he can somehow get ammunition for Greene's handgun that would be lovely.

"If a Pale Stranger comes by, just run. Take the cash and go. Don't worry about me," I say, staring at my new home for the indoctrination's duration. Somehow I have a feeling Levitt won't let anything attack me while I'm indoctrinated. Might be anticlimactic if I died without knowing it.

"Don't die, Walker. We need to kill Renton and his angel."

Paxton closes the door. I am left with the bittersweet feeling of getting rooted for from the sidelines by a psychopath. Beside me are a blank, red notebook and several black pens. Med-kits are on standby across the room in case I come to and am bleeding bad. And finally, in my lap there is the sole entertainment during my ordeal: Joe's red music box.

I want as much time as I can have in peace before I lose myself.

Nothing happens. Not at first. The music plays its soft piece, the steel cools my hands as I count then recount each link of the chain. My eyes wander with nothing to look at but the torn wallpaper and the yellow room. My feet tap the floor as I wait.

Boredom is more likely to kill me than a Pale Stranger at this point.

But soon, memories of another life are coming home.

I hold the music box to my chest as scratches appear on the wall.

Expecting the red spiral hell again, I am surprised when layers of my skin start to float away. A fire burns in my stomach. The flame expands. Before I can react, all my bones explode, turning into powder. My muscles, veins, nerves, blood, and organs hover in zero gravity.

The two things I keep are my eyes and my brain.

I see the insanity of my parts just levitating around. There is no pain, or if there is, my parts are feeling it. I am just a pair of unblinking eyes and a brain, destroyed senses and no mouth to scream with.

Right now, I want that red spiral hell. Instead I get another kind of hell.

The music box melts into a puddle of red and black paint. The puddle expands upward until it splashes on the ceiling. Droplets splatter against the world. Tiny drops turn into a flood of thick paint that covers everything and removes my surroundings.

The powder starts to rearrange itself into a skeletal structure. All my missing parts start to fill around this skeleton. When the skin wraps around this body, I see for myself who it is I shall become: the Yellow Count.

I would tilt my head if I had one. So strange, terrifying, and yet sad. This man I will become chose to live as a Pale Stranger. He was so mortified by what his wife had become, and he had killed his servants to spare them from being eaten. If he knew what he was getting into, why? What is the motivation for a human being to cast aside their humanity to become something so horrible? And why did he let me and Paxton live?

Why don't I remember our encounter?

Find out for yourself.

In front of the Yellow Count's body I see something rise from the red painted floor. A sleek, featureless figure made from this red paint stands impossibly imposing; it's at least fifteen feet tall. He hunches over, his lanky arms snap into a shape that resembles like a praying mantis. His chest opens to reveal a solid eye.

He is the same one who has been haunting me since the beginning. I know it.

The blood knows what it wants to know.

He leans forward, staring past my brain and eyes.

You might like what you see, my puppet. You might want to join.

I'm keeping my humanity, Pale Stranger. I've seen what kind of monstrosities your kind really are.

So you say, like so many before you. All bends to our wills.

He opens the Yellow Count's mouth, then grabs my brain and my eyes. He shoves them down the Yellow Count's mouth. The teeth clinch down, crushing my eyes, my brain matter, until all I'm left with is darkness...

The pillars crack all around me. Immense heat wakes me from a drunken haze. I turn to my side. My royal guards are dead. Not by the hands of the Ghosts in the Mist. They were cut down by an angry blade.

To my side is an armored man. Behind him is a wall of flame. While I can't see his face, I can feel his rage from under his armor.

At his feet is the body of a young, beautiful woman. Her white gown is stained with her blood; her blood stains the knight's dark armor.

"Yes, I murdered her. She escaped a few weeks before with her younger brother. They betrayed me. But I did it to spare her, like everyone else. You know the cost of war, knight," I say. "Death is sometimes better."

He rushes over to me. His gauntlets pick me up by my coat. I am thrown into the fragile stone altar, knocking it down and shattering it into pieces.

"Get up, Count!" His voice echoes across the church. As I pick my head up, I am struck with his blackish greaves. Blood sprays from my broken nose, blinding me. I hold up my arms to keep from being struck in the face. The armored knight grabs me by my hair before yanking me upward. I cough blood on his Yellow Moon tabard. He strikes me in the stomach with the spikes on his bracer. I keel over onto my knees. His closed helm makes it impossible for me to see his face, to understand my attacker's next intentions.

"At least my people are free," I mutter.

"You damned your own by locking them in this castle with that monster downstairs, then hunting them like foxes!" He points to the dead girl. "She didn't have to die!"

I cry, "I had to kill them, I had to kill her. My wife had become a demon. She wanted me to sacrifice them so she could feed her God, this castle. I couldn't do that to them. I sent them to heaven to spare them this hell."

The armored man moves away from me. He stares at the broken altar of the church and clinches his metal hand into a fist. "They never stood a chance, between your madness and the evil outside these walls. You should have executed her the moment she betrayed the Holy Roman Emperor. You could have avoided this!"

"But she is my wife. I couldn't—"

"She's one of the devil's servants now! My men are fighting and dying outside!" The castle walls start to crumble, dust and stone pebbles rain on us. "Even now they are bombarding this castle with catapults. They spread the fires while fighting off the fiends. A necessary sacrifice if I die, so this land can be cleansed." The armored knight unsheathes his sword. "You will be punished for your sins. May God forgive you; die and reclaim honor."

I don't resist. This has to be. I hold my hands together, close my eyes, and begin praying for absolution.

As he readies the blade to strike me down, a howl comes from the hallway. The ground breaks apart, revealing the veins of the plant underneath. Many arms, with the size and thickness of the pillars, pop out. Hundreds of faces and torsos, many of whom belonged to my deceased servants, run across its scaly tendons.

Join us, our master. Join us, our lord.

I cover my ears to drown out their mad requests.

But this armored knight stands tall. The sight does not scare him, nor will drive him back. He holds his sword steady.

"Come at me, wretched abomination," he yells. "I am but a man! Come, try to take my flesh!" The arms extend out like snakes and wiggle high in the air. Half of them go straight for the knight, while the other half try to slam down on him. He moves between each arm and slashes at them. The stones disintegrate as the plant lets out desperate, painful wails. No matter how hard the hands try to hit the knight, he dodges with grace and hacks away at them. To my surprise, his sword is not blemished by the destructive blood, but instead seems to pulse and rust.

So much flesh. Give us flesh.

Hanging from the flying buttresses are three Ghosts. These upside down werewolves glisten with a thick cloud around them. There are endless rows of teeth from endless mouths around their beastly forms. Those eyes glimmer for a moment, then disappear in the darkness.

The armored knight grabs a spear from a dead guard and dips it in the devouring blood of the plant. The metal catches fire and boils, turning into liquid and spilling onto the floor. One of the Ghosts jumps at him, dissolving into mist. He hurls the spear at the Ghost. The burning metal catches the mist, bringing the Ghost back into a solid form. Oil spills from its body as the metal burns away at its form, turning into vapors. The creature cries out in pain and evaporates.

The two remaining Ghosts move back toward the corner of the church, afraid of this man in dark armor and afraid of her.

Your carnage is lovely, Götz the Roggenwolf.

From the fire, she appears. The plant takes its hands away as she approaches us with a slow waltz and a lullaby. She holds a small heart under her breasts; the terrible thing with several eyes and tumors thrashes its tails before resting and wrapping around her body. Tears of blood run down her face, her footprints leave burn marks.

"This place is no use to me anymore," she says. "It's time to go."

"So you're the wretched monster," Götz says.

"Mongrel, you will show me respect. Isn't that right, my husband?"

I refrain from saying anything. Her rotten lip twitches.

Götz points his sword at her, "You are one who craves souls, Countess. As long as you exist, suffering shall reign."

"Aren't you holier than thou? I expect nothing less from a blind zealot of your order most pious yet most malicious." She approaches Götz and lets the blade touch her neck. "Are you angry that your men are dying in my name? Or did they die for someone else?" Götz looks at the body of the young handmaiden. His sword begins to tremble. "So she was your beloved. Her death doesn't have to be in vain."

My countess holds out the deformed heart. With it, she plans on planting many seeds like it all over the forest. With enough time, they will grow. Then she shall spread these seeds over more lands, in different parts of the undiscovered world.

"The dying heart underneath the castle gave me new life. With this one, I can give her new life. Together we can give new life to all. We can create a vast kingdom, with me and my husband as king and queen. And you can be our champion."

My countess tries to extend the heart to him; its vines try to wrap around his arm. Götz stares at the heart, then stares at the body of his beloved. He rips his hand away, tearing the vines from his arm.

He steadies his blade, "May the fires of hell cleanse your impure soul, demon witch."

Her laugh shakes the chapel itself.

Do you think this sword can harm me? Do you think I can be harmed by a mortal man? I am like a god. I am greater than any god, than your God. I will be the greatest queen.

Götz grabs her by the chest and stabs through her stomach. When she screams, the stones shatter and the fires expel from the hallway. Everything rusts, rots, and ages. I can feel the life force in me suffocate and then die, as if several years of my life have been ripped away.

When Götz pulls out his sword, her blood sprays onto his armor, melting what it touches. But before it can harm him, he throws off the burning piece. My countess holds her wound and falls to her knees.

"Blasphemer. A false god can be killed," he laughs. "You will never be queen."

You will die! I will kill you!

The ceiling collapses as a large boulder on fire smashes through. Götz jumps out of the way as the ball hits the ground, igniting and separating me and the countess from him. The chapel quickly begins to catch fire. I crawl to my countess as she holds her chest.

Götz throws the sword across the flames. The blade bounces before landing by my side.

"She is no longer your wife. Redeem yourself, Count," Götz says as he picks up the body of the handmaiden. "Don't let the demon escape into the world of men. Don't let her pass on her seeds, or all will be lost. Do the right thing and end her suffering."

The wall of fire rises so high that I cannot see him anymore.

My wife holds out the heart toward me. Her eyes open, revealing human eyes and human tears. My heart expands and aches for her. This old body yearns for her still.

You don't want to die.

No, I don't.

You don't have to die. You can live.

Yes, I want to live.

It's so wonderful, this power. You can feel what I feel, if you desire.

I want to know what she feels. I want to know her power. I want to be with her, the woman I cast everything aside for.

Yes, let us be together forever. Let us make this world ours.

But I stare at the sword Götz threw at me. Guilt overwhelms me. The faces of my victims haunt me. I cannot sleep. I cannot go on, knowing what wrong I inflicted.

She cannot escape. She isn't my wife. My blood tells me this is the only way.

So my hand reaches for the blade. I reach down and stab the twisted heart. The tiny heart screams, the giant heart underneath the floor groans and shakes the whole castle. My body bleeds from every inch, all from the force of this scream. One of my eyes ruptures, I go deaf in both ears, my bones snap, and my insides rupture.

Then my wife's body collapses, lifeless. She was just a doll all along, just as I feared. The heart had been controlling her, using her thoughts, her words, her body against me. She was never alive. She was dead all along.

I feel so used.

But I become startled when my wife's body suddenly gets pulled at. Something obscured by the fire's shine claims her, and she is dragged underneath the fallen pillars. Veins making up vines wrap around her body, and grab at large stone rubble. The rubble is pushed over her corpse, forming a coffin of rock. Inside the cracks of her tomb I see a pair of eyes glow.

The corrupted heart did not die as I had thought.

You creatures are so useless. No matter. I will rebuild. I will wait for new flesh and start again elsewhere. I will try something different next time. I will find a new way to plant my seeds.

The glowing eyes fade. The heart has gone to sleep.

I didn't finish it off when I had a chance. The cycle will continue. I have failed.

As I cry out of the one eye I can see with, another ball of flame comes through the hole in the ceiling. It crashes down by my side, spreading out its flames and oil outward, like a ravenous animal of hellfire looking to devour everything it touches.

The sea of fire engulfs me. My body becomes immolated. What is left of my insides cooks as the flames enter my mouth. Despite having no voice, I scream louder than that heart under the castle. This unbearable pain shall subside in moments, my agony will cease with my life's end. At least I will sleep now…

It doesn't have to end this way. This place doesn't have to be our tomb. We don't have to feed another who betrayed us.

The pain leaves me. I have no eyes, but I can see. I have no voice, but I can speak. I have no ears, but I can hear. The castle is gone. My world is gone. In darkness it is just me, with my burning body shining bright. A thick mist surrounds me. The Ghosts linger on the edges of the mist. Their numbers have been decimated by the soldiers outside, and by the heart underneath the castle. Only a few remain.

They look like old wolves, battered and tired from the fighting. I can hear them wheezing, whimpering. Their lives extinguish as the mist becomes vapors, just like mine extinguishes as my flesh burns to cinder.

So you are dying too? Just like me?

Yes, we are dying. We were betrayed by our master, our home. He denied us entry so he could gorge himself on this feast. He abandoned us so he could get stronger. Our strength has always been in numbers, but we were routed in the fight. We are dying. We need a new home. Become our new home. Become our master.

But I want to die. I deserve death.

Death doesn't have to be the end. You can be reborn.

Why me? You tried hunting me, aren't we enemies?

Morality is fleeting. Emotions are chaotic. We have no need for them, if some of us ever had them. Some of us are not like you. We are older. We are of another kind. We come from the lords before and the lords after. We come from the deep, from the dark that lurks under the heat of the world's heart. But for those who were once like you, we can tell you that grudges come and go. We do what we must to survive. That is all that matters to us. We can save you, and you can save us.

How can I save you with this immolated shell? It is useless.

New flesh is new life.

New life…is new flesh?

Yes. And with this new flesh, you can have your kingdom.

…I don't want to die…I want to live…I want my own kingdom. I accept this new life. I accept this new flesh.

The Ghosts merge together, forming a large cloud of smoke. The cloud makes its way to my body and enters through my mouth. The flames extinguish from the burned carcass that is my body. Smoke rises from me before turning into vapors. Yes…I wait for this new flesh. Yes…I wait for my new life. Give me new flesh; give me new life.

But my metamorphosis doesn't happen.

I am stuck in eternal black, this unbreakable silence. I am alone.

"Five hundred years is longer for us than it is for you, boy," a whisper runs across the empty darkness. I search around but find just myself. "Over here." I turn my head. His black body is given away by his pale face. Immense heat, volcanic heat, radiates from his figure and burns me at a distance. He walks on ash. His whistling eats away at the absence of sound.

"Who are you?" I ask.

"I'm the man you're pretending to be. But I'm no longer that man you pretend you are."

"No, you're not me. I'm…me."

"It's okay, Claire Walker. You don't have to be me anymore. Despite all the pain, all the things you think you know, they are just memories."

I shake my head and stare at my charred hands. "My name is not Claire Walker. I am a count. The Yellow Count. They also call me Graf Orlok, and Count Dracula. "

"Those are just names others gave you. What is your real name then?" I stutter to give a name, my mind wracks with pain worse than when I was on fire. "Do you remember anything else about your time as a count?" No, it's not true. I am me. I know who I am. I should know my real name. "Don't worry, I don't remember my name anymore. History has forgotten my name, forsaken my name. But I don't need something as insignificant like a name anymore."

No…I am me…I am…

"You've forgotten who you are. What you call indoctrination is leading you to believe you are me. You're not. You just inhabited a lingering memory of me when I was a human." He looks around. "This void is my birth and my death, I have a special connection with this place. I am able to interrupt the breaking of you for a moment, but it won't last. You will return to him, you will return to your breaking."

Claire Walker, where are you?

Who is that? Who is calling me? Why am I responding to a name not my own?

"He is coming to rescue you. He has interrupted me, has interfered with me one too many times. He saved you and your friend at the market. Such is his nature. Oh, how I still burn with hatred that has lasted all these years. That's the only human emotion I still feel inside."

"Who is he?" I ask.

"He originally was part of the Ghosts in the Mist, the very first one in fact. He was their home. He sieged my castle with promises of a bounty unlike any other. Then he betrayed them to have the banquet all for himself. Many humans, many of *my kind*, died to feed his unyielding hunger. He is very ancient, one of the first of our kind to rise, back when the surface was ice. He's the reason you can't remember our encounter. You're just so *precious* to him."

My mind returns little by little despite being in a body not of my own.

With me becoming me again, I stare at this Pale Stranger. I try to analyze his face. I try to reason with him, relate to him. I try to see past this horror incarnate and see if there is still a mortal man inside the mist.

"So why haven't you killed me yet?" I ask.

He stares at his hands. Embers spark from center of his palms. "I was, but I'm here to talk now. I'll kill you tomorrow if I feel like it, or maybe I'll leave you alone. Maybe I'll visit you when you're an old, lonely man. Maybe I'll visit you in those last waking moments, to break you with insanity before I devour you and snuff out your pathetic life." He clinches his fist. "You'll never know until your blood knows, but by then it'll be too late. But we talk for now."

"That easy to switch from killing and talking?"

"It doesn't matter if you live or die, or if you heed my warning about the one who pulls your strings. If you die, he'll just find another after he or another feeds on you. There have been hundreds of others before you. You are not the first, you are not special. But your fate is of your own choosing. I just want to see if you will be my prey or my rival." He comes closer to me and tilts his head. "I want to see if you will betray your humanity, if you'll serve or join." His smile is a vent of smoke. "And I have my answer…"

"Why did you choose to become one of them, Count? After all you saw, all the pain that was inflicted on you, why did you agree and reject humanity?"

"Doesn't really matter anymore. I have no regrets. Power unimaginable. No conscience, no morals. An easy choice."

"How can making a choice like that be so easy?"

"Once a little girl ran away from home, for she believed if she searched and searched, she could become a fairy. Instead she came upon the rotten body of my dead wife in the ruins of my castle. The plant that controlled my wife wasn't completely dead. My kind doesn't die so easily. It survived the fire, survived my desperate blade. It tried growing roots with my wife's body. If left alone the plant would have used the body as a host again, and continued on what it had planned to do. But the little girl ate the burnt remains of my wife and the plant inside, all because she was dying of hunger." He shakes his head. "If she had known what eating the cursed flesh would have done to her, she would have made the same choice. Because it's easy to choose when you have no other choice. She got her wish though. She became a fairy."

"And what did you become?"

"I became a king. But I am a king without a kingdom. One day I will claim my dominion, my birthright. My kingdom will burn with the brightest flame and I rule the fire that covers the horizon on a throne made of cinder. Until then, I kindle the fire within that will create my inherited dream. My queen's dream will live. I will become a true king to rule all."

I cannot relate to him. His soul is long gone. Only hunger, mist and fire fuel his drive.

"What warning are you trying to impart on me?"

He looks away into a corner of the darkness. "All of us have one goal in mind: to feed. But some of us have a plan. He has had a plan all these years. We each have different appetites. Like drinking. The more we eat, the more we need. The hunger is never-ending. Some go out of their way to overeat. Some of us try to do things we are not supposed to. Our food is finite, after all. And we are done talking."

I stare at the darkness around us. "How long am I going to be here?"

The Yellow Count laughs. "Until it is over. Until your body bleeds out, until every bone in your body shatters, until your mind is erased. Or, until your master breaks you."

"Please…I need to know…why me? Why am I being used?"

"You were betrayed long before you were born. Your corrupted fate was decided by another in a single action. But the same could be said that *all our actions* stem from the day he betrayed the Ghosts. The causality of it all has brought you here. And because of it, you're being used for a very specific reason." He sniffs the air. "I'm not into games like he is, or his servant. I'm straight to the point."

From the darkness, I can see a pretty young blonde walking past us, holding a baby in her arms. The cooing of her child makes the Yellow Count grin. From underneath his coat, the mist spreads out, taking forms of humanoid Ghosts in dirty black coats. Their changing faces stare at her. The whispering becomes deafening. I cover my ears.

Sometimes death is better. Sometimes death saves us.

I scream, "No! Don't!"

The Yellow Count pops his umbrella over his head, "Why are you concerned? It's not you being hunted by us. Be happy with that knowledge."

"She's a living human being! She has a child!"

"This is no different than any part of life. We are no different. We are just trying to survive. Like you, like the big beasts in the wild. They hunt smaller beasts, you hunt the bigger beasts, and we hunt you. It's always been that way. We are no different. We all hunger."

The Yellow Count whistles as he walks away from me. The Ghosts in the Mist float around the woman with her baby. They lunge at her. Her screams echo, her baby's cries curdle until they are squashed by ravenous Pale Strangers feasting on them.

Pray we never meet again, boy. Pray your death is quick and clean.

They didn't deserve that. No one does.

I cry out in horror. I cry for them.

No one can hear my cry.

Chapter Thirty-two

Twenty years must have passed since I last saw daylight, talked to anyone, or heard any sounds other than my own voice. I don't think I have moved in over eleven years. Not hot or cold, nor any kind of temperature. There is no up or down, the bounds have no end. Just an endless void; this is what I call my home.

Once I was haunted by the viciousness of that woman and her baby being mauled. I replayed it every day for the first five years. Then the event lost all meaning. What was the reminder of a dead girl and her child going to do for me? I barely remember it now, or anything at all. Sometimes I forget my name. Sometimes I forget why I'm here. I forget to think. What's the point? My mind is shattered by this solitary confinement.

I don't think I exist anymore as a being, or as a personality. I just am an entity floating in empty space. Time is infinite yet imaginary. Nothing stops; nothing begins. Going on forever. I want it to stop. Kill me, God. Or let someone do the job for you if you don't exist.

This is what an atheist must dread when they die and find out that the afterlife exists. That their consciousness is aware of unending nothingness. I'm pretty sure this kind of hell is reserved just for them. But I wish this on no one. Having seen this firsthand, if this is what I have to look forward to, then I don't want to die.

I might choose the existence of a Pale Stranger over this agonizing empty void, this infinite nightmare. Yet all I want to do is sleep forever. I just dream endlessly of a better place, without pain or problems. Please God, let me sleep, salaam.

Then something cold and wet touches my face, sending me into shock. I want to touch, I need to feel with my hands, but I have forgotten how to use them. Tiny cracks of color break through the darkness. Light shines from these breaks.

Is that water leaking from the sky and the ground?

Yes. Water pours from the schisms in the darkness. Bitter, frozen rain defies gravity, aims for me, washes over me. My skin color starts to run, followed by the skin itself. There is no pain other than the subzero liquid pouring on me. The color of me runs into the darkness, creating rivers, lakes, and oceans.

Another layer of me is underneath the running watercolor of skin.

No, it is not my flesh. This flesh belongs to another.

The darkness eventually washes away under a rainstorm. The paint of me becomes flooded mud and grass. Tall trees tower over me, staring down as I lay in this mud. My body is frozen in place, perhaps from the rain itself. I stare at the sky. In between the movements of clouds, I see the brightest stars I've seen in my life. So pure, so honest. Only after having taken them for granted do I now appreciate how they are still above me.

I know how to move my arm again. I reach out with trembling fingers to the sky. If God would just let me grab one of the beautiful stars above, I will be so happy. I won't see my family again. Let me have this one thing before I go. Please God, grant me this one wish before the devil knows I am not dead.

"Get up, Johan!" Foch yells as he grabs me by my forearm. His left eye is covered with dressing; blood seeps through and runs down his chin. The stitches rip as I hobble upward. Thieriot runs past me as dizziness, nausea slaps me around. My side starts to hurt with fiery pain. I look down and see my stomach has a gash. When I stop to check for other wounds, Foch pulls me by my shoulder. "Run!"

That's when I hear the screeches of dozens of the Black Fairy's children. While I can't see them, their howling debilitates us. I can feel blood filling my ear canals. I try to will the pain away as Foch puts his arm around my waist and helps me run.

Tired, hungry, scared, freezing. But we run anyway.

"How much farther?" I ask Thieriot after a few miles of running.

"Not much. The battlefield is close."

When we arrive, I am unsurprised by the endgame of the war effort. But it never gets any easier seeing the desecration of land with dismembered bodies and wreckage. Someone's father and son lay in pieces, sinking further into the mud. The sickening stench of decaying flesh mixes with gunpowder and gas. My eyes water from the horrendous smell and from the overwhelming emotions of my situation.

"Before they get here, let's go search for any survivors, Johan," Foch says.

"Gather any ammunition you can find," Thieriot commands as he picks through the bodies of the dead men. Casualties from the two sides have less than equal spoils. The only thing I see undamaged is a catapult hidden in the trenches. As we trek through, we are greeted with more dead, just in different types. The burnt, bullet-ridden vehicles are unsalvageable; we can't use them for a quick escape down the roads. The hope of finding anyone alive grows slimmer with each footstep. Even if any soldier is still alive, will they help us? Could they help us?

One demon child, after wounding me and being fired upon dozens of times, killed the last two guards before ignoring us to feast on its kill. Then came the others, who swarmed us as we made our escape from the prison. Knowing what happened to the corpses, the Black Fairy used the bodies to host her children. Those children are fast, brutal, small, and inhuman.

I stare at the bodies and wonder when Foch digs through their pockets, "When she is finished with the prison, she will come here."

"What do you mean?" Foch asks.

"Look around us. Hundreds of dead sons are here. Just like in the prison. She will infect their necrotic flesh, and they will birth her children. Imagine thousands of them."

The possibility my heart ache. No, I won't think this. I fall to my knees and punch thick, muddy earth. What if she doesn't stop here? What if she goes past the killing fields and into the villages, into the cities?

"Damn it, man, what are you saying?"

"Millions of her children could be running around. She infects the dead, and her children give her fresh bodies to infect."

"Don't say such insane nonsense, Johan!"

"This is all nonsense, Dr. Foch! None of those things should exist! There are at least two of these nightmare creatures running around. What if there are more? What if they are like her?"

Foch kneels in front of me and holds me by my shoulders. "All we can do is run, Johan. Just like you did."

"But if the Black Fairy doesn't stop, then it will be only a matter of time before there is no place to run on this planet. Her brood will swarm over the earth like a plague of locusts."

The apocalypse. End of the world. Such absolutes I never imagined would happen in my life, much less at all. Maybe I am losing it; I admit I am at my sanity's end. But the horror of this unimaginable situation leads me further down despair with every breath.

Thieriot screams. We run back to where he is. The Black Fairy's brood, thirteen of them, surround and jump at him. Thieriot struggles to avoid the sharp spears coming out of their palms like whips. The bullets hit their slender, tiny bodies, releasing oily blood. They cry like young children, invoking images of my own children crying whenever they got hurt, whenever they became overwhelm with sorrowful emotion. Foch feels the same thing, and we both shout out to Thieriot to stop hurting the children, despite knowing they are not like us. Thieriot hesitates in between shots, only to miss. Foch cannot bring himself to fire on the children, and neither can I.

These wretched are using our paternal instincts against us.

The Black Fairy's loud howl sounds above us as her kin get wounded. She is hidden in the clouds, her insect wings give off a hint of where she might be and how close she is to making us pay for hurting her brood. We try to anticipate where she is going to strike. Yet I struggle to look at the sky as her wings burst from the clouds.

The impossible task of balancing undoes one of us.

Thieriot trips and falls into the mud. She screeches with delight at his fatal mistake. From above she dives, like lightning thrown from heaven. Her speed is so fast she creates an afterimage of where she was. By the time I get to her massive frame impacting into Thieriot, tiny pieces of him are flying in a pink explosion. Her impalement was so strong that we are pushed back by a shockwave that cuts through our clothes and skin.

"Sigmund!" Foch yells and tries to run to his friend, but he stops. Not because it is too late, but because he sees with his own eyes what the Black Fairy looks like. We are dwarfed by her size. From her hunchback grows a large tumor with twelve sharp wings with talons attached; I think of a bat when she spreads them out. Multiple stingers emerge from the bottom of the tumor; I assume that is how she infects or impregnates the corpses of people. Her two legs split into halves, giving her four skinny legs to support her massive upper body. Her front body is lined with hundreds of lesion-like mouths. Her forearms have sharp tusks dwarfing her tiny hands. Balding, black hair swings back and forth. The bottom half of her mouth is that of a normal woman's, but her nose and eyes have atrophied into stumps. Two large, compound eyes prop on the top of her forehead, just like an insect's, but with tiny human eyes.

She tears Thieriot's dangling head off his torso and tosses it to her children. Her children dive to grab his head to suck out the brain matter; they fight with one another just like siblings do over a tasty treat. She holds pieces of him closer to her chest; her mouth-like lesions devour chunks of the deceased Thieriot's.

The creatures aren't interested in us. Not yet. With hundreds of corpses around, the Black Fairy will have new children to sire into our world. So I grab Foch by his shoulder and scream at him to run. But we don't get very far into the forest before realizing we are not alone.

In the trees, I see an army of the Black Fairy's children hanging on the branches, like skinless monkeys. These are the older ones from the prison, the ones who haven't eaten yet. Their faces have become more insect-like; tiny shinning eyes make up two bigger ones. Their transparent bodies seem to be hardening, molting like cicadas; underneath, new flesh slithers and tries to break out. They chirp, screech, and whistle at us despite having no mouths yet.

Foch starts to pray to God for help.

But no one is coming to help us. No one will save us. We can't fight back.

Hopeless despair finally breaks me. I collapse to my knees and sob.

But a familiar sensation starts to itch up my spine. Disorientation, fatigue, sickness…yes, that sickness. Not like the Black Fairy or her children. Very familiar, all from one source, and it's more terrifying than the hundreds of monsters surrounding us.

The feeling my blood knows belongs to the Scarecrow.

There you are, Johan. I missed you.

Foch winces from the sudden voice of my unseen tormenter. The mud underneath us shifts...I knew what was going to happen next. So I jump at Foch and tackle him.

Spikes made out of tongues shoot out of the ground. They poke past the top of the trees, standing so straight and so tall, yet they bend like moving shadows of snakes. The spikes curl, avoiding the trees themselves and seeking the children of the Black Fairy. The children try to escape the chasing spikes, but it is no use. Hundreds, if not all of them, are impaled. Their monstrous, childlike bodies quiver, and they cry out.

"Oh my God," Foch says, motioning for me to look at the corner of the forest. I stare hard to see what he is pointing at.

I almost don't see the Scarecrow. My eyes pass him several times before finally noticing him standing there, feet planted on the ground. His stomach and chest are split open like one large mouth. The four large spikes that now burrow underground emerge from this opening. From these four, the others splinter off into hundreds of smaller, thinner versions.

The Scarecrow has new wounds that are shut together by teeth. The wound on his face from where I had hit him with an ax months ago has turned into a decayed half-smile. Something boils underneath his otherwise featureless face, and then rolls around. He stabs his finger into his face and blood pours out. An eye wiggles from underneath the boil and makes its home in the wound. He holds out his arms as if he wants to hug me. His half-smile turned into a toothy grin.

You had me worried. Hold on. Wait for me, my friend.

I can hear the Black Fairy's angry wail in the distance. The trees start to crack and the mud hardens from her sorrowful rage. She realizes her children are dead.

"Foch, run!" I yell.

No Johan, don't go that way.

The Scarecrow walks toward us with his arms still held out. A wall of spikes shoots out of the ground, boxing us in so we can't run further. The cage clamps down on us like fingers folding together. But they don't harm us or even touch us. The Scarecrow vanishes and appears before us.

She is coming. She'll hurt you. Let me handle her.

Is he really protecting us? But why?

Trees are pushed over. The ground rumbles under our feet. The Black Fairy's growl shakes us from within, then outward. She stops a short distance away from the Scarecrow. She stares at her impaled, lifeless children. She goes to one of them, rubs her face against it. She lets out a chirp as she pushes it with her forehead, following it with a woman's cry when they don't respond.

For a moment, her face turns into that of a normal woman.

But that moment quickly fades. Her terrible visage returns as she turns toward the Scarecrow.

Why did you kill my children?

The Scarecrow looks at the sky and tilts his head.

In time they would have become my rivals. They taste so delicious, despite being so young. But they were a prelude to my actual feast. Your flesh, your gifts, belonged to another. Oh I've been waiting for a very, very long time for this taste. I've dreamed, and I've searched all over for you. I waited patiently. I knew it was a matter of time before you went after my friend. And here you are, at last. My dinner is served.

The tusks from her arms extend several feet, and she flies off the ground. She charges the Scarecrow, screaming so loud all we hear is a metallic ringing. The collision's shockwave rocks against the fleshy prison, making it bleed. Some of the blood hits Foch. He uses his left arm to shield himself, but it is no use. The blood is acidic. Parts of his forearm are starting to eat away; the steam coming off his burning flesh touches his eyes and blinds him. Foch's feeble attempt to roll around in the mud doesn't help him. I try to aid him, but my hand feels immense heat coming off him and the blood of the Scarecrow around us. I feel myself drawn to see the fighting of two monsters more than the condition of Foch, whom I can't do anything for.

There should be guilt, but there isn't, just awe.

The spikes twirl and bend as its master fights with the Black Fairy. Her tusks and her stingers swing at him, but the Scarecrow melts into the earth, only to reappear a moment later where one of his flesh spikes sticks out. He doesn't bother attacking her. He puts up defenses with his spikes, only for her to smash through. She moves so fast I see her blurring in and out of existence. Yet her speed doesn't match the warping of the Scarecrow. Trees splinter from the impact of her tusks, and the ground splits open from the wounds caused by her aftershocks.

From behind the broken trees, the still living kin of the Black Fairy rush at the Scarecrow. Some are impaled on the spikes; a few avoid being stabbed and latch onto him. They claw, stab, bite, and tear away at his rotten flesh. He grabs one by the leg and slams the child so hard into the ground that the body ruptures and its insides fall out. He uses the carcass of the dead child to bat away its inhuman siblings attached to him. In his distraction, the enraged Black Fairy manages to impale him in the shoulder with her stinger. But the Scarecrow laughs. From the wound, teeth form and chomp down on the stinger, severing it. The prison of flesh recedes under the ground, leaving us naked to any attack.

When this is over, the victor will turn their attention to us. The Black Fairy will either devour us or use our bodies to host her children. If what I fear is true, then she can theoretically infect the entire world several times over. But the Scarecrow will continue haunting me all over Germany if he survives this encounter. My tormenter will continue decaying my body and mind until I am a walking corpse.

This is my somber conclusion.

My wife and children will never know peace as long as both of them are alive. This is not a future for anyone. I refuse to let anyone else suffer.

There is no other choice.

"Foch, can you stand up?" I ask as I lean down and help him up. He doesn't respond; he has passed out from the pain. I shake him and give him a few light slaps on his face. "Please, Dr. Foch! I need your help."

Foch awakens. He mumbles, "What, Johan?"

"We are both going to die here."

"I don't want to die—"

"Neither do I, but we need to stop those things."

I tell him about the catapult in one of the trenches. The closest one is fifteen feet away. If we can aim at them and fire the explosives, then possibly we can kill them. Since I don't know how to use one, it falls on Foch's shoulder to fire the weapon as best he can.

"But how are you going to keep them still?" Foch asks.

I take off the loose bandages on my arms. Then I bend down and pick up a fallen bayonet stuck deep in the mud. I begin stabbing the wounds on my arm, reopening some and creating new wounds. The pain is dull; I'm used to this pain. Blood flows from my arms.

"I will get their attention. Hurry, Doctor. Fire everything you have."

"Johan, no! Don't!"

His scream falls on deaf ears as I charge at the Black Fairy, her children, and the Scarecrow. I accept that I shall die here, but so will these monsters. I will finally have my sleep. My blood gets their attention immediately. They forget to fight one another and stare at me, this bloody man running full speed at them. All instinct, all hunger gets the better of them. The Black Fairy's children are the first to react. They jump off the Scarecrow and lurch toward me.

But as I run, I see a light shining high above me. My body is in motion, beyond my control as I run toward the horrors. But this glow captures me. The warmth bathing me is so lovely, so exhilarating; I'm the only one embracing this grace.

I feel great, so carefree…I am happy.

The light engulfs everything. My eyes don't wince from the bright light despite it being blinding. I see a small hand reach down from the light.

"What are you?" I ask without moving my lips.

"Salvation," a woman whispers. "Do you want salvation, Claire Walker?"

"My name is not Claire Walker. You've mistaken me for someone else."

The hand comes further down and softly caresses my forehead. I can feel myself being pulled up from my skin. There is no ripping of my flesh, no violent dissociation of my body. I can feel my soul being lifted into the light. I am floating high in the air, weightless and free.

I look down and see the man I once was, still charging headfirst to the maws of death. But he is not me. I should recognize him, but I don't. The hungry Black Fairy pushes her children aside and lunges at him. But the Scarecrow warps in front of him and takes the slash for him. The children get up and resume their charge. He falls into the mud and holds out his arm to defend himself from being mauled by the Black Fairy's children.

In one of the trenches, I see a wounded old man finish preparing the catapult to launch a bomb at the monsters. The old man falls onto the lever, unable to bear the pain from his wounds anymore. The projectile flings past me, going through me.

And everything turns to eternal white.

"Remember who you are," she says to me.

And I do remember who I am.

"Who are you?" I ask.

She steps out of the light. A naked woman with flowing red hair and two large white wings. I recognize her.

"I'm an angel," Dotty Finley says. "Your angel if you want. Well, am I?"

Chapter Thirty-three

The light starts to dim around me. I take a look at my surroundings. I'm standing on a wooden stage. The stage lights are so bright. My lips crack, and my tongue licks up the sweat running down my face. Off the stage, in the distance, rows of seats stretch beyond where I can see. Behind me, the curtain rises. A mirror standing thirty feet tall shows me my battered frame. I am but a ghost of my former self. The man in the mirror cannot be me. I wish I didn't know him. I wish he would go away.

But my attraction to the mirror means he won't leave.

When I was growing up, I daydreamed of being a different person. I was made fun of because of my name, because of my upbringing—if I was someone else, then I could avoid my torment.

Such was the impatience and ignorance of my youth. Experience taught me to drop the fantasies and move on with my life. It wasn't the best life, and while it got harder, I grew up.

I was never going to make it big. I was on the bottom of the pecking order in this game called life. No way the likes of a guy like me could ever swing upward to a better life. That's why I took the case involving Darius Renton. Maybe I could cheat the system.

Delusions are a powerful thing.

And if delusion were a drug, I would have overdosed a long time ago.

The Pale Stranger gave this deep-rooted desire for the past, forgotten and outgrown, a place to grow like a poisonous weed, an invasive being that destroyed the fragile ecosystem of my body. I was able to become someone else, at the cost of losing who I am. The process was violent, depressing, and fearful.

This man is me, but in a moment, I can change into someone else.

I just want it to stop. I don't want to be anyone else. I want to be me. Please, God, make this stop.

"He doesn't care," Dotty says. I expect her near me, but I see her standing on the other side of the mirror. "If God cared, he wouldn't have made them, if he did make them. His lack of protection proves this."

I look around. "So where am I?"

"Southern Miskatonic's Theater Hall. The happiest moments of my life happened here." Dotty looks around and shakes her head. "This is the best I can remember it. The actual place is more modest, smaller, I think. I willed it into existence to the best of my abilities."

"Why am I here?"

"Because I want you here. Indoctrination is a terrible thing. Look at how you used to be." Dotty points to my reflection. My mirror image turns into my old shell. Standing next to him is me as a teenager, and next to him is me as a small boy. Their bodies are mine, I recognize, but their faces are blank. "Aren't you so handsome?"

This parallel reality is prominent yet depressing.

"So am I going to become anyone soon? My old self? You, perhaps?"

Dotty shakes her head. "No. You've suffered enough. Your body is tearing itself apart, your sanity and memory of your real self are a hair away from vanishing. I know your pain, Claire. We are both victims here. And I just want to talk."

I sigh and rub my forearm. "I'm not in the mood for talking. I never hear what I want anyway. All I get is half-truths baked in a bloody cake called deception."

She approaches the youngest version of me, and pats his head. He stares up at her; I imagine he might be smiling. "He could have shown you the truth from the beginning, could have made you not suffer. But instead, he likes the games. Suffering amuses him."

"Who is he?"

"Somnus."

I ask her who she is referring to.

"The Greek god of sleep, an appropriate name, a needed name. He approached me in my dreaming. In this place, actually. He came to you in your dreams too, didn't he?"

I step toward the mirror. "Is he the tall Pale Stranger who keeps appearing to me yet makes no attempt to harm me?"

"Yes," she says.

So he has a name. My nemesis has a name.

She didn't know just when he first took notice of her, but Dotty believes he had been watching her for some time. Her encounter with him began in flashes during her dreams. A presence would be felt before vanishing, first in small amounts then later becoming longer and more pronounced with each encounter. She saw horrible things and experienced horrible memories, like broken records of lives long since passed.

Her waking days were soon invaded by this pale stranger, who made it a point to never leave her alone. She was terrified at first; his featureless body was hard to look at and hard to tolerate. She felt as if his mere appearance was toxic, radioactive. Everything about him was corrupt, evil.

"He torments you, without ever laying a hand on you," Dotty says.

First went her sleep, then her sanity. Her body had violent reactions every time he visited. Her blood knew what he was: an ancient enemy of life.

Yet like a drug, he tempted her, infected her with a promise.

And she didn't notice until the enthrallment was obvious. Indoctrination.

I nod at her predicament. I might have been the same way, but the obvious was pointed out to me several times.

Dotty moves away from my younger self and grabs the hand of my teenage me. She squeezes his hand and moves him to the edge of the stage, where they both sit down. "His promise to me was to be something greater than I was."

While Dotty dreamed of being a ballerina and performing in theater, the pressure to succeed wore out her soul. She had the skills, but she was losing the passion. She didn't have the grades, and she didn't have the associates or knowledge to secure a way out of her poor existence.

The theater, the dance, was her only escape to a normal life. Her desire to perform was crushed underneath the demand for her to perform beyond her abilities. She wanted to be someone not Dotty Finley. She wanted a better life. She wanted to be free of these responsibilities.

"Somnus had powers. Tempting powers beyond money, beyond sex, beyond the manmade creations, beyond written rules. If I did what he said I could dance forever, free of the chains of man, and beyond humanity."

"The path of a Pale Stranger," I whisper.

Dotty sighs. "God let that horrible monster in my life. While you can attack them physically, there is no defense when they invade your mind. Will power alone won't stop them. Some of them, like Somnus, have been doing this for centuries, for millennia. They know the inner workings of the human mind. They know our desires, our troubles, our weaknesses. And they exploit them."

"Your weakness is you wanted an escape. You wanted to be someone else. An angel."

"Well I never wanted to be an angel, despite what you might think. That meant I'd have to serve someone of a higher power. But an angel I became and an angel I am worshiped as."

"If I may ask, who did you want to be then?"

"Icarus," Dotty says. "I wanted wings of wax to fly away from the prison life had built around me. And if I ever had no need for the wings, I would just fly to the sun and let them melt." She laughs and nods. "It's stupid really. Something so girlish, so childish, so insignificant as life's normal problems. They aren't real, life or death problems. But he chose to attack that because of how insignificant it was. Every day, every hour, every second, he took little stabs at what was a small insignificant chip on my surface. The chip became a festering crater of doubt, pain, and fear. And I never noticed it until he wanted me to. That's when I was broken. That is how they get you. It continues until you give in or until you die. A human life means absolutely nothing to them: they are beyond morals, beyond sympathy, and beyond conscience."

I move closer to the mirror in response. My hand glides over the mirror where her hair might be. While I feel the glass, I also feel the sensation of her red hair somehow. Any fear I had of her was replaced by understanding, by pity.

She tried attacking me in her true form twice before.

I shouldn't relate to this monster, a former person, but I do.

"What exactly did Somnus want you to do for him?"

"Food; all these creatures do is eat," she whispers. "But Somnus is not satisfied with just eating. He also wanted a puppet to play with. Someone he could string along, help him eat, and amuse him. Sick, twisted amusement caused by human suffering and insanity."

I sit down on the floor and stare at the wood floor. "So that's how you got involved with Joe Renton."

"He was always attracted to me, but in a platonic way. He saw beauty in my performances. He only saw me as a dancing glass doll. He hadn't been with a female before. Not that he cared much about it before I came onto him. It wasn't hard. I brought out that untamed sexual beast you saw in the tapes." She stops to stare back at me and says, "You didn't like what you saw, did you?" I shake my head and blush. "Neither did Darius, but he got over it."

"What broke Joe? What was his breaking point?"

"Two things led to his undoing. I was one of them, I admit. He could have been anything he wanted, but why do you think he became an anthropologist?"

"A deeper understanding of the world, I assume."

She nods. "While Joe was a hardcore Christian, he had depressing doubts about there being an afterlife or a higher being. His friend, Charles Benson, the archeologist, was convinced we are creatures that could be solved with science. There was no God, there was no afterlife; everything was arranged by chance, all the answers lay in our very blood cells. Benson further cemented the doubt in Joe's head."

And Somnus saw this as a weakness that could be exploited for his own amusement. Joe would have visions, thoughts, that he needed help deciphering. Dotty would do that for him. She became the mouthpiece of Somnus. Joe accepted whatever she said as canon. Joe in turn would pump his money and his "revelations" into his joint project with Benson. Together, the men would discover hidden quirks about the world and become blinded to their insidious origins; they were focused too much about the glory, not the inherent dangers.

Dotty became a fiend over time. Somnus's poisonous words flowed through her, corrupting her, turning her into a person she didn't recognize. She infected Joe through sex and through her own words bathed in the tainted gibberish dictated by Somnus.

She is quick to say that she wasn't responsible for Benson's madness. His infection came from another source: the sand god. It was the sand god who changed everything.

"After what happened in Afghanistan, Somnus didn't show up. For three years, he was gone from our lives. For a while, I thought it was over…I could go back to the life I was so eager to abandon. Joe was still consumed by his work, but I felt I wasn't needed anymore."

She knows now that creatures like Somnus are a torrent of changing waters.

One moment they can decide to turn cities into salt, while the next can slaughter someone just to watch them suffer. Sometimes they do odd things, like fixate on watching a family grow through generations, or "helping" a man unravel a mystery by guiding him along.

There is no reasoning sometimes behind what they do.

They do what they want, at that moment, because it is of no consequence to them.

But back then she couldn't understand. She was consumed with her want. This divinity, this freedom Somnus promised her was not fulfilled. She was enthralled to him, she was willing to do her part, and yet she was abandoned.

She felt cheated. Such emotions were only human, after all.

Her disappointment quickly turned to terror.

Though Somnus was gone, he was replaced by someone else. Crueler, more antagonistic, the Pale Stranger knew them well because he had been human once; he was involved with everything going on in a way Dotty didn't consider.

It was because of Dotty that he lost his humanity in Afghanistan. Now he was reborn into something much more, much less. And he was given free rein to terrorize the Renton family. First Joe, then Gordy.

Joe began filming everything he did in a desperate attempt to capture the nature of his tormentor on film. He wasn't being perverted when he filmed his sexual encounters with Dotty. He filmed every moment of his waking life to prove there was a devil behind it all.

That devil had a name. A plain name.

"Levitt Brower," I say.

Dotty turns to me. "So that's his name?"

"Yeah. He's the one who got me involved with Darius. He's hell-bent on having you and Darius stopped. Why is that?"

Dotty turns her head to me and stares into my eyes; the sweet smell of honey, strawberries, chocolate, and other sweets rush into my nose. My lips saturate from licking; my heart races with a lustful yet hurtful passion. That glow, oh, her glow, I just want to touch her now…I want to do whatever she says, but I know deep down that it could be a trick. She is a Pale Stranger after all.

Something toxic can become alluring after a while. Like a relationship made of volatile flames, the chemical changes sniffed through the end of a straw, something no good becomes a lifeline to continue existing.

Whatever will there is left, I must resist.

I cover my eyes with my hands and stutter, "What did you two do?"

"To leave here whenever I wanted," she laughs. "What else is there for me to do? Look around you. You have seen it, haven't you? The eternal silence, the void in between my world and your world. What could be minutes in your world is years in mine."

Even if she hadn't cast aside her humanity completely, the separation of time and space would have broken the chains that kept her together.

She would forget herself, long after she had fully given into her predatory nature.

"I wanted to be in both worlds. Somnus did it, as did the plant underneath the Yellow Count's castle and the sand god. They figured out ways to stay in your world. Why couldn't I do the same? I was human once; they are just primal beasts. I should be allowed to come and go as I please. I should be allowed to return to the place I called home." Dotty laughs. "That's why Somnus enjoys messing with people, I think. There is nothing to do here except endlessly search for food. Just imagine how many hundreds, thousands of people came before you Claire. How long do you think he has been at this, refining his technique? How many people have been in your shoes? How many people have been manipulated and suffered because of his machinations?"

I hold my arm, look away, and shake my head. "I don't know."

"But I'm not like him. I can be someone else's angel. Show them the path that I took. And they could join me. Then I don't have to be alone always. Darius took a leap of faith. He'll join me after he's done enough good deeds. I keep my promises."

"So you're doing all this because you are lonely?"

"I can be your angel if you want…" She stops to touch the tip of her nose. "You don't want me. You want her. The girl you call Heather."

"What?"

"She's alive, you know. You've been wondering what happened to her. I can show you if you want. No hidden catch, no strings attached. Just look into the mirror and see for yourself. Think of this as a goodwill gesture."

The mirror fogs over. I stare through the cloudy glass, hoping to find what I seek, what the angel promised me. For a few minutes, nothing happens. Just a dark mirror shines before me. But a mirror is designed to reflect. There is no reflection, at least not of the theater hall.

I see the hallway to my apartment, a place I haven't been to in what might be decades. Kneeling by the door is Heather. A bluish tint colors her skin, she looks strung-out as she bangs on my door over and over. The neighbors are staring at her.

"Claire! Please open the door! Please!" Heather screams.

But I don't answer. Even if I am there, it is not me who is standing under my skin. My body belongs to something else; my will is shackled with invisible chains. Only now do I feel the recoil, the massive weight dragging me to the bottom of the ocean.

The neighbors stare at her. From the looks of their annoyance, more than their indifference, Heather had been at it for quite some time. Her wails are wearing them thin. Having had enough, one or all called the police. They put the handcuffs on her and drag her away, despite her resistance.

My hand reaches out to the mirror, but before I can touch it the image vanishes. Instead, I see myself with Dotty standing behind me.

Dotty says, "She was taken away by the police, she's safe for the moment. I can send Darius to find her if you want. You can see with my eyes on him with the mirror. All you have to do is ask."

The eyes…she can see our world using his tattoos.

So with the drawn eyes in invisible ink she can see into our world just fine. But does it end just there, with her seeing?

Can she do something more?

Can she use the papers to do something like enter our world? Can she summon herself at will to feast on innocent people?

My mouth twists into a smile against my will. I speak without speaking. A loud monotone ring echoes from the deepest bowels. And out of this sharp ring comes a whispering yell of another person.

Took long enough, but you figured it out Claire. I'm so proud of you.

Dotty moves away from me, further back down the mirror.

"How did you find me?" Dotty stutters.

He belongs to us. He is a beacon in whatever darkness he falls in. It was only a matter of time before we found him.

"Let him go. My business with him doesn't concern you."

He is our puppet, not yours. But you were once his puppet.

"No longer. I did what was asked of me. He promised me I'd be blessed if I helped guide Joe. Even if Joe couldn't ascend, I would! But Somnus betrayed me by choosing you!"

Of course. I was stronger, and became stronger because I had my fill of the sand god. All bends to my will now.

"Well, I became this on my own. I worked for what I became. He gave you everything. You're nothing but his dog."

Yes, I am a loyal dog, just like you were once. But you still have a purpose.

"I won't help you or Somnus."

From my pores, pressing against the tiny hairs that stick out of them, tiny strands of silk stab upward. Hundreds, then thousands of them pull out like rope. They coil against one another, forming marionette strings. I can feel my body moving against my will.

There is no resisting. My hands reach forward, and my body lunges into the mirror. I expect glass to shatter, but instead the mirror warps around my hand like a bubble. The sensation of liquid nitrogen burns my skin as I dive in further.

Dotty tries to run away from me, but the bubble bursts. I dash at her and tackle her. Then my hands grip her neck. I squeeze tightly, my cold, burning skin becoming one with her smooth, beautiful, warm skin—a lover's embrace that has no love whatsoever.

All the while, I am laughing mad. My body is hysterical, but I am truly mortified by my actions. Yet this regret doesn't last. Instead, what I see around me is even worse than what I'm doing.

On the other side of the mirror, I see the theater through a madman's lens. The wood has been replaced with ripped and dried flesh. Hundreds of mutilated human corpses stretching back into the darkness fill the seats. They show the marks of teeth and blades, they have been ripped apart and show an eternal agony that serves a reminder of their last moments of unimaginable horror.

Holding her with my grip, I begin to see who these people are. Her memories become mine. Memories of Darius stalking them, her seeing through his otherworldly tattoos, through a glass-like mirror. Their deaths were intimate, personal, wild. I can see her hands stabbing at her friends: the first sacrifices for her ascension. Her hands morph into Darius'. The pleading cries of the people murdered crash against every sense I have. Their pain becomes mine. Absolute agony, even after their lives are snuffed out.

Each death is a trophy to her.

I can feel my will pump through my bloodstream, and I tighten the grip around her neck.

She has to die. This is for the best.

A hand moves over my brain, the touch is warm and soft. I can hear her whisper without speaking; I can see tears that only a human could shed.

"We can save you," she says. "We can save her…you both don't have to die. You don't have to be a slave to them, like I was. You don't have to join me, just help me."

You should have never become one of us. Your flesh was weak, but his flesh is worthy. We will break him in properly. We will make him a weapon unto us. Then he can be us, if he likes.

"You can choose, Claire…choose me…Somnus is damnation." Dotty's essence floods my mind, as if she is trying not only to replace my memories, but also replace my personality with hers.

Just then, the mirror cracks, filling with the red misty fog that has become a part of my life. I hear a voice calling out to me. It's a pleading voice of horror, one I recognize from a time long ago. He is calling my name, telling me to stop.

"Goddamn it, Walker, stop!" His frightened yell weakens my grip on Dotty. With each blink of my eyes, the theater is replaced by something familiar in a nostalgic kind of way.

Dotty herself is slowly replaced by the outline of a man, then by the features of a man. I am not choking him like I was choking her. He is on his back; I am on top of him. In my hand is a piece of broken chain, filed down to a sharp point.

"Walker!" Paxton yells again.

"I'm sorry," I whisper as I fall onto my side. The sudden rush, then absence of adrenaline, almost makes me pass out. On my side, I see the wall where I was chained has been torn down. The shackles are still around my wrists, the flesh it touches is raw and bloodied. All over the walls, floor, and ceiling are pictures of drawn eyes everywhere. The words "Let me sleep, salaam" make up the design of each eye.

Dotty's words echo through my mind.

The past twenty years of darkness echo in my mind.

There is no hope. God has abandoned me.

Chapter Thirty-four

Hunger is a powerful thing. Metaphorically and physically, hunger is what keeps us alive. Our constant, endless searching fuels the engine inside every one of us. We share this with the animals, the monsters, those Pale Strangers.

Right now, the physical aspect has turned me into a wretched slob.

I'm not even cooking food anymore. Eating straight out the can, cold and raw, surrounded by tens of empty cans. I just need to feed. My stomach is ready to burst from all the food undigested, yet I still hunger.

At first, I used my week of absence from the human world as an excuse. I tried to explain to Paxton that I was gone from our world for at least two decades; he accepted my claim despite not comprehending what I experienced. I can do this all day, and I plan on it.

But with each bite, each swallow, each satiated pleasure running across my chest, I grow scared. Am I becoming less human? More primal? Am I becoming not unlike a Pale Stranger?

A chill comes over me as the thoughts tickle me with uncertainty. I shiver, tug on the blanket, and curl my knees closer to my chest. Paxton throws some trash into the makeshift fire pit at the end of the swimming pool to deal with an odd late summer chill that affects only Gordy's former mansion. The fire does nothing for me, except tempt me to jump in and self-immolate.

"So, Walker, let's go over this," Paxton says as he arranges the papers I had written. Moments after attempting to stab him, I had gone into a trance and wrote page after page of the influx of information in my skull. The facts become clear to me, clear like the evening sky above. I would have never known the full scope of what had gone on, yet I do.

A parting gift from Dotty Finley: missing pieces of Joe's research. More like a good will gesture than anything else, but I think it's also an incentive to join her.

"What don't you understand?" I ask.

"It's not that I don't understand. I just don't know which goes first and what goes last."

He hands me the papers. I read off them, notice they aren't in order. So I hand them back and say, "Sorry. Wrote as much as I could when it came to me. Some of it was what I learned, some of it was imparted to me."

To be honest, a sane man wouldn't be able to decode what I wrote.

We weren't sane men anymore, if ever.

Everything started a few thousand years ago in China. The sand god was considered a demon to the Chinese people. He haunted the vast desert of the country for untold generations. Holy men sacrificed themselves to get him out of their land. On a one-way suicide journey, they marched the captured Pale Stranger across the mountains and into Afghanistan. Fatigue, death, and madness made the men abandon their journey and make one of the mountains a prison for the creature. The sand god couldn't escape, so it spread out, like a weed, like a virus, and infected the mountain. It ate away all the vegetation, all the wildlife, and whoever was unlucky to pass by.

"The Sand God chilled under the mountain yet couldn't escape. Got too big and fat. When there was no flesh to feed on, it fed on the rocks, sand, and dirt. I think without proper food the sand god very well could have ate up the entire alphabet on the periodic table that made up the land of Afghanistan, and left a giant crater that could be seen from space."

Paxton scoffs, then rubs his eyes. "Impossible," he says.

"These aren't creatures like us. I'm no scientist, but without a doubt, quantum mechanics and relativity wouldn't be able to solve these things. They eat what they can, which I think is everything. Walking black holes."

This is the reason the ruins of the Yellow Count's castle and the ruins found in Afghanistan yielded strange results in terms of actual age. Quite literally, the sand god turned the very land into brittle sand. The actions of countess and the plant under the castle aged the metal and stone. Everything became older because of the Pale Stranger's influence and presence. They are vacuums, sucking everything dry on a microscopic level in order to feed and stay alive.

I think that's one of the reasons I look horrible, why my body is failing on me. It happened to Gordy, happened to Darius too. It even happened to the Yellow Count before he was turned into a Pale Stranger.

"So what happened next?" Paxton asks.

I shrug. "Nothing that I know of until Charles Benson's expedition led him to the Afghanistan ruins."

Hundreds of years later, thousands of miles away, the sixteenth century rolled around, 1500 CE, Germany. The site of the Yellow Count's castle. A similar scenario with the sand god. A Pale Stranger was hidden inside the castle. I don't know how long it had been there; it had to have been at least ten years but no more.

The plant Pale Stranger lived underneath the castle itself at first; if by choice or because it got stuck, it doesn't matter. The prison was there. Unlike the sand god, the plant had an ample supply of food. Starved and mutilated bodies of traitors and heretics were around for it to feed on discretely. So it planted itself under the castle, then inside the walls. Just like a plant, its roots spread out as far as they could go.

Its influence wasn't felt, or implied in anything, until after the Yellow Count imprisoned the countess. In time, she was either killed or died, and her body was used as an avatar for the plant. It controlled her like a puppet, telling the Yellow Count what to do. She influenced him, while the plant drove his servants mad.

The castle grew bigger, the prison grew larger, and the victims kept on coming. It expanded into that monstrous shape I glimpsed through eyes not mine. Scarring images that echo across generations. The beast wanted more.

"I think the Pale Stranger in the Yellow Count's castle grew much faster than the sand god. Took on the characteristics of a flytrap, or something like that. With all this food coming, there was no reason for it to not grow. The sand god had at least a thousand years to expand on nothing but vegetation, rock, and the occasional passerby."

"How big was the sand god?"

"The size of a mountain, possibly even more. At least a mile long."

Paxton grunts as he stares deeply into the fire pit, my words trouble him. I am bothered by my words as well. Just how big can these things get? What if one ever breaks free? One that large, running around. No single human could stop it.

I try not to think about it as I continue my timeline of events.

The Ghosts in the Mist aren't actual ghosts, but a collective of Pale Strangers. Back then they were more wolf, werewolf even, made of smoke and haze. There is no explaining this to Paxton; he saw them in another, more human form. The ghosts attacked the Yellow Count's castle. I go back to the events that Benson had pieced together, how a boy and his sister ended up running away, only to be chased by the ghosts. The siblings ended up coming across the camp belonging to the Order of the Yellow Moon.

Their leader, a man by the name of Götz, was apparently the beloved of the girl.

"Götz took his men and went to the Yellow Count's castle. He was a badass, from what I saw firsthand. He killed at least two Pale Strangers and avoided the attacks from the giant plant. Those Germans had some insane fighters back in the day."

"So they can be fought? Killed?" Paxton asks with a huge grin.

I nod. "I think the Ghosts were weakened when their original leader betrayed them, but still. Götz's beloved was killed by the Yellow Count. The countess tried to plead with Götz, tried to get Götz to join her. He stabbed her. By then, the castle was engulfed in flames. Götz took his beloved's body and left the castle."

The bothersome part happened next. The countess obviously was possessed, and if I hadn't seen the Yellow Count stab the heart, I would have thought her to be a Pale Stranger. But she was just a husk, used by the plant to act and talk for it freely. A parasite operating the deceased body, just like Levitt.

The plant wanted to move elsewhere, to put its roots down in other places. It even survived death and tried to do just that, starting from zero. Maybe the Pale Stranger was stronger than we thought, or perhaps it survived on will alone. But whatever the case, its plans were quickly ruined when a lost little girl, hungry and mad, ate the remains of the countess and the plant to survive. She became a fairy of myth but with a twisted take: the Black Fairy.

As for the Yellow Count, he was hit with a ball of fire. That should have been his last moment, but he was pulled away by the ghosts and made an offer.

"The Yellow Count was given a damnation or death choice," I say. "He could either die there, or he could become a Pale Stranger and save the Ghosts in the Mist. The creatures were dying, just like him. Their original betrayed them to feed all for himself. I didn't see what happened, or just why this happened, but I believe he is the one Dotty called Somnus. He is the same one who has been popping up to me multiple times; the same one pulling Levitt's strings."

"Question: what did you mean the ghosts were dying?"

I explain what I saw. The Ghosts in the Mist and the Yellow Count were dying. The ghosts were without a form. I think Somnus was the physical host for them, but with him gone they couldn't move around or survive for long. The Yellow Count's body was being eaten by fire but he still could be a host. Not wanting to die, the Yellow Count agreed to let them come into him. The Yellow Count transformed and became a Pale Stranger.

"So the ghosts are like man-o-wars then?" Paxton asks.

"What do you mean?" I ask.

"Well, the man-o-war is a type of jellyfish." Paxton holds his hands out, forming a box shape. "But they aren't jellyfish. It is an organism made up of countless smaller organisms."

"So the Yellow Count and the ghosts are like a jellyfish made up of smaller organisms?"

Paxton shrugs. "It makes sense. They hunt as a group. Prey doesn't stand a chance. Just like a pack of predators, operating as one unit. Without one another, they cannot survive. To survive, the Yellow Count became legion, for he is now many."

The science analogy would have been something I might have imagined coming from Darius Renton, if he was still sane, the religious analogy from Joe, if he was still alive. I didn't even want to think about such biblical demons as real. That they are actually Pale Strangers, actually demons, that they are still lurking out there.

Yet the possibility is real. I move on, pretending that is a fairy tale.

The Ghosts in the Mist, now with the Yellow Count as the host, moved around from place to place. Five hundred years later, they are in the United States, in our town. When they got here, I don't know. They refined their technique over centuries. Practice makes perfect, I guess.

Nothing was to be said for the five hundred years in between. Nothing important, at least. World War I came around. A farmer named Johan and his family were living in Germany around then. On their land was a scarecrow that had been there for an indeterminate amount of time. The scarecrow was actually a Pale Stranger. It remained frozen in one spot for at least decades. How and why it was there was never answered.

While I want to get into details involving what happened at the prison and the presence of the Black Fairy, a question pops in my mind, one that makes Johan's case more interesting.

"Why would a Pale Stranger choose to not kill Johan and his family?"

Paxton stutters words, and then ends with his hand cupping his mouth. For a few minutes, we both remain quiet, trying to figure out what to say. Unlike the other stories, Johan's involvement with the Scarecrow was unlike any other.

The Scarecrow did not try to turn Johan into a Pale Stranger. It didn't even try to harm him physically. It just followed him. At times, it called out to him, waved at him, and was curious about Johan's state of being. The Scarecrow even defended Johan from the Black Fairy and went out of its way to protect both him and Foch when the two monsters dueled.

The Pale Strangers are feral by instinct, predatory by hunger. But Johan was not on the Scarecrow's list. Why?

"Maybe he was trying to indoctrinate him," Paxton says.

I shake my head. "No, the Scarecrow had all of Johan's life to do it. He even had Johan's grandparents, parents, and children to use if he wanted. There is something more. There is a reason he just followed him..."

My ears pick up something soft, quiet. Very faint but audible.

"You know the truth, Claire," Dotty whispers to me. "Just say it."

The familiarity is strengthened by that sickly smell of sweetness. That urge of sensual protection. It is Dotty calling out to me. I look around, then stop. She isn't here. She's reaching across space, time, and reality to talk to me. Her words comfort, yet claw. I feel her course through my blood, bittersweet and toxic with a gentle kiss.

She is flowing in me, there's no way of blocking her out. Yet I want more, like a dying drunk who needs another drop from a fatal bottle. Her wisdom stands on the tip. The answer is there. Just grasp the fucking thing before it vanishes.

My hand presses against my forehead. Immense pain beats louder than my heart. The pool swirls in on itself. Paxton bends, contorts, and presses until he is just a speck of atoms I cannot possibly see.

Instead, I see a battlefield I once took part in as another man. The baking sun devours all. The muddy flakes of grass are covered in death and decay. Blood streams from a million rivers, from caverns of corpses sprawled in the air.

Impaled in their cores are the spikes of the Scarecrow. Raised highest of all are the battered remains of the Black Fairy, above her brood. More than just eating her, the Scarecrow has raised her so far that her shadow is an umbrella.

He is championing his kill. One only accomplished because of one man.

A simple family man who lived on a farm his entire life. A wounded, dying man who was crawling away from the Scarecrow.

Johan, where are you going?

"Please," Johan whispers, tears flowing from his eyes. "Let me die."

Why? There is so much to do, so many places to see, so many to eat. We are friends.

Johan struggles to crawl, then stops. Unable to go any further, he forces himself to his knees. Out of defiance, Johan spits at the Scarecrow. "You've taken everything I held dear away from me. We aren't friends."

I've been with you all your life. I was there when you were born. I was there when you first played, when you first loved, when you first hurt, and when you first feared. Every second I am there. And I will be, forever.

"I don't want you in my life. You are the malice that ruined me. Please, just go away. Or kill me. Do it, monster. That's your nature, monster, so kill me."

"Johan!" Dr. Foch yells, stumbles out from one of the trenches. Despite being crippled, Foch aims at the Scarecrow. Bullets stray, hitting him in the neck and chest. The Scarecrow's wounds fizzle before teeth close them shut. His effort is meaningless, yet he tries until the last bullet fires. The Scarecrow turns to Foch and tilts his head.

So tenacious. The ones that fight till the end taste the best. Almost as good as my kind.

Johan reaches out his hand and attempts to touch the Scarecrow's feet. His hand trembles and his skin ruptures. Wracked with pain, Johan stutters, "No more. Please. Let him go. Just let us be. Let me sleep."

The Scarecrow looks at him, past him. He is looking at me.

Do you want me gone? Do you wish me on someone else?

Johan can't talk anymore. All he does is nod.

I can't talk anymore. All I do is nod.

I want to sleep. Please, God, let me sleep.

Very well, Claire. You will sleep soon. The price will be worth it, I promise.

I feel my consciousness pulled back by a burning pain in my stomach. My teeth crack, the nerves inside rip apart with cold lightning. Water filled with oil and sand floods my lungs, suffocating me. Falling to my knees, I clench my throat; gasping for air leaves me flushed with scarlet fever. An alien has invaded me and rips me apart from inside.

To my side, I hear hooves press against dirt, breaking grass and twigs. On horseback is a knight in shattered, dark armor stained with smoke and blood. In front of him is a wrapped body, slung over his legs. Holding onto him from behind is a tearful, sickly looking boy.

"Götz," says the little boy. "Why must you go?"

"I am a knight of the Yellow Moon, I have my duties. I am needed elsewhere."

"Can I come with you?"

"No, it's too dangerous. One of my soldiers is willing to take you in since you have no family. You will be his son. You will live the life of a farmer, or you can join us when you come of age. That is your choice."

"Will you come home one day?" Götz says nothing as they ride. The boy reaches out for the wrapped body, but his small hands cannot reach. "Did you really love my sister?"

Götz stares at the corpse in the shroud. He brushes his gauntlet against it, turns his head, and nods. Though I know not much of Götz, I know that the time he spent with her was short. Yet his love was true, as is his heartbreak.

What he doesn't tell the boy is the real reason he can't take him.

This knight made a decision that day in the burning ruins of the Yellow Count's castle. War, revenge, sorrow are trivial things compared to the truth he learned there. Among a thousand men, an empire of more, he is alone. Deep inside is a burning rage threatening to possess him. Hidden within that rage is a trembling fear devouring his sanity.

The creatures are still out there. And he is willing to dive into the darkness to stop them.

Death is simple; death is kind. These things are not.

But this boy has a chance to start anew. He has a chance to live the life Götz denied himself, was denied to him. He is never to know the pleasures of living a normal life.

Out of the corner of my eye, hidden in darkness, I see him. I see the Pale Stranger.

The Scarecrow is waving at the boy. He is waving at me.

Hello friend! You will help me. I'll make it your worthwhile.

The pain is overwhelming, this pain called truth. Tiny worms wiggle around in my skull, eating away at my brain. My stomach begins to burst. I feel acid volleying through my throat. My body freezes as I throw up. All the food I ate is emptied out, followed by blood.

I'm back in my world. Reality sets in, and I feel alone more than ever.

Paxton hands me a glass of water. The liquid is cold, yet has no taste. Repulsion fills my thinking, from both the water and from Paxton's helping hand. I try to push him away, but I'm too weak.

I say, "Just kill me, Slowburn. Get it over with. Take your revenge and get out of here."

Paxton shakes his head. "Not this again, Walker. If we die, they win. I need you alive. We have to kill Darius and his angel, remember?"

"Somnus, Dotty, the Pale Strangers, they are all after me. It's gonna get worse. There is no hope for me." My coughs interrupt me for a few minutes. I take extended breaks between breaths, spitting when I can to wet my mouth. "Johan did something for the Scarecrow. Something terrible. The Scarecrow goes back all the way to the Yellow Count. He was after the boy that survived. Whatever Johan did ties back to what happened here."

"What did he do?"

"Johan was willing to do anything to save him and Foch. Foch confessed years later that he was damned for what he did. If there were a hell, he'd burn there. They saved themselves in return, but whatever they did was worse than them dying. And I fear that we are going to have to make a similar choice. But ours is clearer…easier…simpler."

We just have to kill Darius and Dotty.

My ears pick up a solid, distinct scratching against the pool surface. I stare at the fire in the pit, knowing full well there is no point in looking for it. Paxton hasn't picked it up yet. His senses aren't that tuned, not yet anyway.

"Paxton," I whisper, "grab what you can. It's time to go."

Chapter Thirty-five

Goddamn rain finally fell on the way outside the city to Jaune. The radio weatherman said a nice storm was brewing. I can't feel the humidity. Can't feel much of anything anymore. My senses have dulled from the bombardment of pain. The only way to make the painkillers more effective is to swallow a couple dozen with some hundred-proof rubbing alcohol and hope for the best.

I am huddled in the back seat, staring at what I wrote, fighting the urge to doze off into another nightmare. Paxton drives in silence, taking a moment to ask questions about what I learned. I think he does it more to keep me conscious than to endow himself with knowledge. Not like there is much to listen to. Whenever he changes the stations, anything other than weather shoots out massive doses of static.

Maybe the Pale Strangers hate polka music. That is my personal hell. Polka hell. At least I'm spared that fate for now. Our sole entertainment is from my constant turning and replaying of Joe's music box.

I continue the story from where Paxton said I had left off before the last indoctrination. This is the clearest part of the story. Dotty Finley met Joe Renton under orders of the Pale Stranger called Somnus. How this came to be, I do not know, but I saw the end result.

Both Dotty and Joe had irreversible changes. Constant exposure, indoctrination, and the presence of Somnus warped them in body and mind. Somnus had an interest in Joe from the start; through Dotty, he was able to manipulate Joe.

Why did Somnus do this? Why go through the trouble?

The answers were hazy to me but no longer.

To feed. It is all a Pale Stranger really is after.

A few days for me ended up being over twenty years. Maybe he's bored, insane from the theoretical millions of years he could have spent in that realm of chaos.

No wonder their hunger is never-ending, not that I understand their physiology anyway. Curious scientists will throw caution to the wind to study these things. And it will lead to the deaths of many. Darwin would frown upon their stupidity, before handing them an award.

"Something is bothering me, Walker," Paxton says. "This Pale Stranger Somnus, the one behind everything. How did he know which person to choose to get involved?"

I sniff and follow the raindrops splashing on the window. "Not a question of how, but when. If he had been planning this from the start, there had to be some point in time where he got to Dotty. This hole is bothering me, like a small itch of molten pain."

The Yellow Count and Johan have a bridge: their stories took place in Germany and involved the Scarecrow, and to a lesser extent the Black Fairy. From here in America, Benson traveled to both Germany and Afghanistan under the guidance of Joe. After both Joe and Benson's death, Darius got involved. Then Paxton and Greene came into play. All of us were brought together by Somnus, with Dotty then Levitt acting rivets.

Whether I liked it or not, Paxton and I became involved when we fought in that house. Trying to burn the house and that little girl, then me trying to play hero, damned us both.

Yet from the end of Johan's story to the beginning of Dotty's there is no bridge. No rivets, no chains, no connecting the dots. While the Yellow Count is the leader of the Ghosts in the Mist, he has played no role in what is going on in our tales. He is my enemy, but that's further down the road, if we live to see that happen.

"Three people have the answers to this: Dotty, Darius, and Levitt," I say.

"That don't help us much."

I shake my head as I itch all over. "Indoctrination might be the way."

Paxton sours his expression. "Don't say that, Walker. You're a footstep away from falling off the ledge. You're becoming just like Darius."

"And Joe," I scoff. "And Gordy. Johan, Foch. The Yellow Count and his servants. Dotty and Levitt too. All I can name." My heart murmurs; I ache with a breath of panic. My voice strains, but I hit my chest, gasp, and continue in a strained voice. "We are all victims here. Invisible victims. No one will know our misery because they refuse to see us. Not their fault. Their blood knows we're infected. They smell the scent of the parasitic Pale Strangers on us. It's for the best. More people will die. Can't let that happen. No one should suffer our fate."

Paxton nods. "We're almost there. You sure you want to do this?"

"I need to do this before we go to the Vin Forest. I won't get another chance, regardless of what happens to us."

Trying to think about it has become harder than not doing so. I have to remind myself every other minute who I'm going to see. It's a confession that I have yet to make to Paxton, like it would make a difference if I did.

The encounters I've had with these Pale Strangers have done more damage than the scars on my body show. The indoctrination has done its job. My short-term memory is short-circuiting. Places, people, information vanish. My long-term memory is even worse. I can't remember my earliest moments as a child. Not elementary school, not high school, not college. When I think of my parents, when I think of my classmates, when I think of any important figure in the media at the moment, I come up with physical blanks. Their faces are gone. Featureless, emotionless, unreadable.

Not unlike a Pale Stranger, despite being human.

Are they still human? Am I still human?

Such questions bother me for a little. Then I forget. I forget that Paxton and I originally hated each other, and I forget his name until I read what I had written about him. All his crimes, all the vileness he caused is washed away, leaving a clean slate. Only a memento of my handwriting reminds me of what he is and why he is helping me.

Yet I remember them. They stand out with clarity, a blot of white in my eternal darkness. I'll never forget them. I can smell them from those black holes in the universe they reside in. I know they're there. My body knows. The blood knows. That I won't forget; I can't forget. I'll never forget this fear. Something ancient, something primal embedded in my genetic code by breath of God enters my soul.

Interlaced in this fear are the memories of men before me. They are my memories now, having replaced the ones I made on my own. Some fought against the horror. Some were overtaken by the horror. Some embraced the horror. Some became the horror.

The horror is all I know now. All I remember.

But I still remember her. Even through all this, I haven't forgotten her.

Paxton did some investigating while I was chained during my last indoctrination. He found out where Heather was taken. First she went to jail for possession and being under the influence of narcotics. She entered rehab to avoid a lengthy jail sentence.

Turns out our old friend Oliver Greene had done some maneuvering to help her avoid jail time. I assume either he didn't want to deal with her, knowing her link to me, or he didn't want to deal with me in case she was convicted. His scar, and the idea that Slowburn was still out there, put him in his place. Or maybe he felt guilty.

I wish there was some way I could thank him.

No, better he never sees me again. Might get arrested. Might get him and others killed. This is my onus. My fate.

Where are you Claire? I'm waiting for you. Please, hurry.

Her smell gets to me. Pain and ecstasy run together, firing off mixed signals that make me nauseated yet excited. Fever chills me. I shouldn't feel this way, but I do. She infected me when I was in her realm. I need her. Confliction makes me relapse, yearn. I have to have her. She is the drug I've been looking for all this time.

This is the sensation Darius must feel every time he deals with Dotty.

"She's calling me, Chambers," I say. "She wants me, needs me."

Paxton looks at me in the mirror. "Dotty?" I nod. "Why is she calling you and not Darius?"

"I practically am Darius now. At least I know it. Darius is just a shell, a puppet. His mind is scrambled eggs. No different from the lost. No different from the countess. I'm still sane. She needs me for something. I'm just a tool for them to use. I know, I know…" I repeat myself forever, staring around at the car and hoping the world doesn't change on me.

Outside the window, my red, hazy spiral spins further and further in the distance. Like a twister miles wide, it moves along, a cobra's venom running through its veins. Millions of tiny voices susurrus across every piece of skin I have; my ears refuse to listen to the garble. Paxton can't see or hear. Of course not. Only the truly damned can. He's not there yet. I must tell him. I must tell the world what terror lurks around us, through a mirror darkened with blood and fear.

Before I can whisper, the spiral vanishes. I hold the music box closer and shiver.

There is no longer a distinction between reality and nightmares. How long before the next one? How long until I die?

The car slows, and Paxton makes a few turns. The rehab center is very plain, melding in with the city. I wouldn't be able to pick it out from a shopping center. Paxton parks the car a little ways from the entrance.

"Just drive around," I say. "I don't know how long I'll be."

Paxton nods. As I open the door, he taps me on the elbow. I turn to him. "Walker. Our past doesn't matter anymore. I'm not the man I was a year ago when you stopped me from indulging in my flame dance. You're not the man struggling with bills, taking on a job to make ends meet. It's not that we have changed. Nothing has. We are the same people. But our past doesn't matter anymore. So long as those creatures are out there, we are the prey. And the hunter. This is our life now."

I rub my face and nod. I know. "Does that mean you hate me?"

"I would have tied you to a pike and poured boiling mercury on you the moment I got out of prison if none of this happened."

I laugh at his threat. I'm pretty sure he means every word of it. But the past doesn't matter anymore, so long as they are out there. Our hatreds, our prejudices, our quirks, our vices don't matter. It's us versus them. And it's a war we cannot win.

Yet we'll try anyway, with all hope lost and oblivion our only recourse. Because our bodies will keep going. The blood will keep us moving, long after our will to fight ceases.

"Cut it off as best as you can," Paxton says. "No fancy good-byes, none of that. It'll be easier that way. The belly of the beast awaits us just down the road. A long night that just started."

I nod again. When I step out of the car, the cold rain beats down on my wounds like glacier-sized icicles. I wince as I make my way to the trunk. I retrieve the briefcase filled with our war funds. Most of it remains.

A gun in one hand, the briefcase in the other, and wet clothes pushing me down, I watch Paxton drive off. Left alone in this flooded parking lot, I hobble toward the entrance of the rehab center. An orange-yellow glow appears from the lamps above, acting as an electronic beacon in the downpour. I take giant deep breaths as I swing one leg over another. My pain is agonizing. But I march, however slow, to the entrance.

"You're still looking for the truth, aren't you, Claire?" Levitt's voice vibrates through the raindrops whizzing past me. I turn, but he is not at my side. "You have to come to my level if you ever wanna find me…"

Way down low.

Levitt's laugh distorts with splashes. I look under my feet at the water. The concrete is hidden under a corrupted, thick liquid of black. Hundreds of leeches waggle between hundreds of human fingers. They stretch out under my feet, making a hand that is more like a mouth.

Despite being terrified, I'm too tired to run. I will my body to not jump out of its skin. Levitt isn't here to hunt me. He's here to mess with my mind, to taunt me, threaten me until I break or do what he says. But I won't budge. Not this time. I need the truth.

"Yes. I want to know, Levitt, while I'm still me. Might make the end more bearable."

The fingers and leeches melt into the water and are washed down a drain in the parking lot. Levitt laughs. "Go on ahead, lover. She is dreaming of you. We are all dreaming of you. That's all we do. You're always on our minds. Don't keep her waiting."

I continue on and enter the rehab center. The receptionist ignores me. Figures. I look at her entry log of patients who have come and gone. Heather is on this floor. Her room is a few hallways and a turn away.

The junkies waiting for treatment moan restlessly. Homesick, relapsing, withdrawals. They are below the rock, embedded in the muddy hell that is drug abuse. Then I come along, and they all stop. In silence, they freeze. They don't see me, don't even look in my direction. Willful blindness has its perks. But they know the fear. Even with the drugs and the pain, that primal instinct is never dulled. I know that from experience.

All they know is a cursed man walks among them, followed by a Pale Stranger.

I notice the lights have dimmed. When I look up at the fluorescent bulbs, I see bodies of leeches slithering around inside the glass. Levitt's shining eye illuminate them.

"You're such the popular one; everyone wants a piece of you," Levitt says. "But I'm glad you're making time for little old me. Because you had me feeling lonely. You don't write, you don't call. I miss our little talks."

Levitt's eyes float across the leeches. He looks away from me and stares at the junkies. "So delicious. All of them. Can't fight back. So easy."

"Why don't you kill them and eat?"

"There is no thrill in it. The hunter that I am wants game worthy of my presence. And something that tastes better."

"What could taste better than us humans?"

"Pale Strangers, of course."

I rub my temples as I walk down the hallway. As I pass under each bulb, Levitt shadows it out. His words bounce around the glass like wet Ping-Pong balls. His answer, while simple, cannot find a place in my comprehension. "That makes no sense. You feed on Pale Strangers?"

"When we can. I told you we are opportunists. Not many like us, with tastes forbidden."

"So all of this…is so you can eat other Pale Strangers?"

"Bingo. No grand mystery in that, no smoking gun. Just the prize. A Pale Stranger to feed on. Surprised that we resort to cannibalism?"

"A little. The Yellow Count told me there was competition, but this…"

"It's all about survival. Darwinism at its most pure, most chaotic."

"So when you say you want me to kill Dotty and Darius, you really just want to eat them?"

"Dotty, yes. Darius, no. No, I have something in mind for him. He's mine. Dotty belongs to the one you call Somnus."

I stop and lean against the wall. I look at the bulb Levitt's leeches are hiding in. "All this manipulation. The indoctrination. Why? Why me?"

"You were the right man in the wrong place. Just like Johan."

"But why? You can do this on your own."

Levitt laughs and swirls around in the glass. "Have you seen me? My body was blown to bits when the United States government cooked the sand god. It took me years of feeding on its corpse to get this form going. But it works out great." The lights flicker on and off in the hallway. "I'm good at manipulating electronics. I was good at it in life, but let me tell you, nothing can beat what I can do now. What I can do with a body, well, you saw that at Giallo's. I'm a master puppeteer now. What some humans would give to do what I can, with no strings or electronics involved. True magic."

"Before I continue…why did you kill Daniels and West? And those marines?"

The glass cracks and the bulb explodes. "You're so ungrateful, Claire. You said you wanted them gone, you complained at how they ruined your life. So I took care of them for you. It was the least I could do. As for the marines…well, let me just say I had a score to settle with them. A personal grudge that has survived the infinity I've spent in my world. Rankin was always the smart one; he avoided my wrath and hunger. I'll deal with him too, one day."

"Why me, then? Why do I have to suffer?"

You had the best blood, just right and sweet enough in case you failed. While you would feed us just as good, we want more from you. You can be a tool. You can be a weapon of us.

Levitt's monotonous voice deepens into something creepy, yet smooth. "So selfish, Claire. This isn't about you. It's about us. It's about the others who came before you. And it's about the Pale Strangers in each of those stories. The Black Fairy, the sand god, the plant under the Yellow Count's castle. All of them had something in common. You know what that is?"

I stand there for several minutes, trying to think of an answer. Levitt pesters me like an annoying child with a secret. Despite being no longer human, he enjoys a very human game of teasing. But I think hard, as much as my mind will allow me.

Then comes a disturbing thought, the worst thing I can possibly imagine.

My body gravitates toward this.

No other alternative. This has to be the reason.

"The end of the world…"

"Bravo, Mr. Holmes. An end-game scenario, worse than any possible nuclear disaster humanity could inflict on itself, more devastating than the extinction of the dinosaurs. The only thing comparable would be the sun going supernova and turning this planet into a molten rock."

I shiver, and squirm at Levitt's words.

"How is that even possible?"

"Hunger is a powerful thing. For us, it's an addiction. We don't detox for when we overindulge. That's why we wait years in between meals. The hunger overwhelms us if we keep eating without prejudice. Once we become accustomed to a certain quota…well, we have to keep feeding the fiend."

I continue my walk down the hallway after catching my breath. That can't be the only reason. Levitt's slithering makes me think harder.

The countess was a puppet of the plant underneath the Yellow Count's castle. When the castle was bombarded by the Ghosts in the Mist and knights of the Yellow Moon, the plant had itself a seedlike heart. The plant wanted to put down new roots in new places around the world, wrapping around the planet until they covered every inch.

The Black Fairy was able to use the bodies of dead soldiers to produce her brood. Ten bodies meant ten children. A hundred bodies meant a hundred children. The process could be endless. And each litter of children would help her kill more and procreate more.

The sand god was able to convince tribes of people to bring him victims from all around the world, under the guise of human smuggling and other illegal activities. Over a thousand or more years, he had spread out miles under a mountain, and with time and the help of the lost, he would have been able to extend his reach even further until the land itself couldn't contain him.

Dotty figured out a way to see into our world using her glyphs. Something similar happened with the eyes on Johan's skin caused by the Scarecrow, except she took it further. She was able to replicate it with tattoos and even simple drawings on paper. With enough drawings, she summoned herself in my apartment...if she wanted to, she could have refined her technique so she would only need one paper instead of hundreds.

Everything clicks together at last. And my God, the truth is worse than I imagined. I let out a winding cough, a shade too weak to give me a seizure.

Levitt hums, "They cheated the system. Able to come and go as they please, eat more than would normally available. Yet they didn't take into account a simple fact. To sustain ourselves, we have to feed. We must feed nonstop to keep the engine running to keep hanging around. Apex predators like sharks and lions need large quantities of food to keep their engines going. If left unchecked, they would have spiraled into full genocide, devouring all life first, then all nonlife on a molecular level next. That's not good. They have to be stopped one way or another, before it is too late."

Now I understand. In a twisted kind of way, Somnus and Levitt are policing their kind.

"At least you see the big picture, how this is more than just simple competition. The Yellow Count can't see beyond his own bitterness. You know he's always been a thorn in the side of Somnus, if only for spite. The ghosts only further fuel that hatred."

"What would you have done? Somnus betrayed them and left them without a home. Somnus came to devour everyone in the Yellow Count's castle and left him to die. But it was all part of his mysterious grand plan. I'm *so sure*."

"Plan, yes. But you're overanalyzing creatures like him, and by extension like us, and their choices. We have no concept of morality or consequences, or in the case of us former humans, we no longer need them. He got rid of the ghosts because he wanted to, despite them being a valuable asset. It's why he spent all that time building up Dotty and Renton, before dropping them without a moment's hesitation. It's why he abandoned his pursuit of Benson and chose to save me."

"So what are you saying, Levitt?"

"We have all the time in the world. If you die, another can replace you. If our little chess games get messed up, we can play another with the same pawns or start over elsewhere. You're a disposable species. There have been others before and there will be others after you. But don't feel so desperate. You're useful now and needed in our plan."

I sneer. "Aren't I the lucky one? To have the gracious defense of you two. I'm happy."

"There were a few moments you didn't have our protection. Like when you visited the abandoned plant. Dotty almost killed you there. And when we *lost* you during your little chat with the Yellow Count. I'm surprised he didn't eat you when he had the chance, just to fuck with our plans. Most curious. I wonder why."

"Maybe he was hoping a flame would be planted in my heart. Maybe he was hoping, by some impossible chance, I'd kill you both."

Levitt laughs. "Probably. Many have wished that. Except for Joe. He wanted the answers too, just like you. So loyal, so devoted to his cause, just like you. Indoctrination showed him the truth. But the answers broke him. He was too pure of mind, too grounded in his beliefs and in science. He couldn't comprehend the truth."

"The truth you gave him, Levitt? All you did was torture him."

Levitt vanishes from the light, blinding me with the bulb's full glow. I feel a hand reach into my chest and squeeze my heart and lungs with sharp, burning talons. I collapse to my knees and cough up blood.

The circumstances of my evolution didn't have to start with me getting devoured by the sand god. In my last waking moments as a man I suffered. He deserved to die, just like Benson! They got what they deserved!

The clenching releases; like a pipe after it burst, the pressure is relieved, and I faint. I feel an invisible finger poke me. Pain straightens me, gets me off the floor.

"Oh, I'm sorry, Claire," Levitt says, feigning an apology. "I forget myself sometimes. You are not my prey. I'm your friend. We are like brothers, you and I."

"Brothers?"

"I've been looking after you this entire time. I'm the big brother. You're the little brother."

I rub my eyes. "So, bro, why do I have to do all the dirty work for you?"

"What do you care? You get to be the hero. Save the world from those pesky Pale Strangers. Be that super hero you thought you would be when you stopped Paxton Chambers from burning that little girl."

Levitt's offer interests me more than I want it to. All I have to do is kill Dotty. I get to be a hero. Innocent people will be spared my fate, able to live another day in blissful ignorance of these monsters that lurk beside them. Maybe Levitt is lying to me, manipulating me to do the dirty work for him. Maybe he is afraid of dying and being eaten. But what can I really do?

I am a sheep being led to slaughter. This is not to be questioned. Nothing I can do will change my fate. But something bothers me. Something that might have passed by in my brother's grand plan until just now. The two pieces of the puzzle that have no answers.

"What about the Scarecrow? And Johan? What did Johan and Foch do for the Scarecrow that led them down a despairing path?"

Levitt vanishes from reality, and I am left alone physically. But I hear him breathing in my ear. I hear the metallic screech that is his voice.

That mystery will blow your mind.

I wait for him to talk more. Minutes pass; I stand still. Levitt left me to my own devices. His silent departure and cryptic message are brutal. The constant dodging and running around is annoying. Truth, what truth? Find out for myself? What am I looking for? I see nothing between the lines but blank paper. I am blind to what they want me to look for. And it pisses me off. Endless red tape and twisted Confucianism gets me nowhere. This is no different from all the bullshit I have to deal with in my original life. How am I to figure this out?

All this time, I've been searching through grains of sand, one at a time, in endless dunes. Visions and confessions are all I have to go on.

Each hole I jump in is smaller and deeper than the last. My body, my mind are ravaged by what I experience.

What else do I have to learn? When will I finally go laughing mad? Will this revelation be the one that breaks me?

I'm not going to worry about that now. I've reached Heather's room. Her door is open. The coolest breeze from the ceiling fan hits my wet skin in the best way possible. It's relief, so needed, so welcome, even if it's insignificant.

For once, I feel normal. For now, I don't feel cursed.

Her room is dark and tiny, no bigger than the prison cell I called a temporary home. A small TV is on but muted. She lies asleep on her tiny bed. Her colored hair has been stripped to its natural brown roots. Her pale skin shimmers with sweat. She shivers. Withdrawal pains are kicking her around. I don't know how many days she's been clean or when she got here. It's a pain not many people feel, but those who do suffer in agony. If she overcomes, then every day after that will be a struggle. One has to have will to fight the addiction. One has to try and try.

Funny to think that I didn't suffer the same way. But suffering is the same, no matter how you feel it. It just comes in different amounts, depending on a person's tolerance and coping skills.

"Hey," I whisper, putting the gun and the briefcase aside. She responds by shivering more but not waking. All this trouble to get to her, and she won't wake up. I laugh and slide to the floor. "A million things I have to say, a million words going through my mind. It's funny how they only come out too late. I was hoping to talk face-to-face, but here you are asleep. Typical woman."

I watch the old movie on the TV. I'd recognize it if my memory wasn't erased. The floor is freezing; I should get up and try to find something warm to avoid hypothermia, but fuck it. I doubt that will kill me. Levitt and Somnus won't let me die, not when I'm so close to their prize. I'll just rest here for a moment. What I would give for a good night's rest.

"Claire," Heather mumbles. I look at her and realize she is still asleep. Talking in her sleep, she calls my name again.

"I'm here," I say in a louder voice. She doesn't respond. Instead, she moans and tumbles around in the bed. "It's okay if you don't think I'm here or wake up. It's better that way." I stare at my wrinkled hand filled with cuts and ruptures from the indoctrinations of Pale Strangers. "You don't know me that well. No, you do know me well. You wanted to know just about everything I did. You tried to get to know me as best as you could. You saw something in me that I didn't see in you. I am ashamed to say I never got to know you. I never once asked about your family, your history, or your relationships. Never asked you about your likes or dislikes. You were just a woman who came over to have sex, do drugs, and forget your problems. And I know you had some deep-seated problems. Maybe I'm full of shit. Maybe you were just rebelling. Looking to enjoy life, not give a damn. Rock and roll is all you want. That's cool. There's no crime in that. You're young. You can do whatever you want."

Heather moans. I think she wants to wake up, but her body won't let her. Her blood knows I'm tainted. But her desire to talk still comes out. She reaches out to me despite what I am and what is going to happen to me.

That's what I pray is happening. I pray someone will remember me.

"I'm sorry I wasn't a better person to you. I could have treated you better, but I didn't see you past the physicality of what we had. I never tried because I am shallow. It was always about me. I'm selfish. I'm an asshole. But I'm still human. And while I remember you, I want to apologize. I'm sorry for any grief that I caused you, or will. I'm sorry nothing more blossomed between us. I'm sorry I couldn't appreciate the smaller moments with you more, or make something better with the bigger ones. But thank you. Thank you for just being. I'm happy I at least got to tell you something while I can. I hope life for you gets better." I stop to put the briefcase by her side. "Maybe you'll find someone decent. Maybe you can use this money to turn your life around. Maybe you'll blow it on cheap thrills. I can't worry about what you'll do with it, since it's your life. Whatever it is, just do something and never look back. Run. Get as far away from here as you can. Live life in a way I can't." I rub my face and smile. "No more melodrama from me. You're asleep. It doesn't matter what I say."

My body moves upward, using the wall for support. My muscles freeze into place. I let out a loud groan and stumble from a sudden numbness. Holding my side, I shuffle toward the door. Only I stop when I hear her cry. Don't turn around, Claire. It's over. We had our chance, but we can never have this life. We won't get married, we won't have kids, and we won't save the world. We won't be the hero. We won't be living much longer.

All I have left is you, Dotty.

All I have left is to find you and do what must be done.

On this path of thorns I travel. I face the end with bitterness and heartbreak.

Good-bye, Heather.

Chapter Thirty-six

The sun creeps up the horizon. We prowl across the forest. Dry wood and grass crack under our feet, and thick fog blinds us. Rain hasn't reached this place, though humidity burrows under the scabs and wet scars on my skin. I itch all over; I take care not to bury my fingernails too deep.

There are no birds, no insects, and no natural life within the vicinity.

The animal kingdom knows we don't belong. They know that those who prey on matter itself lurk somewhere nearby, stalking us, stalking them.

Nothing but us and the Pale Strangers now.

Paxton carries a heavy load on his back in the form of a gas canister. Connected to it is a homemade flamethrower. He drags a dolly with one hand. Strapped to the dolly are several canisters filled with liquid. Originally, he wanted to use homemade mustard gas to deal with Darius, but then I reminded him it would kill us too if we inhaled any. Then he opted to make homemade napalm and shrapnel. Each of his bombs has a mechanical detonation switch; I dozed off when he explained the details.

I carry the gun and some ammunition, in addition to several bombs housed in PVC piping. All I have to do is light, toss, and run away. But if I can't run away, that won't be a problem. I'd take a page from Johan's playbook and become a suicide bomber.

We know the deal. Neither of us is going to live past today. But neither are Dotty and Darius. But if that's how it's going to be, then goddamn it, we are going out with fireworks. At least my boyhood instincts for blowing shit up never went away.

It is a quiet conversation we have, broken only by grunts, spinning wheels, moving liquid, and clanking metal. Halfway from the car, halfway to there. The fog clouds the emerging sun.

I think of Darius. He ran through this forest when he received a phone call from Dotty, or I think he did. I don't know how his whole situation went down, and I will never know. I have only bits and pieces to go on, and frankly, it doesn't matter anymore. He got infected, he butchered people to feed Dotty, he became indoctrinated, and his personality no longer exists but in small, unfried portions.

But still I smell what he smelled, feel what he felt, and see what he saw. While I can't relate to him as a human being anymore, I understand him. This desire to serve Dotty is all he has left.

So we aren't going there to murder him. Or her, really.

I'm going there to end their misery, to spare them more agony. This is the most, last humane thing I can do for them.

"We're here," Paxton whispers as we arrive to the broken fence leading to the water processing plant. Oh, that fence, the gateway to a hell I never imagined. I cough half a lung up just thinking about how bad an idea it was coming here after I demanded Greene take me here.

"Okay, let's boogie," I say. Before I can move, Paxton presses his hand against my chest.

"You stay," he says with a slow drawl as he pushes me back.

"I'm flattered, but we have no time for this. I know my way around here..."

Before I continue, I notice something about Paxton I didn't pick up on before. His body weight is a little off center. His skin is milk white; the blood vessels in his eyes are ready to burst. I might have mistaken it for fatigue and insomnia, except his nose starts to bleed, and he twitches.

"It's okay, Claire, I'll go set everything up," Paxton says.

"Wait, Slowburn."

He moves the dolly down the stairs and across the concrete bridge. He looks at me and waves. "Why don't you listen to the music box? I'm sure it sounds lovely right now." Paxton lets out a slow laugh as he shuffles away. I try to reach out, but I stop in place. I freeze in horror.

From the entrance, I can see a giant maw of blood, with teeth lining the doorway. Paxton doesn't see it; all he does is slowly laugh as he walks toward it. My own mouth grows small; I shrivel under the weight of my own fear. I close my eyes and clench my teeth, hoping that Paxton's screams don't make my eardrums burst. I scream in silence.

A minute passes before my body relaxes. My eyes open.

Paxton is gone. No mouth, no teeth. Just an ordinary path and an open doorway.

"Goddamn it!" I scream as my hands flinch and I stomp in anger. I don't know whether to run forward to Paxton or back to the car. Doing either won't do me any favors.

I can't take this anymore. I want this to end.

From behind, my ears pick up a sharp chirp. Then another and another. I look in the trees. I see several Pale Strangers, hanging on the limbs like chimps. Their bodies are sleek, silvery, featureless. Their chirps synchronize, and I imagine a whale and hyenas crying before the chirps morph into an owl call. Like they are trying to choose the right animal noise for their surroundings. If I didn't know any better I would have been fooled. But I'm deaf to them.

Could be worse—they could be eating me right now.

This is your new life. They are around you at all times, just like me. But you know this. I'm glad such pretenses are over.

"Who said that?" I whisper.

You know who.

I don't. The voice is too sweet, too kind, too friendly.

Let us talk for a while. Take a rest and listen, my friend.

Something in me stirs. Old wounds, old nightmares, old memories. They don't belong to me. They belong to a personality buried within, a remnant of the time I spent as someone else. Which personality is the mystery; which man is the question.

But I'm too tired, too hurt, and too fucking mad. My mind is devastated from the indoctrination, from all the horrible things I've seen and from the horrors my body has been subjected to. Those Pale Strangers in the tree are going to eat me, or Dotty and Darius are going to eat me, or Somnus or Levitt is going to drive me insane before eating me. Hell, if I make it past today, something will get me. Does it even matter anymore? Do I really care about what I don't know?

I hope you do Claire, because I care about you, my friend.

"Then tell me, Pale Stranger…who are you? What do you want?"

The cries of the Pale Strangers in the trees turn into wails of butchered animals. They scream and scream, they panic and flee. Something more wicked than them is around. Slithering and coiling up the trees are snakelike spikes. They chase the Pale Strangers away and dance where they once were.

The fog thickens, becoming more like a blurry haze. A cold chill, the kind from October, freezes my blood. My eyes squint; I use my hand to shield my face. Standing in the center of this cold haze is the shape of a man. I think it is a man, despite knowing it isn't.

The old wounds on its face give it away. That half-smile made of teeth. The open chest with a mouth and tongues pouring out. Eyes boiling underneath old bullet wounds and popping out to take a peak before slipping back into tiny jaws.

"Johan's Scarecrow." The Scarecrow nods. I laugh against the queasy shivers ravaging my senses and sanity. "Just got here from Germany? Come here for a piece of me too?" The Scarecrow shakes his head.

I've always been here. Since the beginning of man, since the beginning of your journey.

I shake my head. "This is the first time I've seen you."

I have been by your side this entire time.

"Levitt has. Somnus has. Dotty has. You just arrived to the party. Your mind tricks won't work on me. Stop trying to confuse me."

You're not seeing with your own eyes, Claire, you're seeing as Johan. Look past the flesh, and past the memories of Johan. See me for what I am, not as how he saw me.

Might as well humor the monster. I try to look past the living horror he is. I can't do it. I squirm every time I try. But as I blink, something happens.

First the eyes vanish. Then the wounds heal. The snakes in the tree melt away until they become frozen ash. The mouth in its chest closes, becoming ribs instead of teeth before the muscles and flesh clamp over the top. The toothy half-mouth turns into a smile before becoming a frown. Then nothing. No features, no face, no humanity, no life.

Standing before me is a skinny, tall man made in the image of a sleepy blur. And that's when it hits me. I know who this is. He is the one behind it all.

I fall back into the fence. "So that means you're…Somnus?" He nods. "You were Johan's Scarecrow?" He nods again.

Libraries have been written about my many different names. So many lost, so many forgotten, so many unpronounceable by the human tongue. I had many. I have many.

I reach into my pocket and pull out the gun. Not in a sane or thoughtful mind, I point the gun at him and fire. The bullet whizzes through him like he is a walking illusion. No different from shooting at an imaginary monster. He laughs at my failed attempt, so I stop.

I'm not here to hurt you. I want to talk. Me and Johan had some lovely conversations. I was hoping we could have the same.

"Isn't it in a Pale Stranger's nature to chase me? To eat me?" He nods. I start crying and screaming. "Then why am I so special? Why won't you kill and eat me and put me out of my fucking misery?"

Because there are things you can accomplish with ease, that I have a hard time doing. There are things you can do, that I cannot. I need your help to eat, and you need my help to live. We are partners. We are friends.

"But aren't I just a puppet?"

Puppet, friend, they are all the same thing.

"Why was I chosen? Am I—" I stop and laugh at the stupidity of my thought. "Am I related to Johan? Is that why you chose me?" Somnus shakes his head. "Then how does it all relate? How does this all fit together? What happened to Johan? Why are you here? Why?"

But this Pale Stranger doesn't answer.

Instead he just points at me, past me.

His voice is as soft as a breeze on a winter day, yet it hits me with a million splinters of ice. The spell conjures memories I didn't know I had. An experience I never learned about. No, I learned it before. I just didn't realize it until now. Didn't need to until now.

To my side, I see someone walking. An astral projection, a memory, an event, some strange relation to me. A man I know. Standing by his side is a young girl I know. They both were alive once. I wish I knew them then.

"Mr. Renton," Dotty says, "what is so special about this place?"

"The poppies," Joe tells her. "My favorite kind of flower. You know what poppies symbolize?" Dotty shakes her head. "Sleep. And death. They are the same, really, if you think about it. The brothers Thanatos and Hypnos, sons of the Greek god of dreams, Morpheus, represent both. I like their lesser-used Roman names better: Mors and Somnus." Joe closes his eyes and takes in a deep breath of air. "When I'm here I feel like I'm in a dream. When I go to heaven, I hope it looks like this. But being in God's graceful presence will be fine too."

Dotty laughs. "That is wonderful, Mr. Renton."

"Sometimes is, but…" Joe clears his throat before pointing toward me. "Jaune's abandoned water processing plant is a terrible eyesore. Wish they'd tear it down. Vin Forest is too beautiful for that rusted, broken building anyway. Let the wild roam free, untainted and untouched."

"Mr. Renton, there is something I need to tell you." Joe stops and stares at her. Dotty rubs her tired eyes and yawns. She apologizes; she hasn't been sleeping well because of odd nightmares caused by stress and school. "I want to thank you for helping me out. You have done so much to help ease the burden for me and my classmates. You've been a wonderful teacher and father figure to many of us." Dotty bows. "Thank you."

Joe laughs. "Oh, it's nothing. Think nothing of it. I'm just giving back to the community. And I love the arts. You'll be a marvelous dancer one day." Joe holds out his hands and says, "Many awards are in your future."

Dotty looks down and smiles. "That would be lovely." Dotty huffs and shakes her head. "Mr. Renton, you're a wonderful and kind-hearted man." Joe thanks her. "I understand it's your birthday…and I know you don't do anything for it. That's why I asked you to come here. You always talk about it, and I wanted to see it for myself."

Joe smiles. "It's just another day. I have my students, I have my arts, I have my music, and I have God. Life is great. I don't need any more good things; that would be asking for too much." Joe holds out his hand again. "I was hoping that you would be inspired by the beauty here. That is why I come here, to get away from my troubles for a while."

Dotty sighs and reaches into her bag. "Well, Mr. Renton, I was walking down the street one day a while ago and I saw something really beautiful in an antique shop. I know you like to collect things; I had them put a dedication to you…" Dotty smiles and tells him to close his eyes. Joe shuts them tight, puts his arms behind his back, and waits. Inside her hands is a red music box. His face lights up as he takes the gift, winds up the box, and puts his ear near it to listen to the music.

"Happy birthday, Mr. Renton!" I get a cold, hollow feeling.

This is the event that started it all for them, leading them to ruin. Just another in a long chain of events that would include me. Like a cursed bloodline being passed down from one person to another. The blood knows.

I look down at my hands and see the same red music box resting in my palms. I tilt my head, wind up the box, and open it. I wait in agony for the wonderful sounds it makes. But there is no music.

Why isn't it playing music? Why am I not hearing its beautiful sound?

Then I read the inside dedication. And I finally understand as my world crashes for perhaps the last time.

To my slave, Claire Walker.

Inside the center of the box is a deformed face with a crooked mouth, disfigured nose, and an eye surrounded by teeth. The face beats like a heart, releasing the beautiful music I've come to know.

Out of horror, I toss the box away. As it bounces on the grass, blood spills from it and an inhuman cry screeches so loud that my eyes shake.

Like a house suddenly demolished, the world around me breaks. Everything is rearranged until I no longer recognize Jaune's forest. I'm encircled by a thin bubble. It surrounds the area I'm in like a prison and is held together by chains of metal and flesh. Dangling from above is large clockwork similar to the insides of a watch, or a music box. Gears click against one another, rods turn, and metal hums and shakes the bubble with an earthquake of vibrations. Outside this bubble is an ocean of thick blood. I see floating pieces of decaying bodies. Shapes of hands press on the bubble, trying to get in, but they cannot; the chains hold tight but give off a painful wail and a noxious odor.

My God, where am I?

See what I see, through my prison, through my home, through my gateway.

Wait…I'm inside the music box?

Yes, this is your mind interpreting what I live in.

But why are you showing me this?

Not this. Look over here.

My ears turn my head in the direction of the voice. There is a hole inside the bubble like a porthole to elsewhere. I walk over to the hole and stare inside. Inside is a telescope portrait of the Black Forest of Germany. I just know it. The mountains to the south, yes, this is the place. Most of the Scarecrow's crimes happened here. Why did so many horrible things happen in such a beautiful place?

A man is standing in the middle. Behind him are his children and wife. They are looking at something terrifying yet sad. I recognize this man. He was young once, but I remember him.

It is the handmaiden's younger brother, the stable boy. The same one who survived the Yellow Count's castle, the same one who was abandoned by Götz of the Yellow Moon. He has grown up. He has his own family. He has forged his own life despite the tragedies inflicted on him.

But a wolf in the image of a man stands in front of him and waves.

"When will you leave us alone?" he asks.

"Never," says the beast of a man who would be called Scarecrow and Somnus to different people. "We are friends. Feed me."

The man screams. "That's all we do for you! All we do is feed you. All you do is take and feed! Just leave us the hell alone!"

"But we are friends. Don't you want to help your friends?"

"We aren't friends! You're a monster that has been haunting me since I was a boy."

The beast laughs. "It is because of me that you and your sister survived after your escape from the castle. It is because of me you met your wife. It is because of me your children are protected. I've been your guardian this entire time…"

And you will feed me, because you belong to me.

But he's not having any more of the Pale Stranger's demands. I can feel the man's tired anger and sorrow from this tiny porthole. The invisible shackles that bind him to the monster have to be broken; otherwise, he will never know peace.

So he takes a deep breath. He asks, "What do I have to do to free myself of you? What can I do to be rid of you?"

Somnus looks up at the sky. He doesn't move.

This is a wonderful place, your world, but here in particular is perfect. So much potential. The bloodlines stir in your human air. Deception, lust, greed, hate, and the vices of humanity brew in the bloodlines. They mix across the lands, across people, across time. They will boil, then blossom, and then be provoked. Such is the nature of man. Everything will congregate here.

"What is he saying, Father?" one of the children asks.

"I do not know," he says.

"War is coming," Somnus says. "But don't worry. Not in your lifetime or your children's. Not even your grandchildren's. No, it's going to take many years for the time to be ripe. I don't know when, but I can wait. The harvest will come. And I can feed and feed…" Somnus holds his arms out and continues his rant. "This is the perfect place. But you want out…"

What are you willing to sacrifice?

Hours pass by in seconds. Nothing happens. Yet I can feel the age pass through them, through this porthole. I can feel myself age along with them. I see them turn into rotting skeletons then into ash. The forest dies and is reborn with the changing seasons.

Before I know it, almost five hundred years have passed.

And I see a young farming couple buy the land and settle down. They start building on this plot of land. They take great care to build around the Scarecrow that lives not too far away.

"Do you regret it, Johan?" an old voice asks from behind me. I turn my head to a dark corner of the music box. I see a bed surrounded by hospital equipment from the 1960s. Lying in the bed is an old man with wrinkled, leather-like skin filled with scars. By his side is another man, just as scarred, almost as old, smoking a cigarette.

I know them. They were younger once. The last time I saw either was when they were dying in a bloody field during World War I.

"Does it even matter anymore, Dr. Foch?" Johan asks.

Foch nods. "Mr. Friend is persistent in his questions. He wants to know what happened at the prison. I don't tell him. No man should know our story. But I feel my time is coming. I need to cleanse my soul…"

"No point confessing. Just lie. It's easier that way."

"Has he visited you?"

Johan shakes his head. "He got what he wanted. We were but a space on a chessboard for him, I think. At least he kept his end of the bargain. He is tormenting someone else by now, bouncing around from place to place."

"Do you regret it? Killing that music box maker to save us?"

"We traded the lives of hundreds now, thousands yet to come, in exchange for peace of mind. We damned ourselves to hell for letting him escape into the modern world." Johan looks at his cigarette. "But my family is safe. My scars have healed. I can sleep now. Any damnation of my soul was worth it. I regret nothing. I would sacrifice a million more just to keep him away. And I probably have, will. I accept I am subhuman, just like the Scarecrow. It no longer bothers me. I did what I had to sleep soundly again."

Images of Johan begging to be free of the Scarecrow flood my mind. At the same time, images of the stable boy stir together like an oily cocktail. Only when I look into this goblet of blood do I see the truth: how two men, five hundred years separated, made the same choice and ended up with the same result.

It all started with Somnus the Scarecrow offering his own toxic flesh and blood. He let pieces of himself be removed to fulfill his goal. The Pale Stranger wanted a permanent home. He wanted a gateway into ours. He wanted a personal TV to see into our world.

So the stable boy chose a fledgling tree. He opened the tree with a knife and placed the blood and flesh of the Pale Stranger inside. The tree began to rot. Its matter became perverse and molded itself into the visage of the Scarecrow that Johan would come to know. But the blood and flesh were so toxic that the stable boy became very ill after finishing his task. Not long after that, he died in slow agony.

The Scarecrow knew this and probably didn't tell him the risk, for his own twisted satisfaction, I assume. Yet he died knowing his family and his bloodline would be free from the devil that had haunted him since he survived the Yellow Count.

And so Somnus waited. People came, they went. He didn't move. He stayed put as the Scarecrow, and hundreds of years later, Johan's grandparents purchased the land.

When Johan made his offer to the Scarecrow, there was a dilemma. World War I was coming to a close, and the Scarecrow wasn't interested in the next war. The bounty of Pale Stranger food the Scarecrow had was going to be cut off. The area where Johan lived was demolished by warfare. The tree that housed him was split into pieces. And Johan wanted the Scarecrow so far away that there would be no chance Johan would see him again.

It was then that Johan remembered a boyhood dream. His village was well known for its cuckoo clocks and intricate wood designs. But one thing in particular struck him as beautiful: the hand-crafted music boxes.

Johan had learned enough from the legend that surrounded the Scarecrow to not deal with the blood and flesh of the Scarecrow. So instead, he decided to let someone else take the fatal blow.

"You got a music box maker to use pieces of the plagued tree to make a red music box for the Scarecrow," I say to the image of Johan. "He died instead of you, after it was done. And you sent the box off..."

The box traveled from place to place. From his new home, Somnus was able to manipulate others into feeding him, for his own amusement. And after he was done with them, the box would move to another place, to another victim, all doomed by fate and chance.

In time, the box would end up in an antique shop. A young college girl would walk by and find herself drawn to it. In time, she would give the music box to a teacher who showered her with kindness and respect. In time, the box would end up in his nephew's hands as he tried to find out what happened to his uncle and to his fiancée.

And in time, it would end up in the hands of a washed-up journalist looking to score extra money so he could continue living day to day.

How many others have there been like me? How many others like Dotty? Like Darius and Joe? How many more will come after me?

"That was the crime Foch said you had committed, Johan. You damned me before I was even born. You damned all of us just so you could sleep."

As a bell above me chimes, as the gears turn, I fall to my knees. Pressure builds up between each chime, then is released with each turn of the gears. Air comes into me, then expands. Invisible waves rush into me, then out. Like a house demolished by a twister then reassembled only to be smashed again, every inch of me breaks apart then reassembles. Over and over, this happens.

You now know the truth. No more pretenses. No more hints. No more waiting. It is time. But you aren't ready just yet. She tainted you in a play to get you on her side. You need to be cleansed of her. We will break you down, over and over, until you are purified. We will temper you, and sharpen you.

My screams are drowned out by the music box's music.

We will make you a weapon today. All bends to our will.

Chapter Thirty-seven

My eyes open for the first time in ten years. That's how long I have been trapped in the music box. For a time, I was broken by Somnus. For a time, I was tortured. Then I was left alone. All I had was time in that box. To think and to dwell was all I could do; to stare into the porthole and relive everything I learned is how I passed the time.

The music box was my prison at first. Then I got used to the walls.

Then I grew to rely on them, to need them.

It became both my home and my confessional.

The shift back to reality is as sudden as it is jarring. Different from any other time before. There is no more pain or fear. Just an alien numbness. A complete dissociation with my body has occurred during my incarceration.

It is now nighttime in the real world. I am cocooned in dirt and fallen leaves; the humidity and sweat glue them to me. I pat myself off and find my gear still on the ground. The music box is gone. Where it fell, I find my gun. Wind howls across my back, rattling the broken chain-link fence, then down the stairs and through the entrance.

A laugh roars alongside me, carried on the wind.

I make my way into the abandoned processing plant. I wander around in the dark for a few minutes, but I don't need a flashlight. Darius has done the job of lighting the way for me.

The hallways, empty rooms, and wall space are illuminated under black lights. Florescent inks stain every inch. Dotty's eyes are drawn in different sizes and shapes. Mad text, demanding sleep and proclaiming his love to his angel, spreads in every direction. My footsteps splash in the water mixed with diluted blood. The smell of rotting matter reaches my nose, but I ignore it.

The fear is blocked out. On the verge of madness, I feel tranquil, lethal.

Acceptance was the best thing to ever happen to me.

"Darius!" I yell. "Where are you?"

A laugh rings out, echoing through the empty rooms and hallways of the abandoned place. Then a woman's scream swallows his laugh before dying into silence.

He is working to feed his love right now. Where are you, Darius?

Stupid of me. I already know. Where else would he be but in Dotty's room? I make my way slowly down the path I took as a fool both yesterday and hundreds of years ago.

Broken glass cracks under my feet as I reach the shredded door to Dotty's lair. A flickering fire casts shadows across the wall. I peek into the room. The room itself had remained the same—the same mosaic of eyes, the same wallpaper of newspapers—but a new centerpiece was added during my absence.

Chained to the ground is a naked woman covered in blood. She is carved up all over. Eyes have been chiseled into her; broken teeth sealed inside dozens of wax candles surround her. Her face is swollen, and if I knew her, I wouldn't be able to recognize her under the huge bruises. She mumbles and quivers; she probably would be crying if it didn't hurt so much.

Empathy doesn't register. Just a brooding emptiness.

Of course this would happen. Of course it will happen.

"Ma'am," I whisper. She freaks out and starts tossing her body around. The chains make a loud sound but not as loud as her wailing. I shush her. "Hey, I'm not with him." I enter the room and go to her. I keep one eye on the doorway and the other on her chains. "My name is Claire. What's yours?" She tries to speak but whimpers in pain. "It's okay, don't talk." The lock is good and tight. I might have to shoot it off. No, the bullet might ricochet if I miss. I'm going to have to break it off with something.

"Is that you, Walker?" Darius screams from somewhere far away. The naked girl shrivels into a ball. I place my hand over her mouth, causing her more pain but keeping her quiet. "Did you come to join us?"

"Keep still," I say when I move away from her. I lean against the doorway and wait. No need to chase Darius. He will come to me.

After a few minutes, he does just that. I see an outline of him slouched and swaying through the darkness, illuminated by the black lights. He stops halfway down the hall, screwdriver in one hand and hatchet in the other. He is wrinkled in skin and bones. Hollow eyes, crooked, cracked smile. His eye tattoos are infected. His clothes are covered in dry and fresh blood that glows under the black lights.

He looks like a Pale Stranger. By this point, he probably is. If I had come a day earlier, I would be running in terror from him. But I hold my stance. No need to move. No need to do anything just yet.

"Been awhile, Walker," Darius says. "Did you ever get that prize-winning story written about me? About what happened with Uncle Joe?"

"My writing career is over. I'm a man alone."

"So, you going to help us?" I say nothing. "You can join us. We are no different, you and I. We have the same passion. The same lust."

I force a smile with no meaning. "You're right. We aren't different. But I don't serve Dotty. And I am not going to help you."

Darius rubs his forehead with the handle of the screwdriver. "Why? After she's done so much for you. Why must you be a pawn?"

"See, I know I'm a pawn. You don't. Or at least you stopped caring." I step into the hallway to fully see him. "Now that I think about it, we are different. I had a lot of time to accept what I am. Quite a lot. I'm a weapon...*an instrument*...just like you. But you couldn't accept it, could you? You had to be something more. A Pale Stranger. Just like Dotty." Darius paces from side to side. I can feel his agitation, but it doesn't bother me. It should. But I'm carefree.

I finally understand the truth. And the truth has set me free.

Somnus needed an indoctrinated killer to feed him. That's why he chose the music box. He was able to reel me in and slowly break me over time using it. Unlike Johan and the stable boy, there was no way I could say no. It was nonthreatening, beautiful, undeniable. He used indoctrination and the scheming of Levitt to manipulate events so the box would end up in my hands. I took the box with me everywhere. Somnus and Levitt were able to see and show me what I couldn't, as I was able to perform actions they couldn't. And I wasn't completely brainwashed like Darius, leaving me to make choices on my own.

"The truth is, Darius, that Dotty and Somnus have always needed our help. We allow them to eat more, eat better, and eat without them having to expend precious energy searching for food. We are the worker ants. We are the one-ups on the competition. We are what sets them apart from other Pale Strangers." I stare at the gun then back at Darius. "But we are enemies, Darius. Dotty is my enemy. Because, you see, she won't stop eating. She'll just keep feeding and feeding. Her hunger will grow to an impossible dimension. She has the ability to will herself into existence using the eyes you draw for her. Somnus does the same. But he is satisfied with waiting. He is satisfied with us humans as cattle. He doesn't have to keep feeding to be content. He's been doing for a very long time. But Dotty is not him. Her flesh is weak. Her will is even weaker. She'll kill all of us if left alive, all humanity. And I can't allow that."

Darius huffs, his eyes focus on the ground. His hands shake. I laugh. Not at him but at our predicament. It was always going to come to this. Always.

"Why were you chosen? You wanna know?" Darius doesn't answer. I tap the gun against my chest. "Because Joe was originally chosen to do what I have been chosen to do. Johan, the German farmer, came before him. A few people in between them. Johan couldn't do it because Somnus didn't break him in; he let him ride out a normal life until it was go time. The ones before Joe couldn't do it either. Joe had potential, but he was weak. Too grounded in faith and beliefs, too infatuated with her. His mind snapped. And Dotty? She was just a stepping-stone, but she deluded herself into thinking she was going to ascend. She was pissed off when Somnus chose Levitt to become a Pale Stranger. Why Levitt? Because he had potential, and Somnus needed help killing the sand god. But you see, Levitt got blown to bits by the U.S. military. Not much he could do alone as a pile of worms." I point the gun back at Darius. "You had potential too. And Levitt did his best to try to manipulate you, but you see, Dotty got to you first. See, she was going to ascend. She knew how to do it; she learned a lot from Somnus. And you were going to be her pawn."

"Shut up," Darius mumbles as he covers his ears.

"You did your job well." I point to the naked girl inside the room. I can see one of her swollen eyes staring at me. She looks on in fear. Doesn't bother me much what she thinks of me. I don't care. "Dotty knew how to summon Somnus. She sacrificed her friends and strangers over months to do it. Chopped them up right there where that fine little piggy is." The girl moans in pain as I say that and shuts her eyes. "Somnus wouldn't pass up a free meal. He knew she had an agenda, and he didn't care. When he came," I make a slashing motion with the gun, "she chopped at him, took parts of him off. Not that he cared. Because she didn't know his agenda: that he hunts and eats other Pale Strangers. Sure, she would have a piece of him and turn into one of his kind, but in time he would hunt her and repay the favor tenfold. So Dotty ate the flesh of Somnus, just like the Black Fairy did with the corpse of the countess and the plant Pale Stranger attached to it. Dotty's human form died here, but not before calling out to you. So you came. Found her dying. She promised you things. Promised you checks she couldn't cash."

"She showed me the beauty…she will show me salvation."

"Bullshit. She sent you to prison. All the while, she was changing in her grave into a Pale Stranger. By then, you had been tainted. Somnus gave up on you. But something happened that day you got arrested. You know what it was? I stopped an arsonist from setting a little girl on fire. The arsonist went to jail, and I was taken to give a statement. That's when Somnus and Levitt found me. You were in the other room, a wall away, and they found me. I was chosen over a year ago. Had the right smell and taste in case I failed. They learned from previous mistakes. Broke me in little by little. I resisted at first, but now I see everything."

Darius held his face. "Then why did they show us those horrible things? Why did we do the research for them?"

"You know why they showed you what they did? You and Joe? All that research you all found? Because they wanted you to learn from the other players in the game. To teach you how to deal with the competition. To fuck with your heads. To give you purpose. To build up a tolerance in you to them so they could claim you after you were broken. You pick. It's not multiple choice, really, only if you want it. I choose all the above."

His huffing stops. I see a glimmer in his eyes, one of rage and distress. I struck a nerve with the still-human part of him. I could've related to him once, but that boat has long since sailed. 'Cause it just don't matter anymore.

In fact, my talking to Darius is a luxury he shouldn't have. I've given him more than enough time to do something, like run away. Run far, far away. Despite what he thinks, the honest truth is this: he isn't the hunter. I'm the one with the gun.

So why wait any longer? Should have done this a long time ago.

I point the gun at Darius and fire. The recoil sends a tingle down my spine. The explosion of gunpowder silences all other sounds in the small hallway. By the time the sound hits my ears, the bullet had already entered and exited Darius's thigh. I fire another round, this one entering his stomach. The impact pushes him back; he crumples on his knee and drops his weapons. He doesn't scream out; he just stares at me confused, with one hand clenching his stomach. His breathing becomes heavy and short. His blood slowly expels from his wounds, lighting up like a glow stick under the black light.

"It's better this way," I say. "The pain will be over."

"She'll save me," Darius whispers. "I'm going to join her."

I shake my head and look at one of the many eyes drawn on the wall. "She isn't coming. The human side of her is dead. She stares at you, you know, through her little glass globe. And she will do nothing, because she can find someone else."

Darius shakes his head. "No, you're lying…"

"She's a false goddess, Darius, a monster hiding in the decayed flesh of the girl you once loved." I walk to him, my hand extended, the gun pointed at his chest. "I'm not doing this because I hate you. I'm doing this to free your tortured soul. I give you the peace I will never have." He holds up his hand, trying to block and smack the gun away. I move so he misses touching the barrel. I wait for him to finish his tantrum.

"But I don't want to die…"

"Yes, you do. I read your words. You asked to be helped. You didn't want to kill anymore. You wanted to be free of your torment. And I want to free you. You've suffered enough. You deserve your rest. You deserve to sleep again. Close your eyes. This won't hurt."

He stops moving his hand. He does as I say. As much as I expected a fight, I am satisfied with the anticlimactic resolution to our encounter. Maybe the last piece of his original, sane self has come out. Or maybe he's too weak to fight back. Maybe he is thanking me somehow. But I won't wait while he's still calm and in shock.

I steady my aim, point the gun at his head, and fire. The empty shell casing bounces off the wall. The splatter of brain matter, bone, and blood squishes in the water, then his body gurgles and spasms and thuds on the ground.

After a minute, he stops.

His death is quick and clean, unlike those of many people he killed in Dotty's name. I had to put the suffering dog out of his misery, yet there is no moral victory inside me, no sickened horror because I took a man's life, no thrill in committing the gravest of acts.

I tilt my head from side to side and stare at my work.

Something slithers around my feet.

I know what it is without having to imagine what it might be.

Darius's body is pulled past me, sliding across broken glass and bloody water, over his spilled brain matter. Slow at first, the pulling speeds up. I hear the crunch of bones and meat mix with splashing water in the distance.

And that's when I hear Levitt's all too familiar, monotone laugh.

Thank you, Claire.

"You're welcome, Levitt."

You got a surprise waiting for you in the other room. Don't keep him waiting, he doesn't have much time left.

Huh? Who could he be talking about?

Levitt doesn't respond. I wobble around, looking for who he's talking about. I can hear the girl scream in pain, but there's no need to bother with her now. I'll deal with her in a minute.

I search and I search. Where could this mysterious person be?

A groan comes from behind a closed door. I walk over and knock. The groan gets louder. Throwing nonexistent caution away, I push on the door.

Inside, the thick vapors of gasoline burn my eyes. I rub them with my wrist, look around, and see the torn cans that housed Paxton's bombs. The napalm, the pipe bombs, all of it has been torn into little pieces. The devices that would have set them off have been dismantled. There is enough to set this place ablaze real quick, but not from a distance, by remote control.

Stacked against the wall on a small desk are thousands and thousands of blank papers. I grab one and go out into the hallway. Sure enough, Dotty's eyes are written in the invisible ink. Darius had been busy making the replacement papers. In time, Darius could have gone to schools, to businesses, to homes handing them out. People would be oblivious to the eyes of another watching them. They wouldn't know until she reached out from her world and stole their lives.

Yes, I know this to be true. I did the right thing by killing him.

I hear the groan again. I crumple the page and let it fall to the ground. Hidden in the corner I see a mutilated man chained to the wall. From his left foot to his kneecap, I see only bone. Across his right foot and up to his knee, the skin has been peeled off, one layer, one inch at a time. The still fresh sections of the wounds have been cauterized. Hundreds of tiny holes mark the walls, with pieces of the torn skin and muscles hidden in their compartments. The man's eyes have been torn out and sewn shut; they rest in one nearby hole. He can't see me, but he knows I'm not Darius. His blood recognizes me.

"Claire?" Paxton asks.

"Yes. I'm surprised you can talk after what you've been through."

Paxton feigns a laugh. "I blacked out when we got here. I woke up wandering around here in the dark. He got the jump on me. Tried to fight him off, but he was too strong. Tortured me with my own tools. Made me drink my own fuel. Started taking pieces of me for snacks." He smiles. "I'm glad you're alive." I tilt my head. I couldn't really say the same for him. His wounds don't look good, or survivable. "Did you kill him?"

"He's no longer with us."

"I wish I could have done it myself. What about Dotty?"

"She's still here. Don't know what I'm going to do."

"So how you gonna bring her out?"

You know what you have to do.

I do know exactly what I have to do. I tell Paxton I have something to get. So I go back into the hallway and search around for the spot where Darius died. I put the safety on the gun and shove it into my pocket before grabbing the fallen screwdriver and hatchet. I stare at the dull edges of both blades. No way Darius could get a clean cut or stab with either.

How many people did he maim and butcher with these? Plenty, no doubt. Now they have become my tools, my weapons.

I will put them to good use.

I return to the room. Paxton lifts his head. He uses his ears to search for me, to hear where I am. Poor fool. I'd feel bad for him if things were different. But they aren't. It is what it is. So I won't hesitate; not anymore.

A swift, heavy strike embeds the sharpened screwdriver into his neck. The shock hits him. His body shakes. He can't scream; I probably struck his vocal cords. His hands open and clench; he tries in vain to close his gushing wound. If he could will his legs to move, I'm very sure he would.

"Why?" Paxton mouths.

Because it's the only way.

"Because it's is the only way," I repeat. "Don't worry, this will be quick. Just close your eyes." I pull the screwdriver out. Blood flows, and he slumps over. "Sleep for the both of us. Sleep for me, since I never will." Paxton gasps for air; the blood is filling his lungs. Soon he will choke to death, but not before passing out.

A faint heartbeat thumps within me. I can't leave Paxton like this. I can't let a man like Slowburn die this way, especially after all the help he has given me.

No, he needs to go out in the way he loves.

I go the table filled with papers and overturn it. The papers scatter on the floor. I break open the unbroken pipe bombs and spill the gunpowder all over the papers. Then I dip them in gasoline and napalm before throwing some on Paxton. I go to the candle shrine room with the chained woman. She tries to get away from me, but I shush her; I'll deal with her soon.

I pick one of the candles up then go back to the room with the dying Paxton. I don't enter the room; that would be stupid. Instead, I stare at the flickering ember. The candle wax spills on my hand, but I feel no pain.

"In memory of you, Slowburn," I say with a fake smile.

Then I toss the candle inside and move away. The room instantly illuminates with an orange glow. A flash of flames exit the doorway into the hall. The flames narrowly avoid me, yet I feel no heat. Miniature explosions of gunpowder fire into the wall; shrapnel tries breaking through but can't.

I'm sure Paxton would've died with a smile. I just know it.

The smoke and flames quickly eat the roof of the building. Smoke inhalation is my bigger enemy now, more than the roaring inferno or any spooky Pale Strangers hiding around the corners. Time to go.

"Help me," a woman's voice cries out.

Oh, I almost forgot about her. Can't leave her here alone to burn up.

So I return to her. Hatchet in one hand, I grab one of her chains with the other. She winces, thinking I'm going to strike her with the dull blade.

But I'm not going to be that cruel. No, Darius did horrible things to her. What I do instead is strike a link in the chain. I hit it over and over so hard that the chain weakens and breaks. I do this to the other one. She moves away from me when free.

"Can you move? Walk on your own?" I ask. She nods. "Well go. You're free."

Without a moment's hesitation, she gets up and limps away. She goes away from the flames and smoke, the only way she can go.

You just torched Slowburn's body. We need her now. Don't let her escape.

"I know, Levitt...but I have to give her a head start. Wouldn't be fair. I'm kind."

I was broken in a way no man would ever know.

I am a weapon of them. All bends to my will.

Chapter Thirty-eight

My fingers press on the typewriter. The keystrokes don't make any coherent sentences; the blood on my fingers sticks to the keys and jams them in place. But there is no paper to type on, and the ink ran out long ago.

I forgot how to write anyway. So it doesn't matter what I press.

Gordy's empty home echoes with every creaking bone, every slow but heavy breath, every keystroke. All of the sounds imprint. I found a new place in this abandoned home.

One day, the kids will tell stories of me, about how my ghost haunts here. My very own haunted house! It's a shame they don't know about the other ghosts that inhabit this place alongside me. I look the part, though. Wrapped in bloody bandages soaked with alcohol over pale, cracked skin, I am a mummy.

From one of the boarded-up windows, I can see the thick smoke and orange glow of Vin Forest ablaze, despite its being miles away. A huge inferno has been raging in the forest for the past day. Most of Jaune had to be evacuated because of the potential for the fire to spread and devour the city. Poor Joe would be rolling in his grave if he found out what I did to his beautiful forest. At least the old water processing plant is gone, just like he wanted.

I sit in Joe's room. Had to break open the seal and demolish the locked door to get in. Gordy was right about the wretched smell. All over the walls are thousands of deep scratches, probably from Levitt or from another Pale Stranger wanting to get into the house.

I am right about another Pale Stranger wanting to get into the house.

A room away, Darius's old room, I hear the crunching of bones and flesh. I stand up and exit to the hallway. Then I peek around the corner. Inside Darius's former room are several trash bags filled with the body parts of the girl Darius chained. She gave me a good run around Vin Forest. But three little buddies from the gun were faster than she, and a fourth to the brain gave her a much deserved reprieve.

The bags have been ripped open. The hands and feet are being gnawed on by a naked woman. Well, half of her, the upper half, is human. The bottom half is bubbly, oily, and scaly; her feet are hooves. Her back is turned to me. Her angel-like wings are but skeletons with hanging tendons and a few bloody and dirty feathers.

"Hello, Dotty," I say. She turns around in a panic. Her dislocated jaw snaps back to form her normal, human face. Her shimmering eyes become humanlike. "Caught you red-handed. Should have asked for permission." She moves a ways off with the food still in her hand. "I'm just joking. That was for you. Always was." Dotty seems lost as she looks around the room. She might have a hard time remembering, so I remind her that it's Darius's old room. I'm sure she had fond moments here.

"Why did you torch Vin Forest?" Dotty asks.

"That's all you want to know? Funny. That was an accident. I meant to just blow up the building, but that didn't work out the way I planned. Nothing did."

Dotty looks scared of me. Why should she be scared of me? Before I could react, she could tear me in half and eat me. I'm just an ordinary human. I can't do anything to her. I should be afraid of her.

But she should never have taken me in and tried to reason with me. She should have never gambled on me to join her. I've seen her for what she truly is. A beast. A monster hiding under the skin of an angel.

"You really are no different from an animal, you know that?" I say. "Look at you. You actually came for an easy meal. All it took me was a few swirls of paint on the ground to call you out. Really, you Pale Strangers are so pathetic sometimes, so predictable." I wave my hand at her. "Don't mind me, though. Enjoy your meal."

I turn my back to her and walk to the living room. Every inch of the living room is covered in new sigils and signs, written by me. Drew them with paint until I ran out, then with ink until I ran out, then with my own blood until I passed out.

My knees ache; painful arthritis breaks through the dull senses. So I sit down in the middle of the floor and massage my knees.

"Why did you choose them?" Dotty asks, her footsteps inching closer behind me. "Why did you choose damnation? Why did you choose to be a slave?"

I turn my head toward her. "And what would I have been if I chose you?"

"Free. You could have joined me. You could have ascended."

I shake my head. "I saw your idea of free in Darius. It would have all been the same, no matter who I chose." I stare at my wounded hands. The healing process isn't working. My health has taken a turn for the worse. "You know, all I had was time inside Somnus's music box. I started thinking. All the horrors around me. The reason no one was broken in properly by Somnus. Resistance and will do so much. Then a moment of clarity came. I'm not Joe or Darius. But I am no different than Johan. Yeah, me and Johan have much in common." I scratch my chin and nod. "Me and the Yellow Count have a lot in common too. But I relate more to Johan since he was still human. Our choices were exactly the same."

"What do you have in common with Johan?"

"This, Miss Finley..."

A figure appears from behind her. I can feel the cracking of her spine, the ripping of her skin and insides. She's pushed forward, her stomach ruptures, and her guts spill out. The hatchet used on so many of her victims is hacked into her. Then as quickly as it went in, the blade is removed, and she falls to the ground beside me.

Surprised dismay appears on her face. She sees I am still on the ground, in her presence the entire time; there's no way I could have attacked her.

Then who? Her oily blood spills from her mouth as she tries to talk.

"Say hi to Darius," I say. Dotty turns her head. Her face becomes washed in fear. Standing above her is Darius—or I should say, someone who once was Darius. You can tell something is off by the worms coming out of his left arm, burrowing into and bulging through his skin. His eyes glimmer a different color—they are not his eyes, not human eyes.

No, his body is just an empty husk, a perfect husk. If it had been any other body, it would have long ago deteriorated. But his body was being readied, primed to ascend and become a Pale Stranger. Even after his death, the body is still ripe. It will last much longer than a normal body.

And now it belongs to Levitt Brower. Darius's body is now his home.

"I told you the flesh was weak," Levitt says. "But you just wouldn't listen to reason, would you, Finley? You just had to become one of us." He tilts his head and looks down at her. "Why are you so surprised? You knew this was coming. The moment you decided to show up and eat something free, you doomed yourself. But you couldn't just walk away, could you? You had to give in and feed that fiend inside. You grew so accustomed to eating, to that lifestyle of yours." Levitt tosses the hatchet aside.

Dotty turns away from him and focuses on me. "This didn't have to be."

"But it is," I say. "For the first time in my life, I'm on the winning side. Might not get a good night's rest, but I chose peace, salaam. I would damn a million more just for peace. Just like Johan. We did this to appease another."

Levitt starts to sing as he moves away from her. He sings louder when he opens a door to an empty closet and leaves.

The closet is empty, except for the red music box sitting on the floor.

The music box starts to play on its own. The lid pops open.

Standing behind the box, I see a Pale Stranger from afar. He waves.

From out of the music box, hundreds of snakelike spikes slither out. They shoot at Dotty and hook into her.

"No!" she screams.

Dotty is pulled toward the music box. Her claws and fingernails stab the floor. Blood breaks from every pore of her skin. She bleeds from her mouth, from her eyes, and from her nose. She struggles to crawl toward me.

"Please, Claire, help me! I don't want to die! Please help me!"

My heart bleeds for her. Not because of her sweet but toxic scent. Not because of her puppy-dog looks, not from lust for her body, not because of her eternal promises.

My blood knows that underneath all her terrible, monstrous flesh is something human. Underneath the Pale Stranger is a young girl who got in over her head, got put into this position and corrupted. Terrified and remorseful at all the things she has done and experienced. Her essence of humanity gets under my skin.

The part I thought was broken in is not so broken.

Feelings of regret, terror, and sadness overcome me. All the atrocities I just committed and will commit in the name of Somnus sicken and frighten me. Everything I do in my master's name, just to feed and satisfy him, ruins me. Immediately, I wish I could undo everything. God, please take all of it away. Please don't forsake me.

"Dotty," I say. I reach out for her. She reaches out to me. Her fingers inch into my hand. We clench together, and I hold on with all my strength.

Maybe I can save her. Maybe I can do one last decent thing while I can.

"Thank you, Claire," she whimpers.

Come to me, Dotty, I hunger.

Her hand rips out of mine, slicing deep into my palm. Her body is yanked backward. Her claws and fingers are torn from their sockets. She is dragged across the floor and into the closet.

Dotty's screams last long after she vanishes into the music box.

I stare at my wounded hand in horror.

Oh my God, what have I done? My God, what have I become?

"And you belong to us now. You can be one of us if you want one day, when you're ready." Levitt laughs. "But you must get rid of those useless emotions. You're not of their world. You are of ours. You are primal, just like us." Levitt moves away from me and goes to the closet. He stands and watches as Somnus devours Dotty. All he does is stare and laugh.

I feel like the first cosmonaut, the first human to die in space. Lost in orbit, his ship malfunctioning. He came crashing to Earth in a blaze of metal. Damned and abandoned, his descent became his death. Unable to be saved, he is heard crying in rage.

I cry in rage. I cry for what must have been hours in minutes. My rage flows in my tears. I curse everything. I damn everything.

But my crying turns into something else.

Laughter. Mad laughter. Mad laughter of rage. My laughing lasts for minutes that become hours. I wander around the empty house laughing. I laugh at the horror. I laugh at the madness. I embrace everything with my mad laughter.

I do this to drown out the dying screams of Dotty and everyone else who came before her. I do this to escape my nightmare for just a moment.

My body collapses into the doorframe. I slide down and fall to my knees. I'm too tired to cry anymore, too tired to laugh.

Through the boarded windows, I see them. They are outside by the hundreds. They march toward the mansion. Behind them is the red spiral hell. The tornado of souls is home to a thousand more Pale Strangers. Above me I can hear running on the rooftop. I can hear the scratching, the banging, the clawing. I can see hands warp the paint, and try to push through.

They know I'm in here. I can hear them call out to me. Their whispers are so loud, so pronounced, they become the only sound in the world.

But all of them are unaware of the monsters that wait for them. They are unaware that the glyphs meant to summon Dotty are also being used to draw them into this trap.

My blood is in the water to attract the sharks for the hunter, my master.

My body is a tool to bring the sacrifice to his alter.

All will become a sacrifice to feed this monster among monsters.

I hunger.

All this pain, this stress, this sorrow, this horror. For what? So I could become like Icarus, and gain wings to fly into the sun? No, I'm something much worse.

I've lost my humanity. I am the villain.

Everything bears down on me like a cross made of heavy stone. I'm burdened by the sins and tragedies of the people before me. I am chased and haunted by the monsters within the void. I never asked for any of this, yet I will shoulder the terror like a broken messiah, without a cause or salvation. The pain inside is unbearable. The pain is there to remind me this is real.

On a path of thorns I walk. I face this nightmare with bitterness and sorrow.

Please, God, just let me sleep, salaam. Let this nightmare end.

But it won't…it never will…the Pale Strangers are always there. They always will be.

And I will become a stranger from afar, to crave on souls from afar.

Because the blood knows.

The blood knows.

Acknowledgements

I would like to thank my parents Raquel and Jesus "Chucho" Perales, my siblings Ernest Perales, Lori and Jeanette Guevara, Armando Salas, Jerry Perales, John and Jim Fairley, and to their immediate families. Special consideration to the Mendiola, Contreras, Fernandez, Guerra, Gonzales, and Shellenburg families. Extended consideration to the entire Reilly family and the rest of the Perales family, because they are numerous like the Pale Strangers.

I also would like to thank my professors over the years for caring and nurturing me whether I wanted it or not, Sheila Kizzart, Jane Foch-Hansen, Gary Partridge, Carol Reposa, and Ernest Tschalis. I would like to thank my close friends who had been along for the ride, whether they wanted it nor not, and I apologize for dragging them kicking and screaming across the finish line, Ned Lesesne, Selina Gutierrez, Richard Bost, Charles Benson, Alek Fisher, Spencer Sumner, Paul Brown, Augustine Gonzales, and Luke Reilly. To my early bird readers for all stories, including this novel, I thank you Raquel Stark, Karen Montalvo, Eli Guajardo, Jacqui Carona, Chris Martinez, Liz Sanchez, Steven Delgado, Jonathan Cabrera, Samuel Rankin, Kristin Vakey, Jerry Martinez, David Torres, Rebecca Barrera, and Samantha Lopez. Other friends I would like to thank are Chip Foch-Hansen, Ashley Rodriguez, Jonathan Whitlock, Will Wright, Charles Sibley, Tristan Bulgrin, Michael Tudyk, Christian Fernandez, Katie Reilly, Amanda Gonzales, Vanessa

Rankin, Laura Anima, Arturo Haces, Christa Haces, Krissi Taylor Leslie, Facil Yohannes, Philip Franklin, Frank Gonzales, Nate Torok, Michael Garza, Patrick Bruno, Jacob McBride, Elena Garcia, Chris Ramos, Morgan Schaar, Erica Guerrero-Torres, Jacquee Nico Rodriguez, Stephanie Lopez, Eddie Perez, Christy Medlock, Sean Robinson, Valerie Gonzales, Eric Lopez, Ladelthia Mohnen, Marguerite Richardson, and Bob Riddle the owner of Big Bob's Burgers.

Sorry if I don't remember more of you all, it's been a blur and I apologize if I didn't put you down. Please don't hurt me. For those who I did intentionally forget, I told you I'd get you back. Ha! Please don't hurt me. In seriousness, I'll get you all next time, I promise.

I thank all of you for putting up with my weirdness, my laziness, my hilariously random temper swings, and my inability to settle for a normal job. It took me longer than expected, and I promise next time it will take a fraction of the time. Also I will do other books that aren't as dark and depressing, so the whole family can read. Maybe.

All I can say is thank God it's over!

Again, thank you everyone and remember that the best is yet to come.

Made in United States
Orlando, FL
30 March 2022